BISHOP'S WAR

A THRILLER

RAFAEL AMADEUS HINES

For my mother, Margaret Mary Duncan, whose love of the arts, literature, and passion to create fueled my imagination and guided me towards becoming a writer.

"Got it done, mom. Rest now my darling—rest in peace."

And a special thank you to my son, Rafael John Alan Hines, the legendary Carl Younger, Mike Barrett, Rick Bellusci, Martin Sierra, Oliver Carlin, Linda Matias, Jonathan Canter, and Tade Reen for your unwavering support and constant encouragement.

CHAPTER 1
THE PEACEMAKER

Mexico

HOURS BEFORE THE deadly desert sun rose above the low hills in the east, Clayton Unser walked over to one of the Valdez prison guards to ask a few questions. The moon had been full, bright enough to cast shadows, and the guard wore NVG's (Night Vision Goggles), but Clayton made sure the man heard him coming. No reason to startle anyone in the dark when they're holding an AR-15 assault rifle and wearing .45 Colt Commander in a hip-holster. Clayton raised his hands palms up as a sign of reassurance, not surrender, and to make it an easy reach for the 9mm Glock 17 in his shoulder rig in case things got dicey.

Fortunately, the guard turned out to be a calm and alert seasoned soldier working the graveyard shift who didn't mind company, and after a few minutes of small talk about the cool night and the blazing heat that lay hidden below the horizon Clayton got to the point: "I hear the prisoners have an interesting name for the ceremony."

"Ceremony? Strange word for it. More like an ancient

Aztec ritual, but yeah, the inmates call it El día que Dios duerme," the guard said.

"The day God sleeps," Clayton translated. "Why?" he asked.

"You'll see for yourself in a few hours."

"Come on, man,"

The guard shrugged. "Every year on this very day two guys beg, plead, and pray for death, but so far God's been sleeping and never answers. The rest of the inmates pray their asses off that God stays asleep and *don't* wake up 'cause if he does they know they'll be the next ones begging to die."

Clayton had nodded his head in thanks, then turned and walked away. Now, six hours later, he watched a group of prisoners making final preparations for what definitely was a gruesome annual ritual. Sweating hard through their light-blue uniforms, they hurried around the dusty yard below the main house setting up steel tables with built-in drains and gutters for the blood, and then laid out a medieval array of metal probes, bone saws, long knives, and short handled razors.

Clayton shook his head as he watched them work. *I'm getting too old for this shit,* he thought. He'd buried his father years ago, but it was Big Earl Unser's gravelly voice that still scolded him from the grave:

Always fucking complaining. Be thankful you're drinking iced coffee in the shade instead of baking down there with those poor bastards.

The high porch of the main house faced west so the mid-morning sun hadn't hit him yet, but the night chill of the Sonoran desert was long gone, and Clayton already felt the heat. Taking his daddy's advice, he enjoyed a long cool caffeine shot and then got himself refocused.

He put down the coffee, picked up a pair of Steiner

military binoculars, and scanned for threats across a flat tree-less plain that stretched for miles in all directions. In addition to the armed guards, the compound was surrounded by a multilayered security system and hidden sentries, but Clayton hadn't survived this long without taking his own precautions.

He zoomed in and out, searching the beige and gray barren desert for any activity, but the only movement came from a flock of small birds flying fast and low towards the house, and from the sand eddies swirling far off in the distance.

Clear and quiet, Clayton thought. *Maybe too quiet... Maybe.*

If there was something out there he couldn't see it or feel it so he flexed his shoulders and rotated his neck to release the tension.

After his internal threat meter gave the all clear he lowered the binoculars and turned his attention back down to the sweating, grim-faced prisoners. Their work done, they stood in a straight line with their heads bowed, silently roasting in the sun.

"Going to be a hot day," Clayton said.

"Hot and bloody," Gonzalo Valdez replied, which brought a nod of agreement from Clayton.

Clayton and Gonzalo sat a few feet apart on the open-air porch, both with their backs against the rough white-washed wall of the old ranch house.

Clayton's chiseled features, crystal blue eyes, thin mustache, and the neat part in his dark brown hair made him appear more like a British stage actor than a spy. The CIA's Deputy Director of Covert Operations was one of those rare unreadable human beings. His age could be anywhere between thirty-five and sixty, and although his calm demeanor and movie star smile immediately put people at ease, there was something else there that told you he could take your life without wrinkling his suit or breaking a sweat.

In contrast, few people ever felt relaxed around Gonzalo Valdez. His face and hands were scarred from years of bare knuckle boxing on the streets of Panama when he was a boy. His body was marked by knife cuts and bullet wounds, and his dark skin, shaved scalp, high cheek bones, and yellow cat-like eyes gave him the predatory look of a stalking panther. You didn't need to know he was the head of the notorious Valdez crime family to instantly fear the man.

Clayton's chair creaked as he stretched his legs out, crossed his suede Oxfords at the ankles, and began reading a thick military personnel file. It was the John Bishop file and Clayton shook his head in disbelief as he went through it. The Special Forces sergeant had a career that was beyond impressive, spectacular really. The report cited Bishop's countless acts of heroism, detailed the twenty-three times he'd been wounded, and listed all the medals he'd received. More than any soldier since Vietnam.

"Jesus," Clayton said, without looking up. "You know John turned down the Medal of Honor? Flat out refused it?"

Gonzalo was staring intently at a framed photograph resting on the wooden table in front of him. He only nodded subtly in response to Clayton's question. His eyes stayed fixed on the image of a happy couple. Clearly pregnant in her gown, the tiny bride and the tall-tuxedoed groom both had big toothy smiles on their wedding day.

The comfortable silence shared by two old friends was only disturbed by the rapid turning of pages as Clayton scanned quickly, searching for answers. He finally sighed in resignation, dropped the file, then steepled his fingers under his nose to help him concentrate.

After a minute he gave up: "Why?"

"Why did my nephew refuse his nation's highest honor?" Gonzalo asked.

"That's it."

"John's always done things his own way."

"So he never told you."

"No, but if he got the Medal they would've pulled him out of combat. Back then he wasn't ready to walk away from war."

"And now?" asked Clayton.

"We'll see. He hasn't been home or spoken to me in years."

"So out of the blue he quits the Army? Leaves Special Forces?"

"Your point, Clayton?"

"Your nephew is probably the deadliest man on the planet. Now he's coming home, practically on the anniversary of his parents' murder. I'm kinda wondering what his plans are."

"After I'm done here we'll meet with the Mexican cartels and broker this peace treaty. Put an end to this senseless violence," Gonzalo said. "Tomorrow, *if we're still alive tomorrow*, we fly to New York for John's welcome home party so you can ask him all about his plans."

"We can't have anymore cartel murders on our side of the border," added Clayton.

"Yes, my friend, they understand that kidnapping and killing American citizens has to stop."

"Maybe get them to stop killing each other, too," said Clayton.

"Maybe, but there's a lot of bad blood between these families. Expect the meeting to start with each side dumping a bag of heads on the negotiating table. Then, well, who can say…" Gonzalo shrugged his shoulders and raised his palms to bring home the point.

"You broker this deal for us, you'll have a new title at Clandestine Services," Clayton said. "From now on you'll be known as 'The Peacemaker.'"

"Will that go on a business card?" Gonzalo asked.

Clayton laughed. "The title will be unofficial, but as always, the United States of America will be extremely grateful for your assistance. Anyway, I'm looking forward to finally meeting John."

Gonzalo reached for the framed photo of his sister Christina and her husband, Michael Bishop. "Hard to believe it's been so long."

"John was in the car with them that day?" It wasn't really a question. Clayton knew the whole sad story, but sensed that Gonzalo wanted to talk about it.

Gonzalo looked up for the first time. "The Davis brothers were gunning for me. My baby sister had her whole life ahead of her when they shot her down. They slaughtered her and her husband in front of John and put that scar on his face. He was just a boy when it happened."

"And you've kept them alive all this time?" The *them* Clayton was referring to was Tom Tom and Skeeta Davis.

"The prisoners here are all condemned men. They live only as long as they keep the brothers alive," Gonzalo said.

Clayton thought about what that meant. In addition to the five inmates standing in the yard, he'd seen about twenty armed men around the ranch when they landed at Gonzalo's private airfield just before sunrise. Gonzalo was a careful man, so Clayton knew there were hidden security teams for miles around. Another twenty? Maybe more? That was close forty or fifty men including the surgeons and a full medical staff all dedicated to keeping two men alive—what was left of them anyway.

The isolated twenty-thousand-acre property in the desert was a private prison, specially designed and built for Tom Tom and Skeeta Davis. Kept in an underground dungeon, once a year they were carried up to the surface. Carried because they would never walk again. Carried, because every year on this day, the anniversary of his little sister's murder, Gonzalo Valdez personally removed a body part from each of the brothers.

Clayton had witnessed many horrific events throughout his long career at CIA: genocide and torture, unspeakable atrocities that haunted his dreams, but in all his years in the field, he'd never encountered such a brutal and long-term commitment to vengeance.

Four burly Valdez soldiers wearing shoulder rigs with Glock 40's over their white tees carried the stretchers into the yard and placed the Davis brothers onto two of the steel tables that were set up in front of the house. Both brothers were naked and they squirmed and rolled trying to keep from being strapped down onto metal tops that were already super-heated by the sun. Once they were firmly secured the soldiers bowed to Gonzalo, then stood at parade rest behind their charges.

From the other side of the yard the medical team came out of a small white wooden house trimmed with red around the door frames and shutters. Two surgeons and three nurses walked over with seven more prisoners trailing behind with the equipment: oxygen tanks and masks, coolers with blood bags, IV's, clamps, sutures, heart monitors, defibrillators, and the various drugs that the surgeons would use to save their patients, as they had done time and time again.

When all was ready the medical team and the men around them stood at attention. Tense and sweaty, they waited in silence. The land was silent too. The birds stopped chirping, the flies stopped buzzing, and the wind died so abruptly it was as if the whole world paused in anticipation of what was about to happen.

Gonzalo kissed his baby sister's picture, carefully placed it on the table, then stood up and unbuttoned his guayabera.

"Why ruin a good shirt," he said as he hung it on the back of his chair. He stepped off the porch, walked down the short flight of wooden stairs that led to the yard, and strolled over to confer with the doctors who would clamp off arteries and repair the damage he was about to inflict.

Clayton watched him walk amongst the prisoners, marveling at his power. At over sixty and only five-nine, Gonzalo was by far the most lethal-looking man he'd ever seen. Dark, hard, and lean, his muscles rippled across his chiseled back as he moved, but his physical strength paled in comparison to his persona. He walked freely and fearlessly past twelve men who stood next to a table full of weapons. Men whom he'd made prisoners and condemned to death. Any one of them could grab a scalpel or long knife and gut him before the guards could react, but his fierce yellow eyes kept them cowed and resigned to their fate... a fate that only Gonzalo Valdez would decide for them.

He spoke briefly to the doctors, then turned back to the tables and picked up a pointy eight-inch metal probe and began inspecting each of the brothers. Tom Tom and Skeeta were painfully aware of the purpose of examination. Naked and strapped down across their waists and chests, they twisted frantically as Gonzalo searched for the best place to start.

"There's not much left to cut," he said to them. "In a few more years I'll have to find new ways to remind you of your crime."

Clayton came over to take a closer look and quickly

wished he hadn't. Twenty-five years ago Gonzalo started with their hands and feet and systematically continued up each appendage until their arms were gone just above the elbows, their legs were cut off at mid-thigh, and each brother was missing an eye and ear. When Clayton made the mistake of looking down at the rough jagged scars that covered their groin areas he swallowed the bile that bubbled up into his throat and unconsciously grabbed his crotch for reassurance.

"You first this time," Gonzalo said to Skeeta.

Skeeta's screams were garbled and inhuman when Gonzalo slowly began slicing him with a scalpel to mark where he'd make the deeper cuts with a heavier blade. He'd taken both their tongues many years before.

Did I just call him The Peacemaker? Clayton asked himself as he walked back up to the porch and tried his best to ignore what was happening just a few feet away. He picked up the picture of Christina and Michael Bishop and thought about their son. The once traumatized little boy was now a man and wherever he went death followed. John Bishop was heading home, and once again, Clayton wondered if New York was ready for what was coming.

CHAPTER 2

CENTRAL BOOKING

New York, NY

THE HEAVY RAIN had stopped on Manhattan's Lower East Side, but the officer kept the windshield wipers going to sweep away the tail end of the storm. Handcuffed, with their wrists behind them, the prisoners in the back of the police van braced for impact: feet planted, pushing up with their legs. They groaned and cursed when the van slammed into another deep pothole as it splashed along Chrystie Street heading downtown.

"Yo, you *tryin'* to hit all them holes, man!?"

An evil grin on his face, the police officer behind the wheel glanced over at his partner, accelerated, then aimed for a big crack in the street. The van hit harder this time, sending prisoners airborne. Most landed back in their seats. The few who were dumped on the floor struggled to get up while the driver reduced speed and scanned ahead for his next target.

"Punk ass cop!"

"Take these cuffs off and see what happens!"

Ignoring their pissed off passengers, the two officers in front continued their private argument over the Yankees starting lineup and whether the Bronx Bombers could win another World Series. Bored by the nightly routine of prisoner transport, they passed the time "pothole hunting," and cruising along at an easy pace through Lower Manhattan. The guys in the back of the van had already been arrested. There wasn't any reason to rush them down to Central Booking.

Almost all of the prisoners were used to the routine as well. The veterans knew what to expect and played it cool. When they weren't cursing at the cops in front they joked with each other and laughed easily. The one newbie was sweating and nervous, uncertain and afraid of what lay ahead. Staring through the steel mesh covered window, the passing street lights flicked his strained features in and out of shadow.

"What they pop you for?" asked the heavyset Puerto Rican on the seat next to him.

Too scared to speak, he sat there frozen, his eyes darting back and forth.

"I ain't gonna bite choo. You don't wanna talk, it's cool."

He glanced over, preparing to concoct an elaborate story about his arrest, then quickly decided it was best to stick to the sad simple truth. "Failed the breathalyzer," he said, trying his best to put an edge on it.

"First time?"

"Yeah, I mean yes. I've never done anything like this before."

"I ain't your lawyer, man. Long as you didn't hit no one you'll be home tomorrow after you see da judge."

"They told me I'd be home tonight."

"Most days you might, but jail's gonna be real busy. No way you're out tonight."

"Why?"

"Why what?"

"Why is it going to be so busy?"

"Moon's almost full."

"So?"

"Fuller the moon, fuller the jail."

"You're kidding me, right?"

"Nah, straight up. Human beings man, we're some primal motherfuckers."

"That's hard to believe."

"Believe it, papa. Even if you don't, you'll see for yourself once we get inside. Name's Fletcher," said Fletcher Vargas. Short and chubby with high combed back hair from his old school DA, and a close beard flecked with gray, he was a lifelong hustler who often sold drugs to support his heroin habit. His motto was "dress to impress" and today he was rockin' what he called casual cool. Fletcher was arrested wearing white and green high top Adidas, bright green satin shorts, and a green Boston Celtics Tiny Archibald throwback jersey.

"I'm Tucker," said Tucker Harrison. He was tall and slim, blond and clean shaven, with a West Hampton tan. A Morgan Stanley Investment Banker and lifelong yachting enthusiast, Tucker often drove home drunk after client meetings. Along with handcuffs he wore a dark grey Zegna suit, a white pin-striped shirt custom made for him in Hong Kong, and black Ferragamo loafers.

"Am I going to be okay?" he asked, just as they arrived at Central Booking.

"Tucker, don't let anyone tell you different, jail sucks, man. Even for one night, it ain't where you wanna be. You're gonna be locked down with some stone cold killers, but there's citizens in here too, and the guards don't want no tax payer like you dyin' on their shift. Too much paper work. So yeah, we walkin' into a jungle, but it's a jungle that got rules. Don't worry, I'll school you. You listen and do like I say, you ain't gonna have no problems," Fletcher said to the Wall Street executive just as the gates of the Manhattan Detention Center closed behind the police van.

MDC, better known as Central Booking, is located in the downtown New York court district. It's one of those old non-descript buildings with lots of angled corners that almost disguises the fact that you're looking at a prison. If you ever get arrested in Manhattan you'll spend some time there.

Tucker and Fletcher had been last in, so they were the first prisoners out of the van. They stepped down onto the cracked, rain soaked pavement in the center of a wide court-yard surrounded by high fences topped with razor wire and glaring flood lights. Their NYPD drivers handed them over to the Department of Corrections. A heavyset DOC officer with brown smoke stained-teeth and a low gut that hung way down over his belt clamped his thick fingers tightly around Tucker's left elbow. He farted loudly, then guided Tucker and Fletcher to a white hash mark four inches below the surface of a wide puddle. Told not to move, they stood up to their ankles in the dirty foot bath. Fletch cursed at the fat guard for getting his kicks wet, while Tucker kept quiet about his plans to throw his seven hundred dollars loafers in the trash when he got home.

Staring down at his ruined shoes, Tucker's eyes fixed on a bright reflection in the water before he slowly tilted his head towards the heavens. His whole body shuddered when he looked up at the night sky. The moon sat high above peeking through the scattered clouds, its hazy glow bathed everything in an eerie, ominous light. Since they were both shackled, Fletcher nudged him with his shoulder.

"Hey Nantucket! You best keep your head out the clouds and focus on what you walkin' into here, man."

Along with six other prisoners they were ushered to the main building by several DOC guards.

"I'll tell you one thing, I'm sober now."

"Good."

"What're you here for?" Tucker asked, trying to mask his nervousness as they passed through the main doors.

"Had an outstanding warrant. Won't see the streets for at least a year, man." Fletcher didn't add that he was going to have to kick his dope habit cold turkey. Even though the evening was warm and sticky, thinking about his long nights ahead filled with convulsions and vomiting made Fletcher shiver in a cold sweat.

They were searched again, then slowly moved through processing before being taken up to the holding cells. As soon as the steel doors clanged open on their assigned floor the noise hit them like a sledge hammer. The sound of nearly five hundred men talking, laughing, and shouting in a confined space blended into a constant roar that made Tucker's legs shake uncontrollably. Then the smell hit him like a punch in the face. Sweat, shit, piss, puke, and the chemical sanitizers used by the Department of Corrections all hung heavily in the air like a thick rancid fog that made his stomach turn.

The holding cells in central lockup are oversized cages, each of them made to hold about twenty guys, but they manage to squeeze in over sixty on the weekends. Designed for function rather than comfort, every cell has floor to ceiling bars on three sides, a bolted down metal bench running along the back wall, and one stainless steel open toilet that sits in the corner. The bright overhead lights stay on twenty-four hours a day.

As they were escorted down the long hallway towards their cell Fletcher passed on some final words of advice: "Keep your mouth shut and stay sharp. If you gotta take a shit you'd best hold it. With this many dudes in here you don't wanna be squatting down with your pants around your ankles."

"Thanks."

They both automatically moved to an open space along the back wall next to the bench as the barred door slammed shut behind them. They were locked in with forty-eight other men who had been arrested for a wide range of crimes. Most were in jail for misdemeanors like smoking weed, disorderly conduct or drunk driving. Others were in for assault, armed robbery and murder, so lifetime offenders and those new to the system were all thrown in together. A couple of guys were sleeping on the concrete floor using MDC's inedible bologna sandwiches as pillows, while some were talking in small groups, sharing stories of how they ended up in jail on a warm Thursday night in June. A few stood or sat alone, dwelling on the long years they faced in prison, or first timers like Tucker that were too scared to talk or make eye contact.

One man sat quietly at the end of the bench, deep in thought, but clearly unafraid. Every man in the cell had done a double take on him. First a quick glance, followed by a longer look over. Then they didn't look again. Even Tucker, who was trying his best to become invisible, snuck a peak at the soldier in full military dress uniform.

Above the sergeant's stripes on his left shoulder his dark green tunic bore an arrow head shaped patch with a sword and three diagonal lightning bolts running through it. Above the patch his arm read, AIRBORNE. Above that, RANGER, and above that, SPECIAL FORCES. A light blue Combat Infantry Badge was pinned over his left breast, and below the CIB were rows and rows of ribbons and medals. Purple Heart with cluster, two Bronze Stars with V's for Valor, the Silver Star, and the Distinguished Service Cross were all on display.

Initially it was the uniform that drew all the attention, but it was his face that made everyone momentarily stare. A deep jagged scar ran down his forehead like an angry river, gouging through his right eyebrow, and zig-zagging its way into his cheek. The ancient wound was impressive, but the eyes of Sergeant John Michael Bishop were what pulled you in. Amber, luminescent, and cat shaped, they were both fascinating and disturbing.

John Bishop ignored the nervous glances from his cellmates and tuned out their chatter. Although he appeared calm and relaxed he was working really hard to control his emotions. Inside he was raging, furious at himself and at his cousin for ending up in jail on his first day back home.

Bishop had been in the military for the past fourteen years, twelve of them as a Green Beret. He fought, killed, bled, and buried friends all over the world, and it was only two weeks ago that he went on his final mission as a member of Team Razor, a roaming Special Forces unit based on the Afghanistan-Pakistan border. Now he was done. He put in his papers and walked away free and clear.

He didn't leave the Army because of his questions about the war, which were many. He didn't leave because he was tired of all the killing, which he was. He didn't leave because of the painful memories of so many comrades lost, which would haunt him forever.

He left to get his life back. He left to finally reconnect with his family after being away for so many years. Most important of all, he left to win back the woman he loved.

Sergeant Bishop had been in almost constant combat throughout his military career after he joined the army at eighteen, first as an Airborne Ranger and then as a Special Forces weapons sergeant. Wounded twenty-three times, he was one of the most decorated *living* American soldiers, but his medals meant nothing to him and he never wore them. Except for today. Today he had reluctantly made an exception because he knew how much they meant to his uncle. His uncle was the man that raised him and the man he truly loved like a father. His uncle, Gonzalo Valdez, was also the head of the one of the largest organized crime families in New York. Maybe the largest in the country. Gonzalo was throwing him a huge welcome home party tonight, but John never made it. Instead he was in jail waiting for bail or processing.

Other than Fletcher, the only person he knew in the holding cell was his cousin Felix Valdez. First cousins, but there was little family resemblance. While John was fair skinned and clean shaven with brown curly hair, Felix was dark with a thin goatee and a short afro. They were both exactly six feet tall, but John was a tough, hard, and lean one-ninety while Felix was two hundred-ten pounds of pure muscle and power. While John had always been self-conscious of his scar and grinned cautiously, Felix kept a bright white infectious smile plastered on his face.

If you stood the two of them next to each other you would never think they were related. At least not until they looked at you. Then you knew. Their eyes were the same. Yellow, cat-like, and unblinking. Of course, Felix the Cat had been his childhood nickname. Now it was just Cat.

John sat there brooding and wouldn't even look at Felix. He was so mad at his cousin he wanted to kick his ass, but chuckled at the thought. Felix was a legendary street fighter and a black belt who worked out three hours a day, six days a week against the best that Tiger Schulman's Karate School had to offer. With all of John's training in hand to hand combat a fight with Felix would be touch and go at best.

"You be extra careful now," Fletcher whispered to Tucker. "That's a real gangster right there," he said nodding towards Felix. "He even looks at you wrong you won't make it out the building. Guys will *do you* just hoping to get in good with him."

"Shut up Fletch."

Tucker's head snapped back, banging into the wall. Fletcher stiffened, then carefully turned and moved forward to look closely at the soldier sitting nearby. Then his eyes went wide.

"Johnny!? Damn papa, didn't see you there. Looking good bro. Welcome home."

"Why're you talking that shit about Felix?"

"Hey John, no disrespect to your cousin, I'm just trying to school this rookie here. But papa, what you doing in jail?"

"Last warning, Fletch. Shut your mouth."

Fletcher could see the mood that Bishop was in and moved back to his post against the wall.

"I guess you should have followed your own advice about keeping quiet," Tucker whispered.

Fletcher turned to face Tucker, his playful eyes now hard and flat.

"He can talk to me like that. You can't," he said to his former student and then hit Tucker with a crisp open hand slap across the face.

Felix heard the exchange and looked over. Bishop shook his head no, but Felix stared silently at Fletcher and Tucker for several tense moments.

Both John and Felix had looked up to Fletcher when they were kids and neither one had really forgiven him for turning into a dope fiend. He'd been a legend in the neighborhood and one of the greatest ball players they had ever seen before the drugs consumed him.

"You havin' a fight with your girlfriend, Fletch?" Felix asked.

They both stood rock still with their backs against the wall, heads down, and sweat pouring off them. Tucker had tears of humiliation rolling down his checks from the slap.

"Uh, no Felix, just a misunderstanding," Fletcher said.

"Don't bring any drama up in here. You two kiss and make up," Felix said, which brought nervous laughter from around the room. "Nice throw back. Tiny was the man back in his day, even if he was a Celtic. Those green shorts are a little over the top, but I respect the level of commitment to your costume."

"Well, okay, uh, thanks Felix," Fletcher said uncomfortably.

His yellow, unblinking eyes bore into them for another moment until both men exhaled slowly when he finally turned back to his conversation.

Felix was a wild and dangerous dude, but he loved to laugh and tell stories. He had fun wherever he went, jail or prison were no exception, and he was surrounded by four young guys that were hanging on his every word.

"Yo, you guys down with midgets?" Felix asked the group of youngsters.

"Say what?"

"Big titty midgets, man. You think about 'em?"

Felix looked over at John and winked at him, and John smiled back momentarily. He'd heard Felix's "little people" story before, and it was hilarious, but he drifted back to his own thoughts, rewinding the tape, trying to figure out how to explain this mess to his uncle. He'd started his day as far from jail as one could imagine, thousands of miles away, excited to see his family and begin a new life…

CHAPTER 3
COMING HOME

BEFORE LEAVING HIS Combat Outpost (COP) in Afghanistan to start his long journey to a jail cell in NYC he said goodbye to his "family." The Special Forces Operators on his A Team, Team Razor, were more like brothers than friends. The goodbyes had been hard, the packing was easy. After fourteen years of front-line combat duty the few items he cared about, including his parent's wedding picture, all fit neatly into two duffle bags. The bags were light. It was the dead that weighed him down. The friends and family he'd held in his arms as they died and the many men he killed all traveled with him. Wherever he went, they were always there, lurking, moving about in the shadows. He knew his dead would follow him home.

The first leg of John's trip was a military flight from Khost that took him to Hamburg, Germany. In Hamburg he read an e-mail from Felix giving him a heads up about the big welcome home celebration so he showered, shaved, and put on his dress uniform, probably for the last time. John knew he wouldn't have time to change once he got home and he knew how disappointed his uncle would be if he showed up at the party in civilian clothes.

A military police jeep drove him to the private airfield where a luxury Gulfstream G200 was powered up and waiting. John was the only passenger and after settling into a soft leather recliner he was sound asleep before they reached cruising altitude. Seven hours later Felix met him on the tarmac at JFK in a brand new Range Rover and after a long embrace they loaded up the bags, hopped in, and headed to the city. They didn't say much until they crossed the Williamsburg Bridge into the Lower East Side of Manhattan. The locals call it LES (pronounced L.E.S.), or simply The Lower.

"Man, it's good to be home, but everything looks different," John said.

"My dude, you been gone so long you're gonna need a tour guide. You're right though, the neighborhood's changed. Now it's million dollar condos, yuppies, and wine bars."

"You're kidding."

"Nah, I'm serious. Rich folks done bum rushed the hood, man," Felix said.

"That's crazy. I remember when cabs wouldn't come down here," John said.

"Police neither."

"True."

John was stunned as they drove by all the new luxury buildings and high-end restaurants. There were still lots of rough edges, but it was fast becoming a very upscale part of the city. LES had always been an immigrant neighborhood where Italians, Ukrainians, European Jews, and many others came through the gates of Ellis Island and settled into the thousands of five story brownstones throughout the area. Then, in the 1950s and 60s a huge influx of Puerto Ricans and African Americans moved in along with John and Felix's family who came from Panama. Black, Latino, Italian, Ukrainian and Polish populations all lived side by side, making LES a true melting pot that was one of the poorest and toughest neighborhoods in all of New York City.

Throughout his years at war he would dream of how things once were. Sleeping in jungles, deserts, or high in the mountains he would float back to the burnt-out ghetto of his youth. Even though everything looked different now it was still home, and the sights, the sounds, and scents of the neighborhood were like an electric current running through him as all the memories of his childhood came roaring back.

"You remember the congas?" John asked. They grew up hearing calloused hands banging on drums night and day, giving LES a rhythmic sound and pulse as if the neighborhood were a living thing.

"Ba bum bum bada, ba bum bum bada," Felix sang as he drummed on the steering wheel.

"How about the baseball and barbeques on the East River? Man I used to love those Sunday afternoons."

"That we still do. Remember the basketball games at Tompkins Square?" Felix asked.

"Those were wars."

"The run is garbage now. All one on five bullshit," Felix said.

"What about the viejo who sharpened knives?" John asked. The old traveling knife sharpener worked a foot pedal to turn his large wheel shaped stone that gave knives a razor's edge for a dollar.

"I can still hear that grinding sound."

"There'd be twenty or thirty dudes on line waiting to get their blades shined right there in the street."

"Sure was," Felix said.

"Hide and seek in the abandoned buildings!"

"Running round in the dark with hundred pound rats and fifty pound junkies. Why would I wanna to forget that?"

"Then we'd all go up to fight on the roof and Auntie would have to cut the tar out of our hair."

"Everyone would snap on us 'cause we were walking round with holes in our heads!" Felix said, laughing.

"Man, we used to beat the shit out of each other."

"Those were some good times, primo."

"The best," John said.

They were still reminiscing when Felix pulled up in front of Castillo's restaurant on Rivington Street to get a quick bite. John's mouth was watering when they walked in and inhaled the rich aroma of simmering beans and pork slow cooked with garlic and cilantro. The owner sent over rounds of beer and platters of food on the house, turning a snack into an hour-long meal that ended with John and Felix holding their bellies in satisfaction. They looked at each other and shrugged, both knowing without saying a word that their aunts had cooked a feast and they were going to have to eat again shortly.

When they left Castillo's Felix threw him the car keys. "She yours," Felix said. "And don't bother sayin' no. She's signed, sealed, and *legal*, all in your name."

After a long pause John smiled. "Gracias Felix, she's a real beauty."

"I was gonna put shoes on her. Make her even sexier with some chrome rims, but Tio said you wouldn't like the flash. I did upgrade the sound system and added a radar detector in case you ever wanna put your foot on the gas."

"I don't know what to say, man. I can't thank you enough."

That was true. John could never thank his cousin Felix

for what he'd done for him and the new SUV had nothing to do with it.

More brothers than cousins, they grew up doing everything together, and were once inseparable. That all ended on John's eighteenth birthday after a long night of drinking and dancing when they were confronted by five big guys in the West Village.

It should have just been drunken teenagers having a fight, but things quickly got out of hand. After a few punches were thrown by each side one of the attackers snuck up behind Felix and smashed a bottle over his head. John rushed in to protect his stunned and bleeding cousin. He braced himself with feet spread apart for good balance, left foot forward, chin down, elbows tucked, and fists close together just like his father, and then later, his uncles had taught him. When the first kid came in range swinging wildly, John ducked the punches, faked with an overhand left and connected with a vicious right handed upper cut, pushing up with his legs. It was a knockout blow that literally had the dude out on his feet, swaying back and forth. Unconscious and tumbling backwards, he seemed to be falling in slow motion until his head smacked the fire hydrant on the curb. The impact was like a giant egg cracking. Everyone knew it was bad. Fight over. The guy's friends went to help him and John and Felix took off running.

They almost made it past Avenue A, to Tompkins Square Park and into the safe zone of their home base when the cops caught up to them. They were both running flat out with John slightly ahead when Felix tripped and fell over a crack in the sidewalk. John stopped and turned back, but Felix waved him on.

"Go! Go tell Tio."

From across the street John watched the police swarm on Felix. They formed a circle and hit him with their night sticks. One of the officers asked Felix if he liked killing college kids while he struck him again and again. That's when John knew things were way past serious. The boy he hit was dead and cops were mercilessly beating his handcuffed cousin in the street.

The next day the papers were all over it. The boy who died was a Yale student and a rugby player from England and the story told by the New York press portrayed Felix as a vicious armed robber. They said he attacked the Ivy Leaguers without provocation and described how he pistol whipped the victim when he didn't hand over his wallet fast enough. "Yale Honor Student Beaten to Death by Mugger," was just one of the many headlines.

There was never any mention of an accomplice and Felix of course never said a word about John. In fact Felix never said anything at all, refusing to give a statement. His uncle was a powerful man who got him the best lawyers money could buy, but New York had so much racial tension at the time and the case received so much national attention that prison was inevitable.

John was with Felix, their uncle, and Felix's parents when they got the bad news.

"Felix, they offered a deal," his lawyer said.

"How much time?" Felix was still swollen, bruised and battered. Even though he spoke softly the big split in his bottom lip opened up and began bleeding from asking the simple three word question.

"Ten years, but you'll be out in less than half that," the lawyer stated, handing over a handkerchief that Felix used to gingerly dab at the blood running down his chin.

"You don't have to take the deal, but the DA will come after the family if you don't," Gonzalo said. "It's the press. If they weren't college kids and the case wasn't in the news we could make this go away, but they're all over us on this. Still, the decision is yours Felix. It's up to you if you want a trial."

"No Tio. I'd lose anyway, and the family has to be kept out of this. I'll do the years," Felix said.

"Wait a minute! Just wait a fuckin' minute here! He's innocent!" John shouted. "We all know I did it. Go tell the DA and let me take the deal."

"Felix has already been convicted in the papers and identified by three of the four witnesses. Unfortunately, he's going to prison whether or not you turn yourself in. If you want to keep him company that's your choice, but we don't recommend it," said the lead counsel.

"No Johnny, I don't want you with me," Felix said.

"Felix, we can protect each other... We can... You're innocent God damn it! I can't let you do time for something I did."

"Like the man said, I'm getting jacked regardless. It's okay primo, I'm good with it. Go home Johnny. Just go home. Tio, make the deal."

And so it was. Felix served four and half years in Elmira, a maximum security prison known as "The Hill" in upstate New York.

They had never really talked about it, but in his heart John knew that Felix had done those years for him and he'd never forgiven himself for letting his cousin, his brother, take the fall alone. The day Felix was processed and sent upstate to start serving out his sentence John walked into the Army recruiting station in Times Square and signed up.

It pained them both that things were never the same

after that fateful night. John was overseas when Felix was released from prison and they had seen each other only a few times during his infrequent visits home. They still loved each other deeply, yet neither knew how to say what needed to be said, and now there was a distance and an awkward tension between them that neither wanted to be there.

As John drove them north on Essex Street Felix pulled out a big bottle of Hennessy, cracked it and raised it up.

"Here's to you primo, welcome home." He took a deep pull and passed it over.

Stopped at a red light, John looked over. He grabbed the bottle and took a long drink himself before handing it back.

"I wish I had been here for *your* homecoming." He paused and went on. "We've never really talked about what happened. How you took all those years for something I did. I feel ashamed... I feel like a coward and I owe you a debt I can't ever repay."

Felix looked at him unblinking for a moment, thinking deep before he said anything.

"America's most decorated soldier feels like a coward? Come on, man." Then in a softer voice he continued. "Look cuz, the only thing that would've happened is that you would've been stacking' time with me, and that would've been bad. Real bad. You being the pretty boy that you are, I would've spent all my time protecting your sorry ass and the family honor. Make sure they didn't change your name to Juanita."

They both laughed and Felix went on.

"Listen J, we're brothers, and I know you would've done the same for me. They say misery loves company and prison's a miserable place to be, but believe me when I say it, there was never, *ever*, even a single day I wished you were there with me. That's the truth, man."

Felix took another sip.

"Besides, I got to spend those years with uncle Nestor, and he's got his own army in there."

"Isn't he getting out soon?" John asked.

"Between us, I hope he never gets out. He's our uncle, but the streets just ain't ready for that man."

"He's been inside for almost thirty years. That's a lot of time. People change."

"Not uncle Nes. He went away for one body, but he's killed more than twenty dudes since he's been in."

"Come on."

"For real. He did at least five on his own, and ordered dozens more. Nes points his finger at someone and they're just gone, man. He's a real scary dude J."

"Alright, we can talk about uncle Nes later. Right now there's something I've gotta say."

"You don't have to. We're good, bro."

"Cat, I know you're cool with it, but I'm not. I still feel like shit, and I'm so sorry. I'm so fuckin' sorry," John said staring straight ahead, his eyes tearing up. Then he turned to look directly at his cousin.

"I love you, Felix."

Felix smiled and said, "Don't guilt yourself over that night. I'm happy in my life and you're a fuckin' war hero. We're two bad-ass homies from LES. LES for life baby, and don't you forget it! Oh yeah, and I love you too… John!"

The last line was followed by a swift punch to John's right arm that left him numb. The fact that the light had changed and John had pressed the gas a little too hard as a reaction to the unexpected blow started the chain of unfortunate events. The traffic ahead came to a sudden halt halfway through the intersection, and John's lightning quick reflexes weren't fast enough to stop the Range Rover from slamming into the rear bumper of the car in front of them. The impact jarred the open bottle out of Felix's hand and spilled cognac over both of them.

When the two undercover police officers exited the dark blue Chevy Caprice they had just rammed both cousins knew they were in trouble, or at least John was since he was the one driving. They had sucked down the beers at Castillo's and even though they had each taken only a few swigs of the hard stuff they both reeked of booze from the spill.

The lead officer was an ex-Marine and was sympathetic when he looked at John's uniform. His partner wasn't. His partner had been driving the unmarked police car without wearing his seat belt and the collision slammed his face into the steering wheel. He was pissed off and bleeding from a deep cut on his forehead. Screaming and cursing, he ordered the cousins out of the car.

There was no doubt about the outcome and right away Felix started mouthing off to the cops.

"Hey jerkoff, you see those medals on his chest? Today's his first day back from the war, man."

"That's great news, 'cause the boys in city jail will make him feel right at home."

"Bitch-ass motherfucker!"

"What're you doing, Cat?" John asked while they were both being frisked.

"You think I'm showing up at your party without you and telling Tio that you're locked up?...That I couldn't even get you home from the airport? You're outta your fuckin' mind," Felix replied. "I'd rather go to jail than face that," he added.

Turning to the officer he said, "Write me up for disorderly or resisting. I'm going with him."

"Sorry pal, not gonna happen," the officer said.

"*Look*, write it up!" Felix shouted.

Then in a low, sinister voice that made the cop involuntarily take a step back he added, "Don't make me smack the shit out of you, cause believe me I will. Save yourself the embarrassment. Either let us go or we go *together*. You understand?"

And that was that. They were getting locked up for a few hours if not for the night and they were going to miss the party. Far worse was that they would soon face their uncle.

CHAPTER 4
EL GATO NEGRO

FORMERLY KNOWN AS "Happy" because of his bright smile and easy-going nature, the desk sergeant at the 9th Precinct had been a football star at his Long Island high school who married his childhood sweetheart. Happy now wore a permanent scowl on his face and had the hard sad eyes of a cop who's experienced way too much pain and suffering to ever feel love or joy again. He was six-two and heavy, on his way to getting heavier, but stood ramrod straight and spent each shift trying to suck in his gut.

"You clowns know who you just brought in?" he asked the two plain-clothed officers that had arrested John and Felix.

"Didn't see warrants on either of 'em," said the lead officer.

"The Green Beret? He someone famous?" the other cop asked.

"Yeah he is. You saw his chest. He's a God damn war hero, and you bring him in cuffed like a fuckin' perp?"

"If it was just the DUI we'd of given him a pass, but we've got a busted car, and I may need a stitch or two in my head."

"One whole stitch?"

"Look, Sarge, we wanted to let 'em go, but we just couldn't figure how to do it without jamming ourselves up."

"Shit!" the sergeant shouted, slamming his fist down on the desk. "This is bad. Real bad. You really don't know who he is? Who *they* are?"

"Okay, we give. Who are they?"

"You heard of El Gato Negro?"

"Yeah, that gangster, Gonzalo Valdez. So?"

"Those are his nephews."

"Serious? They don't even look alike."

"They're not just his nephews, they're his adopted sons."

"No shit. I hear Valdez is big time."

"And then some. He's the biggest this neighborhood and probably this city has ever seen."

"That's a bold statement, Sarge."

"Yeah, well I stand by it. The guy's run a multimillion-dollar crime syndicate for forty years, and he's never spent a day in jail. All I know is he's the worst kind a gangster there is."

"What kind's that?"

"Smart, ruthless, and low key. None of that Gotti flash that gets your name in the papers."

"Sounds like you admire the guy."

"Admire him? No, but I have a healthy respect for the man and I learned the hard way not to fuck with him."

"How's that?"

Happy looked away and thought back to his days as a narcotics detective in the Major Case Squad. Ten years with commendations up the ass, and he took down some heavy hitters before he set his sights on Gonzalo. Decided that it was his mission in life to take him and the whole Valdez family down.

He started from the bottom up, busting low level

players, and trying to flip them to get to the big fish. Problem was he couldn't get anyone to roll. Guys wouldn't even say the man's name when they were facing twenty-five inside with no parole.

People were terrified, and Happy heard some wild stories about a house of horrors in a Valdez private prison. He dismissed those rumors as urban legend, but one thing was clear, Valdez severely punished traitors, and generously rewarded loyalty. Anyone who got busted, even at the street level, had the best lawyers fighting for him, and if he had to do the time, his family got taken care of—with houses, cars, cash for the wife and kids—grannies, too.

The same "never give up" mantra that had made him a star on the football field had Happy more determined than ever to bust Gonzalo. Working off the clock, sleeping in his car, going through trash, and squeezing every source he had for info, he finally caught a break when he popped a mid-level Valdez dealer carrying ten keys of coke. Desperate for anything that would get him close to the boss, he temporarily cut the dealer loose after he shared that Gonzalo was taking the Amtrak down to DC for a big meeting the next day. Happy tagged Valdez at Penn Station, followed him down there, and took a bunch of pictures of him meeting with some suit in a fancy restaurant.

Happy couldn't wait to get back to NYC, develop the photos, and ID the suit. He pictured himself showing them to the Chief of D's, getting a few atta boys, and then building a real case against Valdez. None of that ever happened. He was sitting in a DC cab, daydreaming about being a hero when he got boxed in by two SUV's. He was abducted at gunpoint in broad daylight by Delta Force operators with aviator shades and ear pieces.

Driven to an abandoned warehouse, they held him naked and cuffed to a table for two days. In between beatings he found out the suit Gonzalo met with was a top CIA spook. They were on their way to the land fill when someone called and ended it. The operators were actually pissed off that they couldn't kill him, and one of them told Happy it'd be better for everyone if he spent some time investigating worms from underground. Before they let him go they told him to keep his mouth shut or they'd finish the job—said he was messing with the wrong people and to consider this his once and final warning.

When he got back he was booted out of narcotics, and barely managed to keep his job after being suspended for a month with no explanation. The icing on the cake was getting permanently assigned to the front desk at the 9th Precinct right in the heart of Valdez country, but the nut shot was a gift box delivered to his house by messenger. It was all wrapped and ribboned up, and Happy and the wife opened it together. Top layer was chocolates and truffles, the bottom had his Valdez snitch's chopped off hands holding a picture of himself in cuffs with Happy walking him into One Police Plaza. The wife left him that day, and he'd been sitting at his desk and staying out of Gonzalo's business ever since.

He couldn't share his story with the two undercovers who arrested John and Felix, but still felt obligated to warn them about the shit storm that was coming their way.

"Look fellas, all I can tell you is that Valdez is all the way connected. He got a lot of power in this town, and he's gonna be seriously pissed off at you two."

"Come on, Sarge. We're NYPD. Nobody fucks with us. I think you've been sitting behind that desk for too long.

You need to kick some ass on the street with us for a few days and get your bal… your head back in the game."

Happy knew it was only the chevrons on his sleeves that made the officer say "head" instead of "balls." It pissed him off that they saw him as a timid house cat, but he kept his cool.

"All I know is there's a big welcome home party just a few blocks from here for the war hero you just processed and he ain't gonna make it. Both nephews are in the system now and we can't undo it, so you'd best get 'em outta here. Did they make a call?" Happy asked.

"I asked the soldier if he wanted to use my phone, but he said he didn't want to get in trouble," said the lead officer.

"Actually, what he said was that he didn't want *you* to get in trouble. I didn't think anything of it at the time," his partner said.

"Well, at least he's looking out for you guys. That's a good thing, but too many people know 'em and the word's gonna hit the street. As soon as it does this building's gonna be surrounded by an angry mob." Happy didn't add that he'd already been captured once and wasn't about to let it happen again.

"Get a car right now and take 'em down to Central Booking before the shit jumps off," Happy ordered.

"You think that'll be the end of it?"

"Can't say for sure. You apologize hard enough to the cousins on the way downtown they might put in a good word for you."

"Apologize for doing our job?"

"Up to you. From what I just told you, you know Valdez is a serious player with lots of pull, and the man definitely holds a grudge."

"Gonzalo Valdez, huh?"

"Yeah, the one and only Gonzalo Valdez."

"Fuck me."

"Just hope he doesn't."

Gonzalo was born in Panama in nineteen-fifty, the eighth of Maria and Juan Valdez's seventeen children. The Panama of his youth was a daily adventure filled with fun and excitement with the country in a flurry of activity after World War II. Life was good in those early years. The Valdez family had money, was well respected, and they lived in a big house near the Canal. It was good until his father Juan, who ran a small club and gambling joint for GI's, was killed in a shootout with corrupt Panamanian police who tried to rob him. The same crooked cops who killed their patriarch confiscated the house and overnight the family was in a freefall.

Within weeks Maria was forced to beg for food and shelter to keep her children alive. Life became a daily struggle and everyone had to contribute. Gonzalo earned money entertaining the same U.S. troops that used to drink at his father's club by fighting in bare knuckle boxing matches. The winner takes all purse was a dollar, and driven by hunger, Gonzalo rarely lost. He literally grew up fighting for survival and his mother would hide her tears when he proudly handed her his winnings each night. "Gracias Negrito," was all she could manage to say as she cleaned and bandaged his handsome face that quickly became battered and scarred for life.

They were a proud family. They fought hard to keep it together, but as time went by their plight became increasingly desperate. Each dawn brought on a new struggle that slowly crushed their morale. No one spoke of it, but there was a collective sense of defeat and the realization that their days as a family unit were numbered.

One dreary night during the rainy season when the heavy clouds dumped bucket after bucket on the muddy city of Colon, a soaked Gonzalo angrily stomped into their temporary shelter feeling dejected after being knocked out for the first time. His mother called to him from a dirty mattress on the floor. She had been sick and bedridden for a week. Her voice had faded and was little more than a coarse whisper.

"My son, you must promise me something."

"Yes, mama."

"You've fought so hard to keep us all together negrito. You're the one who everyone looks to. Even your older brothers know you are the strongest."

"What are you saying?"

"You must lead the family now."

"Lead us? Lead us where? How can I do it? I couldn't even bring you a dollar today."

"The family is lost Zalo. We stay here we die. You will go to America and send for your brothers and sisters once you're settled. Take this." From under her worn blanket she handed him a thick wad of cash wrapped in rubber bands.

"But how?" he asked, staring wide eyed at the fortune.

"Your father's final gift to us. He buried it years ago in case anything happened to him. I waited until today to dig it up. Now there is no choice and no time. You're the only one who can save us."

"I'm not strong enough."

Using the last of her strength Maria pushed herself up and slapped him hard in the face before falling heavily back down onto the bed.

Wheezing from the effort, Maria croaked, "You have

the strength of your father and his fathers before him. Don't you remember the stories they told you?"

"It just seems so long ago."

"Zalo, you must never forget. *Never*. Always remember who you are. You come from men who fought and died for their freedom in those mountains out there. You come from great Kings... and now, now it is your turn... You must wear the crown my son. You must lead this family to a better life."

That moment, sitting next to his ailing mother on the floor of that broken-down shack in Panama, changed his life forever. His back straightened and his spirit lifted upon remembering the stories his father and grandfather used to tell him of his lineage. He could feel his own power for the first time and knew that there was nothing that could ever again stand in his way.

"And the promise?"

"Promise me that you will keep the family together. Bury me next to your father, then go to New York. My nephew is there and he will help you, but promise me that you will send for all your brothers and sisters."

"Bury you? I'll send for you first."

"No, my son. It is my time, and your father has been waiting. I go to him now. But I can die happy once I know my children are safe in your hands... Promise me! Promise me, Gonzalo."

He took her hands in his and swore that they would all be together.

"Good. Never forget who you are, and the power of the blood flowing through you my son. Now call the others so I can say goodbye."

And she did. The entire family gathered around her and she explained to them what they all must do. Maria died that night and right after the funeral Gonzalo boarded a ship bound for New York. He kept his promise and within a year his eleven brothers and five sisters had all joined him on the Lower East Side.

Maria's nephew was a small time dealer who introduced them to the drug trade and with his brothers behind him, Gonzalo and the "Valdez Boys" quickly became a powerful force on the streets. LES in the 60's, 70's and 80's was a war zone with almost as many abandoned, boarded up, and crumbling buildings as those that were lived in. Most of the neighborhood was just an open drug market where dealers, junkies, hookers, pimps, and gunmen strutted the streets that the police rarely bothered to patrol.

Gonzalo planted his flag, staking claim to an area known as Alphabet City. Running from Avenue A to D, and from Houston to 14th Street, he "owned" about twenty square blocks of prime real estate. There were many casualties over the years. Four of the brothers were gunned down in the early days, another was sent to prison for thirty years, and Gonzalo himself had been shot several times as they fought and died to build their multi-million dollar drug and gambling empire. Then, in the 1980s with his power base secure, he became careless with security, and the family suffered its most devastating loss.

Christina Valdez was the youngest of the seventeen siblings. She was tiny at just five feet, with beautiful bright shining eyes and a dazzling smile. She spoke very little English and had such an amazing voice the neighbors from all the adjacent buildings would open their windows wide so they could hear Christina singing from her kitchen. A happy little bundle of energy, she touched every person who ever knew her, infecting them with her joy of life.

In contrast, Michael Barrington Bishop was a feared Valdez enforcer who spoke little Spanish, stood tall at six foot four, and was pale skinned with long tangled dreadlocks. He grew up on the mean streets of Kingston, Jamaica and had a thick island accent.

With the language barrier, and the foot and a half height differential, Christina and Michael may have seemed like an unlikely couple, but for them it was love at first sight.

Gonzalo liked the young man a lot, and after warning Michael not to break his little sister's heart, he gave the happy couple his blessing. John Michael Bishop was born soon after they were married and Christina, who named him for her father Juan, only called him Juanito.

Madly in love and inseparable, they doted on their baby boy and only child. Those early years with his parents were happy times for John even though his cousins used to tease and torture him for his light skin and his gringo name. He used to come home in tears of rage and his mother would comfort him by pulling him to her breast and sing softly to him in Spanish. His father, being more practical, taught him how to fight and the teasing stopped soon after.

On a warm summer morning when John was nine, Christina asked Gonzalo if they could borrow his new car for a family outing. He sent the Cadillac over with his driver and they piled in the back, excited to take a trip out of the city. Heading south on Avenue D, the Bishop family was laughing and looking out of the dark tinted windows when the world exploded all around them.

Christina screamed as machine gun fire ripped through the doors and windows. Michael pushed John down to the floor a second before the tires were blown out and the car crashed into a bodega on the corner. The attackers didn't let up. Bullets twanged into the car's metal frame and thumped into the seats. Then Michael was thrown back by a shot to the chest. Husband and wife stared sadly into each other's eyes. Badly wounded, Michael coughed up blood, then dove onto Christina to shield her body with his. "Mi amor," she whispered just as the next fusillade of steel jacketed shells came in through all sides, killing them both along with the driver.

When the shooting stopped John was the only survivor. Blood poured down his face where a sharp piece of metal from the crumpled door frame had viciously slashed him from his forehead deep down into his cheek. He sat up trembling in fear, covered in gore, staring in horror at the bodies of his parents. From above the shoulders it looked like they were sleeping peacefully with their arms wrapped around each other in what John would always remember as a warm and loving embrace, but below there was only carnage where they had both been struck multiple times by the high velocity rounds.

The hit was aimed at Gonzalo. The killers thought he was the one sitting behind the tinted back windows. His street name, "El Gato Negro," The Black Cat, was given for his luck at surviving the many attempts on his life as much as for his dark complexion and yellow cat-like eyes.

Gonzalo was wracked with guilt for being so careless. He blamed himself for the death of his beloved little sister and even vengeance did nothing to cleanse him of his grief. The shooters themselves were quickly tracked down and slaughtered, although it took him another year to capture the two men who ordered the hit: the Davis brothers.

After the funeral Gonzalo brought the heavily bandaged Juanito home with him. His wife Grasiella could not have children of her own and Juanito became the center of their lives. Gonzalo reduced his workload in order to care for his nephew full time and together he and Grasiella were tireless in their efforts to bring the little boy back to life. They tried everything, but months after the attack he had retreated into his own world. Frantically rocking back and forth, he would constantly touch his own face like a blind man following the contours of the jagged scar. He refused to speak, rarely ate, and would wake up screaming from the nightmares that tortured his sleep. Each night Grasiella and Gonzalo lay on either side of him trying to make him feel safe and loved while he sobbed for hours in their arms.

Fearing that Juanito was at the point of no return, Gonzalo finally approached his younger brother Carlos who was Felix's father. Felix was two months older than John and they had been playmates since birth.

"Carlos, I have something very serious to ask of you. To ask of you both," Gonzalo said to Carlos and his wife Marci.

"You're the head of this family, mi hermano. There is nothing you can ask of us that we can deny."

"I'm not asking as the head of the family. I'm asking only as your brother and you or Marci can say no. Her answer is just as important as yours in this."

"What is it?"

"Will you give Felix to me?"

"*What?!*" screamed Marci.

"I am asking you to let Felix come live with me and Grasiella to save Juanito."

Carlos closed his eyes. "You ask too much," he said.

"Yes, I know. I knew it was too much before I came. Still, I'm here. I had to come, and I have to ask. If we don't act now Juanito will be gone forever. Also, know this.

Grasiella and I will never, *ever* try to replace you. You are his mother and father and always will be."

Marci and Christina had been best friends. She loved Christina and Michael and their beautiful boy so much that after many tears she too agreed that it was their last hope. The next day they delivered their son.

For John it was a blessing. Felix had always been a terror and his energy was infectious. Soon after he moved in John was up and out, playing, eating, and being a kid again. Even the nightmares gradually faded, but his face and heart were scarred for life. A shadow remained over him, a darkness and a deep pool of anger. It was something he would use to his advantage in the military many years later.

John, Felix and Gonzalo went everywhere together and because they were the only ones in the Valdez clan with the "yellow eyes" they were soon known as "los tres gatos," the three cats.

As the years went by the bond between the three grew stronger and stronger, and although they always called him Tio, both boys truly loved Gonzalo like a father. He taught them all he knew about life, the family's long history going back almost two-hundred years and the journey from slavery in Panama to riches in America. He taught them about the streets, about leading men, and being the head of a family. He also taught them to play chess. In return he demanded that they would not be fools.

"You'll make choices every day for the rest of your lives. Some are small, but many, many will be big life-changing decisions. Think before you make them. Think before you act." He repeated this over and over again to them until they could hear him saying it even when he wasn't there.

CHAPTER 5

SWEET DREAMS

BACK IN CENTRAL Booking Bishop sat on the bench brooding, reflecting on his life, and thinking about how he wound up in jail on his first night back home. In the end he knew it wasn't Felix's fault that they'd been arrested. If anything he was just angry at himself. He shouldn't have been sipping on Henny and driving no matter what the occasion. Most important of all he didn't want his uncle to think he was a fool after all he had taught him and after all these years.

"Hey Fletch," John said.

"Yeah Johnny, what's up?" Fletcher said eagerly.

"My bad for jumping down your throat like that. Been a long day and I'm missing my welcome home party."

"Don't sweat it, man. It's great to see you back, but sorry it's in here. Listen papa, there's a Muslim dude against the bars over there who's been scoping you," Fletcher said.

"Yeah, I saw him. Thanks for the heads up. How much time you looking at?" John asked.

"Probably eleven months."

"I'm gonna get someone to look into your case, but

you know if you don't wanna do the time, you'd have to go to rehab. You down with that?"

"Yeah, sure. I mean, thanks Johnny. Really, papa, thank you."

"You're getting too old to run these streets, Fletch. You get yourself clean, there's a job waiting for you when you get out."

"For real?"

John nodded his head.

"I don't know what to say, man. Getting busted today turned out to be the best thing that's happened to me in a long time." They both laughed and shook hands.

While John was in his reverie he'd sensed someone watching him and the man Fletcher had just warned him about was standing with his back to the bars across the room, still staring intently. He looked Middle Eastern with dark curly hair, a close beard, deep set eyes under a heavy brow, and a freakishly long hooked nose that gave him an almost hawk-like appearance.

Clearly enraged, he was scowling at John and started clenching and unclenching his fists. John didn't want any trouble. For a moment he stared back impassively, but looked away just as the guy screamed out, "Allahu Akbar!" (God is Great) then reared back and spit at him. The thick gob landed just short of his polished boots. John sat there looking down at it for a moment, then exhaled deeply.

Damn it, he thought.

Okay pal, you asked for it. Nobody spits at this uniform.
Make it quick, but whatever you do… don't kill him.
I'll try my best.

John ended his private conversation and eased up off the bench. His cellmates quickly formed a wide circle so they could all see the action. The spitter edged forward with fists cocked, eager to fight. John stood casually, waiting for his opponent to come in range when Felix jumped in front of him. He should have known that his cousin wouldn't be waiting around for some nut to throw the first punch.

Felix closed the gap in two short steps then fanned his left hand in front of the spitter's face. The quick simple hand feint created an involuntary blink reflex and in the split second the eyes were closed Felix followed through with a devastating straight right that echoed like a gunshot in the cell. His rock hard knuckles flattened the big beak nose and sent blood spraying from both nostrils. The spitter's eyes rolled back in his head and he went down and out.

"Damn!"

"Yo, you see that shit?"

"Sweet dreams mothafucka!"

Felix barely heard his shouting cellmates. Looking down on the unconscious man he stepped back to get more leverage in his kick and was about to inflict some permanent damage when John wrapped his arms around him and pulled him away.

Felix struggled to get free. "This bitch-ass punk spit at you, cuz! I ain't even close to done!"

"Easy Cat, easy. We wanna get outta here tonight. You already put his ass to sleep. Let's leave it at that, okay?"

Felix was losing it and fought to get free. His eyes blazing and muscles popping as John held him close.

"Cat, Cat. Be cool, be cool. You did your work, and we're never going to see this Jihad motherfucker again," John said into his ear.

Felix eased off and then turned to the group of youngsters standing close by.

"Pick up that piece of shit and throw his ass under the toilet."

Eager to please, they picked him up and roughly threw him in the corner with his bloody face pressed up against the steel bowl.

Felix turned to address the room. Taking his time, he looked every man sharing the cell directly in the eye.

"Anyone asks, he slipped and fell when he was trying to take a drink. He ain't from this country and thought the toilet was a water fountain. We clear?"

Every head nodded in full agreement. When his eyes met the Investment Banker's, Tucker's bladder involuntarily let loose. Felix shook his head as he watched urine drip out of the man's six thousand dollar suit and onto the floor.

Fletcher walked over to the unconscious body.

"Leave him be Fletch," Felix said.

Ignoring him, Fletcher took a tiny pin out of the waist band of his shiny green shorts. Pulling up the spitter's right pant leg, he carefully inserted the pin into his Achilles tendon and walked back to John and Felix.

"He won't even notice it when he wakes up, but within a week that tendon's gonna pop. Fuckin' asshole," Fletcher said.

Felix was laughing now. He put him in a head lock and then gave him a big bear hug.

"Nice job Fletch. Wish I could be there to see that thing bust," said Felix.

"Me too, but like I said, we'll never see that piece a shit again," John replied.

CHAPTER 6
TEAM RAZOR

Khost Province, Eastern Afghanistan

SPECIAL FORCES SERGEANTS Bobby Floyd and Able Diaz were that typical size and shape of American front line combat soldiers. Bobby at five-ten, a hundred-eighty-five pounds and Able at five-nine, one-seventy. Tough strong and lean, they were guys that never quit, guys that can take on anything and get the job done.

Bobby came from western Kentucky. He grew up hunting in the mountains and was considered by most to be the best tracker in Special Forces. People called him Tick, short for Bluetick Coonhound, some of the finest hunting dogs ever bred. Modern technology had nothing on Bobby "Tick" Floyd. He could read the land and find the enemy. Bobby was a man hunter.

Able "The Mexican" Diaz was born and raised in Detroit, Michigan. His parents were from El Salvador and got factory jobs in the auto industry after becoming U.S. citizens. He grew up in a poor all-black neighborhood where fighting was a way of life. Always small and lightweight, he learned early on that he had to fight or be victimized by the bigger guys. Then he had to fight because he was different. After a while he just fought because he liked it. Able was street smart and street tough. That, combined with Special Ops training, made "Mex" one bad-ass soldier.

Able and Bobby had been fighting side by side for five years, and they moved as one, each a mirror of the other. Best friends, they considered themselves true brothers and went everywhere together both on and off the battlefield.

The two Special Forces sergeants were standing in the central square of the tiny Afghan village. The rough road was made of dirt and tiny rocks. The houses were all mud and stone. There was no electricity, and the only well was a quarter mile away along a treacherous footpath farther up the mountain. The village had been there for a thousand years, sitting high on a plateau to help defend itself against neighboring tribes.

"No wonder these people are hard as nails. Man, there's nothing soft in this land," Bobby said, looking around at the harsh lunar landscape.

"Roger that. Even the goats look ready to throw down," Able said.

"And the women."

"Shit, they look meaner than the men," said Able.

"Uglier too," Bobby said.

"We need to thank Allah they cover themselves up."

"They really want to win this war, all they've gotta do is take the veils off."

"Game over," Able said.

"I know I'd surrender," added Bobby.

"Okay, you two, knock it off," said Chief Warrant

Officer Bear Bernstein as he ambled over with Sergeant Mace Hendricks.

Each twelve-man Special Forces A team was made up of ten sergeants, one captain who was the commanding officer, and a chief warrant officer (CWO), who was the second in command. Bear was aptly named at six-four, two-thirty. He grew up outside of Chicago, his parents both surgeons. Bear was following in their footsteps when he quit school to join the Army twenty years ago. They never forgave him for "throwing his life away," but Bear had never looked back or second-guessed his decision. He was a happy man and loved Special Forces.

"We're just getting warmed up, Chief," Able said.

"Warm? I'm not even moist," said Bobby.

"What comes before foreplay?" Able asked.

"Enough. You comedians start mingling and winning some hearts and minds," Bear said while looking around the square at the cold faces and hard stares they were getting from the men of the village.

"Those guys appear very progressive. 'Animal House' probably just opened here," Bobby said.

"Can we dance with yo dates? is my opener," Able said.

Bear and Mace were trying their best not to laugh, but Tick and Mex were good. After serving together for five years they had their routine down pat, and they prided themselves on always having fresh material.

"C'mon guys," said Bear.

"Chief, you know handing out Snickers bars to these dudes ain't gonna help our cause here. We need to help these people get a new water supply so they can grow bigger rocks," Bobby said as he reached down and picked up some pebbles from the road.

Mace smacked his pants leg, raising a cloud of moon dust. "We'll need to fly in a few million metric tons of top soil before we can even discuss farming," he said.

Sergeant Maceo "Mace" Hendricks was a musical prodigy. He was born in Washington DC, and by age three he could play any instrument placed in front of him. An accomplished Jazz composer and performer by his early teens, everyone expected him to have a long and successful career. It all ended at nineteen. He never told anyone the reason why, but he stopped playing and stopped writing. A few months later he joined the Army, six-one, chubby and out of shape. He quickly worked off the fat and excelled at everything the Army threw at him. Within a year he was offered a shot at Special Forces and had excelled there, too. His new instruments were weapons of war and once again he had mastered them all.

"Seriously guys, we're Green Berets. The fuckin' A Team. We're not called Team Razor for your sharp wit. You know the four of us standing here have more knowledge of these people and a better understanding of their culture than the entire Army, Navy, and Marine Corp combined," Bear said.

"Agreed," said Able. "But with all our knowledge these guys are still looking at us like we just came from outer space."

"Suggestions, Chief?" Bobby asked.

"Let's mosey over and get some conversations going. Maybe we can gain some intel. Find out if they're really pissed off at us or someone else. Major Burke's meeting with their head honcho, and when he's done we can give him some feedback from the man in the street. Worst case we'll get some close ups and maybe recognize some of these guys next time they shoot at us," Bear said.

"That's why you're in charge, Bear," Bobby said.

"Just don't stand too close to me, Chief. If they pick up on your Zionist roots we're gonna have to fight our way out of here," Able said.

"I'll gladly keep my distance, Sergeant Diaz. You skip the personal hygiene class back in basic? Man, you stink."

"His last bath was when he swam the Rio Grande, sneaking into America," Bobby said.

"Fuck all a' you. My people are from El Salvador."

"So you're southern Mexican?" Mace asked.

"I was born in the States, dipshit, and I don't stink." Able lifted his arm up over his head and sniffed his armpit. "Do I?"

Mace, Bobby, and Bear looked at each other and smiled and then they all turned towards Able shaking their heads in pity.

"Let's go," Bear said.

"Lead on," said Bobby, always wanting the last word as they walked toward a group of men who were smoking and drinking strong coffee in the dusty afternoon sun.

All four Green Berets wore tee shirts and flak jackets with khaki cargo pants over their mountain boots. Each carried an M4A1 assault rifle in his hands and had a pistol strapped across his chest. With their thick beards and sun glasses they looked like bikers, but their confident strides, headsets, and fire power identified them as elite fighting men.

They were, in fact the best of the best. Along with the rest of Team Razor they were trained in hand-to-hand combat, explosives, weaponry, communications, counter-insurgency tactics, and intelligence gathering. Between them they knew several local languages, and they had all studied the history and culture of the region, which is mandatory for Special Forces Operatives.

What really made these guys, like all Green Berets, so unique was that they worked in autonomous twelve-man Operational Detachment Alpha Teams (ODA's) or A Teams. Acting independently, with little or no oversight, they lived among the locals on the front lines.

Mace, Bobby, Able, and Bear were part of ODA 851, also known as Team Razor. They worked closely with ODA 834, Team Saber, and together had won the trust and respect of the Afghanis within their Area of Operation (AO). The team had traveled from its Combat Outpost (COP) twenty miles away to this small village near the border with Pakistan to try and win their trust as well.

Afghanistan is a tough country, but Khost is an especially brutal region made up of high barren mountains and shallow valleys that isolate the area from government control. For years it's been a safe haven and training ground for terrorist fighters who launch attacks from across the border in the frontier region of Pakistan.

While trying to increase local support on the Afghan side, U.S. forces were also trying to coordinate their actions with the Pakistani military. Together they shared information and targeted enemy bases, but even with this new joint effort the insurgent forces continued to gain strength.

Afghanistan's border with Pakistan, three miles east of the village

The five Afghans sat on rugs laid over the dirt floor of a tiny one-story rock-and-mortar hut that had been at the base of the treeless mountain for over two hundred years. All were heavily armed, with AK-47's across their laps and pistols stuck in their gun belts. Several Rocket Propelled Grenade launchers (RPG's) leaned against the wall. The road had been heavily mined above and below the meeting place, and there were over fifty fighters spread out nearby to protect these men against a surprise attack.

Usually communicating by encrypted messages delivered by courier or through coded websites they rarely saw each other face-to-face. Today was different. They were being hurt by the joint U.S.-Pakistani efforts in the region, and over the last two months had suffered heavy losses with more than three hundred men killed, wounded, or captured.

Aziz Khan had dark deep-set eyes that drilled into a man with an intensity that made even the bravest falter and turn away. Dressed in black from his turban to his boots while casually stroking his long full beard, he was the undisputed leader and the others waited for him to begin. He took his time.

Aziz had been at war his entire life and one of the many lessons of war was patience. Another was never to show mercy to his enemies. Aziz never did. He had a heart of stone, hardened when he began fighting the Russians as a young man, and hardened further when he watched his entire family slaughtered by the Soviet invaders. After sending them home in defeat he fought other warlords for power and control of his country. Then came the Americans. Now there were also the Pakistanis.

Aziz believed in war. Whether from outside his country or from within, there was always an enemy that needed killing. He didn't hope for peace as peace only made his people weak and unfocused, while war kept his men strong and determined.

"This new push by the Americans… it is a coincidence? They cannot know of our plans?" he asked.

The question was posed to the group, but it was Salman Hamidi, his Oxford-educated senior intelligence officer who answered.

"No Aziz, mission security is intact. Your nephew in New York has personally seen to everything, and he's done an excellent job. If there were any leaks or a breach by U.S. Intelligence our friends would have alerted us by now. We are ready to begin operations, praise be to God," he said.

"Salman, you speak kindly of my nephew, but he wears his anger on his face for all to see. He devised the plan, and I gave him command. It remains to be seen if he can control his temper. This mission requires discipline and patience for it to succeed, and he is not known to possess either of these virtues," Aziz said.

The next to speak was Tariq Hassan. His family home was hit by an aerial bomb when he was a baby and he was badly burned. A scar covered most of his face and only allowed his beard to grow in irregular patches. The youngest of Aziz's commanders, Tariq was in charge of military operations in Khost and in the neighboring Peshawar Valley of Pakistan. He had also spent two years training and fighting with their ISIS brethren in Syria and Iraq and had been instrumental in convincing Aziz to launch an all-out assault on New York City.

"The Americans are attacking us in our country, in our homes. We will continue the fight here, but we *must* bring the war back to American soil! Their women and children will know suffering as ours do. We killed thousands on 9/11, but our martyrs have killed only a few hundred since then. Our attacks will bleed them like they've never bled before. Allahu Akbar!"

"Allahu Akbar!" was repeated by all.

"Yes Tariq, they will bleed. The Americans are fighting here and against our brothers in Iraq and Syria while the U.S. economy is weak. This mission can be the fatal blow, praise be to Allah," Aziz said.

Aziz then spread out a large map of the region. "Now let us turn our attention to operations here and discuss this new threat from the Pakistanis."

As they surveyed the map and discussed strategies they had no idea that they were being monitored. Two weeks prior to this meeting a Special Forces Operator had placed a voice activated digital recorder in the ceiling when the shack had been identified as a potential location where high value intel could be gathered. In addition to the recorder inside, there was also a camera with a live satellite uplink positioned on the front door. The audio from the recorder would have to be retrieved manually at a later date, but the camera shots were available immediately.

Still photos of all five terrorists were downloaded from the satellite and sent to the NSA, CIA, Homeland Security, FBI, and Special Operations Command (SOCOM). The pictures were then entered into databases with facial recognition software. Members of the Most Wanted List of international terrorists produced a red flashing light when one was identified by the system and it was a senior analyst at

CIA headquarters in Langley, Virginia who was the first to see the "hit" on his computer screen.

"Bingo," he said when he saw Aziz Khan's name flashing. The "bingo" was soon followed by "holy shit" when Tariq Hassan and Salman Hamidi's names also blinked bright red. He quickly sent an urgent e-mail to all the department heads and the Director of Middle East Operations just as two more names from the world's top one hundred bad guy's list popped up. He ran down the hall shouting, "High Value Targets! High Value Targets!"

The news quickly moved up the chain of command and finally reached Colonel Paul Edwards, the local U.S. commander with "boots on the ground." All five names were already on his High Priority Kill or Capture List and as soon as he determined that they were together in a fixed location within his AO he immediately sent three Black Hawk helicopter gunships and twin A-10 Thunderbolt ground-attack jet fighters streaking towards the target. Surveying the map he saw that Team Razor was only three miles away.

"Get Major Burke on the horn, pronto," he ordered.

The meeting with the tribal leaders, the local elders, and the Imams had just ended when Major Burke was given his orders. After he ended the transmission with Colonel Edwards, Burke gathered the team to fill them in.

"Okay Razor, we have five HVT's less than two clicks from us. These guys are all senior management. Birds and fast movers are on the way, but we're going in first to see if we can grab some of these guys alive. Let's assume they've got a security force so if we're outgunned we'll fall back and wait for the flyboys to take them out. Questions?"

"Can we get an eye in the sky, sir?" Bear asked, referring to the UAV's (Unmanned Aerial Vehicles) known as

Predators that had infrared sensors and air-to-ground attack capabilities.

"SOCOM sent one our way, but it was on over watch way down south so we'll get there first."

"Understood, sir," said Bear, knowing that the jets would wipe these guys out before the Predator arrived.

"Okay Razor, mount up and move out," said Burke.

They climbed into the three armored Humvees and took off, bouncing down the rocky road at fifty miles per hour.

As he was now mandated to communicate with his Pakistani counterparts when operating in the border areas, Colonel Edwards called General Ghulam Mohammed to give him a mission update. He made the call reluctantly. It was common knowledge that a large portion of the Pakistani Army and Intelligence units in this frontier region held strong tribal allegiances to the Taliban, Al Qaeda and now ISIS. Even at the highest levels, security was a key concern.

One minute after Edwards made the call to update General Mohammed an encrypted phone in Aziz Khan's tunic started vibrating. His eyes narrowed as he read the text message in his native language of Pashto, "Run!"

Aziz jumped up. "A warning from Ghulam. The Americans are coming. Move out quickly. We will take the passage through the mountain. Tariq, your men will cover us."

"Gladly," Tariq Hassan hissed through gritted teeth. They all bolted out of the shack. Each of them paused for a second to look at the American armored vehicles in the distance before they turned and quickly ran up the mountainside while Tariq shouted orders to his men.

Each of the three Humvees held four men, except for the lead with Major Burke which carried three. One member of their team, Sergeant John Bishop, had just left the service and rotated back to the States. They were still temporarily a man short.

Burke had been in the Army for seventeen years, all of them in Special Forces. He trained and worked side by side with his men. He trusted them because he knew they were the best. He trusted them because they'd all shed their blood together in battle. His guys were smart, self-motivated, highly skilled warriors, and he loved them all like the sons he never had.

Burke spoke into his mic: "Eyes up for shooters or RPG's."

"We've got fucking bad guys with AK's up there on the slopes," was the quick response from Chief Warrant Officer Bear Bernstein, the second in command who was traveling in the follow vehicle. "Sir, I suggest we lay back until the birds get here," he added.

Bobby "Tick" Floyd was driving and sitting next to Bear. He chimed in. "Chief we're driving into a fuckin' ambush here. Tell the major we need to stop and back up before they hit us."

"I see 'em Bear and there's movement from the target," Major Burke said. He could see figures running out of the hut less than a quarter of a mile away. They were now driving up a steep hill on a narrow road with high slopes on each side. It was a perfect place for an ambush. He turned to the driver, Sergeant Dan "DC" Collins. "Slow 'er down DC. We'll wait for air support."

"Bobby says we're about to get hit. We need to stop now and back up, sir," Bear said.

Major Burke trusted Bobby's instincts more than his own. He looked over at DC and was about to give the order when they hit the IED (Improvised Explosive Device). The massive explosion lifted the five-ton truck off the ground before it slammed back down, landing in the crater. The Green Beret manning the heavy machine gun on the roof was killed instantly by the blast. Sergeant Collins was more stunned than hurt. He was semi-conscious, but trapped in his seat.

It was the right front tire that hit the mine, detonating directly under Major Burke. Blown out of the passenger door and catapulted skyward, he landed in the middle of the road. His right leg was gone below the hip, his left leg ripped off at the knee. Blood quickly drained out of him from torn arteries spraying from both stumps. Lying on his back Burke's hands were shaking uncontrollably as he looked up at a cloudless blue sky.

Following fifty feet back, the second Humvee skidded to a stop the instant the lead vehicle hit the IED.

"No! No! No!" Able shouted.

Bobby was on the radio calling for a CASEVAC when one of Aziz's men with a long tube on his shoulder popped up on the ridgeline above them. Mace was in the gun turret manning the .50 cal. "RPG! RPG!" he shouted, then started blasting away with the heavy machine gun. Mace hit the man low. The rounds shattered shins and knees, ripped through thighs, then gutted him before they blew through his spine and kept right on going. The dying fighter was doubling over when he pulled the trigger on the RPG. The grenade came in low, exploding five feet away from the Humvee. Shrapnel bounced off the armored grill and engine block, but ripped into the front run-flat tires, crippling them both.

From the ridges on either side of the road dozens of Aziz Khan's soldiers appeared on the high ground. Several of them were thrown backwards when Mace tore into them with the 50. The survivors concentrated all their return fire on him and a torrent of AK-47 rounds came at him from all sides. Bullets pinged off the armored gun turret, a ricochet slapped the back of his helmet, another creased his forearm. It didn't hurt yet, but his wrist and hand were instantly slick with blood. Time to move. Mace slid down from the gun turret, through the Humvee, and out onto the road.

Bear, Bobby, Able and Mace got behind the disabled vehicle. Bear and Mace were shooting right, while Bobby and Able found targets on the high ground to the left. They each fired in controlled, five shot bursts.

The third Humvee pulled up behind them. One of the Green Berets stayed up top firing the roof mounted M2 .50 cal while the other three sergeants jumped out and began shooting from ground level.

"Hey Bear! Ready to move?!" Bobby shouted.

"Let's go!" Bear shouted back as he killed two more enemy fighters on the ridge above them.

Before they took a step, they all saw a bottle with a burning rag stuffed in its mouth fly through the air. A fireball erupted when the Molotov cocktail broke apart on the crumpled and smoking Humvee that had hit the IED. Still trapped in the driver's seat, Sergeant Dan "DC" Collins, screamed and frantically beat at the flames.

Mace charged ahead with rest of the team providing covering fire and running behind him. He ignored the enemy rounds chewing up the dirt at his feet. Everyone on Team Razor was tight, but DC and Mace were best friends.

The Humvee was engulfed in flames by the time he reached it. Mace could see DC fighting to get free, violently throwing himself back and forth. He managed to get his head through the window, but his uniform and hair were already on fire. Burning alive, he turned and locked eyes with Mace.

The battle was loud. Beyond loud. It was a ceaseless, deafening, heart-stopping roar. DC didn't shout, but Mace heard him as clearly as if they were alone together sharing a beer in a quiet room.

"Kill me, Mace. Please kill me."

Mace nodded. Knowing he couldn't save him, he aimed his M4A1at DC's burning head, but then quickly lowered it and ran to try and yank him out. DC pulled his head back into the flames, grabbed his pistol shoved it under his chin.

"Nooooo!!!" Mace screamed.

"I love you brother," he said to Mace, and then pulled the trigger.

There was no time to stop and mourn. Bobby and Able ran forward up the left side of the road while Mace and Bear zig-zagged up the center. Two more Team Razor sergeants, Brian Ilchuck and Jimmy Waters, raced from behind the last Humvee and moved up on the right. All six Green Berets fired as they raced towards their commanding officer.

Major Burke felt himself going. He pulled out the family photos he carried inside his flak jacket—knew he was looking at them for the last time. He whispered a prayer, asked God to watch over them and said his final goodbye to his daughters as he kissed each picture. He died with his eyes open, staring at the image of his wife Amy.

Bear slung his M4A1over his shoulder, bent down, and easily picked up the torn and bloody body of Major Burke. Bear held him like a baby in his arms and watched the family photos slip through Burke's lifeless fingers.

"Let's go Razor. Able, grab the pictures of Amy and the kids," he said grimly.

Able bent over to retrieve them just as Sergeant Ilchuck was shot in his right shoulder. It spun him around, but he stayed on his feet and kept firing. Jimmy Waters got hit next, shot high in the left leg. He was on his back and firing nearly straight up at the ridge line. Mace stood over Jimmy to provide cover while the large force of fighters relentlessly fired down on the bloodied Green Berets from three sides.

"Let's go!" Bobby shouted. He sprinted across the road with bullets and tracer rounds coming at him. Shooting his M4A1with one hand, he grabbed Jimmy Waters with the other and carried him on his hip until they were behind the last Humvee. The surviving members of Team Razor were right on his ass. The steady flow of enemy AK-47 rounds pinged off the armored truck with a deadly rhythm.

Sergeant Raymond Riley was up top, furiously working the Humvee's .50 cal. Emboldened by the sight of the burning trucks the enemy became reckless. They abandoned their cover and came charging down the slopes. Now out in the open, Ray and the other Green Berets blew them to pieces, knocking down one bearded and turbaned figure after another. Ray was frantically rotating the turret and blasting away when he was hit in the back of the neck by an unseen shooter. Richie Lugo was pulling him down from the gunner's platform when he was hit multiple times in the gut and groin. The bodies of both sergeants fell down onto the rear passenger seats just as two RPG rounds smashed into the front of the Humvee. The blast rolled over the rest of Team Razor, leaving all six men lying silent, twisted, and unmoving in the Afghan dirt.

Flying in low, the pilots had a clear view of the battlefield. From above they could see the three burning vehicles and knew they were too late to save some of their friends.

The A-10 Thunderbolts released their ordinance disintegrating the lower face of the mountain and the Black Hawks streaked in with missiles and mini-guns. The pilots looked down upon the scene with grim satisfaction at the upturned faces below. Turbaned heads, arms and legs disappeared in a red mist as they shredded the enemy that had just killed some of their own.

CHAPTER 7
FAMILY

Long Island, NY

JOHN AND FELIX were released on their own recognizance early Friday morning after pleading not guilty before a judge. They were now sitting in the study inside the home of another uncle, Calixto Valdez. John squinted at the setting sun, its orange rays shining brightly between the tall trees, over the football field sized lawn, and through the huge bay windows he was facing. The house was really a mansion with sixteen bedrooms, tennis courts, a pool house, and guard's quarters. Calixto and his son managed all the legitimate family businesses, and although they were started years ago with street money, they were now completely separate and generated millions of dollars a year in revenue.

When news of the arrests got out, the party was rescheduled for Friday and moved from LES to the sprawling Long Island estate. Security was always tight at any event Gonzalo attended. In addition to the armed security on the grounds, there were roving patrols driving in concentric circles for miles around, and two small planes flew lazily overhead observing everything from the high ground. Everyone, including family, was thoroughly searched, and all cell phones were left at the gate.

The two cousins felt like they were in detention back in public school while they waited for his arrival. They sat patiently for a long twenty minutes when Gonzalo walked in and silently looked them over. He was an intimidating figure, and at almost seventy his life force still filled a room with an electric current. His scarred face was so dark and regal, and his yellow eyes so penetrating, that he often reminded John of the trumpeter Miles Davis. Always dressed impeccably, today their uncle wore a Ralph Lauren Purple Label ensemble with a black blazer, white silk shirt, grey slacks, and black loafers.

They both stood and nervously said, "Hola Tio," at the same time.

"Dos piasos," (two clowns) was his flat response. He crossed the room holding his arms out wide and then wrapped them tightly around John. He stepped back, but then came right back in for another warm embrace.

"So many years," he said sadly. "I've missed you."

"Me too, Tio. Sorry it's been so long."

"And you, I'm not even speaking to you," he said to Felix, yet pulled him in for a hug and kiss on the cheek nonetheless. Disappointed as he was he couldn't stay mad at his boys; the only sons he would ever have.

"So, how was your night in jail?" Gonzalo said jokingly.

"It was my fault, Tio," Felix said.

"Of course it was."

As they all sat down he added, "I thought you were going to wear the uniform one last time for the family."

"Lo siento (I'm sorry) Tio. I wore it on the long

flight and then after the night in jail... Well, I hope you understand."John was dressed simply in a white linen guayabera, with jeans, and black shoes.

Gonzalo waved his hand dismissively, changing the subject. "So, what are your plans John? Maybe get married and start a family? She's here you know."

"She," was Maria Williams. John and Maria had been in an on again off again love affair since junior high school. He hadn't seen or spoken to her in three years, and he couldn't wait to see her.

"Tio, all I want is some peace and quiet. Special Ops had me running all over the world and I feel used up. Think I might get in my new car and drive to Idaho... maybe Montana. Just camp out for the summer. Fish and hunt for my meals," John said, trying to hide how eager he was to see Maria.

"Go fishing for the summer? Well, it's your life, and you're too old for me to tell you what to do, but can I give you some advice?"

"Of course, Tio."

"Don't make it too quiet. Like me, you're a man of action. I know about some of your missions from my contacts at CIA, and I'm sure there's much more I don't know. From the briefs I read and the stories I've heard, you're the Army's Michael Jordan. I'm so proud of what you've done, and the man you have become. We all are. Still, part of me worries for you."

"Why?"

"Why? Because it's hard for a trained athlete to just turn it off, shut it down, and walk away. That's why Jordan kept un-retiring and that's why boxers fight into their 40s.

That's why soldiers always say they hate war, but keep going back to it."

"What about gangsters still being gangsters in their seventies?"

"Only sixty-six, but point taken. All I'm saying is, I don't want to see you become a Rambo. A man without a mission fighting the local sheriff and his deputies in Idaho… or Montana." They all laughed.

"Don't worry, Tio. I won't lie to you, I miss my friends. The guys on Team Razor are like brothers to me, but I'm not looking for another cause or another fight. And now that you mention it, I think time with a pretty woman sounds a lot better than being alone in the woods with mosquitoes and a fishing rod."

"Good. I hope you stay close so we can spend time together."

"Me too, but what about you? When are you going to retire?"

They both knew a great deal about their uncle's business. He had shared all his knowledge of the streets as part of their upbringing, but never gave them any active roles in his criminal enterprise. Although early on Felix was being groomed to take over, once he had the manslaughter conviction Gonzalo refused to let him be a part of it. Felix now ran the security teams that protected all the family's legitimate operations.

"You both know I love games. I taught you chess so you could use your minds and see how one move, one action, can change the entire outcome of the game. Change the outcome of life. Well I've played the ultimate game. I played for survival and freedom. The rules were simple. If you lose you're dead or in a cage for life."

"So you're in business all these years for the excitement, not for the money?" Felix asked with a sly grin.

"More money I don't need. What I want... what I have always wanted is for our family to be safe and secure. I want you both to know that the Valdez family is no longer involved with drugs. That is all far behind us now."

"Really glad to hear you say that, Tio," John said.

"The truth is I'm semi-retired already. I've turned most of the day-to-day operations over to your cousin Antonio and your uncle Sesa. From here on, I just maintain our high level relationships here and overseas."

"Maybe you should come fishing with me then."

"Maybe the three of us will go. Los Tres Gatos ride again."

Now being serious Gonzalo added, "You know, the business has changed. It used to be all about territory. You had to fight to get it and fight to keep it." He paused, a shadow falling over him as he remembered his slain brothers and little sister, John's mother.

"It painted a big target for our enemies and for law enforcement. They knew where you were and what you were doing. That's why your uncle Nestor's been inside for thirty years. Now we're behind the scenes. We're a mobile army, we're always on the move and we move everywhere. What's more important is that we don't need the drugs to make our money anymore. Don't get me wrong, I know the local narcos, the DEA, and the FBI all have long memories. Especially the Feds. I've never spent a day in jail. Never even been in a courtroom, and I know they want me bad. But I'd have to make a big mistake for them to get me now. Informants have always been the wild card in this game, so I talk to no one except you two, Antonio, and my brothers. As long as we all stay quiet and low key and don't draw any attention, everything will be okay. We all know from Felix's troubles years ago; it's when your name gets in the paper that they come at you. That's it. So you two keep out of trouble and stay out of the news. Okay?"

"Yes Tio," they said together.

"Anyway, enough about business. It warms my heart to see you both together again. We've missed you, Johnny, welcome home," Gonzalo said, hugging him again. "Bueno, there is much to talk about, but we'll talk later. Go. Enjoy your party... and go find her!"

Both cousins got up to leave when Gonzalo pointed at Felix.

"You? Where do you think you're going? Sit down, Señor Felix the Cat. You and me, we talk now."

Turning to leave, John looked back at Felix and gave him a big better you than me smile. Felix just rolled his eyes.

As John walked out the door and down the long hallway he thought about his uncle's advice. He would have to find something to do that would keep him satisfied both mentally and physically. He didn't need money either. Through Calixto's legitimate arm of the Valdez Empire, John, Felix, and all the inner family members had trust funds and property in their names. Calixto's son Nelson was known as a real tightwad, but he had an MBA from Harvard and had made everyone financially secure. John knew he was too young to lie around counting his money for the rest of his life, but he'd think about all that later. Right now he wanted two things: to see Maria and to have a very quiet and very peaceful summer.

The party in his honor was going strong on the great lawn with banquet tables of food and drinks, a live band, a packed dance floor, and banners with "Welcome Home

John" hanging everywhere. He moved through the crowd, stopping to speak with everyone and catching up on details from friends and family he hadn't seen in a very long time.

His cousin Silvia ran over and threw her arms around him. She was his Uncle Sesa's daughter, and they'd been really close as kids. Everyone called her Silvi and she was someone he could always talk to.

"So cuz, you're one badass super hero, huh?" she asked.

"No, nothing like that," he said humbly.

"Well I hope you've been training."

"What'ya mean?"

"Look around you, dude. Every chick in here is ready to pounce on you, man. If you listen close you can hear their coochies calling your name."

"Very funny."

"I ain't kidding. Some of them just want to give you a welcome home ride, but most of 'em are thinking about how cute your kids will be."

"You're still crazy, Silvi," John said laughing.

"Maybe, but I hope you brought a case of condoms cause all those putas scouted out Calixto's house so they know which rooms they can pull you into," she said with a devilish grin.

Just then her brother Antonio Valdez, Gonzalo's heir apparent, walked up to them with his top lieutenant and enforcer, Benji Medina.

"Hey Johnny, welcome home. It's really good to see you, bro," Antonio said as they embraced.

"You too, Antonio. I see you're still wearing the sweater." Antonio was the tallest in the Valdez clan at six four, but what really set him apart from the rest of the family was his hair. Balding on top, everything up to his neck was covered in a thick kinky mass. Antonio took the good natured ribbing from those close to him, but from no one else. He was no joke, and when it came to gangsters he was the real deal.

"Yeah, I'm still the family gorilla," he said smiling.

"Seriously T, Tio just told me the good news. You're going to be Don Valdez soon. I know how hard you've worked for this. Congratulations, Jefe."

"Thanks, but I'm still learning from the best."

"Tio is putting the family in your hands, and I'm proud to have you lead us."

"That means a lot coming from you. Thanks Johnny."

"Hey Benji! I see you're still watching my cousin's back," John said.

"Since the first grade. Good to see you bro," Benji said.

"You too, man."

Benji Medina was not an imposing figure. In contrast to Antonio, he was only five-eight, had a pock marked face and a slim build, but he gave men pause. He was known as "Medicina Medina" because a single dose of Benji was always fatal.

"What's up Steel Mags?" Silvi said to her brother.

Antonio flinched and hastily said his goodbyes, saying they'd talk and catch up later. He quickly walked away towards the main house with Benji at his side.

"Steel Mags?" John asked.

"He was babysitting my kids last week when I went to a friend's wedding. I come home and he's on the couch in tears, crying like a baby."

"Why? What happened?"

"He was watching that movie, *Steel Magnolias*, with

Dolly Parton and Julia Roberts. Some big time gangster, huh?" Silvi said, cracking up.

"I think you were a little rough. He practically took off running."

"That pendejo tortured me my whole life. It's time for some serious payback. You want to hear something really funny? Benji and his crew think "Steel Mags" has to do with guns or something. Like it's a tough guy nick name. The tag may stick!"

"Ouch," was all John could say. *Man it was good to be home* he thought as Silvi ran off to stop her kids from ripping down one of the big banners with his name on it.

The Valdez clan was huge. He had forty-two cousins living in and around New York and most of them were married with kids so Calixto's estate was quickly filling up. John spotted his uncle Macho in the crowd and walked over to say hi.

Macho had been a great boxer in his day. A Golden Gloves champion, undefeated in six pro bouts, his son Chris was born the night of his last fight. There were complications and Chris' mother died in childbirth. Macho quit the ring to raise him. Chris was his only child and his pride and joy.

Even though Chris was almost fifteen years younger than John they shared the common bond of both having lost their mothers. They always kept in touch and had written each other long letters when John was overseas.

"Where's Chris?"

"Right behind you."

John turned and was stunned to see the mischievous, gangly teenager he remembered replaced by a strong, handsome and confident young man. More than anything else it was the Army uniform that Chris wore that had him tongue tied.

"This one's following in your footsteps, John," Macho said, his voice filled with pride.

"But when? How? Why didn't you tell me?"

"I wanted to surprise you. "

"Are you serious?"

"He even got promoted already. You're looking at Private First Class Christopher Valdez "

"This is unbelievable!"

"There's more. Tell him Chris."

"I got accepted to try out for Special Forces. I start the course in three weeks."

"Come here, boy." John wrapped his arms around Chris. "So, I've got three weeks to get you ready? That course almost killed me. In the meantime let's see what you've got."

They squared off, throwing jabs and a few light punches at each other until John moved in and grabbed him in a head lock.

After Chris tapped out John said, "Seriously, congrats cuz. I see you're in great shape, but we're gonna do some insane workouts together before you head out to SF training."

"Yeah, that would be great Johnny. Thanks!"

"Thanks? You're the one doing me the favor. Now that I'm retired I'm already feeling soft," he said winking at Macho.

"Yeah, sure. I can tell, real soft. I'll call you tomorrow and we'll set up a schedule," Chris said as he and his dad went to get drinks.

Even though John was having a great time he was still looking for Maria. He finally spotted her sitting on a lawn chair away from the main party talking with his Aunt

Grasiella. He stood there watching them from a distance and realized his palms were moist and sweaty. He'd known Maria his whole life and she still made him nervous.

Maria's father was from Scotland and her mother was Filipino. She was the first girl he ever kissed and she was still the most beautiful girl he'd ever seen. Her complexion was a creamy mocha, her long jet black hair flowed down her back, her Asian eyes were dark, soft and shining, her lips were full, and her body was simply ridiculous. More important than her good looks, Maria had a huge heart, and was "wicked smart." She volunteered at the local Boys and Girls Clubs, had an MBA from Columbia, and was a Senior VP at JP Morgan.

Grasiella and Maria saw him and waved franticly as he worked his way over. He picked up the aunt that raised him, his favorite person in the whole world and gave her a tight squeeze that made her giggle.

Then he turned to Maria and gave her a hug and kiss on the cheek that was more formal than he meant it to be. After an awkward moment he decided it was time to speak and managed to croak out, "Huh, hi Maria."

"Wow! Really? That's what you got for me? After you were done saving the world I dreamed you'd come charging in on a white horse and carry me away. Even without the horse I was expecting a lot more than a huh and a hi."

She pulled him close and gave him a long lingering kiss that made Grasiella blush and smile with approval.

CHAPTER 8

THE EVIL THAT MEN DO

Union Square Park, Manhattan

"EVERYTHING IS READY, Amir. The men will not fail you, but you should not be here," said Khalid Mulan.

"I must be certain. There has already been one mistake, and the mistake was mine alone. Aziz will not tolerate another," said Amir Khan, standing with Khalid next to their off-duty cab on the west side of the park.

Amir couldn't hide his tension and ignored Khalid's disapproving stare. He wanted to be at the scene even though he knew his battered face was attracting unwanted attention. His smashed in nose had been poorly reset. It looked unnaturally crooked and both his eyes were swollen and black with green highlights around the edges. The dark sunglasses he wore did nothing to stop the sun's rays from repeatedly stabbing him in the brain and he was still seeing spots from getting "sucker punched" during his night in jail.

Amir still could not believe his own stupidity. He wound up in jail because he forgot his wallet and driver's license at the safe house. He was heading here to the park to scout it out one last time and was focused on the mission instead of the road when he was pulled over for going through a red light. Just two days before the operation that he'd planned for years he gets arrested and then gets his nose broken.

Right away he had known he was in big trouble and it only fueled his anger. He was angry at himself for getting arrested. He was angry that he lost his temper and spit at the soldier. More than anything he was angry for getting beat up. Amir also knew that if this mission did not go as planned he was a dead man. His organization was unforgiving and family or not, his uncle Aziz would have him eliminated.

"You know, they will call on you to kill me if anything else goes wrong, Khalid."

"Amir, we have been friends since we were boys. You are my brother, and I will gladly give my own life to protect yours."

"Let us pray that Allah keeps us both alive. At least until our work here is done."

"Have faith my brother, and look around you. Allah has blessed us with good weather and the target is filled with infidels," Khalid said, as they surveyed the park. They had picked Union Square because of the large crowds and light security. One of the few city centers without check points and security cameras, it's a central hub for New Yorkers with eight subway entrances and six different subway lines that keep the park crowded with lots of through traffic.

Busy year round, warm weather increases traffic tenfold, and every Saturday from spring through fall there is a bustling farmer's market surrounding the park where they sell homemade pies and breads, grass fed beef, fish, fresh fruit, and locally-grown vegetables. Dozens of stalls are set up for the thousands of shoppers that pass through.

This Saturday in June the sky was clear, the sun shone brightly, and the light, easy breeze made it one of those perfect summer days. The park and surrounding market were filled beyond capacity, people shopped to the island rhythms of a decent reggae band, and some talented teen-age break dancers put on a show for the crowd.

Amir looked on with indifference at the scene in front of him. He saw no beauty in the tall trees that shaded the benches where people were eating lunch and relaxing. The happy hum of children's laughter from the large play-ground at the park's north end did not touch him. The many families and women with strollers walking nearby meant nothing to him. These were his enemies, nothing more than moving targets.

"Fucking Americans. I wonder how many we will kill today?"

"Many Amir, many."

Amir and Khalid were both of the Pashtun tribe and grew up in small Afghan villages east of Kabul. Amir began fighting by his uncle's side when he was a boy, first as a lookout climbing the high rocky bluffs and mountain peaks in search of the enemy, and later, given his own rifle, he became a deadly sniper. He shot his first man at age eleven and there were many more after that. Despite his bad temper and insatiable appetite for killing, his uncle Aziz had seen intelligence in him. Amir spoke seven lan-guages including English and some broken French. A long term planner, Aziz ordered Amir to go to America, "to help destroy the enemy from the inside."

Given a false identity, he arrived in New York and for

the past five years his uncle had been sending him men and money. He had also recruited his own soldiers and established cells throughout the city.

Amir patiently planned for the day when they would strike and that day was today. Once this mission was completed three more massive strikes were to follow that would cripple the city and maybe even the entire country. His dream was to bring America to its knees. He wanted the world to know his name. He wanted the world to know that a poor mountain boy from Afghanistan destroyed the superpower that dared to invade his country.

"Go now, Khalid."

"You're not coming?"

"Soon, soon. You go on ahead. I will meet you later to celebrate and prepare for the next attacks."

"As you wish, Amir, but don't stay long. Everything you see, including the ground under your feet will be gone very shortly."

"God willing."

"It is God's will that these devils all die today, my brother."

"I know it is Khalid. Go now and get the other teams ready."

As Khalid walked away Amir gazed upon the thousands of men, women and children all around him. He hated them all and wondered again how many they would kill today.

CHAPTER 9
MARIA

Queens, NY

WHILE AMIR WAS thinking about murder John was thinking about love. He and Maria had talked for hours at his party the night before and once they got to her house in Queens there had been no pretenses. They both desperately wanted each other and clothes were coming off before the door closed.

The sex had been violent at first. Fast, rough, and angry. Only after they had purged the pain of their past hurts did they slow their pace, becoming more tender and more passionate. Drenched in sweat, they gripped each other tightly as they came together. Afterwards, bathed in the warm light of the full moon, they lay staring into each other's eyes, saying I love you without a word being spoken.

John slept deeply and slept late for the first time in a very long time. He was still on a combat schedule and usually shot up an hour before dawn with his senses keen and alert. Today he woke up at nine with a lazy smile and Maria's sparkling eyes on him.

"I know you just got back and you just woke up so I'm not trying to put any pressure on you, but there's something I need to say," she said in a soft voice.

John sat up and laced his fingers through hers, waiting for her to speak.

"I've loved you my whole life, Johnny. I love you, and I've been waiting a long time for you. Waiting without any promises. Waiting without knowing if I've been waiting in vain. Worrying that you might get hurt again or even killed this time. Worrying that you might have met someone else and come home married." She paused, wiping away tears and trying to maintain her composure.

"I love you, I want to marry you, and I want us to have lots of kids together before I'm too old to have them. Sooo... what's it gonna be big guy?" she asked with a fearful smile.

Looking back at their long love affair, all their breakups had been over stupid things. Although it seemed big and important at the time it was always something insignificant that tripped them up. They would argue over things that he couldn't even remember now and a disagreement would escalate into a fight and the next thing he knew they were broken up. Before either of them could take back what had been said he would be on a plane heading into another war zone.

In his heart John knew that he had been unfair to her. He'd been running from Maria and from himself for a long time. The death of his parents, accidentally killing the Yale student when he was eighteen, and Felix going to prison for his mistake had all haunted him. These were his demons and they had eaten him up and driven a wedge between them. Not anymore. Now he felt more at peace than he had ever been.

Less than two months ago he had been talking and laughing with his buddy Sammy Mills in Kabul. John and Sammy had gone through Special Forces training together. They became fast friends and were both unofficially adopted and mentored by their CO Tommy Burke. They were separated when John was assigned to the 7th Special Forces Group that operated in Central and South America because of his fluent Spanish. But later, with all the action in the Middle East, he re-united with both Sammy and Tommy in Iraq and Afghanistan as part of 5th Special Forces.

John and Sammy were sipping morning coffee at a small café in Kabul when a young kid on a bicycle rode up to them. They smiled and waved at him, not realizing the kid's intentions. He raised an ancient, large caliber revolver, steadied it with both hands, and casually shot Sammy in the face. John killed the kid, who couldn't have been more than thirteen, then bent down to check on Sammy. His lower jaw was gone, teeth and bone fragments were stuck in his throat. He held him tight, breathing into the gaping hole that used to be his mouth, waiting for the ambulance that never came. Sammy died in John's arms, staring into the eyes of his best friend.

Men die in war and John had buried a lot of buddies over the years. You stay on the front lines long enough you bury friends, or friends bury you. Period. He lived this, he knew this, and still he just couldn't get past Sammy's death.

Finally, after starting three fights on base and volunteering for every hot mission he could Major Burke pulled him into his tent and sat him down for a talk. "Look Johnny,

I know Sammy's death hit you hard, but you've got to let him go."

"I'm trying, I'm really trying."

"We've known each other a long time, and I care too much about you not to tell you the truth when it needs telling. Johnny, you're probably the greatest fighting man I've ever seen or ever heard of. That's the truth. You're the best. Not 'cause you're the bravest, though you are one heroic son of a bitch. No, you're the best cause when the lead's flying and the bombs go off, most guys, no matter how tough, no matter how brave, and no matter how well they're trained, still get a little nervous. They'll flinch, or hesitate, or rush, or do something foolish that gets them or their pals killed. Not you Johnny. You stay cool. I've seen you, man. It's almost an eerie cool. It's like you slow everything down and you kind of float across a battlefield. You always seem to know which guy to take out first or last. Somehow, you instantly know the sequence. It's like you're playing chess out there Johnny, and it makes you real special, but it scares the shit out of a lot of guys who are some pretty scary motherfuckers in their own right. When it comes to killing you're one spooky dude, my friend."

"What're you saying, Tommy?"

"What I'm saying is this man: you've got to bury your dead. You told me a long time ago about your mom and dad being murdered in front of you, and you've seen a lot more death since then. You have 'em all wrapped around you like a blanket and it makes you one deadly motherfucker out here, but it's not letting you have a life, man. Outside of your patchwork quilt of dead family and friends you've got nothing. You're afraid to go home. You're afraid to live."

John was shaking with anger and ready to rip Tommy

Burke apart for what he'd just said, but Tommy continued on. "Johnny, I can see you want to kick my ass right now. All I can say is, do what you gotta do man, no hard feelings. Just know that I'm saying what everyone else out here knows, but are too chicken shit to tell you. They're too scared of what you might do to them, and too scared that you might lose your edge and not be there to save their sorry ass in the next fire fight."

He'd looked down at his feet for a moment, then added, "Johnny, I love you, and I don't want to see you get wasted out here. You've done your share. You're not even fighting the enemy anymore. You're just trying to kill your own demons. That is guaran-damn-teed to get you blown away, son. Bury your dead and leave them here. Go home and get a life, man. Marry Maria if she'll still have you."

"What about you? Majors don't lead A Teams, Captains do. So why're you still out here?" John asked in a shaky voice.

Burke had shaken his head slowly and then with disappointment in his eyes said, "You already know the answer to that. First off, you guys on Razor are the sons I never had, and I can't put my boys in the hands of a stranger while we're at war. I called in every favor I could, and then had to beg and plead to keep my command. Second, I'm a working man. My whole check, every dollar I earn goes directly to Amy and the girls. I've got seventeen years in this man's army. Three more till retirement and a full pension, then no more humping through the mud shedding my blood. It's watching my lawn and my baby girls grow, giving them all lots of TLC, and waking up with Amy in my arms for the rest of my life. And I'll tell you something else. If, God forbid, I catch a bad break and get blown away out here, I'll be real sad about it, but I'll also accept it and die a happy man. You wanna know why?" Burke asked looking deep into John's eyes, piercing him.

"The reason is that I gave my country the full measure of my devotion and service, the same way I gave my wife and kids all the love in my heart. So I'll be real sad that I won't get to walk my girls down the aisle and grow old with Amy, but I'll die knowing how much they loved me, and how much I loved them in turn. With my last breath I'll whisper their names and ask God to protect them for me."

Burke started getting angry then.

"Johnny, the only two guys out here who've known about your money are me and Sammy. Sammy's dead, and I've never told a soul and never will. I've never thought less of you for it, or that you were some rich punk with something to prove. But, the fact is you don't need to be here, man. You don't need this job. Your papers are here. I took it upon myself to have them prepped and ready. In a month you can be back home. Walk away Johnny, walk away. You saved my life four times out here, and I'll miss you, but do it. Go home before it's too late. Walk away before you've got nothing left inside. It's time to stop the killing and start the living."

John had stumbled out of the tent feeling drained and beaten by Tommy's words. It took him and his battle buddy two days to fully digest it all. Then the storm clouds in his head parted. He realized that almost everything he believed in was a lie. He'd warped his own truths to cover up his guilt, sorrow, and anger. He'd run away from his family and from the woman he loved. He'd lied to himself and to her. He knew he'd wasted a lot of years of their happiness and he was suddenly desperate to get to Maria and to start a real life with her.

He signed his discharge papers that afternoon. He'd had many more talks with Tommy Burke over the next few weeks while he waited for his release and his ticket home. He told the major that he'd saved his life and he wanted him to be at the wedding. Tommy had two weeks of R & R in August so they would schedule it then.

"Don't you think you better propose first?"

"Planning on it, sir."

John had gone on his last mission just before his papers came through. He traveled through the mountains near the border and placed surveillance equipment in an old shack that was a suspected enemy meeting place. It took him and his battle buddy two days to make the round trip. They could have done it in one if they'd killed the enemy scouts and lookouts they came across, but his fighting days were over. He chose to go around instead of through them.

He said goodbye to his many friends, the operators from his ODA, Team Razor, and he told Tommy he would send a letter with the wedding invites for him and his girls. John felt like a new man, as if he'd been reborn. He felt lighter because he was. He left most of his dead in Afghanistan. Most of them. The final moment of cleansing had been his talk with Felix and even though they'd gone to jail right afterwards it was well worth it. The last of his demons were gone and he could finally start living a real life.

He'd planned to tell Maria all this in time. He just didn't want to blast her with everything on their first day together.

"I'm so sorry, Maria," he said.

She immediately burst into tears, falling face first into her pillow.

"No baby, you don't understand," he said pulling her close. "I'm *sorry* for all the years I wasted for both of us. I'm sorry I kept running away. I've loved you from our first kiss. No, from even before that. From the moment I first saw you in the fourth grade. Then it took me three years to get up the nerve to kiss you. I loved you then, and I love you now more than ever. I left the service, honey. I left to come home to you. We're getting married in August. Tommy has leave then and he has to be there."

Maria pounced on him and screamed at the top of her lungs, squeezing his neck until he could hardly breathe. They kissed and laughed and kissed again. Then she pulled back and said, "Two things. One, you didn't kiss me first, I kissed you. I waited and waited for you to make a move, but you were such a big chicken I knew I had to do something or end up an old maid. I kissed *you* first, you big liar!" she said and gave him a punch in the chest.

"Okay, okay you kissed me! What else?"

"What else and second is this: What kind of lame ass proposal was that? You didn't even ask me to marry you. You just said we're getting married in August. How do you know I'll even say yes?"

"What? You just told me that you wanted to… You're driving me cra…" He stopped in mid-sentence and composed himself. He picked her up and gently sat her on the edge of the bed. Getting down on one knee he asked her.

"Maria, will you marry me?"

"Yes! Yes! Yes!" she screamed, then quickly kissed him and ran to call her mother.

Feeling dizzy from the morning's events, he leaned back against the bed and shook his head. He smiled while he listened to Maria squealing on the phone and realized that for the first time in his life, or at least as far back as he could remember, John Michael Bishop was truly a happy man.

CHAPTER 10
ALWAYS A GREEN BERET

MARIA WAS GOING dress shopping with her mother and the newly-engaged couple planned to meet for dinner around seven. John called Felix and met him at his apartment on East 9th Street. When John told him about the wedding plans Felix immediately grabbed him in a tight head lock.

"It's about fuckin' time, man. That woman is a saint and she's finer than Beyonce, J Lo, and Halle Berry all rolled into one. You know, she hasn't gone on a single date in the three years you've been gone. I don't know why, but Maria's always loved you, man."

John slipped out of the hold, pulled Felix's arm up behind his back and flipped him lightly onto the rug.

"You're getting soft, Cat. You been sparring against little kids?"

"I don't wanna send you back to Maria all broken and bruised. Plus, I figure I owe you for last night."

"Owe me for what?"

"Man, you had all those chicas at your party primed and ready. When you left with Maria there was nothing left but drunk, jealous, horny women. You used to be my cousin, my brother. Now I'm just gonna call you my fluffer!"

"So I guess you did your duty and took care of 'em all."

"To the best of my ability, son," Felix said, giving a mock salute. "Calixto has a big house and I left wet spots all over it. I'm drained, bro. I got to Angie last and she wore my ass out."

"She's a big girl."

"Yeah she is, but big girls need love too, and whenever I drink I tend to go heavy. I'll tell you one thing, whoever ends up with that heifer is gonna need steroids and Viagra mixed in with their cornflakes just to keep up. That woman is no joke."

"Sounds like marriage material."

"I could do worse. Hey, you remember that big sister who ran the laundry on Avenue D?"

"You're talking about Willemina? Now that woman was huge. Looked like she had bowling balls in her bra, and that ass. Yikes."

"Well, I used to jerk off to that hefalo every night before I went to sleep."

"Yeah, I remember you making love to your tube socks all the time. Didn't know it was big Willemina making you rub yourself raw."

"Yeah it was, asshole. Anyway, Angie reminds me of her."

"Whatever makes you happy, primo."

They laughed and talked some more and decided to have a fancy brunch to celebrate. They headed to Blue Water Grill at Union Square Park and passed through the basketball courts in Tompkins Square on the way.

"Remember how I used to light your ass up out here when we were kids?" asked Felix.

"You know you never came close to beating me, and I used to let you score just to keep it interesting."

They borrowed a ball and John put on a dribbling exhibition in front of Felix, who kept lunging for steals. John had been a real magician when it came to hoops, but hadn't played in years.

Putting the ball effortlessly through his legs and behind his back while Felix kept reaching, John said, "Speaking of name changes, Cat just doesn't fit anymore. You're looking real slow and sloppy out here, Dancing Bear."

"I'll let you dribble all day long, but you ain't gonna score."

"You know, I just realized something," John said, still quickly moving the ball from hand to hand.

"What's that?"

"I'm jealous of you."

"That's understandable."

"No seriously. I can't see myself play. I'm jealous 'cause you get to watch me."

"Whatever," Felix said, rolling his eyes.

"So, tell me the truth. All those times I busted your ass, was it as good for you as it was for me?" As he finished his question, John lifted off the ground from twenty three feet out, and in one smooth motion effortlessly shot the ball over Felix's outstretched hand. With perfect rotation and a high arch it sailed into the hoop, ripping through the net.

"Why punish yourself like this?"

"Asshole."

"By the way, you're my best man at the wedding."

They left the court with their arms over each other's shoulders and walked the ten blocks to the restaurant. They toasted the upcoming wedding, tossed back fresh oysters, and ate steamed lobsters. After the meal they stepped out into the bright afternoon sun and onto the crowded sidewalk facing the park.

"I need a new pair of sneakers," Felix said. "Wanna walk me to Paragons?"

"Think I'll just wander around the market till you get back. I'll stay in this area, but call me if you can't find me in the crowd."

Amir Khan was restless and full of nervous energy as he sat in the cab next to Blue Water Grill. He saw the two men exit the tall front doors of the restaurant. He could only see his profile, but the one with the crew cut was vaguely familiar. He couldn't remember where he'd seen him; just that something about the guy bothered him. It nagged at Amir for a moment, then he dismissed it and focused his attention back on the mission. His teams were in place by now and his palms were wet with anticipation.

Man he was feeling good. The sun was shining, people were laughing, and he finally felt right again with Felix. Best of all he had Maria back. And, oh yeah, he was out of the army and getting married. Take his night in jail off the table, and it was one hell of a home coming.

Looking at all the afternoon shoppers he was amazed at the amount of children. There were boys and girls riding on their fathers' shoulders and mothers pushing strollers everywhere. It made him realize for the first time in his life how badly he wanted his own kids.

Soon, he thought.

John was happily strolling from stall to stall when the hair on the back of his neck stood up and alarm bells suddenly began ringing loudly in his head. His "Spidey Sense" as he called it had saved him countless times against unseen enemies, and it was now telling him that he was once again in harm's way. Hearing the laughter of children and seeing all the smiling faces around him he thought he must be imagining things and tried to dismiss it.

Probably just decompressing from combat.

He slowed his breathing and did a three hundred and sixty degree scan of the area, then shrugged. "I'm losing it," he said aloud a split second before he spotted two men standing rock still in the middle of the moving crowd. They were both wearing matching black long sleeve jackets, which was odd for such a warm day and their weathered skin and dead eyes reminded John of the Tali and ISIS soldiers he had just been fighting against. One of the men had his head down and seemed to be talking to himself while the other was tensely scanning the crowd.

These guys were wrong. John edged closer. Moving casually with the flow of tourists and shoppers, he angled his way towards the two men. He stopped a few feet behind them, but kept his back turned and pretended to be reading a text message on his phone. He did his best to tune out the background noise and zero in on what the guy with the book was saying. John immediately recognized the man was speaking in Dari and realized he wasn't talking to himself, but reciting an excerpt from the Koran. John turned slightly to get a peripheral view. He stayed relaxed when he saw the hand held detonator and the wires running up into the sleeve of the terrorist's jacket. The other man had an unzipped bag at his feet and John could see the butt of an automatic weapon poking out of the top.

Most suicide bombers act alone. After a few had been

stopped and overwhelmed by crowds before they could blow themselves up there were now instances of two man teams. One is the bomber and the other acts as security, ready to shoot down any good Samaritans that try to intervene.

What made the scene so incredible was that no one else noticed or paid any attention to these guys. People were just walking by and standing next to two suicide bombers in the middle of downtown Manhattan!

John was glad that no one noticed. If someone shouted an alarm the crowd would panic and the terrorist would release the trigger and detonate. John knew he had to act fast.

Retired or not, civilian or not, he would always be a Green Beret. He took the Swiss Army knife he always carried out of his pocket, opened the blade, and slid in behind his two targets. He didn't hesitate. His body coiled like a spring, from two feet away he exploded forward with deadly speed and precision, plunging the knife into the back of the security guard's neck. The blade entered right above the shoulders, severing the spinal cord so swiftly and forcefully that the man was dead before he could make a sound.

The bomber was unaware of what just happened and was finishing his final prayer when he saw his partner fall forward. His mouth shot open and his eyes bulged wide with surprise. They bulged even wider when John hit him with the same knife blow from behind, instantly killing him where he stood.

He knew the dead man would spasm so he grabbed the hand with the detonating button before the terrorist's thumb released the trigger. Holding on tight, John fell to the ground with the body.

Dozens of people had just seen two men killed in broad daylight. They screamed and ran in panic.

"He killed them! He killed them!" one hysterical woman shouted as she charged through the crowd.

In the sea of human chaos John stayed cool. Holding firmly onto the firing button, he pulled open the dead terrorist's jacket to make sure there were no trip wires or booby traps that would detonate the thick wads of plastic explosive strapped to the body.

As an 18C SF weapons sergeant John was familiar with all types of ordinance. Tuning out the noise around him, he focused on disarming the device. The mechanism was a simple yet lethal design. You hold the four inch tubular device in the palm of your hand with your thumb depressing a button at one end. When the button is released the bomb goes off. This ensures that if the bomber is shot, or killed before detonating the device himself, it will automatically go off when his fingers relax. If John hadn't grabbed the terrorist's hand and held the trigger down in the same instant that he killed him they both would have been blown to bits along with hundreds of innocent people.

The wires ran up the limp arm and into the back of the vest-like rig. He took his time examining each wire and then double checked before he cut the lead from the pack, making the button in the firing tube useless. He looked down at the long brick shaped strips of C4, or plastic explosive. Each "wad" had small ball bearings, marbles and nails imbedded in it, as did the vest itself. The bomb was designed to kill and maim. He estimated that everyone within thirty yards would have been dead or seriously injured.

"Jesus," he said.

John stood up and looked around. Although some

of the crowd had run far away from the grisly scene many remained close by. They stared at him and the lifeless bodies at his feet with morbid fascination. Both terrorists had blood pools expanding outwards around their heads and people were actually standing there taking pictures and phone videos. Ignoring them, he reached into the black nylon bag and removed the AK-47. After checking the magazine, he turned the selector to semi-automatic and cocked the weapon.

That got everyone moving. He felt, no he knew, that these two bad guys were not alone and people were stopping after fleeing only a short distance. They still weren't far enough away to be out of danger so he said, "fuck it," then fired four shots into the air. He watched with satisfaction as the crowd let out a collective scream and took off running for their lives.

His yellow eyes were scanning the area for threats when he recognized the familiar echo of a nine millimeter pistol. In the fraction of a second it took his brain to process the situation, he recognized that his attacker was an excellent marksman. After the first two rounds hit the pavement at his feet, the shooter quickly adjusted fire sending the next shots whizzing by John's head.

In one fluid motion John crouched, turned to his left with the rifle pressed to his shoulder, got the sights on his target, and fired a quick three shot burst. The terrorist was mostly concealed behind a cab twenty yards away. John knew he couldn't shoot through the engine block, so he aimed above it, sending rounds tearing through the top of the hood. He fired four more times and heard the grunt of a man who had just been hit and hurt.

The terrorist stood up and John was about to finish him off when two things stopped him in his tracks. The first and craziest was that he knew this guy. He didn't actually know who he was, yet there was no mistaking the face. It was the same long nosed asshole from jail who'd spit at him.

"No way," John said.

The second thing was the police officer standing behind him, screaming at the top of lungs. "Okay Mohammed, drop the weapon! Police! Drop your weapon!"

John watched the man who launched a loogie at him two days before and who shot at him just now run off holding his side as he slowly lowered the AK to the ground.

"Officer, I'm Sergeant John Bishop, U.S. Special Forces," he said, turning to face the officer who was screaming at him.

"Stand still! Don't fuckin' move! Put your hands behind your head!"

"Officer, these two dead guys were suicide bombers planning to blow up the market. I put them down."

Police officer Louis Johnson Jr. was shaking from the rage and adrenaline running through him. His father was a firefighter who died on 9/11 and he joined the force right after he buried his dad. Like most New Yorkers, and more importantly, anyone who'd taken a personal loss on that terrible Tuesday morning in September, he'd always dreamt of revenge. He now had what he thought was a live terrorist in his cross hairs.

Louie heard what John was saying, but the words didn't match up with what he was seeing. First of all, the guy claiming to be a Green Beret looked like an Arab and he'd just seen him shoot a machine gun in the center of Union Square Park. Louie wasn't taking any chances.

"Last time motherfucker. Put your hands behind your head and get on your knees!"

When John slowly moved his arms up to comply, the

Swiss Army knife he'd tucked in his shirt sleeve slipped out and hit the ground with a loud clack.

With the bodies in front of him, the gunpowder in the air and the sudden sound, Louie reflexively pulled the trigger just as Felix kicked his gun hand skyward. The forty caliber round passed over John's head by less than six inches. Louie quickly turned his gun towards his attacker. Felix swiveled in with perfect balance, punched up and in and cold cocked Louie with a terrible blow to the jaw. Catching him as he went down, Felix gently laid him on the cement.

"My second knock out in two days!" he said. "Johnny, you okay!? I'm gone five minutes and you're standing over dead bodies and a cop's shooting at you. Dude, what the fuck?"

John picked the AK back up. "Terrorist attack, Cat, and I don't think it's over. Grab the cop's gun and let's take cover until reinforcements arrive."

At that moment the blast wave from a huge explosion at the south end of the park hit them like a punch in the gut, sucking the air from their lungs and knocking them off their feet. The ground shook. Dust and debris rolled over them.

John had been put on his ass by high explosives more times than he could count. He'd seen soldiers that were untouched by the blast get so disoriented by the aftershock that they walked right up to enemy positions with their hands held out in greeting and been blown away. Still on his back, he shook his head from side to side to help clear it before he sat up and looked down at Felix.

"Am I dead?"

"Just shaken up," John said. "Take it slow. You're going to be off balance for a few minutes."

"Holy shit," Felix said. John helped him up and

brushed off his cousin's hair and clothes. They each had a few nicks and cuts, but otherwise they were unharmed.

"Aw Christ! I hope they didn't get any kids. There were a lot of kids here," John said.

They stood in silence for a moment watching the huge smoke cloud rising skywards. Small branches and leaves fell from the trees all around them.

Sirens were wailing and people were running towards the scene. Then the awful screaming started. The primal sounds of shock and fear, of death and dying. Felix started to move towards the carnage when John put a hand on his arm.

"We can't help those people right now. Stay here."

"Stay here? Why?"

"Because there's an unexploded bomb at my feet and a bag full of evidence that these terrorists didn't expect to be found. This attack may not be over and we can't walk around with guns in our hands without getting blown away by cops arriving on the scene. Let's grab the weapons, the bomb and the bag and take cover over there," John said, pointing to the steps leading towards the now empty playground.

"Whatever you say, primo. You're the man when it comes to this shit"

"Okay, I've got the explosives and the AK. You bring the bag."

As Felix reached down to pick it up John grabbed his hand and held it firmly. They looked at each other and John shook his head slowly back and forth. "Just dawned on me that I never checked it for booby traps. Let me take a look first."

A shot rang out and they both crouched and turned towards the sound.

"Police! Freeze!" Six angry cops ran up and surrounded

them. Each one glanced down at the unmoving officer Johnson and the two dead bodies. John and Felix knew that if they moved they were both dead. They slowly dropped their weapons and put their hands behind their heads.

"This cocksucker had Louie's gun in his hand," said Officer Martin Sullivan, Louie's partner.

"On the ground! On the ground!" and they went down with hands locked behind their heads.

Even lying face down Felix knew the kick was coming. He couldn't protect himself in his prone position so he exhaled a second before the heavy shoe hit him in the right side just below his rib cage.

"Hey! We're the good guys here," John said.

"We'll see about that" said another cop who had just made the "10-13" officer down call on the radio.

More cops came running and the cousins were frisked, roughly handcuffed and dragged to their feet.

Felix wasn't saying a word, which John knew made him even more dangerous. He was staring intently at Officer Sullivan.

"What are you looking at, asshole?"

"Making sure I never forget you."

"Felix, cálmate (relax). We'll deal with that shit later."

"Yes we will," he responded. His yellow eyes bore into the cop that kicked him.

A police captain and an FBI agent arrived on the scene and took control.

"Captain, I'm Sergeant John Bishop, U.S. Special Forces. I put down these two suicide bombers. This is my cousin Felix."

"Yeah, we'll check you and your story out downtown, but for now the cuffs stay on."

The Captain turned to look at Officer Johnson who was now sitting up, shaking his head from side to side and gently rubbing his jaw.

"How did my man get hurt?" the Captain asked.

John disregarded the question. "Captain, I just got back from Afghanistan. I've seen these types of coordinated attacks and I don't think it's over. Once responders arrive on the scene they usually set off a car or truck bomb. They use the suicide bombers as a smoke screen to go after the real targets. You and your men. You should check every vehicle in the area and any apartments or offices facing the park."

There was a long three seconds where no one said a word. Everyone looked at John differently now and although he was still cuffed the officer that had been firmly holding him by the arm involuntarily released his grip.

While staring directly at John, Captain James Ryan got on his radio. "Command, we need ESU and the Bomb Squad up here now to check vehicles for explosives."

"They're on scene Captain, holding at 14th and Broadway."

"Bring 'em in. Start checking cars and trucks on Union Square west and expand from there, over."

"10-4 Captain," came over the radio in response.

"Next, I want officers to check every apartment, storefront, or office with a park facing view and all the surrounding rooftops. We may have more terrorists in the area. Take down doors and proceed with caution, over."

"Roger that, sir."

Hearing that there could be more terrorists in the area put everyone into overdrive. More cops continued to arrive on the scene, sprinting in every direction. They all wanted the same thing, a chance for some payback.

"You should also get on the horn about the other terrorist," John said.

"The other terrorist?"

"Yeah, and he'll be hard to miss. Mid-forties, five-ten, dark hair, long broken nose, and a bullet in his left side just below the chest where I shot him. He ran west on 16th Street."

After putting Amir's description out on the radio Captain Ryan turned back to face John. "Sergeant Bishop, we're going to move you and your cousin out of this area to our command center south of the park. Procedure dictates we have to keep the cuffs on, but assuming your story is true we all owe you our thanks for what you've done here today," he said, putting his hand gently on John's shoulder. "And quite possibly an apology as well."

"Thanks Captain. It's my cousin who needs the apology, but right now focus on making sure no one else gets hurt," he said, turning to look at the cop who kicked Felix.

Officer Sullivan put his head down and fumbled around with his belt buckle as John and Felix were walked to a squad car.

While he was being escorted away John looked back at Ryan and added casually, "By the way, there's a bomb at your feet."

Everyone froze.

"I defused it after I killed the guy over there wearing it. The nylon bag belonged to them too and it may be booby trapped so be careful with it. Also, the one still wearing the jacket could have a nasty surprise on him so you should let your bomb guys examine him too."

"Command, this is Ryan."

"Go ahead, Captain."

"Would you mind sending bomb squad members to my location? I have an unexploded device at my feet."

"Say again, sir?"

Ryan stared intently at Bishop as he was led away.

Chapter 11
Meecham

26 Federal Plaza, Downtown Manhattan
New York FBI and Homeland Security Headquarters

JOHN AND FELIX were briefly held at the temporary command center south of Union Square before being taken downtown to 26 Federal Plaza. They had each been placed in separate interrogation rooms and John figured about five hours had gone by since the door closed. He sat on a hard metal chair that was bolted into the floor in a tiny room painted stark white.

He knew they were busy. There was a lot going on and they'd get to him eventually. Still, he wanted to know how everything played out and more importantly he needed to call Maria. She knew he was going to Union Square for lunch and must be worried sick.

The door swung inward and two bulky Homeland Security Agents in matching blue suits and dark ties entered the room.

"Sergeant Bishop, will you come with us please." The delivery was polite, but it wasn't a question.

John got up, fascinated by their identical outfits. On any other day would have asked them if they shopped together. Today was too serious.

The twins escorted him to a large conference room that had a long oak table with fifteen black leather seats on each side, perfectly spaced and neatly lined up. There were twenty men standing in a tight group at the far end of the room. John knew a few of them and some of the others he'd seen on TV.

General Marcus Palmer, the head of SOCOM (Special Operations Command) was in the center of the group. John knew him well, though he hadn't seen Palmer for several years. The last time was when the general presented him with the Distinguished Service Cross, the nation's second highest military honor.

Only average height, the general's bearing and air of command made him appear much taller, and he was a man John both liked and respected for being tough yet fair. Palmer was also one of only a handful of senior officers that had come up through the ranks of Special Forces. He understood their tactics at every level and fought to get his troops everything they needed from training, to funding, and equipment. The general was both a legend and a hero to the men under him.

Captain Ryan of the NYPD was there as well. His uniform was dusty, his face looked drawn and haggard, but his blue eyes were sharp and alert. The corners of his mouth rose slightly when he saw John come in and they each nodded a hello.

A feisty little man in a sharp custom made gray suit quickly stepped into the room with a nervous assistant trailing behind him. The atmosphere immediately changed when he came in, and John could sense that everyone was suddenly tense and guarded. General Palmer shot John a look that said, watch out for this guy.

"Well, Mr. Bishop, you've had quite a day. My name is Michael Meecham, Deputy Director of Homeland Security." Meecham's words and his movements were exaggerated, almost theatrical, designed to inspire fear and intimidate those around him. It didn't work on John. He stared into Meecham's grey lifeless eyes for three long seconds, noting the pointy, almost rodent-like features in his face.

Dismissing him without acknowledging the introduction, John turned his back on Meecham and came to attention. He crisply saluted General Palmer and the two light colonels at his side who were his aides. They returned the salute and the general simply said, "At ease Sergeant."

Meecham, not one to be ignored said, "He's not in the army any more so there's no need for all that. Bishop, we need you to tell us exactly what you saw. Every detail of what happened, what you did and why."

"General, where is my cousin, Felix Valdez?" John asked, still keeping his back to Meecham.

"We'll get to that later. First we need answers, Bishop," snapped Meecham.

Looking over his shoulder John addressed him for the first time. "You get Felix in here now weasel, or I've got nothing to say."

"What did you call me? You understand that if you don't answer my questions to my satisfaction or impede this investigation in any way I'll have you arrested and held without bond."

"Arrest me then, because until I see Felix I've got nothing to say. And once he gets here someone other than you better ask the questions or I'll put you over my knee and give you a spanking. I'm in no mood to be barked at, or threatened."

Meecham's head snapped back as if he'd been struck and his face flushed with rage. He was about to explode, but was cut off by another man wearing a smart dark blue suit with a bold red striped tie.

"Mike! This is counterproductive, and we have a lot of work to do here." He pressed a button on the phone bank on the table. "Agent Matthews, bring Mr. Valdez in here now."

"Sergeant Bishop, my name is Terry Hall. I'm Special Agent in Charge of the New York FBI office." He walked over and extended his hand. He had a firm grip and looked John directly in the eye when they shook hands.

General Palmer added, "Let's all take a seat and start over." Looking over with contempt at Meecham he turned back to speak to John.

"John, you understand why you're here. I hope we can count on you to help out."

"Absolutely, sir. I just want to make sure my family's okay."

"Understood."

The large mahogany door with a hand-carved emblem of Homeland Security opened silently and the twins brought in Felix, still wearing handcuffs.

"What is this? Is he being charged with a crime?" John asked.

"Not by us," Captain Ryan said.

"Then why is he still cuffed?"

"Deputy Meecham's orders," replied Agent Matthews nervously.

"He's a convicted murderer and he assaulted a cop

today. He should be in jail and definitely not in this room with us," Meecham said.

"That cop mistook *me* for a terrorist. Not his fault, but he almost blew me away. Felix saved my life. Is the department pressing charges here Captain?"

"No we're not. The officer involved corroborates what you just said. He made a poor assessment of the situation and accidentally discharged his weapon. Take those cuffs off him," Ryan said.

Agent Matthews waited until his boss, Meecham, nodded reluctantly and then released Felix. Felix rubbed his wrists to get the circulation back then walked over to John and gave him a warm embrace.

"Glad you're okay."

"You too."

Just then Tony Kolter, Director of the National Security Agency, entered the room with his deputy. He was five-ten and two hundred-fifty pounds, with pock marked cheeks and a nose that had been broken several times. A former wrestler and Army Ranger, even at sixty-five he was still a bull of a man. A bull that didn't take any bullshit.

"Where are we?" he asked simply.

"Just getting started," Terry Hall said.

"Then let's get going. The president is waiting for my call and I want to hear this young man's story first," Kolter said.

"What can you tell us about the events in the park today John?" asked Agent Hall.

"Well, after I proposed to my girlfriend and asked my cousin here to be my best man, me and Felix walked over to the Blue Water Grill to have a lobster lunch to celebrate. We finished eating at 2PM and I walked around the market while he went into a store. After about ten minutes of strolling around the northwest side of the farmer's market I got a bad feeling."

"You got a feeling?" Meecham said sarcastically.

"Shut your mouth and don't interrupt him again," General Palmer said venomously. Palmer knew he'd just made a new and powerful enemy, but he wasn't about to sit back and see a man like John get abused.

"Continue your report Sergeant."

"Thank you, sir. I thought I was imagining things, but after doing a quick recon of the area I spotted the two terrorists in the middle of the crowd."

"What gave them away?"

"At first glance, the fact that they were both wearing matching black jackets, which was odd for such a hot day. Also, the way they were standing completely still in the middle of a moving crowd really got my attention. My gut told me these guys were wrong. So, I moved in closer from their blind side and when I got within five or six feet I heard the primary bomber reciting his death prayer in Dari. Dari or Farsi is the dominant language of Afghanistan. From his accent I could tell he was from the Eastern part of the country and Dari wasn't his first language. He probably grew up speaking Pashto or one of the local tribal dialects in the frontier region."

John paused and looked over at several aides franticly taking notes. "Am I going too fast?"

"No John, you're doing great. Your report is being recorded and transcribed. Please continue," Terry Hall said.

"I then observed what I will again call the primary bomber holding a thumb depressed detonator in his left hand. There were hundreds of people: women and children everywhere. There was no doubt about his intentions. He was going to blow himself up and it would've been a blood bath. I knew I had to act fast, so I moved I moved in from behind them and engaged the second subject, killing him with a knife blow to the back of the neck."

"Why him first and not the bomber?" Terry asked.

"Well, the bomber had his head down in prayer. Terrorist two was security and he was there to shoot anyone who tried to interfere. I didn't mention that I observed a bag at his feet with the butt of an automatic rifle sticking out of it. I knew if I went after the bomber first, the second terrorist would engage me to try and pry the thumb button free, and boom, game over."

This was the first accounting of the day's events for Felix and he was awestruck listening to what happened.

"I then neutralized the bomber utilizing the same knife blow to the back of his neck. In his case, as I struck him I had to grab his hand and keep the pressure on the release button. I managed to do that and defuse the devise," John said nonchalantly, as if this was something people do every day.

"What happened next John?"

"There were people standing around watching and taking pictures. I knew the attack wasn't over. They wouldn't waste their time with just a single two man team. I removed the AK-47 from their bag and after firing four warning shots to get the crowd moving I was fired upon by a third terrorist from across the street at 16th and Union Square West. I returned fire and hit him once on the left side of his torso below the chest. I believe he's hurt, but not critically wounded assuming he finds treatment. I also believe he was the leader of the operation."

"Why?" General Palmer asked.

"Sir, he was only carrying a pistol. Nine mil. I'm pretty sure it was a Berretta from the gun's profile. If he was a primary operator he would've been packing more firepower." He paused. "From his position it was the perfect place to observe and coordinate the mission without being trapped on a rooftop. I didn't see radios on any of them so I don't think he was in direct contact with the two teams of bombers, but my gut tells me he was in charge. Just one soldier's opinion, sir."

"I see."

"Then there's the fact that I kinda met him two days ago."

There was stunned silence from everyone in the room. Even Director Kolter had a physical reaction to this piece of news. His back stiffened and he placed both palms carefully down on the table.

"What! You know this guy?" Meecham screeched.

"Don't know him, but we crossed paths. We were both arrested on Thursday night," John said nodding towards Felix, "and the guy I shot was in our holding cell. I was in my dress uniform on my way to my homecoming party when we got locked up. My uni really set this guy off. He spit at me."

"Hold up. You can't be serious. That long-nosed dude I knocked out is the same guy you shot today? No way," Felix said.

"Crazy, but yeah, same guy."

"Spooky."

"And then some," John added.

"You're saying you assaulted this man, Mr. Valdez?" Meecham asked.

"Damn right I did. That son of a bitch spit at John. Felt his beak break on impact, and lights out, baby."

"You two morons don't even realize that you probably caused this attack by your actions in the jail."

Felix jumped up from his chair. "Morons!? Who are you anyway? You're talking about my cousin? My cousin who's got more medals than any soldier since World War II? The guy who saved hundreds of lives today, maybe thousands? Hey pal, whoever you are, go fuck yourself."

"Valdez, you are about to find out what a mistake it is to curse at the Director of Homeland Security," Meecham said.

"You just promote yourself, Meecham?" John asked. "It was Deputy Director a few minutes ago."

"I misspoke. I…"

John ignored his fumbling and looked at Tony Kolter. "Sir, there's no way this operation wasn't planned months in advance. This wasn't some pissed off loner. It was a well planned, coordinated group attack."

"I agree." Kolter had had enough. "Meecham, take a hike. When I brief the president I'm recommending he fire your ass for impeding this investigation."

Meecham balled his fists at his sides and his whole body shook in anger. He regained his composure and stared long and hard at John and Felix and then menacingly pointed a thin index finger at each of them before storming out of the room.

Captain Ryan had already picked up the phone and gave terse commands.

"Get me names and photos of every person we had at Central Booking on Thursday night. And I need them ten minutes ago!"

Kolter turned to John and Felix. "Sorry about that. Meecham's an asshole. He thinks he's the second coming of J. Edgar Hoover. I hear he even has his own team of private investigators collecting dirt on people so he can coerce them to do his bidding. He's one of those evil little pricks that gets real pleasure out of creating problems, but don't worry, you won't see him again."

"That's what my cousin said about the guy who spit at him in jail. Just like that terrorist I think we're definitely going to be seeing and hearing from Meecham again," Felix said thoughtfully.

"Bank on it," John said.

Tony Kolter had his hands behind his head, staring up at the recessed track lights as he digested everything John had reported.

"As Napoleon once said, 'give me a man who's lucky.'" Turning to John he said, "Well Sergeant, you've had quite the homecoming. You saved a whole bunch of lives today, son. Thank you for your service and your decisive action."

"What happened after we left the scene?" John asked.

"You were right about everything you warned us about," Captain Ryan said. "We found a flower truck a hundred feet from where we were standing packed with enough C4, TNT, and gasoline to take out three city blocks. The bag with weapons was booby trapped too. It was designed to blow when someone picked it up."

Felix reflexively grabbed John's arm and squeezed hard. "Shit, you saved my ass, primo," he said and exhaled deeply.

"How many casualties from the bomb that went off?" John asked.

"Good news, at least in the context of what might have been if you hadn't been there. The second team blew themselves up when the park had been mostly cleared by your warning shots. We have just over twenty injured. Three are serious, but they're all expected to pull through. Most of the others are just cuts from flying debris. No fatalities. The two terrorists did not survive the blast of course and they blew the head off the statue of Gandhi. You saved us all John."

General Palmer stood up walked over to him. "Sergeant, you saved thousands of lives today. Job well done." He snapped to attention and saluted formally.

All John could say was, "Thank you sir," while standing and returning the salute.

The Q & A session lasted another hour. They both identified Amir Rashid from his mug shot. His picture was sent out city, state and nation wide and forwarded to Interpol.

Kolter had stepped out to brief the president. When he came back he said, "The president will be contacting you both personally. Can we count on your assistance if anything else comes up?"

"Absolutely," they replied in unison.

"Now, is there anything we can do for you? You can reach me on this number day or night," he said handing them each his card.

"Two things," John said.

"Name them."

"One, our names stay out of the paper. I know this is big news, but I want us to stay anonymous. I don't want CNN and Oprah calling us for interviews."

"Done."

"Two, this guy Amir Rashid or whatever his real name is has seen us both. He obviously has resources and plenty of firepower at his disposal."

"Agreed. So?"

"I want concealed weapons permits for both of us. Felix is as good a shot as I am, and I don't want to get arrested again if we have to protect ourselves."

Kolter looked at John for several seconds before answering.

"I'm a no bullshit guy. We know who your uncle is and what he does." Turning to Felix he said, "Felix, I don't think you're a drug dealer, but you've got a felony manslaughter conviction so there's no way we can give you a permit." He paused for another long moment and then said to Ryan, "Make it happen. Give John a permit and I'll write up a thirty day get out of jail free card for Felix with my mobile number on it so he won't do time if he's arrested with a weapon. You two be careful and stay close in case we need you," said Kolter over his shoulder as he walked out.

"Give me a few minutes to get you outfitted," Ryan said.

Palmer was one of the few generals outside of an active war zone that insisted on carrying a side arm. He unclipped his holster from his belt and handed it to John. Colonel Masters, the aide at his elbow did likewise and handed his piece to Felix. It was the ultimate act of respect. For a soldier at any rank his weapon is part of him, constantly cared for and kept ready for the day it's called upon to save his life. Both pistols were 9mm Glock 19's.

"I don't want you boys having anything less than the best if you get into another firefight," Palmer said.

"I'm honored, sir." John said.

"Me too. It's an honor," Felix said.

Palmer stepped in closer and put his hand on John's shoulder. "Son, I know you've had a long hard day, but I have some bad news."

"Sir?"

"Major Burke and four Team Razor sergeants were killed yesterday."

John doubled over involuntarily as if someone had just punched him in the stomach.

"Oh no, not Tommy," he whispered. A tear rolled out of his right eye and traveled down the jagged scar. "Who else besides the major?"

"The Team was ambushed east of Khost. Sergeants Collins and Jacobs were killed by the IED that got Major Burke. Riley and Lugo were shot and killed. Ilchuck and Waters were shot and wounded, but they're not critical."

"The shack at the base of the mountain?"

"That's right," Palmer said.

John fell into a chair upon hearing the names of so many friends. He put his head in his hands and closed his eyes for a moment, letting the reality sink in.

"Their families have already been notified in case you want to make any... well, I'm very sorry Sergeant. I know you've had a rough day and this just made it a whole lot rougher, but I thought you should hear it from me here and now."

Felix moved closer, gently putting his hand on John's shoulder as the general and his men said their goodbyes and the meeting adjourned.

Captain Ryan was still there and it was clear there was something serious on his mind.

"John, I'm really sorry about your friends. I know this is a really bad time, but I want you guys to listen carefully. You both need to watch your backs, and I'm not talking about terrorists now. Felix, you were right about Meecham. The man has a lot of power, a shit load of money, and he uses them both to destroy people. I hear he's border line psychotic, but he's got pull in Washington and you two just cursed him out and more than likely got him fired. He's coming after you for sure and it probably won't be straight on. He'll find some way to back shoot you. I'll protect you if I can, but I'm just a city cop and he carries a bigger gun. Thought you both should know."

"Thanks Captain," they both said.

"Call me Jimmy, and thanks for not jamming my guys. That was stand up. Now, let's get you your permits and a ride home."

When they walked out of the building they were surprised to see their drivers were none other than Louis and Martin. Louis and Martin were Officers Louis Johnson, Jr. and Martin Sullivan. The left side of Louie's face was already purple and swollen from where Felix hit him. His jaw was probably broken and he needed to get X-rays, but he waited on the hospital until he could speak to the cousins directly.

"Look, I made a big mistake and I'm here to apologize," he said through gritted teeth. "I'm sorry for shooting at you." He turned to Felix. "And no hard feelings about the jaw. I box and you pack one hell of a punch. You saved your cousin's life and saved me from being the fuckup that would've killed a hero."

It was Martin's turn. "I'm sorry too. I saw Louie on the ground and you had his gun so I thought... you know... I just... point is, that kick was way out of line. I'm really sorry, and understand if you want to file a complaint or even hit me back."

"We're cool," Felix said. "I probably would have done the same or worse if I thought someone had wasted my cousin here. I knocked out your partner and you cracked my rib. Let's call it square," he said offering his hand.

They shook hands all around, compared pain levels and discussed the best ways to reduce swelling.

"Here's both our cell numbers. You guys need anything, I mean anything at all, just pick up the phone," Martin said.

They were driving home in an unmarked car when he finally called Maria at 11PM.

"Hi honey."

"Ohhh baby, where are you?" Maria asked.

"On my way to you."

"Are you okay? Are you hurt?"

"No baby I'm fine."

"Thank God. We've been watching the pictures of you all night. You're amazing. I'm just glad you're not hurt and you saved all those people."

"Pictures? What pictures?"

"Pictures, video of you in the park. It's on CNN, You-Tube. You're on every news channel Johnny. They don't have your name so they're calling you the Unknown American Hero and the Hero of Union Square. I recognized you right away. You look so fuckin' hot shooting that terrorist. I can't believe those bastards came at us again. Thank God you were there to stop it."

Not good, he thought. He hoped they would never get his name. Celebrity status was something he definitely did not want, especially after his uncle had just warned him about staying out of the news.

NEW YORK TIMES

Special Sunday Edition
Terror Cowards Stopped By Unknown Hero!

The largest coordinated terrorist attack on U.S. soil since 9/11 was thwarted by an unknown hero (pictured below) in Union Square Park yesterday. This Citizen Superman single handedly killed two terrorist suicide bombers before they could blow themselves up in the middle of the crowded farmer's market. He then confiscated one of their weapons and shot and wounded the terrorist leader known as Amir Rashid who is now a fugitive (pictured right). Rashid, the name is believed to be an alias, was actually arrested on Thursday night in downtown Manhattan for driving without a license and running a red light. He was released on Friday morning only to lead this cowardly, bungled attack the next day.

The mysterious hero who saved hundreds of lives was briefly taken into police custody before being released. His name and whereabouts remain unknown.

The story was covered in every major newspaper and news broadcast around the world, with John's picture front and center right next to Amir's.

CHAPTER 12

RETURN TO THE BATTLEFIELD

Khost Province, Afghanistan

"WE FOUND TWO more mines. One south and one north of the hut. We disarmed and cleared the one on the south side so you can go up there now. My men'll have the other one cleared in twenty minutes in case you need to go further up, Chief."

"Thanks, Lieutenant. We're moving in now. It looks quiet, but the Predator stays on over watch to make sure no one's hiding under a rock," Bear Bernstein said.

"Understood."

"Chief?"

"What is it?"

"We're all real sorry about Major Burke and the team. Let us know if you need any backup, or if you've gotta go off the reservation on this one. We want in regardless."

"Thanks Loo, I'll let you know."

Bear, Able, Bobby, and Mace were the remnants of Team Razor. Traveling up the same dirt road where they fought for their lives two days earlier, they stopped next to

Major Burke's Humvee. It was mangled from the explosion and burned black from the fire. The charred body of Sergeant Dan "DC" Collins had been removed after the battle. What was left of him.

They all stared in silence, looking on at the wreckage that was also a grave stone for their five brothers.

"Mace," Bear said.

"Yeah," he replied, his jaw flexing.

"I couldn't have done it either." He didn't have to spell it out. They all knew Bear was talking about when DC begged Mace to shoot him.

"He did it himself so I wouldn't have to carry it," Mace said.

"That's the type of man he was," said Bobby.

"Every time I blink I see his face," Mace said.

"I know, but I'm gonna picture him smiling when we kill everyone that had a part in this," Bear said.

"We're gonna find these fuckers," said Able.

"Find 'em and waste 'em," Bobby said.

Mace didn't say anything. He just spit in anger and flicked the safety on his M4A1on and off.

They walked across the road to the other two disabled Humvees. Bobby looked down at the engine block of the third vehicle that had taken the two RPG rounds.

"Good thing we welded that front plate on last week."

"Without that hillbilly armor we all would've been dead instead of just put to sleep," Able said.

"My ears are still ringing," Mace said.

"Mine too," said Bobby.

They had all been standing behind the last Humvee when the RPG's hit. The impact knocked them out cold, but no one was seriously hurt from the blast.

"Let's see if they left anything for us," Bear said.

They drove the quarter mile up to the tiny one room shack which remained intact even after the aerial barrage. The pilots had been alerted that there was potentially valuable intel inside and they skillfully placed their ordinance down on everything around it. There were impact craters, blood stains, and bone fragments everywhere, but no bodies. The enemy had come back after the battle to retrieve its dead.

"All clear up there?" Bear said into his headset. The Predator UAV was circling high above and could detect the heat signature of both man and weapon.

"All clear Chief," was the quick response from the UAV Command and Control Center thousands of miles away back in the States at Creech Air Force base in Nevada. There was no ambush today and no booby traps other than the mines that had already been detected.

"Wish we'd had that Predator when we came up this road the last time," Bobby said.

"Would've saved all our guys," Able said.

"We didn't, they're gone, and we're still here so let's stay sharp and see if we can get some info to help track Aziz and his guys," Bear said.

All heads nodded silently in agreement. There was no joking around now. They were all professionals and war was their business, yet each knew that the fight was now very personal.

Even with the all clear they approached the hut cautiously with M4A1's pressed to shoulders and safeties off. They checked all four sides of the small mud and stone structure that had one entrance with an ancient wooden door on rusted hinges and no windows. Mace kicked open the door and looked in on the dark sparse interior. There was a small wood burning stove and a few old rugs lay over the dirt floor. That was it.

"Shit. This is mission control?" Bobby asked while pulling up the rugs.

Mace looked up at the ceiling: "Jonny said he hid it over the door in the roof. How'd he get up there without a chair or a table?"

"How Johnny Bishop did most of the things he did has always been a fuckin' mystery to me. Boost Able up past the door frame," Bear said.

Mace and Bobby each held a leg and pushed him up. Able switched on his helmet light and searched the wall, feeling for anything loose with his hands. Frustrated, he was about to give up when he spotted a small piece of straw stuck between two stones. He pulled on it and the rocks fell away revealing a small hole where the microphone and recorder were hidden. He grabbed it and the guys lowered him down. There was a note wrapped around the recorder.

"Asshole," was all Able said after reading it and passing it around.

JB was here. Miss you guys.
P.S. How long and how many of you dipshits did it take to find this?

"Fuckin' Johnny," said Bear after reading it and passing it to Bobby.

"Wish he was here," Bobby said.

"Then you're wishing him dead cause he would've been riding lead with Tommy," Mace said.

"Fuck me. I wasn't thinking straight. I just miss the guy is all," Bobby replied.

"We all do," Able said.

"Play a song Chief," Mace said.

Bear hit the play button on the voice activated digital recorder. They each listened to the conversation in Pashto from the meeting two days prior.

"Motherfucker," Mace said.

"Yeah, they were tipped off," Able said, shaking his head and looking out of the doorway at the ambush site.

"Yeah, we've got a mole for sure. No doubt about it. Some other good info here besides that. The nephew in New York must be the one that led the attack. He's probably the one Johnny shot, so this Amir Rashid may actually be Amir Khan," Bear said.

They had all been briefed on the Union Square attack and their former teammate's role in thwarting it.

"Johnny retires and still finds time to kick Jihad ass on the weekend," Bobby said.

"You gotta love it," Able said.

"And then there's this part about a secret passage through the mountain," said Bear.

"We going up there now, Chief?" Mace asked, eager to be on the hunt.

"Not today. We've got leave. We're all going stateside for a week to attend the funerals," Bear said. He took a final scan of the hut to make sure they didn't miss anything. "Okay, mount up. Let's get this intel to SOCOM ASAP."

As they headed back down the road they each pledged a silent vow of vengeance and retribution against Aziz Khan for their fallen brothers.

CHAPTER 13
THE KHANS

The mountains of Eastern Afghanistan

AZIZ KHAN SAT on an old ammo crate with his elbows resting on a rough wooden table. He was in a small chamber within a large cave high in the mountains. The caves had been ideal for evading the Russians, who rarely left the cities or the main roads. They tried and failed to win the war by air power. The Americans, especially the Green Berets and Army Rangers lived in the mountains and were better fighters than the Russians, though far less ruthless. Aziz had a network of these caves throughout his country and they all had secret passages and escape routes. It allowed him and his men to go through the mountains instead of around them like their enemies.

He knew he needed glasses, but considered them a luxury item he could live without. Although Aziz made millions from his poppy fields and heroin labs in the south, he took nothing for himself. The money bought weapons and was distributed to those in his territory that needed it most. He lived as the poorest of his people did. His clothes were worn and dirty; his boots were scratched and needed resoling. He didn't smoke, drank coffee for breakfast, and ate little. Refusing to sleep in a bed, each night he lay on his father's old rug, which had been his father's before him. Aziz lived only for war.

A portable generator powered the lights that hung on the jagged stone walls and allowed him to read computer printouts describing the failed operation in New York. After squinting at the fine print he stared long and hard at the mug shots of his nephew before re-reading the description of how Amir had been arrested two days before the attack.

Aziz worked hard at staying calm and in control. He had learned from seeing so many men die early deaths by acting in anger and letting their emotions cloud their judgment. He put the papers down and sat for twenty minutes in silence.

His trusted lieutenants sat on thick rugs along the cave wall waiting patiently for orders. They followed him unconditionally and respected how deliberate he was in everything he did. Deliberate in his calculations and decisive in his actions.

He stood up and summoned his men. "Send in Omar," he said simply.

The curtain at the entrance of the chamber parted and a small figure seemed to glide across the stone floor. Omar the Blade, also known as the Sword of Allah, was Aziz's top assassin. A killer who focused only on selected high value targets. Omar had never failed to execute an assignment.

The only discernible features were Omar's black lifeless eyes. Everything else was covered by a turban, mask, thick robes, and soft boots. Even the hands were gloved. Except for Aziz, every man in the room stiffened slightly in the presence of such an instrument of death.

"Assalaam alaikum (Peace be upon you)."

"Waalaikum assalaam (And peace also upon you)," replied Aziz.

"My target?"

"Targets. First, Amir Khan," Aziz said without emotion. He had already determined that his nephew must die and actually felt annoyed that he was still alive. "And then his second, Khalid Mulan."

"It will take several days to get to New York."

"May Allah keep you safe in your travels. This will assist you in finding them." Aziz handed over a CD that had photos and backgrounds on all of Amir's known contacts and the location of all his safe houses.

"Is that all my lord Khan?"

"The American Hero," Aziz added nonchalantly. "We must redeem ourselves from this set back. The media is calling us incompetent and unprofessional. Perception is everything when it comes to public opinion and his meddling caused..." Aziz paused for a moment. "Make an example of him. A bloody public statement as retribution for his interference."

"Does he not remain unknown?" Omar asked.

"He does for now, but his name will surface in the next few days. Someone will identify his picture and we will have our man."

"And then so will I. It will be done."

"May Allah protect you," Aziz said.

"And you," Omar said without looking back, gliding silently out of the room.

Brooklyn, New York

With six thousand seven hundred and fifty-five miles between them, Amir Khan had been reading the same news clippings at the same moment that his uncle was. He put the papers down and thought about his Uncle Aziz. Amir knew he was a dead man and figured he had a week to live if that. If he could keep all his local cells insulated and prevent any direct contact with leadership back home then his own men wouldn't be the ones that killed him. They would send someone though. That would give him at least a week, or maybe more if he was careful. And that was time enough to get even.

The throbbing in his nose was now a minor annoyance compared to the searing pain that made him tremble with every breath. He was fortunate that he had been turned sideways when the bullet tore through the hood of the cab. If he were facing straight ahead it would have killed him on the spot. Instead, it made a deep gouge right below his chest that broke two ribs before it went through the bicep of his left arm.

After being wounded he ran west on 16th Street and jumped into a cab on Fifth Avenue. He'd made it to a safe house in New Jersey where he was patched up before being moved to this hideout in Brooklyn.

He stood up shakily and looked himself over in the full length mirror. He had a broken nose, two black eyes, fifteen stitches in his chest, two broken ribs, his left arm was swollen tight and seeping blood from both the entry and exit wounds and his right Achilles tendon was throbbing steadily. He looked like shit and felt even worse. The only thing that kept him going was his rage and his need for revenge.

It wasn't until he was alone and replaying the events

that he realized the man that shot him was the soldier from his jail cell. It had to be a coincidence, just bad luck, but he had no doubt it was the same man. The pictures in the paper showing the scarred face had just confirmed what he already knew.

Everything was put on hold and the "unknown hero" was his new mission. He now had to kill this soldier before Aziz killed him.

He sent all the cell members out in their cabs in hopes of spotting the soldier in downtown Manhattan and each had a picture of him taped to their dash board. It was a long shot, but it kept all his men busy and out of contact with Aziz. He felt he was due for some good luck anyway after such a string of unfortunate events.

Part of him knew that he should stay on plan and hit the other targets as scheduled, but his need for revenge consumed him. Once the soldier was dead he could then launch the next round of public attacks if there was time. Time, as much as the soldier, was now his enemy.

Amir had taped an enlarged photo to the wall and he hawked a gob of yellow phlegm that hit John right in the face this time. Amir winced in pain from the sudden movement as he watched his spit roll down the black and white photograph of his nemesis.

"I am coming for you soldier," he said aloud. "I am coming."

CHAPTER 14
PLANNING

Brooklyn, New York

LIKE AZIZ AND Amir, Gonzalo Valdez was reading the papers and watching the news.

"Didn't I tell them to stay out of the papers? They never listen to me," he said more to himself than to the others in the room. His brothers, Sesa, Carlos, Macho, Victor, Fiero, and Calixto and his nephew Antonio were all sitting quietly in leather seats surrounding a large glass coffee table as Gonzalo watched another report on CNN.

"Okay," he said.

He turned off the TV, stood up, and walked over to the window. They were in a twentieth floor penthouse apartment with a spectacular view of the East River and the sun setting behind the Manhattan skyline.

"They have his picture, but not his name," Macho said.

"They will soon. This story is too big and too many people know who he is. By tomorrow, if not sooner, they will name him," Fiero said.

"Yes, Fiero. One day or less," added Gonzalo. "Where are they now?"

"John dropped Maria off at her mother's house and met Felix at his place. They're still there and Chris is with them," Antonio said, looking over to his Uncle Macho, Chris' father.

"How many men do you have watching them Antonio?" Gonzalo asked.

"Six Tio. Three on each of them."

"Make it twenty. Keep an eye on any cars driving in the area and take down license plates. Let's not take any chances. If anyone even appears threatening have them taken out. These people are walking bombs so shoot first and ask questions later. Your only job now is protecting the boys. Me entiendes?"

"Yes Tio," he said.

No one spoke on a phone when Gonzalo was present so Antonio got up and walked out of the room. He called Benji Medina who was down the block from Felix's place and passed on the orders to expand the security team and gave the green light to engage. He came back with news.

"They're on the way. We'll have the area completely covered in ten minutes."

"Good," Carlos said.

"The Feds are there too," Antonio said. "Benji said they had cars on Felix and more were following John when he arrived."

"Interesting, very interesting," Gonzalo said. "Let's think about what that means later, but first the main threat. These terrorists worry me. If their leader is still alive he will come at John and Felix with everything he's got once their names are released."

"He's a fugitive. Won't he just run for home?" Carlos asked.

"He has no home now. He's a dead man walking," Antonio said.

"Very good, Antonio. Yes, you see it," Gonzalo said, while Sesa beamed with pride at his son's understanding of the situation.

"Not sure I do," Calixto said.

"He embarrassed his organization. He got arrested right before his mission and his mission failed. In one of two ways he will die shortly. One, his men here will kill him on orders from their superiors. Or two, if his power is very strong here, they will send a hitter from back home to take him out. Either way he's a dead man. So we must plan for the worst case," Gonzalo said.

"That he has loyal followers here and they will target John and Felix?" asked Antonio.

"Yes, in part. But, the worst case is he and his men come after your cousins and his superiors also give their names to their assassins. The same ones who may be coming to kill this local terrorist leader may also come after the boys."

"So we may have two separate threats coming at us from the same organization," Antonio said.

"Four threats," Gonzalo said.

"Four?" asked Calixto.

"Four. The two separate threats from the terrorists and then there is this Michael Meecham who has made a vendetta against us."

"That's only three," said Carlos.

Gonzalo looked over at Antonio, waiting for his prized pupil and heir to the throne to answer.

"The fourth is our own government," Antonio said.

"Yes, exactly. We don't know where they stand. And there are many agencies at work here. CIA, FBI, NSA, ATF, Homeland Security, local police and who knows who else. Are they simply using John as bait, or do they have a more sinister agenda towards him?" Gonzalo raised his hand dismissively before anyone could speak. "I know they are coming for me now, but first we protect the boys. Nothing else matters."

"You can be just as effective from Mexico or Brazil, mi hermano," Sesa said. It was the first time he had spoken as he was a man of few words. Gonzalo paused before answering. Sesa had tremendous vision and Gonzalo would not be where he was today, or even alive for that matter, if not for the counsel of his older brother.

"We're at war now, and I can't leave until these threats to them are completely wiped out. I'd gladly spend the rest of my life prison in order to keep them safe. After, if there is an after for me, I'll leave. But not now. Now we plan and review."

"Okay, this Meecham," Gonzalo said. "Find out everything you can. The police captain told John and Felix that he's coming after them. That means he's also coming us, la familia Valdez, so we go after him, too. He's an evil one, and must have made many enemies over the years. Find them. Once we have more information we'll meet again and decide his fate."

"Let's get our intelligence people studying these terrorist organizations. None have claimed responsibility for the attack because it failed. Still, we should look into them. See if we can find any patterns that will help us against them," Victor said.

"Excellent. Next, your men, Antonio. Tell me who you have and who else we may want to bring in," Gonzalo said.

Antonio gave him a detailed run down of every man he had, discussing their strengths and weaknesses.

"Let's call the Bank Robbers. They're the best planners I know and they helped us in our past wars," Fiero said.

"Yes, but they don't rob banks anymore. They work only as consultants now. Double their fee and if they're already on an assignment triple it. I want them working for us full time until this is over," Gonzalo said. Fiero nodded and left the room to make the call.

Once Gonzalo was satisfied and Sesa also nodded his approval he stood up and stretched. Pouring a glass of water for each of them he said, "Now we start again. See if we missed anything. Now we are planning and studying the board. Soon we will act, but without planning we can never make the correct move. So let us begin again."

CHAPTER 15

PRO KEDSS

Queens, NY

KEVIN MITCHELL PULLED back the heavy curtain and looked out of the window for the third time. He huffed and resumed pacing back and forth in the spacious living room.

"Where the hell is he? We're on the clock now."

"Easy Kev. He'll be here soon," Danny Jones said.

"*Easy*? The Valdez Boys are at war D. That means that as of two hours ago so are we. Gonzalo doesn't like excuses, especially when it comes to his family."

Remembering Tom Tom and Skeeta Davis and knowing what Gonzalo still did to them every year, Danny nodded his head in agreement. They had helped plan the abduction of the Davis brothers after Gonzalo's sister had been killed. Danny had even designed the underground dungeon which was now their permanent home in Mexico.

Danny was sitting on a chocolate brown leather couch with his legs stretched out in front of him staring intently at a scuff on the tip of his black cowboy boots. Kevin was halfway through another lap across the room when Ed Taylor pulled into the driveway and hurried through the door.

"Hey guys, sorry I'm late," he said when he came in.

"Where the fuck were you?" Kevin asked.

"Upstate. Hit traffic on the way in."

"We've got full time work now. Fiero called. We're on retainer indefinitely and he tripled our rate," Kevin said.

"Sweet. Who are the Valdez boys at war with now?"

"Whoever's behind Union Square," Danny said.

"No shit?" Ed said. It wasn't really a question.

"No shit," Kevin replied.

"Glad we're getting paid, but I would've done this work for free. We've got a brother in the White House fellas. He's already got enough on his plate without these terrorists runnin' round blowing up shit in our own town. We're working for Gonzalo, but I'm doing everything I can to help the black man with the plan."

"I'm with you on that," Kevin said.

"Let's get to work," said Danny.

All three were well dressed and in their early fifties. They were a tight knit team that had robbed over sixty banks around the world over the last thirty years. None of them had done any time, or even been arrested. They were that good.

Master planners and experts at identifying weaknesses in security, between bank heists they worked as consultants for the Valdez family, Columbian and Mexican Cartels and African Dictators. After each of them put away several million dollars they gave up robbing and became full time security professionals.

They called their highly specialized and very secret consulting company Pro KEDSS, which stood for Kevin, Ed and Danny's Specialty Services. Kevin had an engineering degree from MIT, Ed learned combat tactics and demolition as a Force Recon Marine, and Danny was a computer genius capable of hacking into any system. Together they made a formidable team and now made more money protecting governments, crime families, and even banks than they ever did stealing.

"Here or in the van?" Danny asked.

"Let's start here and then go mobile later tonight. We'll sit down with Gonzalo and his brothers tomorrow morning, but we've got a lot of work to do between now and then and we're already behind schedule thanks to me," Ed said.

They all turned when the motion sensors around the house sent a vibration through the room.

"That's the cavalry," Danny said, looking at the surveillance monitor. "This job may get bloody so Fiero sent over Christmas, Boogie and Minty. I told them to tool up in case things get hot right away,"

Danny opened the front door and three rough looking men walked in. They each brought something heavy to the war: themselves. Christmas was an ex-Navy SEAL, Boogie had been a CIA operative for years specializing in wet work, and Minty spent twelve years in the French Foreign Legion. They were the elite fighting force within Gonzalo's army.

They each carried duffel bags and merely nodded their heads in greeting, as they were in the midst of a heated discussion.

"You shouldn't even be talkin' since you ain't never had game to begin with," Minty Jackson said. They called him Minty because of his bright green eyes. He was five-seven, with a barrel chest and massive arms from his daily morning workout of a thousand dips and a thousand push-ups before breakfast

"I'm a fan of the game motherfucker. Just 'cause you played a little ball don't make you no authority on this here. And don't start with your shit about how many points you scored back in the day," Boogie Washington said. Everyone called him Boogie because he ran ten miles a day rain or shine. Tall at six four, his frame was lean and wiry.

"Neither one of you knows shit about the Knicks so your opinions don't count," said Randal 'Christmas' Owens, who was also in tremendous shape from a combination of muay thai kick boxing and Brazilian jiu jitsu.

"What're ya'll squabblin' over?" Danny asked.

"Best Knick all time," Christmas said.

"Any position?"

"Yep."

"For me it's Frazier," Danny said.

"You see? Here's a man knows what he's talkin' about." Christmas gave Danny a high five.

"I still say it's Patrick. Stats don't lie and he's the all-time leading scorer."

"Fuck the stats. I've got Frazier, Monroe, and Bernard all ahead of Patrick," Boogie said.

"Don't we have work to do?" Minty asked.

"Yeah we do," Kevin answered.

"Are we rollin' out now or are you guys headed downstairs?" Christmas asked.

"We're going down for an hour or two, but we'll give you a heads up before it's time to move out unless something jumps off," Ed said.

"Cool. We'll recheck our gear. Hey, I'm sure you

already know, but we take our orders directly from you on this Op... unless."

"Unless?"

"Unless from a military perspective the three of us feel your leadership skills are lacking."

"Then what?"

"If there's time we contact Fiero. If there's not we try to work it out between us. If we can't all agree to the best course of action we stand down. Look, this is just worst case scenario shit. We know you guys are pros and we're not here to second guess you. We cool?"

"Yeah, we're good. Fiero already broke it down to me and Danny, but I wanted to hear it from you directly and make sure Ed heard it too."

"Okay then."

"What're you packing?" Kevin asked.

"We've got it all. MP 5's with sound suppressors, a Harris M86 sniper rifle, grenades, Claymores, lots of hand guns. We've even got a .50 cal that can knock out a truck or take down a steel door from half a mile away. We're under your command for this op, but I'm sure you already know that if we light off any of the heavy stuff the whole world's gonna take notice. How do you see this going down?" Christmas asked.

"We've always tried to be subtle and silent when it comes to ending lives, but you're weapons free on this. Terminate with extreme prejudice by any and all means necessary."

"Good. The opposition?"

"Right now we're estimating enemy strength at between fifty and a hundred split up into small two to five man teams. That's really just a guestimate, but we can't picture more than that or they would've had security leaks by know. A hundred max, but I bet it's less than half that. The numbers work for you?"

"Yeah, no problem. The three of us can handle that many and I've got four more deadly motherfuckers on standby, locked, loaded, and ready to roll in case we need 'em. Main problem I see is finding these assholes. They sure ain't gonna charge us all at once. How you gonna draw 'em out?"

"Working on that."

"Cool. Now, some a these terrorists are gonna be experienced fighters from back home, but a good number of 'em are probably just true believers whose only trigger time's been on a shooting range. That said, we ain't taking 'em lightly. These dudes blow themselves up," Christmas said.

"Understood. We'll have more info for you soon, Christmas, but for now you guys just sit tight."

"You got it, Kev."

"Let's get it on," Kevin said as he pressed in the eye of a large samurai warrior statue three times. A section of the wall slid away, revealing a reinforced steel door. He entered another code on the frame and it too silently opened inwards.

Kevin, Ed and Danny walked through the doorway and down the rubber padded steps that led to the basement. The room looked like the control center at NASA or NORAD. Every wall was covered with multiple giant screens and there were three consoles set up on the inner side of a large C shaped desk. They each sat down in wheeled captain's chairs and began typing furiously.

CHAPTER 16
BUNNY RABBIT

JOHN MET WITH his uncle early Sunday morning and gave him a complete run down of everything that happened the day before. They talked a lot about Meecham and being careful. He spent the rest of Sunday and Monday with Maria trying to decompress and making some difficult calls. He spoke with Amy, Tommy's widow, offering condolences and making plans to attend the funeral on Thursday as a pall bearer. He'd also called the widows and mothers of his other four fallen brothers from Team Razor. Logistically, attending all five services was going to be tough, but he had to do it. Maria worked out the itinerary and they were leaving on Tuesday afternoon.

He wanted to speak to his uncle again, but he never used phones of any kind. John had to make several calls to get through the layers of Valdez security and finally reached his Aunt Grassiella. He let her know he was leaving town for a few days. She would pass the news on to Gonzalo and she also cautioned John to be careful until the terrorist leader was captured or killed.

His last and longest call was to Felix. Felix seemed

really shaken by Saturday's events. After an hour on the phone they planned to meet on Monday night to do some hard drinking to celebrate being alive.

John had been on an emotional and physical roll-ercoaster. Throughout it all Maria was right there to offer advice, to listen, to make love, and then to let him rest, which was what he needed most.

On Monday night he dropped Maria off at her mother's house on the Upper East Side and then met up with Felix at his place. Their cousin Chris Valdez was there when he arrived and John explained that there was a former member of his Special Forces unit that he had to meet with to tell him what happened to Tommy and the guys. They all wanted to have a few drinks anyway and "Bunny" was bartending.

The three cousins walked into Still Bar around eight and it was crowded for a Monday night. "Johnny B!!!" Bunny shouted as soon as he saw them. He came running and grabbed him in a bear hug. Bunny, whose given name was Valentino Brown, was black and Italian. He had a face like a model and was built like an NFL lineman. A serious power lifter, Bunny was a massive man at six-five and two-seventy. He'd saved John's life on more than one occasion and was a true friend.

"Hey Val!!!" John said, hugging him back. They gave each other a kiss on the cheek and solid pounds on the back.

"Val, these are my cousins Felix and Chris."

"Call me Bunny," the big man said, extending his giant hand to each of them.

"Saw your picture in the paper Johnny. That was a fine piece of soldiering."

"Just glad they don't have my name."

"Big news man. Gonna be hard to stay anonymous on

this one. Hey, I worked the day shift today and I'm just getting off. Hope you're here to do some drinkin'. What're ya havin' fellas?"

"Hennessy and Heinekens all around," Felix said.

"Doug, make that four times and these guys don't get a check," Bunny said to the bartender who had just come on shift.

"Bunny, we need to talk," John said.

"Walk with me."

They went into the open back room that had an empty bar against the far wall. Felix and Chris watched the exchange and saw Bunny collapse into their cousin's arms. The big man was sobbing and seemed inconsolable after John gave him the sad news about the death of so many friends.

Wiping his eyes as they walked back, Bunny grabbed a snifter of cognac and raised his glass high.

"To fallen heroes! Gone, but never forgotten!" he said solemnly.

"Gone, but never forgotten!" was chorused by the entire bar.

Bunny downed the drink in one swallow. "Doug, give us the bottle and make sure there's plenty of cold ones on ice. It's gonna be a long night."

"Sure Bunny. Anything you need," Doug said. He refilled the glasses and left the bottle on the bar before moving away.

They drank hard and steady, but John knew he had to fly with Maria the next day to attend the first of the funerals and was trying to pace himself. He and Bunny told stories about each of their friends, describing embarrassing situations and countless acts of bravery under fire. They repeatedly toasted to each man's life and his valor.

"So Chris, I hear you're gonna to be one of us," Bunny said.

"As far back as I can remember I've always dreamed of it, sir. I can't believe all the stuff you and John have done. I just hope I can finish the course and put on that Green Beret."

"You will. We'll fill you in on what to expect. Just do your job, work your ass off and learn all you can. Piece a cake."

"I never heard SFAS referred to as a piece a cake, sir."

"Will you stop calling me sir for fucks sake? The name's Bunny."

"How'd you get the name?" asked Felix

"We were in Iraq. In Fallujah. I was on point and walked into an open area with no cover. Three little fellas with AK's screamin' about Allah this and Allah that opened up on me from a rooftop twenty feet away. They started shootin' and I started hoppin' and boppin' and runnin' round in circles till Johnny here took 'em out. Bam, bam, bam. Three shots and he put all three of 'em down for good. See your cousin here did his part to support the war by not wasting any ammo."

John laughed, but both Chris and Felix were in awe and hanging on every word.

"I shoulda been wasted, but didn't even get a scratch. Just some Iraqi sand in my eye from the ricochets. So anyway, after that everyone called me Rabbit on account a how I hopped away from those bullets."

"How'd you go from Rabbit to Bunny?" Chris asked.

"When we found out he took ballet as kid it was just a natural progression." John said.

"Seemed to fit," Bunny added. "My whole life, even when I was a Green Beret, I always dreamed of being a dancer," Bunny said as he put his hands high over his head and did a dramatic twirl. "Billy Elliot is my fuckin' idol."

Beer sprayed out of Felix's mouth when he laughed and choked at the same time and Chris and John were doubled over.

After they caught their breath and settled back down Chris finally asked, "Why'd you leave the service Bunny?"

"Got wounded. Couldn't hop away from these rounds," he said lifting up his shirt. Above the Heckler & Koch .45 he had tucked in his waist band with the barrel going down his butt crack there were two dime sized holes in his back on either side of his spine where the bullets went in and massive scarring across his stomach where they came out.

"Bunny should have got the medal that day. He saved my life twice. He got shot in the back cause of me and I ended up getting the DSC."

"We've got to hear this," Felix said.

"Nah. I hate talking about that stuff."

"Come on primo, tell us," Chris said.

The bar patrons had given the four of them their space, but those within earshot stopped their conversations and leaned in to hear what few civilians ever do: the truth about war, told by true warriors.

"Okay, okay. The Team was still in Iraq. We were on escort duty. Two senators and a congressman on a fact finding mission in a war zone. They requested a Special Forces unit for security and we got the job. We were traveling in a caravan of six SUV's."

"They didn't wanna use armored Humvees because, and I quote, 'They wanted to blend in,'" Bunny added.

"So here we are driving through Indian country looking at sand and goats with a big sign on us that says shoot me."

"And they did," Bunny said.

"Yeah they sure did. We entered a small vill with only one main road and that's where they bushwhacked us. They hit the lead and tail vehicles first which blocked everyone else in. I was in the last car with three CIA operatives we worked with. All three of them were shot and killed with rounds coming in from both sides," John said.

"Were *you* hit?" Felix asked.

"I was, later, but not then. Not in the car." A shadow came over him and John paused for a moment. "I froze. I was in that shot up car in Iraq and it was like I was nine years old again riding down Avenue D with mom and dad. I couldn't move. I'd never let my team down or hesitated before, but I was frozen in my seat and scared to death."

Knowing how difficult it was for John to talk about his parents, Felix gently put his hand on his cousin's shoulder as he continued with the story.

"The car kept taking rounds, but I didn't get a scratch." He unconsciously touched the scar on his face, which was a constant reminder of the pain and loss he felt over his parent's murder.

"I remember screaming at the top of my lungs and not being able to hear a thing. Just silence. I was gone man. And then the back door flies open and there's Bunny. He was sayin' something to me, looked like he was shouting cause I could see his mouth moving, but I couldn't hear a word he said. I just sat there staring into space."

"And that's when I hit him. Really cracked him too. Found out later I broke his cheek bone," Bunny said.

"Yeah, well he almost knocked me out, but it woke me up too. Snapped me out of it just in time. Bunny pulled me out two seconds before the gas tank blew and the SUV turned into a fireball. He was lyin' on top of me to protect me from the blast when he took the two rounds in the back. They went right through his flak jacket, front and back and stuck wet and bloody to the front of mine."

"The vests weren't shit back then. No stopping power. They're much better now though," Bunny said, roughly clapping Chris on the back. Chris smiled back nervously.

"Even with his guts hanging out he rolls over and blasts the guy that shot him. Then he turns to me and says, 'I'm hurt bad. I need you to kill these Hajji's so we can all go home.'"

Bunny took over. "And that's just what he did. Half the team was dead or wounded, the other half was pinned down, and both senators and the congressman had literally shit their pants. But then here comes Johnny Bishop to the rescue, an MP 5 in each hand mowin' down bad guys like it's a fuckin' video game. He's runnin' back and forth shootin' one guy off the roof with one hand and blastin' another out of a doorway with the other. I saw him take out fifteen of 'em before I passed out. The total body count for that day was five from our side and thirty-seven from theirs. In the after-action report the rest of the team only claimed eight kills so your cousin here did the rest all on his own. He was runnin' down the street, chasing 'em into houses. He was..." Bunny looked up at the ceiling fan trying to find the right words. "He was an unstoppable force. A one-man army. Still is by what he just did in the park."

"Jesus," Chris said.

John was lost in thought remembering the details of that bloody day. He'd been a berserker. He'd killed in every way imaginable, using his guns until he was out of ammo, then attacking with a knife and finally with just his bare hands. As much as he'd been a Special Forces Operator that day he'd also been a raging nine year old kid avenging his parents' death by killing everything in sight.

"He was shot three times and didn't even know it."

"One was just a graze."

"He saved us all. After the senators got the doo doo out of their drawers they called the president. Usually takes a year, year and a half to go through the chain of command, but they fast tracked it and they were gonna give Johnny the Medal of Honor a month later. He begged, pleaded and called in every favor *not* to receive our nation's highest honor so they gave him the Distinguished Service Cross as a consolation prize."

"*What?!* You *turned down* the Medal of Honor?" Felix asked.

"Why?" Chris asked.

"Because they pull you outta combat. Make you an Army poster boy. Your cousin here couldn't face life away from the front lines," Bunny said.

"Unbelievable," Felix said, shaking his head. "Unfucking believable."

"Don't listen to his shit bout how he don't deserve it, which is what he says about all his medals. This is the motherfuckin' man right here. The badest of the bad and the bravest of the brave."

"Come on, Bun, knock it off. You saved my life twice that day, and it was my fault you got shot. He spent a year in the hospital and had to leave Special Forces."

"Offered me a desk job, but just couldn't see myself pushin' papers around for the rest of my life."

"I've sent him my DSC four times and he keeps sending it back with a new thank you letter each time."

"That's 'cause you're my hero Johnny boy," he said,

easily picking him up and squeezing him so hard John's face started changing color.

"Mine too," Felix added. "You saved me, bro. I was this close to picking up that bag in the park. Man I would've been gone." He took a long pull straight from the Hennessy bottle.

"We both would've been gone Cat. We're still here. We're alive, so don't waste your time thinking what might have been," John said putting his arm around Felix's shoulder.

They all kept talking and drinking until Felix was leaning on the bar with his head down near the hand rail. John came back from the bathroom and walked up to him.

"Johnny, that you?" Felix asked without lifting up his head, still bent over and staring down at the floor.

"Yeah, it's me."

"Thank God. I've been looking for your shoes."

"Think he needs some air," Bunny said cracking up.

John walked Felix outside to see if he was going to throw up. The cool evening breeze cleared his head and they talked for ten minutes before going back inside.

While they were out front every flat screen around the bar showed pictures of John and this time Felix as well.

"Turn the music down and the TV's up," Bunny said.

The cousins walked back in just as the report came on.

"The Unknown Hero of Union Square has been found! His name is John Bishop and until two weeks ago he was a sergeant in the Army's Special Forces serving in Afghanistan. On Saturday he single handedly killed two suicide bombers using only a Swiss Army Knife and then shot and wounded the suspected terrorist leader after confiscating one of their weapons."

"Former Sergeant Bishop was a highly decorated Green Beret and was awarded the Distinguished Service Cross in

2007. Beyond his military achievements he is most famous or *infamous* for his lineage. John Bishop is the nephew and adopted son of New York crime boss Gonzalo Valdez, also known as El Gato Negro, or The Black Cat."

"Though never convicted, Valdez and his syndicate have been linked to countless murders, in addition to drug dealing, and gambling. It is unknown what role Mr. Bishop plays in his Uncle's crime family. Although hailed as a hero for his actions in Union Square, Mr. Bishop, who resides at 215 E. 7th Street in Manhattan, is a person of interest and may face indictment by several law enforcement agencies."

All the news networks had similar stories. They continued to cover the terror attack in detail, but they all insinuated that John was a career criminal rather than a war hero. One network even suggested that he had been dishonorably discharged and may have worked with the terrorists before turning on them at the last minute in order to regain his hero status. There were also pictures of Felix and reports that he assaulted responding police officers during the Union Square attack. They called him a known gangster and a street thug convicted of armed robbery and murder.

"Shit," Felix and John said at the same time.

Brooklyn, NY

Amir was hoping his luck would change and it did in a big way. Five minutes before the news cast came on and gave him the name of his target he received a call giving him the soldier's exact location. One of his men stopped for coffee and was sitting in his cab right outside Still Bar when John and Felix stepped out for air. Taking his time to make sure, his man confirmed it was Bishop, carefully noting the scar on the right side of his face.

Excited by this golden opportunity, Amir's pain was gone, masked by the adrenaline rushing through him. He got his people moving and his top man Khalid Mulan was waiting downstairs in a Lincoln Town Car with darkly tinted windows. As he walked out the door he spoke to the picture on the wall.

"As Allah is my witness, I will watch you and your cousin die tonight John Bishop."

CHAPTER 17
NOTHING

Still Bar, Downtown Manhattan

JOHN'S PHONE RANG and he saw it was Captain Ryan.

"John, Jimmy here. How you holding up Sarge?"

"Pretty pissed off Cap. Our names being out there are bad enough, but they're practically calling me a terrorist and Felix, Al Capone."

"I checked around and this smear campaign comes directly from Meecham," Ryan said.

"Fuck me."

"Yeah, well that's exactly what he's trying to do. I told you he'd come after you and believe me he's just getting started. I'll bet he's got copies of your service record with his people going over every page to see where they can hurt you."

"Anything else?"

"Just that he's angling to get indictments against Felix and your Uncle."

"What are the charges?"

"He's still fishing. Trying for assaulting an officer

against Felix, combined with a RICO indictment against them both. My guess is he'll try to convict them in the press first, then force the DA and the Justice Department to do his dirty work."

"Son of a bitch."

"That he is. Look, I've contacted friends in the press and told them this story is pure bull, but these people are sharks and they smell blood in the water."

"But none of this is true!"

"John, I learned long ago that truth and the news are mutually exclusive. All these people do is try to sell more ad space or get higher ratings, the truth be damned."

"Okay, thanks Jimmy, I'll be in touch."

"Same here. I'll let you know if I hear more."

The place had cleared out as it was now approaching midnight. There were only two people sitting at the front of the bar speaking with the bartender, but John still moved Felix, Chris and Bunny to the back room to talk in private. He passed on everything that Ryan had said and stopped to think for a minute.

"You know, he never asked me where I was."

"So," Chris said.

"I think he already knows," he said taking off his belt. He examined it closely and found the small incision where the microphone and GPS tracker had been inserted. He found an identical device attached to the battery in his cell phone and one more in his wallet.

"These are the only items that I had with me when we were held at Homeland Security. How about you?" he asked Felix.

They only found two on Felix since he'd put on a new belt. All five devices were state of the art. They put them all in a bag and Chris took them to the front of the bar where the music was loudest.

Felix shook his head. "Who's tracking us?"

"We can't know for sure. Meecham maybe? Director Kolter just to keep tabs? Question is, are they using us as bait so this Amir and his guys come after us, or are they trying to get some dirt on us for an indictment?"

Having already seen their Glock 19's when they took their belts off Bunny said, "I'm glad to see you guys are armed. Saves me the trouble of getting you outfitted, but from here on I'm on both of you night and day. Twenty-four hour security."

"Thanks Bunny, appreciate your help."

"What about me? I can help too," Chris said.

"Chris, I know you want in on this, but you don't have the training. Not yet anyway. You can be a huge help though. Get to Tio and tell him what's going on here. Being the master planner that he is I'm sure he saw all this coming and probably has guys outside watching us. Still, make sure he knows everything," John said.

"Okay, I'll call dad and find Tio. Hey, before I go, can I get a picture of the three of you?"

They were posing for photos along the far wall when shots rang out in front of the bar. All three had their guns drawn when a man staggered in spitting blood with an explosive device strapped to his body. Bunny and John fired a moment ahead of Felix, and Chris reflexively pressed the button on his mini camera. They saw the terrorist falling backwards from their three head shots right before the bomb detonated. There was no place to hide and no time to move. The blast came at them like a sonic freight train… There was nothing after that.

CHAPTER 18
NATIONAL SECURITY

Washington D.C.

THE PRESIDENT, ALONG with his National Security Advisor, the Directors of the CIA, NSA, FBI, Homeland Security, the Secretaries of State and Defense and several generals, including Palmer, were all seated in the Situation Room of the White House for the late night meeting. They all listened intently to the translation of the tape recovered from the hut in Afghanistan.

"Tony, what's your assessment?" the president asked Director Kolter.

"Mr. President, that tape has given us some valuable intelligence. We know that Aziz Khan is behind the attack in New York and is responsible for the death of our five operators in Khost Province. After debriefing Colonel Edwards and examining the timeline it is clear that General Gulam Mohammed of the Pakistani ISI is Khan's ally and warned him that our troops were on the way. It is also clear that it was Khan's nephew, whose alias is Amir Rashad, who planned and led the attack in New York."

"What do we know about Khan?"

Bill Webster, the CIA Director, fielded the question. "Mr. President, Aziz Khan is a powerful warlord from eastern Afghanistan. We armed and trained him and his militia to fight the Russians. After that war ended he carved out a big piece of territory for himself and was close to taking over the whole country. We estimate he has about four thousand men under his command. He has strong tribal ties and even blood relations in Pakistan. He finances his army through heroin production and distribution, but takes nothing for himself. Reports are that he lives in a network of mountain caves and gives all his wealth to his men and the local population. Khan is fiercely independent and nationalistic and takes orders from no one. He definitely built strong ties to both the Taliban and Al Qaeda, but for the past few years he's also been working with ISIS leadership. We know he's currently sending and receiving soldiers to and from Syria. Bottom line, sir, he is one tough and ruthless S.O.B. who views war as a way of life."

"How do we catch him?"

"Sir," said General Palmer, "we definitely missed a great opportunity to capture or kill him last week. To be candid, Mr. President, we have no idea where he is now. I would suggest we try tracking him through the Pakistani traitor, General Mohammed."

"We are working on that now Mr. President," Director Kolter said.

"Gentlemen, we are fighting wars in Iraq and Afghanistan. We barely survived the worst economic crisis since the Great Depression and we have just endured another terrorist attack in New York. Word will soon get out that the attack is the work of an Afghan warlord with ties to

ISIS and Al Qaeda. Aziz Khan will be called the next Bin Laden. We need a win here. Somewhere. Where are we with the nephew Amir Khan?"

"We're building from the ground up, Mr. President," said Terry Hall. "We recovered a lot of evidence they didn't expect us to find. They had military grade C4 and lots of it. We recovered three hundred pounds of it from the flower truck alone. We are tracking that with the help of ATF and we should know its origination very shortly. As to the whereabouts of Amir Khan, that information is unknown at this time, but we are using every resource including the media to track him down, sir."

"Thank God Sergeant Bishop was taking a stroll through that park. If that truck bomb had gone off thousands would have died."

"We're tailing him, sir, just in case the Khan's go after him," Kolter said.

"We're using him as bait?"

"Not exactly. We've got mikes and trackers on him and we're following from a distance. If anything we're protecting him. If Amir crawls out of his hole and makes a try for Bishop we'll be there to stop and arrest him. It's a long shot anyway, but so far our sergeant has been in the thick of things, so we're sticking to him."

"Don't let anything happen to that young man."

"Yes sir."

Cell phones around the room went off simultaneously.

"Mr. President, there's been another bombing in New York."

"God damn it! Where?"

"The terrorists went after Sergeant Bishop and his cousin directly. They blew up a bar in downtown Manhattan where they were having drinks. The entire building was destroyed. The number of casualties is still unknown sir. We had surveillance teams on site and video is coming in now," Terry Hall said.

They all looked over at the giant wall monitor. The video was shot from the roof of a surveillance van parked across the street from Still Bar. It showed a cab pulling up in front and a man exiting the back door with a large explosive device wrapped around his torso. Before the terrorist reached the bar's front door two men ran towards him and shot him multiple times. Badly wounded, he still managed to stagger inside. As the first of the gunmen put his hand on the door handle he disappeared in the bright light of the huge explosion that blew outwards and across the street directly towards the camera.

In the aftermath the two-story building was completely demolished. Cars were smashed and burning, and even the street itself was ripped up. The camera panned to show the wide path of destruction. The adjoining buildings were on fire and debris floated in the smoke-filled air.

"Son of a bitch!" the president shouted. After a brief pause he asked, "Terry, were those your men caught in the blast? The ones shooting?"

"No sir. We believe the uncle had his own security team watching them."

"So even with FBI agents and a private security team for protection these terrorists can't be stopped. They're executing our citizens while we watch and take pictures."

"Mr. President, although your trip to New York is still a secret, I strongly recommend that you postpone it until after we get these guys."

"I think my surprise visit to the U.N. will show the

world that we won't be intimidated. I'll be there tomorrow, Terry, but I still want it kept under wraps until my arrival."

"Very well, sir. If you'll excuse me I need to get up there. I'm going back to New York to be on scene," Terry said and stood up to leave.

"Gloves off, Terry. The Patriot Act enables you to execute no knock warrants on any persons of interest. Use it. We all know what's at stake here, gentleman. They've brought the war home to us. These terrorists must be stopped immediately. Killed or captured I don't care which. Do you have all the resources that you need?"

"I could use a hundred more agents."

"Done. Now let me be clear. We've all seen the movie 'Siege' with Denzel. I'd hate to have life imitate art here; however, we will declare Martial Law in New York if we don't get some quick results. Understood?"

"Yes, Mr. President. I will give you an assessment once I get there, sir.

"Very well."

"Special Ops teams, Terry?" General Palmer asked.

"On standby, so I can use them if I need them, General."

"Keep me updated regardless of the time."

"Yes, Mr. President," Terry said as he rushed out of the room with General Palmer at his side. They were both on their cell phones giving terse commands as they headed towards the FBI helo that was revved and waiting.

CHAPTER 19
WE'RE ON OUR WAY

Brooklyn, NY

THE VALDEZ BROTHERS and Antonio were watching the news reports about John, Felix, and Gonzalo.

"We expected their names to be released, but this? What is this mierda they are saying about them?" asked Fiero.

"This must be Meecham," Gonzalo said. "They even gave out John's address."

From across the river a huge fire ball rose above the skyline. They all stared at Manhattan in silence, fearing the worst.

Antonio saw the call on the cell phone that was only used for the most extreme emergencies. He didn't bother to leave the room this time and knew it was bad news before he picked it up. The breach in security protocol alerted all the brothers that something was indeed very wrong. Antonio's face was ashen as he listened to Benji. Then he simply said, "We're on our way," and hung up.

He turned to his father and his uncles.

"A bomber got out of a cab in front of the bar where John, Felix and Chris were. My men shot him in the street… but he… he got inside and detonated. The building was destroyed," Antonio said, trying to keep hold of his emotions.

Carlos and Macho exploded out of their seats and ran out of the room to get to their sons. The others raced close behind. Antonio stumbled after them, but Gonzalo pulled him aside.

"Whatever has happened is not your fault, Antonio. We all approved your security measures."

"But Tio I should have…" Antonio said helplessly, his eyes welling up with tears.

Gonzalo cut him off with a crisp slap to the face and said, "No tears and no weakness. We are at war. Learn from this moment, Antonio. Let us pray they are alive, but whatever the outcome, make sure this night has made you stronger. To be the head of a family, to lead *this* family, you have to be stronger than everyone else. Even when you don't want to be. Learn from this and remember, we still must find and kill our enemies."

They quickly embraced each other and then hurried out of the room, racing to the city to discover the fate of the three cousins.

Queens, NY

Kev, Ed and Danny were all watching the CNN reports about John, Felix and Gonzalo while they continued their research. All three stopped multitasking and stiffened when they heard the first reports of another bombing. Kevin's cell phone rang. The only people who had the new number were his partners sitting next to him, the soldiers upstairs, and the Valdez brothers.

"This is bad news, fellas," he said before answering. He picked up and listened to the steely, heavily accented voice on the other end.

"We're on our way, Fiero," was his only response.

"They blew up John, Felix, and young Chris at a bar downtown in front of the FBI and Antonio's security team."

"Motherfuckers," Danny said.

"Chris... isn't he Macho's son?" Ed asked.

"Yep."

"We went to his baptism."

"Yep."

"Are they all gone for sure?" asked Danny.

"No confirmation, but it don't look good. Let's mount up. Grab the gear. I'll brief our soldiers and get the van started," Kevin said. He ran up the stairs shouting to Christmas and his men.

They all knew that their mission intensity level was now off the charts. The three of them had to do what all the branches of law enforcement were trying to accomplish with the government's unlimited resources: find every person involved in the bombings. The catch was that Kevin, Ed and Danny had to find them first.

Upper East Side, Manhattan

Maria was printing out the travel itineraries for her and John's weeklong trip. She was sitting at her father's desk when she heard a groan and dishes breaking in the living room. She rushed in to see what happened and saw her mother on her knees sobbing in front of the television. The cup of tea and the plate of cookies she had been holding lay broken and scattered across the wood floor.

Maria didn't comprehend what she was seeing at first. Her vision was blurry as she stared at the images of the collapsed and burning buildings. From someplace far away she barely heard the voice of the reporter repeatedly saying the name John Bishop. Then her father ran in and put his arms around her. The fog cleared in her head and Maria let out a primal scream.

"Nooooooooo!"

The phone rang and Maria's father passed her to her mother before he took the call. He stared into his little girl's fearful eyes as he listened to the voice on the other end.

"We're on our way," he said softly.

"That was Antonio. A suicide bomber blew up the bar where the boys were drinking."

"He's not dead, Daddy. Johnny can't be dead. Not now."

"I know, baby. I know. Get dressed. We're all going down there."

LES

The boys were known by everyone and word traveled fast through the neighborhood.

"What up fellas?"

"Yo dog, you heard what happened to Chris?

"Nah, what?"

"Those jihad motherfuckers blew him up. Him and his cousins."

"Chris? You serious?

"Dead serious."

"Those motherfuckas."

"When?"

"'Bout half an hour ago."

"Where at?"

"At that bar up on Third Ave. We're on our way up there now. See if we can help."

"And find out who needs to get got."

"You packin'?"

"Fo sho. Locked and loaded."

"Wait up, lemme get mine. Call the rest of the fellas. Tell 'em to tool up and meet us there."

"I'm on it."

Hundreds of people, both family and friends rushed to the scene in cars, on bikes and on foot.

Atlantic Ocean, 75 miles off the East coast of the United States

They were headed to Andrews Air Force base in Maryland when the pilot patched the call through. Bear was stone faced. He listened without saying a word.

"We're on our way, sir," Bear said and hung up the phone. The Air Force transport made a sharp turn northwards.

"Listen up."

"What's up, Chief?"

Bear's voice was monotone. Each sentence short and flat. "A suicide bomber blew up Johnny and his family. Leave is cancelled. We're changing flight plans. We fly into New York and meet General Palmer at the scene."

There was a long stunned silence as each man reflected on what he'd just heard.

"This is unreal. Johnny gets wasted by an Afghan terrorist a week after he left the army and stopped fighting Afghan terrorists," Able said.

"This is one cruel and twisted world," Bobby said.

"Someone's gonna find out just how cruel real soon," Mace said.

"We're burning these fuckers down," Bear said.

JFK International Airport, Queens, NY

The flight attendants uniform was the perfect cover and the trip through customs was quick and easy. Gliding casually through the airport as every screen displayed CNN's coverage of the latest bombing, right away Omar knew that this had to be a direct attack on the soldier. Amir wouldn't waste his resources on such a small target after the failure in the park. Omar decided the bar was a good place to start the search and directed the cab towards downtown Manhattan.

"We're on our way," said the friendly driver as they pulled away from the curb.

"Excuse me?"

"I said here we go, we're on our way."

"Yes. Yes we are, aren't we," said Omar the Blade.

CHAPTER 20
GHOSTS

THE CROWD, FILLED with spectators, friends, and family, continued to swell and was running out of patience as they watched fire fighters pound water onto the smoldering mass of rubble that had once been Still Bar.

"I need you all to back up!" said one of the cops straining to control what was quickly turning into an angry mob.

"You back the fuck up!"

"That's our people in there!"

"What's taking so long!?"

"How come they're not going in?"

"If they won't I will!"

"We all will!"

"Who's in charge?"

"Those dudes over there drinking coffee."

Captain Ryan, along with FBI, Bomb Squad, ATF, and ESU team leaders were getting an update from the Fire Chief when Special Agent in Charge Terry Hall jogged over.

"Where are we with this mess?"

"The fires are pretty well contained. The main problem now is the structural integrity of the two adjacent buildings.

I don't want my people or yours digging around for bodies and then have one or both of those six story monsters come down on top of them."

"Can't we shore them up?"

"Yeah we can, but we need cranes and braces."

"Do it. How much time?"

"It'll take at least an hour, maybe two to get all the equipment here from the Bronx and probably another four hours after that to make it safe. Its 2AM now, so by 8 we can start digging."

"Make it happen. Jimmy, can your guys give the cranes a police escort and clear the streets so we can save some time?"

"Can do Terry."

"Now, everything on this goes through me. Everything. And I want everyone sharing what they've got, whether it's hard evidence or just a hunch. We clear?"

Heads nodded in agreement all around the circle that had formed on Terry.

"I'm reporting directly to the president on this so let's not screw this up. The other thing is no one, and I mean no one, speaks to the press. Get the word out to the rank and file. Anyone talks, they lose their badge on the spot. I'll make a short statement now and we'll give a full press conference in the morning after we start digging. All right, let's get to work," he said as he walked towards the screaming reporters.

"That's Terry Hall from the FBI," Gonzalo said.

"You know him?" Fiero asked.

"Met him once."

"Turn the TV on so we can hear his statement."

Calixto picked up the remote and pointed it at the wall mounted flat screen. They were looking down on the scene from a third floor apartment directly across the street. Benji Medina kept his head after the bombing. He acquired their new HQ by knocking on doors until he found the young couple willing to take twenty grand cash to vacate their home so Gonzalo and his brothers could see without being seen.

They all listened to the Terry Hall give his public statement on the TV behind them, but their eyes stayed glued to the smoking pile of twisted metal, split beams and crumbled bricks across the street. The boys were somewhere in that wreckage.

Carlos was nervously hitting his thigh with his fist. "This is taking too long," he said.

"They're worried about the side buildings coming down."

"We can't sit here for six or eight hours. They're in there! They need help now!" Macho shouted.

Antonio burst through the front door with Benji. "You remember Manolo? He works for us and knows the back building. His sister lives there. We can go through her side window and it's about twenty, maybe twenty-five feet down to the alley that connects to the back of the bar."

"I'm going," Carlos and Macho said at the same time.

"One of my guys was a medic in Iraq and I've got another who was an EMT," said Benji. "I'll get some of the kids to jack an ambo for supplies and load it into backpacks. I already ordered the rope ladders so give me ten minutes and we can go in."

As Benji ran out of the room with Carlos and Macho, Antonio made another announcement.

"There's someone downstairs in the lobby waiting to see you, Tio."

"Who knows we're here?'

Antonio handed him the business card that read CIA with the title of Deputy Director under the name.

"Ah. Bring him up. He is an old friend."

Clayton Unser entered the room a minute later and Gonzalo directed him to the bedroom so they could speak privately.

"I'm very sorry about your nephews."

"Is that why you are here? To tell me the CIA is sorry for my family's suffering?"

"No. CIA doesn't care about your family, but I do. The sorry is from me, Don Valdez."

"Then thank you, old friend. Now what does CIA want?"

"Help." Clayton handed over a thick manila folder. It was a complete dossier on Aziz Khan, his history, known associates, and all the intel that had been gathered so far on the attacks in New York.

"You understand this is personal for me. When I find anyone involved they stay alive only long enough to tell me who else is involved."

"You'll have no interference from us. Just do what you do best."

"That's it?"

"Yes... oh, there is one more thing," Unser said. He handed Gonzalo a second folder.

"There always is." Gonzalo opened the folder and smiled for the first time. "Now I know you need something from me in return."

"Yes I do."

"What?"

"Don't kill them all. Get what you need, but save a few for us and fill me in on any information that can help us in the war on terror."

"That's it?"

"That's it my friend. Will your people need assistance with international travel arrangements?"

"Yes. I will let you know when."

"Good hunting, Gonzalo."

"Thank you, Clayton."

He walked Unser to the front door and turned to Fiero.

"Send them in."

Kevin, Ed and Danny were working from their van parked a block away when they were ordered to come up. The mood in the room was tense and somber so other than head nods all around there were no formal greetings. Gonzalo handed over the folder on Aziz.

"This is the man responsible. Find him."

"Aziz Khan? A lot of people have been trying to kill this guy for years."

"You have a much shorter time line."

"Yes, Don Valdez. We understand," Kevin said uneasily.

"While you're working on that you must first help us eliminate his entire local organization led by the nephew."

"Anything else?" Kevin asked, as Danny began carefully taking pictures of each page with a high speed digital camera so they could upload them into their own system and leave the originals.

"Yes. This," Gonzalo said. He dropped the second folder on the glass coffee table.

"Michael Meecham," Kev said reading the file's title aloud.

"He's the Deputy Director of Homeland Security," Ed said without opening it.

"He was."

"Take action?"

"Him you just research for now."

"We're on it."

"Gentlemen…"

"Yes sir?"

"Work fast. As you can see… this is… very personal," Gonzalo said, pointing to the open window that framed the destruction across the street. "Fiero, Antonio and Benji are your direct contacts for everything. Keep us informed."

Ed finished photographing the Meecham file just as Danny finished the one on Aziz.

"The soldiers are nearby?" Antonio asked.

"A block away."

"There were three suspicious vehicles in the area before and after the bombing. One was the FBI; another was a civilian looking for parking. We checked inside after she found a spot and it's clean. The third was a Lincoln Town car with tinted windows that arrived ten minutes before and left right after. We followed from a distance. It's at a warehouse in Brooklyn in Redhook. Here's the address. We also tailed the cab that dropped off the bomber. It's parked in front of a house in Queens, but an FBI SWAT team is there too so go to Redhook and my men will watch what happens to the cab driver."

"Alright. You want more men with us?"

"You remember Chepe?"

"Sure. Good man in a firefight."

"He's downstairs waiting for you with five more soldiers, all ex-military. They will back up Christmas and his team. Now listen to me very, very carefully. Tell Christmas to make sure they leave some alive. Alive, you understand? We will have questions for them."

"We'll make sure, Antonio."

They were hurrying down the hallway when Kevin put a hand on each of his partners.

"Remember when we said we wanted to help the president on this one?"

"Yeah. So?"

"Well I think we are. In the Aziz file there were copies of the President's Daily Brief. The fuckin' PDB man! The National Intelligence Advisor hand delivers it to the pres first thing every morning. That's as top secret as it gets and Gonzalo just gave it over like it's something he reads every day."

"Our man is well connected."

"That's all the way connected. This is one time when we can't let our bosses down."

"After just looking into those murderous yellow eyes I'm a lot more worried about disappointing Gonzalo Valdez than I'll ever be about our president," Danny said.

"Me too," Ed said. "Me too."

Kev called Christmas as they walked down the street and away from the crowds with Chepe.

"Mount up. Rolling out in sixty seconds."

"Roger that. Rolling in sixty."

Two blocks away Bobby, Able, Mace, and Bear walked up to the Mack truck that was the mobile Special Operations Command Center. They all came to attention and saluted General Palmer when he met them at the side door.

"At ease, gentlemen."

"Any word on our boy, sir?"

"They can't go in yet because the adjacent buildings may collapse."

"Let us go in and get him out."

The general shook his head, "I have a mission for you. We tracked the cab that delivered the bomber. I'm glad you're already in civilian clothes. No military uniforms while we operate on American soil. There's a weapons locker in the back. Gear up and be ready to move out in five."

"Yes sir," said Team Razor.

"Listen men, I know how you feel about Sergeant Bishop. If he's alive we'll get him out shortly. You're going to be the tip of the spear on this Op, and I can't have you guys climbing on that pile of rubble with the whole world watching."

"Understood sir," Bear said. "Alright, you heard the general. Night Vision Systems, comm gear, vests, weapons, ammo and ready to roll out in four minutes."

Back at the bomb site Maria was at the front of the crowd with her mother and father. Grassiella, Marci and Silvi were standing with them.

"Oh God, why is it taking so long? Where's Gonzalo and his brothers? Can't they do something?" Maria asked.

"The family is at war now," Silvi said.

"At war?"

"Yes, my sweet girl. Gonzalo will figure out a way to help the boys, but he will also find all those responsible for this," Grassiella said.

"Shouldn't he leave that to the police?"

"That is not our way. You should know that since you are about to marry into the family."

"You know it too, don't you?" Maria asked.

"Yes, I know it. I know Juanito is alive. I feel him like I feel my own heart beating."

"Then where is he?"

"Trying to find a way out of that," she said looking across the street.

The bright flood lights illuminating the destruction created a stark contrast with the night sky. The crumbled building continued to send up wisps of smoke that looked liked tendrils of morning mist reaching up towards the heavens. Anxious to see something happen, everyone stared intently, their tension mounting. Family, friends, policemen, firemen, even reporters all took a sudden and audible intake of breath when they saw two chalk white figures emerge through the haze. Looking down on the crowd from the highest point on the pile they seemed to generate their own light, glowing like angels.

"Ghosts!" a young girl shouted.

"Those aren't ghosts. Those are the boys," Grassiella said, her eyes welling up.

"We need some help over here, God damn it!"

"That's John! Johnny!" Maria screamed.

"We need a crow bar and a blow torch!"

"And that's my Felix," Marci said.

"But where's Chris?" Silvi asked fearfully as the crowd surged forward.

From a window in the back building Macho came down the rope ladder with Carlos right behind him. Ignoring the danger they madly scrambled up to John and Felix. They were both bleeding from numerous cuts and scratches by the time they reached the cousins.

"Where is he?!" screamed Macho. He grabbed John's shirt with both hands, his eyes pleading. "Where is he?!"

"He's way down there in the basement, Tio. My friend is with him. He's hurt and we can't get him out without tools."

"Let's go," Macho said. "These guys are medics. Felix you wait for Benji. He's getting the torch. Take this phone and press three to call him. Tell him anything else you think we need."

"It's a maze down there. The flashlights make it easier,

but be careful. This thing wants to bite and stab you at every turn," John said as he crawled back down into the small black hole.

Carlos was the last to go in and he held his son Felix for a long moment. "What's this white powder all over you?"

Felix looked down at his clothes seeing the white dust for the first time. "Plaster. Flour… I don't know. Chris is all fucked up, Dad. He's trapped by a heavy steel beam and a pipe went right through him."

"We'll get him out," Carlos said. He lovingly put his hand on his son's face before going down to help his wounded nephew. The touching scene was replayed over and over again on every network.

Across the street and a few feet behind Maria it was also witnessed by a lone figure who looked on with both fascination and indifference.

"You failed again Amir Khan," Omar whispered.

CHAPTER 21

TWENTY-FOUR SECONDS

Redhook, Brooklyn

THEY ALL KNEW they were in the right place given the tight security around the facility, but the assault on the warehouse was taking longer than expected. Cameras faced the street, the windows were boarded up, and a sophisticated alarm system added to what the inhabitants thought was a safe blanket of protection.

"Danny says he needs five more minutes to neutralize the alarm," Ed said.

"Then we wait," Christmas said.

"I always meant to ask you, where'd the name 'Christmas' come from?"

Kevin chuckled. "You don't know?"

"No. Know what?"

"Go ahead Christmas, we've got time. Tell Ed how you got your name."

"Alright," he said, pausing for dramatic effect. "I was still a SEAL at the time. Just finished six months of heavy action and came back stateside for the holidays. I met this hottie before I went on my tour, and she wrote me letters begging me to come stay with her for a few days. So I show up at her house the day before Christmas Eve, the blood barely washed off, still smelling like death. Anyway, turns out she's a general's daughter and we're staying at the family compound up in Connecticut."

"He must've loved you."

"He was a retired desk jockey from the Pentagon, but still soldier enough to recognize a killer when he saw one. The man was none too pleased. He put me in a room on the other side of the house as far away from his little girl as possible."

"Surprised they didn't have you stay with the help."

"Man, him and his wife were so chilly I would've been warmer sleeping in a tent outside in the snow."

"So what happened?"

"Well, keep in mind I hadn't had sex in months. I knew the daughter was gonna clean my pipes good, but I couldn't get near her. Anyway, I slept in on Christmas Eve and the whole family had gone to town to do some last minute shopping. So I'm chillin' in the living room, eating cookies, and looking over at their ten foot tree when this one ornament catches my eye."

"Angel?"

"Far fuckin' from it. It was this little burlesque type figurine with huge tits, a fat ass, and juicy red lips. It was even holding up two purple feathers like she was ready to put on a show."

"Freaky."

"Yeah, well I ain't never seen a slutty Christmas ornament before or since, but I couldn't take my eyes off it. Next thing I know I'm rock hard and ready to bust. I shoulda just gone back to my room, or yanked it in the bathroom, but that dirty little thing had me going."

"You didn't."

"Yeah, I did. The whole family walked in right when I shot my load. A perfect shot that sailed high and hit the ornament right in the tits. The rest was hanging off a branch like wet tinsel."

Ed was cracking up. "You sick fuck."

"Talk about trimming the tree," Kev said, shaking his head.

"Yeah, well I didn't even bother asking for a ride. Just packed my shit and walked out the door."

"Wow."

"When I got back to the Teams my CO threw me under the bus. In front of twenty SEAL's he says, 'Randall, there's a retired general going around saying that you jerked off on his Christmas tree in front of his wife and daughter. Can this be true?' After I confessed I was branded Christmas for life."

"You still think about her?"

"The general's daughter?

"No, the slutty ornament."

"Yeah, I do, and I've been banging thick, big titty women ever since.

"Unrequited love."

"It's a powerful thing."

The go signal came through their headsets, indicating that Danny was ready.

"Okay, here we go. Danny's gonna shut it down it in exactly sixty seconds from... three, two, one, now."

"Minty's on the roof, Boogie's going in through the back and I'm hitting the front. See you in a few," Christmas said. He exited the van. Dressed as a bum, he stumbled down the street like a drunkard.

"There's seven guys in there. Three are near the back and the other four are in the center of the room. Remember, we need some for interrogation," Kev said into the microphone.

"Done," Christmas said. Getting in character, he took a swig of water from a quart sized vodka bottle.

Sitting in the van a block away, the Pro KEDDSS team watched the action unfold on a computer screen linked to their custom-made ultra-wide-band heat and motion detector which allowed them to literally see through walls. The choreography was perfect. Danny shut off the alarm and the cameras, then turned out all the lights, throwing the five thousand square foot space into total darkness. A second later Minty came through the sky light, Christmas breached the front door and Boogie blasted through a back door on the loading dock. Wearing night vision goggles they could clearly see the seven terrorists stumbling around and shooting blindly.

Two of the fighters had been in combat. They stood back to back, calmly firing their pistols in a shoulder high arch. They couldn't see anything, but still provided decent three hundred and sixty degree cover for each other. Christmas' took aim with his silenced MP 5 and squeezed twice. Both terrorists crumpled to the floor from the head shots.

From above Minty watched two bearded men pull machine guns from the trunk of the Lincoln Town Car. They were just cocking the AK-47's when he opened up, giving each double taps high on the forehead. The blood spray glowed bright green through his night vision sensors.

The final group of three was trying to go out with a bang. Fumbling with wires in the dark, they tried to attach a detonator to a big block of C4. Boogie slid in behind one of them, stabbing him in the heart, lungs and throat with quick, precise and powerful strokes. The two remaining terrorists didn't know their comrade was dead when Boogie silently moved in. He cracked one in the temple with the hilt of his combat knife, knocking him out cold. The last man standing still couldn't see, but heard the noise and turned towards Boogie, gun in hand. Boogie came in low under the weapon, extended his enemy's arm out over his own shoulder and pulled down hard. The elbow bent the opposite way, snapping the bones with a loud crack. Its owner's high pitched scream was cut short when Boogie pulled his arm around the man's throat and choked him to sleep.

"All clear."

"Clear."

"Time?" Christmas asked.

"Twenty-four seconds," Kev answered back from the van.

"Okay, make sure you save the tape. We'll review it later."

"You got it."

Danny turned the lights back on and Chepe came in his with men. He walked up to the three killers and bowed formally, showing his respect. Chepe himself was a skilled warrior, but these men were in another league.

Kev and Ed drove the van to the back of the warehouse, coming in through the loading dock while the two unconscious survivors were bound and gagged.

"Those two are in for a world of hurt," Danny said.

"Fuck 'em. I got no respect for any man that kills innocent people," Ed said.

"I'm with you on that. Alright fellas, let's get to work. Gather any evidence and get photos of everything, including the bodies," Kev said.

"We're leaving them?"

"Yeah, they stay."

"God damn!"

"What?"

"Take a look at this."

Everyone walked over to look at the back of a big Con Edison utility truck. It was packed with explosives. U.S. military C4 still in its original casing was stacked eight feet high and ten feet deep.

"The truck comes with us," Kev said.

East Elmhurst, Queens

The FBI helicopter had been flying high overhead when the bomber exited the cab in front of Still Bar. They tracked the cab over the bridge to this three story house in Queens and waited until an FBI SWAT team arrived on the scene. The SWAT team stayed out of site and waited for Special Ops to do the assault. They wanted a live body for interrogation, but once the FBI took someone into custody their hands were tied in terms of how the prisoner was treated and de-briefed. Special Ops was off the radar on this and no such restrictions applied.

"Johnny's alive," Able said, as they exited the truck two blocks from the house.

Mace pumped his fist. "That's what I'm talking about!"

"We all know our boy is hard to kill," Bobby said.

"He's gonna be pissed at the people that tried," Bear said.

"Johnny's always deadly, but when he's actually mad at someone they might as well just shoot themselves in the head and get it over with," Mace said.

"Be less painful," Bobby added.

"Alright, let's get this terrorist alive if possible, but don't get yourselves killed trying to do it," Bear said to his team as they approached the SWAT commander.

"What's it look like Captain?"

"The cab's parked in the driveway. There's been no movement since he entered. The curtains are drawn, but the second and third floors have lights on."

"Means he's probably in the basement."

"That'd be my guess. It's been quiet so I can't tell you how many are in there."

"Think he spotted you?"

"I don't think so. We came in stealthy and you can barely see the house from here. The bird's still up there, but it's so high you can't even hear it."

"The dude drove straight here so unless he's a complete dipshit this is a setup," Bobby said.

"A setup?"

"Yeah, that house is gonna blow as soon as anyone steps inside. A hundred bucks says there's a tunnel in the basement leading to another house nearby," Bobby said as he scanned the neighborhood. His eyes locked on a two story home about fifty yards away. It was isolated and had lots of hedges and trees so you could barely see the structure. "There. That's where he is."

"Just like that?" asked the SWAT Captain.

"Just like that."

"I've been doing this with him for five years now and he ain't been wrong yet. He always knows which hole the gopher's in," Able said.

"Captain you should expand your perimeter in case their tunnel has more than one exit," Bear said.

The house was dark and quiet as they approached

silently through a world turned fluorescent green by their night vision goggles. Moving past the hedges each member of Team Razor got into position. They checked for alarms or booby traps, then went into action. Their timing down to the split second, Bear and Bobby fired concussion grenades through the windows on the top floor, Mace tossed one through the front door, and Able threw his through the small basement window. All four grenades went off simultaneously, rocking the house on its foundation.

They rushed in two on each door, Bobby and Able in the back and Bear and Mace through the front. Bear immediately saw an enemy fighter working to clear his head. He had blood coming out of his eyes and ears and both his legs were shredded from the blast. He was trying to raise a twelve gauge shotgun when Bear shot him twice, heart and head, with his MP5.

Able charged up the stairs with Bobby close behind. They quickly checked every room and gave the all clear on their headsets.

Mace ran down the basement stairs and saw an arm extending an army issue .45 towards him. He opened up on full auto and in less than a second the arm was ripped from its owner's shoulder and lay bloody and twitching on the basement floor. The now one armed terrorist stepped out into the open and looked down in shock at his own appendage before collapsing forward.

There was one more man around the corner in a separate room. He'd been sitting at a desk when Able's concussion grenade went off. The desk shielded him from the shrapnel, but the shock wave knocked him out of his chair. He was lying flat on his back with arms and legs spread wide, alive, but out cold.

"Clear."

"Clear."

"I think that's all of them, but let's find the tunnel and make sure," Bear said.

"Will you look at this."

They all gathered around the table. The monitor showed a three hundred and sixty degree view around the other house with the cab in front of it. A flashing red button with wires running across the basement floor was obviously the trigger.

"They lit up the top floors so they could see us coming. Anyone assaulting that place would've been blown sky high."

"Nice work Bobby."

"Alright now that we're done jerking each other off let's call in the troops. Put some pressure on that wound and see if we can save the one armed bandit over there and secure the sleeping bomber."

Bear spoke into his headset, "We're done here, sir. Three bad guys. One dead, one alive and one badly wounded. Lots of evidence here for the FBI to sift through,"

"Well done, Chief. Leave the body, extract the prisoners and exit the premises before the lights and cameras get there. I'm out front with transportation."

"Yes sir."

"You heard the man, Razor. We're outta here."

"By the way, how'd we do, Bear?" Mace asked.

"I had us clocked at twenty-four seconds."

CHAPTER 22
DECORATING A SOLDIER

BLOOD WAS DRAINING out of him so they had to move quickly, but it took another hour to get Chris free and carefully bring him up to the surface where firemen and an ESU team loaded him into a rescue basket attached to an extension ladder. Macho gripped the cables above the basket with one hand and held his son's hand with the other while they were both lifted to safety. Everyone else climbed through the pile of rubble and made their way down to street level.

They loaded Chris into the back of a waiting ambulance and the medics immediately went to work on his multiple injuries. Macho and Silvi climbed in and the instant the doors slammed closed the ambulance raced down Third Avenue towards the Beth Israel trauma center.

John, Felix, Bunny, Carlos, Benji and his two men were all covered in dirt, dust and blood. Some of it came from their own cuts, but most of it had come from Chris. They stood in the street staring after the ambulance as the crowd cheered and the reporters screamed questions at them.

"That's the bravest kid in the world," Bunny said.

"He sure is," Felix said.

John's face was grim. "He's got a tough fight ahead of him."

They were each saying a silent prayer for Chris when a loud crashing sound behind them made them all jump. They turned around in time to see the six story brick building to the right of what had once been Still Bar crumble at its base and topple over onto the pile. The impact rocked the already shaky building on the left and a moment later it too came crashing down, sealing what would have been their tomb.

Beth Israel Hospital

John needed stitches and was waiting for the doctor to come back. Maria was wiping away blood and dirt from his face and hands when SAC Terry Hall and NYPD Captain Jimmy Ryan walked into the small hospital examination room.

"Hey soldier, you okay?" asked Ryan.

John was cut, scraped and scratched from head to toe and his shirt and pants were ripped up.

"Am I okay? Nah, I'm about as far from okay as I can possibly be."

"Really sorry about your cousin," said Ryan.

"Same here. Think you're up to telling us what happened?" Terry asked.

"Yeah why not. Rather do it now than later." He took a deep breath and exhaled heavily.

"Take your time Sergeant."

"I was out cold and I think Bunny was the first to wake up."

"Bunny?"

"His given name is Valentino Brown. We served together in Special Forces before he was wounded in Iraq. Everyone calls him Bunny."

"Okay, thanks."

"I remember shooting the bomber when he ran in and then after that I was waking up in total darkness with Bunny pulling on my foot. The floor under us must have collapsed from the explosion 'cause we found out we were in the basement with a two-story building piled on top of us. It's just dumb luck that we're not all dead."

He looked over at Maria who was being really brave and doing her best to stay calm. Her back was straight, her eyes were clear, and her palms dry as she held his hand firmly. He was so proud of her. He knew that she was holding it together for his sake and he gently brushed a few strands of hair away from her eyes before continuing.

"It's funny how life sends you messages."

"How so?"

"Me and Bunny were trapped in the dark once before. We called in an artillery strike on some Hajjis in Iraq and the rounds came in short. Hit the building we were in and messed us up. We were both wounded, it was pitch black, and we couldn't find our gear. After some Marines dug us out we both went and bought matching flash lights. Swore that we'd always keep 'em handy." John pulled the mini Mag light out of his front pocket and held it up.

"We never would've made it tonight without 'em. Anyway, we both had crap pinning us down and it took a while to wiggle free. I found Felix a few feet away on an old sofa. Don't ask me how he managed to land on that thing. The concussion from the blast knocked him out like the rest of us and then the couch saved him 'cause there was a bunch of nasty stuff down there that would've torn him up if he'd fallen on it."

"And Chris?"

John looked down at his shoes for a moment, trying to compose himself. Maria handed him a bottle of water and he took a deep swallow.

"Bunny found Chris under a pile of bricks and sheet rock. The three of us cleared a path. We were working fast cause we could feel the room heating up from the fire above us and smoke was seeping in. We thought we could just pull him out until we saw the heavy support beam pinning his leg... and then the two inch pipe sticking out of his chest."

"Shit," Jimmy said.

"We tried clearing everything around the beam, but it was wedged in good and was way too heavy. We couldn't budge it. When my uncles came down with the blow torch we tried cutting through the thing, but it was slow going and the heat was literally cooking him. You could smell his skin burning."

"Jesus."

"You know through the whole thing he never cried. Didn't even scream when I cut off his leg."

"You what?"

"I amputated his left leg below the knee with a machete and no anesthesia while his dad was holding one hand and Felix held the other... You know what he said to me before I did it?... He said he knew how hard this was gonna be for me. Hard for me! Told me not to feel bad. He said he knew we wouldn't leave him so it was the only way we'd all get out of there alive. Said he'd gladly give his leg to save the people he loves. He was more worried about us than about himself. His only regret was that he'd never get to be a Green

Beret... I've seen a lot of wounded men in my day and with something like this they all pass out. Not Chris. He stayed awake the whole time... talked us through it." John's voice was cracking and Maria couldn't hold back the tears. She buried her head in his shoulder.

"Brave kid."

"He's in surgery now?"

"Yeah. We had medics down there with us. They clamped off the arteries in his left leg. His right leg is badly broken and he's got about twenty small wounds. Chris was taking our picture when the bomber ran in. Me, Felix and Bunny were kind of against the wall in the back room, but he was standing in the middle and out in the open when the bomb detonated. He got hit with a lot of shit from the blast, but it's the chest wound that worries me the most. It collapsed his right lung and he lost a lot of blood."

"Anything we can do for you John?"

"Yeah, one thing."

"Name it."

"Stay out of my way."

"Excuse me," Terry said.

"You heard me. I'm going to find every person that had a hand in this and I don't want the FBI following me when I do."

"You know you're a civilian now. We have laws."

"Laws? Since when is it legal to put bugs in people's clothes and listen to their conversations?"

"John, please, just let us handle this. We can protect you and your family."

He exploded up out of his seat. "What! Protect us? How many FBI guys were outside the bar when we got blown up? And how many stood around for three hours while we dug ourselves out of our own grave?"

"Look I'm sorry that…"

"Terry, save your sorry for someone that gives a fuck. My little cousin is in there fighting for his life. My family protects itself from here on and I'll find the guys responsible faster than you ever will. Just leave us alone."

"Sorry you feel that way, but I can't sit back and watch you kill people. You understand that even though I'll hate doing it, I will arrest you if you break the law."

"Yeah I understand. No hard feelings from me when you put the cuffs on."

"I really hope it doesn't come to that. Think about your fiancé here."

Maria's eyes were blazing. "Don't you dare! Don't you dare try to use me to get what you want. If you were smart you'd go take a vacation and come back when he's finished. A thousand of you and your men can't do what he can. Now get out and leave us alone!"

Terry's face was red as he walked out of the room, stung by Maria's words. Ryan hung back.

"Johnny, I want to help. Let me know if you need anything. No strings and no interference. You understand what I'm saying?"

"Yeah. Thanks Jimmy."

Captain Ryan tipped his hat to Maria before leaving to find Terry.

"I love you, baby."

"I love you, too. You know you need a shower and some new clothes."

"After the Doc stitches me up I need to talk to Tio. Then we'll run home and come right back."

Everyone was there. His aunts Grassiella and Marci, his cousin Silvi, some of his other cousins and a few of Chris' closest friends were in a large group on one side of the waiting room while his uncles Gonzalo, Sesa, Macho, Fiero, Carlos and Calixto were talking quietly in the corner with Felix and Antonio when John walked over.

"Any word?"

"Nothing yet."

"It's been five hours," Macho said.

"He's strong, hermano," Gonzalo said.

"Any leads on these guys, Antonio?"

"Yeah, Johnny. We took out five and Benji is interrogating two more. They'll tell us all they know shortly. We watched some ninjas take a few other terrorists out of a house in Queens so it looks like the FBI might be doing its job for once."

"If it was the FBI."

"Hey Johnny."

Everyone in the room turned to look at Team Razor as the four "ninjas" strutted over.

"What're you doing here?"

"Good to see you too, man."

"Didn't mean it like that, Mace. You got leave?"

"We did. Now we're working. How's Chris?" The team shared each other's mail from back home and they had all read some of Chris's long letters.

"They're still working on him."

"Sorry, man."

"Where's Bunny?" asked Bobby.

"He's with Chris. Won't leave his side, even during surgery."

"That's Bunny," Able said.

"How's this gonna go down?"

"Come on, Johnny. What kind of question is that after all we've been through?" Bear asked.

"No hard feelings guys. I've got a lot of people to find and just need to know up front if you're with me on this."

"Anything you need. Shooters, weapons, anything. We stand with you, Johnny. You hear me man? We're here for you."

"Thanks guys, really glad to hear that. What'd you get from the cabbie in Queens?"

"He lost an arm and is still asleep, but we took out another live body that'll be giving it up soon. You'll know when we do."

"Alright. This is my uncle Gonzalo, the head of the family, and these are my uncles and my cousins Felix and Antonio."

Introductions were made all around and they all moved into a tight circle to strategize without being overheard. They spoke quietly for half an hour before the surgeon came in. His face was tight as he spoke directly to Macho.

"Mr. Valdez, you raised a very brave and very tough young man. The good news is he's alive. The bad news is we had to remove his right lung and two of his ribs. There was a lot of other internal damage and we repaired most of it."

"Most of it? Why not all of it?"

"His body just couldn't take any more. We removed sixteen pieces of shrapnel from him and stopped all the major bleeding. His heart stopped twice and we brought him back both times. It's really a miracle he survived the surgery after experiencing so much trauma and losing so much blood. That said, he's young, strong and he's obviously a fighter. That's more good news. Now we wait. His body needs rest to heal, but he should wake up in a few hours."

"Let me use your phone," John said to Bear after the Doctor left. "Is he on speed dial?"

"Who?"

"General Palmer."

"Yeah. Press one."

After making several calls John went home with Maria to shower and change. His body was drained and he was having trouble mentally managing all the strategies for his next moves. He put up only token resistance when Maria forced him to lie down. He jumped up four hours later feeling refreshed and re-energized.

Chris was just waking when they got back to the hospital. His complexion was gray and his voice was a staticky whisper, but he smiled when John walked in.

"Hey cuz. Glad to see you're awake. You had us all worried."

"My surgeon was the one that was worried. The nurse told me Bunny put a gun to his head," Chris croaked.

"He started the operation with a lot of negative energy. The man needed an attitude adjustment," Bunny said, looking down at his shoes in embarrassment.

"I hope he doesn't transfer before he checks on me."

"Not a chance. He decided to give up all his other patients so he can devote himself to your recovery full time." Bunny looked ferocious, like a mother bear guarding its cub. He had cuts and scratches all over him that were sealed with dried blood. Under his hospital gown his clothes were torn into rags. No one, including Macho tried to get him to leave. They all recognized that he was part of the family now.

Gonzalo came in and said, "They're here."

"Who?" Chris asked.

General Palmer and Team Razor marched into the room formally, all wearing their best dress uniforms.

"Chris, this is General Marcus Palmer, head of Special Operations Command," John said.

"Hi Chris. I'm proud to meet you," the general said gently taking Chris' hand in his.

"Great to meet you, sir. I've heard a lot about you... well read a lot... I mean John wrote me about you.. Sorry, I'm still a little punchy. Can't get my mind and mouth to work together."

"That's okay, Green Beret, you've been through hell."

"Green Beret?"

"You heard me, soldier."

"I don't understand, sir."

"Even though you didn't go through Special Forces training yet you already went through basic with flying colors. That, combined with your heroics during and after the attack makes you a perfect candidate for us." General Palmer pulled out a green beret and placed it on Chris' head, adjusting it at the proper angle.

"Come on. I've got one leg, sir. I appreciate what you're doing, but we all know I can't wear this on my head. Not when I didn't earn it."

"A Special Forces Operator is intelligent, resourceful, adaptive, and selfless. You've already exhibited all these qualities under extreme duress. And as to earning it, believe me, you will. Once you heal up we're going to give you the most advanced prosthetic limb there is. You're going to be assigned to my personal staff, and I guarantee you'll need two legs to keep up with me, Private Valdez."

Chris was trying not to cry. He always dreamed of wearing the Green Beret. Of being a part of something so special and a member of the elite. To be the best of the best. He tried boxing to please his father and then went to school for his mother. While his mother was pregnant with him she told everyone that her baby was going to be a doctor. Neither one worked out because he knew when he was just fourteen that he wanted to be a soldier. He wanted to be like John.

"Thank you, General. Thank you so much."

"Special Forces Operator Valdez, it is my honor to be the first to salute you.

Atten-hut!" The general and Team Razor all came to attention and saluted Chris. He couldn't raise his right arm at all, but got his left one a little past his chin in return.

"There is one more piece of business we have to take care of Private."

"Sir?"

The door opened and the distinguished black man in a blue suit and red tie walked in with his secret service detail.

"Am I dreaming all this?" Chris asked, weakly.

"I sometimes ask myself the same thing," the president said.

"Wow."

"Private First Class Valdez, let me first say that there is a clear connection between the war in Afghanistan and the bombing last night. It is the same war, only now we're fighting it on American soil."

"Yes, sir."

"Chris, when I heard your story this morning I simply had to meet you. You know, people often talk about true sacrifice and selflessness, but few actually know what it means and fewer still choose such a difficult path when confronted with it. Last night, your selflessness and sacrifice saved the lives of many others. By your actions, by making the decision that others would not and could not, by instructing Sergeant Bishop to amputate your own leg, you stand amongst the most exalted heroes of this great nation. Young man, it is my great honor and privilege to present you with one of the highest awards for valor that the United States Army can bestow upon one of its members." The president opened the felt box and placed the bronze star attached to a small red, white and blue ribbon solemnly on Chris' left breast.

"The Bronze Star. Wear it with pride young man." He shook his hand and then stepped back and saluted."

"My God… Thank you, sir."

"Chris, I'm on my way to give a speech to the United Nations to show the world that we will not be intimated by these cowardly acts of terrorism. If it's all right with you I would like to share your story. You're a shining example of the will and strength of good versus evil and of character triumphing over cowardice."

"Sure, I mean, of course, Mr. President."

"Before I go is there anything I can do for you?"

"One thing."

"Yes, Private?"

"Can you take a picture with me? Otherwise I won't believe any of this ever happened."

"Of course, son." The president leaned in and Silvi took several shots with her phone.

Chris was beaming as he looked around the room. He touched his Green Beret, felt his medal and smiled up at his dad. He saw the love and pride in his father's eyes. His father who had given up so much for him when his mother died. His father who taught him about love, honor and sacrifice. He felt himself weakening so he beckoned him closer.

"Thanks, Dad."

"Gracías por que?" Macho asked.

"For everything. I love you so much."

"I love you with all my heart, mi hijo. I'm so proud of you."

Next he called Silvi over. She had been his surrogate mother since the day he was born when his real mother died. He spoke briefly to her and she turned away laughing and crying at the same time. After a quick exchange with his homies he called over John, Felix and Bunny.

"John, you and Felix have always been the older brothers I never had. And now with Bunny I have another one. Thanks for looking out for me and for all this. You guys are my heroes."

"Chris, we've all been around. Between the three of us we've seen and done a lot of things, but none of us have ever witnessed anything close to what you did in that basement" John said. "This is for you. I could never wear it again." He carefully laid a medal on Chris' chest.

"Your DSC?"

"Yours now. You're the bravest soldier I've ever known."

Chris held up the medal and waved to his father, Gonzalo, the president, General Palmer, Team Razor, Maria, and all his other family and friends. His eyes were wet and had a mischievous sparkle as they slowly closed. He was still smiling when he took his last breath and the heart monitor flat lined.

CHAPTER 23
LIONS

Trappe, Maryland

SEVERAL HUNDRED MILES south of the hospital, two men were having an animated discussion about John Michael Bishop.

"You sure you want to pursue this, Mike?"

"I don't understand the question," Michael Meecham said.

"I'm asking if you really want to go after this guy. He's a fucking war hero for Christ's sakes," said Blake Alston, the FBI's Deputy Director.

"If we find shit on him he goes in the toilet with the rest of his family before I flush it."

Alston adjusted his glasses and picked up his secure Blackberry to re-read Terry Hall's report on the New York terror attacks and John Bishop's involvement with both.

"Says here he cut off his younger cousin's leg in order to save him. Terry adds that the kid is still in surgery and will more than likely die on the table from his injuries. Seems to me Sergeant Bishop has already been through hell."

"Doesn't change a thing, and means less than nothing to me," Meecham snapped.

"You always were a vindictive son of a bitch, Mike."

"Lions can be vindictive."

"So you're a lion now?"

"I've been one all my life and yet despite my powerful sense of self I didn't fully realize it until I went on safari in Kenya last year. We slept in the bush and tracked a pride for five days. It was very enlightening. I strongly recommend it, Blake, especially for someone like you. I believe it would be extremely helpful."

"Someone like me?"

"A man without ambition. You lack the will and the force of nature to strive for more."

"What are you talking about, Mike? My father was a house painter and I'm the Deputy Director of the fucking FBI!"

"My point exactly. You father was content to mindlessly move his brushes up and down, laying on coat after coat of Benjamin Moore, just as you are content in your position. How long have you been deputy?"

"Eight years."

"And two men have been promoted over you during that time."

"Yeah, I took a few kicks in the nuts. Anyway, it's going to happen. I just have to be patient."

"A lion would never be so cavalier. He'd fight for what he wants, destroying anyone who stood in his way."

"Lion huh? What about you Mike? You were only the Deputy Director of Homeland Security and you got fired. Why'd you take that thankless job anyway?"

"It was merely a stepping stone."

"To what?"

"The presidency."

"Come on. You really thought you were going to be president?"

"I will be president. I've known that for many years now. The unfortunate incident with Mr. Bishop and Mr. Valdez is merely a slight detour. Once I'm vindicated it may even accelerate my timelines."

"Vindicated how?"

"By destroying them and every single person who was present in that room."

"So, in addition to John Bishop and his cousin Felix, you're going after SAC Terry Hall, General Palmer and NSA Director Kolter?"

"Yes, them and several others. There can be no survivors. I will ruin them all one by one. That's the only way, although I will add that I'm really going to enjoy doing it."

"Yeah sure. Why don't we get back to your little trip through the jungle."

"It was the Savannah, and again I strongly recommend you make an effort to go."

"Maybe someday."

"Yes, yes of course. Anyway, you do at least know that lions and hyenas are ancient and mortal enemies?"

"Sure. I've seen them fighting it out on TV."

"You should stop watching that thing. It stunts your growth. But at least you should have a vague conception of what I'm about to tell you. Our guide explained that the dominant male lion in the area and the female matriarch of the hyenas had been feuding for years and the feud went far beyond the normal degree of hatred that the two species instinctually engender. The legend was that this lady hyena had bitten off the tip of the king's tail before he became the king and he never forgot it. For a long time he'd been trying to get even, but the bitch was either too smart or too lucky to get caught."

"Isn't this a Disney movie?"

"It could be. Walt Disney was a fucking sadist. People always wonder why this country is so violent, meanwhile their children are in the next room watching those homicidal cartoons."

"This story keeps derailing, let's get back to the lion king," Blake said, shaking his head.

"We followed the lions on several failed hunts. Three days they ventured out, and three days they failed to make a kill. This was the dry season when prey was scarce. They were exhausted and starving. On the fourth day we saw them take down a cape buffalo. It was an epic struggle for survival. The bull gutted one of the lionesses with his horns before he was finally overwhelmed by their numbers. It was unbelievable. The power. The brutality. The beauty. The whole pride was eating this magnificent beast alive. You could hear the buffalo panting and screaming while fifteen females and their cubs ripped him open. We were close enough to smell it."

"Wow. Sounds intense, Mike."

"It was. But I kept wondering where the male was. He's supposed to come down and eat first. I asked our guide and he pointed to some thick bushes nearby and indicated he was in there. I didn't understand until the hyenas showed up. About forty of them charged in to steal the meal and just when the lions were about to retreat he made his move. It was an explosion. His power, his anger, his determination were all directed at one thing: his lifelong nemesis. He charged through the chaos of the battle, straight at the hyena queen and once he got his jaws around her head you could actually hear her skull cracking. He didn't eat her and he didn't even kill her right away. He took his time and slowly ripped her to pieces, raking her with his claws and stripping off flesh with his teeth. Her desperate screams were remarkably human. When the act was complete his joy in triumph was palpable. He roared and strutted, all the while swishing and flicking his bitten off tail."

"And in some primal way you identified with the lion?"

"Blake, you know I find sarcasm very distasteful."

"Yes, I know," Blake said with a smile.

"What you fail to grasp here is that the lion's first instinct is to eat. Food is survival and the next meal can be a long way away. Despite his hunger, this lion suppressed his natural instinct and overcame his genetic pre-programming. He sat there in that bush planning, plotting and waiting patiently to take his revenge when every part of him was screaming to go and eat that buffalo before it was gone. I didn't just identify with him as you so crassly described it. In that moment I saw myself in him and him in me, because like that beautiful beast I place vengeance above all else."

"Come on, Mike. We've known each other a long time. For most of our lives. I know you're not a forgive-and-forget type of guy. All I'm saying is be careful. Bishop seems like a good kid."

"And why do I need to be wary of this so called good kid?"

"You don't. It's his uncle you should be concerned with. One thing for sure, Gonzalo Valdez is one big, badass lion."

"He's street trash that should have been serving life without parole a long time ago."

"Don't underestimate Valdez, or he'll be coming out of a bush and cracking your skull."

"I find your analogy offensive on two counts. One: that

you just compared me to a female hyena and two: that you think a small time gangster would dare to physically attack me."

"Okay, enough. I see you're committed, but my question is just how committed?"

"Look around you," Meecham said, spreading his arms wide.

The two men were sitting on matching sofas that faced each other in Meecham's massive study. There were eighteenth, nineteenth and twentieth century portraits of Meecham's forefathers and many more paintings of the frigates that had made the original seafaring family so wealthy. Above the art work the high walls were adorned with the heads of animals that had all been killed by Meecham men.

"You didn't kill all these Mike. I remember this jungle scene being here since I was a kid. I used to be scared to death of the gorilla."

"You're right Blake. I've only added one to the collection."

"Which one?"

"Behind you."

Blake Alston turned and looked up at the magnificent head that was far more regal and ferocious than any other trophy in the room. It looked as if it was still alive and coming through the wall with its beautiful flowing mane and enormous bared fangs.

"That's him?"

"That's him. And that's what I do to big, badass lions."

"How could you kill him after everything you just told me?"

"You know Blake, I always envied you for your time in the Army and law enforcement."

"Thanks, but with all your money and all you've accomplished, I don't know why you would."

"You miss my point as you often do. Your employment allowed you to kill men with impunity. I envy you for that. I've always wanted to kill a man."

"Come on Mike, even you can't be that sociopathic."

"There is so much beauty in suffering. You know I love destroying people. Taking away everything someone has elicits a powerful reaction, and the more they have, the more profound that reaction becomes. Only three of the men I've ruined have actually killed themselves, but I consider them my best work. I only wish I could have had a more direct hand in their deaths. There they are," he said, pointing to three framed photographs hung on the far wall. "I look forward to adding Bishop's head to my collection."

"I've known you for forty years, but until now I've never known just how twisted you are, my friend."

"Be thankful we are friends, Blake. That's the only reason I haven't destroyed you too. I don't like to envy anyone or anything, as you can see from my lion on the wall. I shot him in the guts so his death would be long and painful. I watched him twist and writhe in his death throws for hours and it was better than sex."

Mike Meecham came from old money, as they say. His great, great grandfather was a sea captain, a part-time pirate, and a full-time slave trader who created the family fortune. It had grown as it was passed down from generation to generation and Michael Baskin Meecham had made his ancestors proud by multiplying his inheritance more than twenty times over.

His hundred-fifty year old home was called "The Castle" and it wasn't far from it. The beautiful thirty thousand square foot mansion sat high on a hill overlooking the Atlantic Ocean. Outside, there were five hundred acres of carefully sculptured landscape with decorative gardens, lush pastures where thoroughbred horses ran free, and a private golf course. Inside, there was a priceless art collection that would make any museum proud, a luxury spa, and full-time chefs hired away from some of the world's finest restaurants.

"Let's take a walk," Meecham said.

"Where to?"

"You asked me about commitment. I want to show you something."

They exited the study through a side door and entered what appeared to be the main floor of a working office. They were greeted by a beautiful long legged blond assistant who immediately began updating Meecham while they walked amongst his employees who were either on the phone or typing away on computer keyboards.

"What is this?" asked Blake.

"I had my people drop everything else to work on Bishop and the Valdez family full time. There are three working groups so far: military, criminal and corporate."

"How much is this costing you?"

"So far I've allocated five million towards this project, but we're still in the early stages. We've only been operational for two days. These guys are all top notch investigators who can find dirt on anyone or in any organization."

"Mike, this is crazy."

"Weren't you listening before? Money is not a concern. Five, ten, twenty million, whatever it takes. I only want results, and the results can only be one of three things. Death, prolonged incarceration, or my own clearly defined form of total destruction." Turning to face the room he said, "Okay teams, form a circle. Where are we so far?"

"Sir, there is clear evidence that Felix Valdez assaulted

police officer Louis Johnson during the Union Square Park attack. NYPD is refusing to follow up on the incident, however we can get the story on the front page of the New York papers as well as the Washington Post. After that we start pressuring District Attorney Fishman's office behind the scenes. We have no doubt Fishman will issue an indictment a few days later."

"That's a good start. Keep digging. He cursed at me in front of NSA Director Kolter. I want that foul-mouthed young man back in prison for a long, long time. Next. The Uncle?"

"Nothing concrete yet on Gonzalo Valdez, sir. We are following up on some rumors of his personal involvement in murder and kidnapping."

"What rumors?"

"First, we know that Gonzalo's father Juan Valdez owned a bar in Panama during the 1940s and 50s. When he refused to pay for protection he was immediately killed by the Panamanian police. Five years later, all four policemen that were involved in the shooting were abducted from their homes by masked kidnappers. Their dismembered bodies were laid out in front of the bar's former location. The chopped up body parts spelled out the name JUAN. The rumor is that Gonzalo and his brothers Sesa and Fiero were responsible, but this will be a hard case to prove forty years later and, of course, the crime did not take place on American soil."

"What else?"

"The youngest Valdez family member, Christina, was accidentally shot to death in New York along with her husband twenty-five years ago. It was a hit aimed at Gonzalo by rival drug dealers, the Davis brothers. The word is that Gonzalo kidnapped both brothers and has kept them alive all this time. It seems he personally removes a body part from each of them on the anniversary of his little sister's murder."

"Find out where he keeps them."

"Yes sir. We also thought you should know that the murdered sister, Christina Valdez and her husband Michael Bishop were John Bishop's parents. John was in the car with them when they were gunned down and that's how he got the facial scar."

"Thank you," Meecham said without emotion. "What do you have on Mr. Bishop?"

"I have something here Dad!" said Caleb Meecham.

"Blake, you remember my son Caleb."

"Sure," Blake replied, barely disguising his distaste. Caleb was rail thin with a sickly pale complexion and the darting, lifeless grey eyes of a reptile.

"Dad, I've been researching the incident when Felix Valdez was convicted of manslaughter. In the original police report it says there were two assailants that attacked the group of Yale students."

"Two?"

"Yes sir. I have copies of each statement made by the four students and something's fishy. These three statements all indicate that there was only one assailant, the soon to be convicted Felix Valdez. But look at the dates. All were made two days after the incident took place. Why only three witness statements and why weren't they made the day it happened?"

"The police had them revise their stories to get an easy conviction," Mike Meecham said.

"That would be my guess. I dug deeper and found one hand-written report from the fourth witness and it's from the actual night of the murder. It states that there were two muggers. It says here and I quote, 'The guy who did it was a real mean looking kid with an ugly scar running down the right side of his face.' I'm leaving for New York now to see what else I can find."

"You do that, Caleb, and call me the second you get anything."

"Yes sir."

"So, Blake, it appears your war hero isn't such a good kid after all." Turning to his blond secretary he said, "Get Josh Fishman, the New York DA on the line. It's time to reopen a sixteen year old murder case."

Chapter 24
Lambs No More

Bronxville, NY

THE SECLUDED FOUR bedroom home could barely be seen from the road making it an ideal location for those who cherished their privacy. Thick untrimmed bushes and ancient trees with low hanging branches made the entrance almost invisible.

The off duty police lieutenant missed the unmarked turnoff on his first attempt to find it. He drove slower the second time and eventually spotted the old tree with the arrow carved in its trunk. He didn't turn in. He kept his foot on the brake and sat there thinking.

Don't go in. Just keep driving and never look back.

I can't. Where would I go?

Anywhere. Start a new life.

A new life? I owe too much for the one I have now. I owe too much.

He knows that. He will use it against you.

I know, but I have no choices here. There is nowhere to go. Nowhere to run.

Then be prepared.

For what?

Death.

He turned the wheel and hit the gas a bit too hard, spinning his tires and tearing up the gravel driveway. Once past the dense foliage the property was well kept and opened up so that no one could approach the safe house from any direction without being seen.

Even with the air conditioner on high, the lieutenant was sweating as he guided the Jeep Cherokee towards the house. He pulled over near a set of lawn chairs where a lone figure sat casually in the midday sun. The shirtless sentry was a man in his sixties who appeared to be working on his tan. He spoke to him in Dari and instructed him to pull into the garage. The officer parked, stepped out of the SUV, and and adjusted the .40 caliber Glock on his hip before he stepped through the doorway into the main house.

"Hello Atal," said Amir Khan.

"I haven't been called that in long time, Amir."

"Do you know why you're here?"

"Yeah, sure. Your picture and your fuck ups are all over the news."

"Be careful, Atal. Or do you prefer to be called Adam?"

"I know who *I* am. Your uncle Aziz got us out of the refugee camps and sent us here. He gave us new names and we built a new life. I've never forgotten my debt to him. No one can question my loyalty. I am still Pasthun. The question is, do *you* know who the fuck you are, Amir Khan?"

Amir's temper once again got the best of him. He jumped up out of his chair too quickly and was overwhelmed by the pain. He glared at Atal Wazir as he slowly sat back down.

"I see you still have control issues. Just so we're clear,

if you try to stand up again, or if your hands leave the table I'm going to shoot you and call it self-defense," said NYPD Lieutenant Adam Harbey, his hand casually resting on the butt of his pistol.

"You would have a lot of explaining to do."

"Really? I don't think so. It's called probable cause, asshole. I'll just say I made a wrong turn and saw your big broken nose in the window. That schnoz of yours is on CNN night and day. Shit, they'll give me a medal for bagging public enemy number one."

"Enough! Who are you to question me?" Amir said through gritted teeth.

"I am a soldier of God and a Waziri warrior. I fight for my tribe, my country, and for Aziz Khan. Who do you fight for Amir?"

"I am no less loyal, Atal."

"Is that why you're waging war and wasting men against one man, this John Bishop?"

"He is a symbol of America. He must die."

"He's an ex-soldier who broke your nose and killed your men before he shot you."

"It was his cousin that broke my nose."

"Whatever. Bishop and his cousin are not your mission."

"The bar was a mistake, but now there is no turning back."

"Why?"

"The warehouse was attacked. Five of my men were killed by assassins and two more were taken alive. Khalid and I were a block away, otherwise we would be dead too."

"I haven't heard anything about it so it wasn't NYPD. Who were they? FBI or CIA?"

"It was the FBI that killed Nazir and his men at the safe house in Queens, but the warehouse in Redhook was something different. They were in and out in ten minutes. I believe they were the uncle's men."

"Fuck. Well that's bad. Real bad. Gonzalo Valdez has his own army. They call him El Gato Negro, and like Aziz, he's a power unto himself."

"I knew nothing about Bishop's family when I went after him."

"You went after his family, and now Valdez is coming after you. Alright, he killed some and captured some. They can't know much. The good thing is you have more men."

"But not more explosives."

"What?"

"They took all the C4 and TNT."

"Then it is over, Amir. You shouldn't have called me. Now you're a lamb hunted by wolves. There's no place you can hide."

"I once was a lamb, many years ago. But never again. We will get the explosives back and I will finish what I started."

"How? They could be anywhere."

"Bishop will bring them to me."

"For a man that looks as beat down as you do, you sure sound confident. What time is Bishop stopping by?"

"Not long after you kidnap his woman."

"I hope you've got a backup plan, because that one ain't happening."

"You really sound like an American. I would never know you are one of us."

"I'm a mole. It's my job to blend in. You know, you're not gonna be alive much longer. You sure you wanna waste what little time you've got left discussing accents and phonetics?"

"Listen to me, Atal. You are the only one that can get close enough to do it."

"You're nuts. Where is she, at the hospital?"

"Yes. Khalid's daughter saw her there. Here is her picture."

"Pretty," Atal said looking at a color photo of the Asian beauty. "But this is a suicide mission and that's not in my job description. She's going to be surrounded by family and like I said before, Gonzalo Valdez has his own troops. She'll be protected."

"The injured cousin is still in surgery, but people are constantly going in and out of hospitals. You can get close enough to observe without arousing their suspicion, and when the opportunity presents itself, you take her."

"How the fuck do I do that? This isn't a spy novel or some action movie! She's in a crowded public place with tight security. She sure ain't gonna follow me out and get in the car. Or should I crack her in the jaw and just walk out the main doors with her body over my shoulder? I'm thinking someone might notice."

"You must be patient, yet decisive."

"You're the last man who should be preaching patience, my friend. It's your lack of it that created this mess."

"Yes, you are right. It is my fault. Going after Bishop got our men killed and the explosives stolen. I cannot change what's been done, but together we can still win this battle for our people. I can't do it without you, Atal."

"Okay, I'll play along. Assuming against all odds I manage to get her. What then?"

"I remember the day my family was killed as if it happened only moments ago."

"You have my condolences, Amir, but let's not lose focus here."

"I am more focused now than I have ever been. Do you remember Kurram Valley?"

"How could I forget? We could see the valley from our refugee camp. Kurram looked like paradise from our dusty hell hole."

"It was a magical place, though now the trees are all gone and the grass grows only in scattered patches."

"War kills our people and scars the land. Thanks be to Allah that our women bear more children and the land will heal itself in time."

"Not there. God has cursed that patch of earth."

"Why?"

"Let's have some coffee. You can either take your hand off the gun or shoot me," Amir said. He carefully got up from the desk and limped over to the couch.

Khalid Mulan, Amir's right hand man, walked in carrying a tray with three steaming cups of strong black coffee that were already heavily sweetened. Atal sat down and exhaled heavily to help release his tension. They each took a sip and placed their mugs down at the same time as Amir began his story.

"The clan was gathered for my grandfather's eightieth birthday. He was a respected elder and had reached an age that few men in our land ever hope to achieve. Many came from great distances to honor him. The Russians killed our people on sight so we traveled by night into Pakistan in small groups, climbing the mountains in the dark. We thought there was safety across the border and we reached the valley at Kurram on the fourth day. I remember the air was cool for mid-summer and the grass was the greenest of greens. I ran through it laughing with my sister. The wind blew from the west and pushed us along as if God's own hand was on our backs."

"I can see it," Atal said with his eyes closed.

"My father, Aman Khan was clan leader then. I have not been blessed with his height. He stood a head taller than most men and he was a great and fearsome fighter. He killed every man that dared to challenge him and he was an expert at killing Russians. With all their weapons and all their technology they couldn't beat him. In the end they put a large bounty on his head."

"Was he betrayed?" Atal asked.

"Yes... Yes, he was."

"By who?"

"Over the years I have very slowly and very painfully killed many men trying to find the answer to that question. It remains a mystery."

"What happened in the valley?"

"My uncle Aziz was my father's younger brother and his second in command. That afternoon I was with Aziz and his two sons scouting high up on the mountain slopes. We were looking down on the valley when the infidels sprang their trap. The Soviets always relied on their airpower, but on that day they surrounded our people with a ring of soldiers on horseback. My father and his men surrendered, knowing their own deaths were certain. They did it to protect the women and children. It was a mistake. The Soviet commander had them tied up so they could watch the women being raped. I saw my mother and sister defiled by those animals before the soldiers shot them all, one by one. Even the youngest of the children were not spared."

"Why doesn't anyone know about this?"

"Those who know are ashamed."

"Ashamed?"

"The Russians could not have crossed the border and

surrounded the clan without help from the inside. It was one of our own people that led them there."

"Who lived?"

"Only me, Aziz and his two sons. His sons were just kids like me back then, and they're both dead, killed later on by a landmine. I know it wasn't me and Aziz watched his wife and his daughters being raped before they were murdered. No man could endure life after being the cause of so much suffering to those he loved most."

"I know I shouldn't even ask, but what happened to your father and his men?"

"They laid my father, Aman Khan, on the ground and tied each of his arms and legs to four horses. They ripped him apart. The riders laughed as they dragged his limbs behind them. The rest of the men were shot where they stood."

"My God."

"My cousins and I shed the last of our childhood tears that night. With the moon as our guide Aziz took us up to the mountain's peak. We stood at the summit with the clouds below, the stars just above and the spirits of our loved ones whispering on the wind. My uncle spoke softly to us and explained that we too were dead. We had all died in the valley below along with everyone else. He said that before the massacre we had all been lambs, laughing and playing like sheep waiting to be slaughtered. We were lambs no more. From that day forward we lived only to avenge our loved ones. We were instruments of death that would kill without mercy.

The next morning we went back down to our people. It took the four of us five days to bury all two hundred and thirty eight of them. I never cried once, not even when I carried my six year old sister to her grave."

"I don't know what to say Amir. I didn't know. I'm

sorry. And sorry I called you a lamb before. I know you're not that."

"Look Atal, not every man has the will to choose his own destiny or the strength to decide his own fate. Only a select few of us have the power to die for something we believe in. This is Tuesday, June fifteenth. I know you didn't wake up this morning thinking today is the day I give my life for my country. And it still may not be, but the question is: are you willing to die today?"

Atal Wazir, better known as NYPD Lieutenant Adam Harbey stared down at the plush Persian rug under his feet. He tried to follow the intricate pattern, but his eyes refused to focus. Amir said something else to him, but the voice came from far away. The world around him was muted by the sounds of rushing water in his ears and the hammering of his heart beating uncontrollably in his chest. He didn't want to die, and up until this moment had expected to live a long life. His mind was racing so he forced himself to take his time. He knew he was at the crossroads. Whichever path he chose had monumental consequences. Death, or worse yet life in prison, on the one hand, and dishonoring himself and his family on the other. He took a deep breath and the world slowly came back into focus. His heart steadied and his ears cleared.

"Funny, I can hear that bee outside the window," Atal said. Suddenly, he felt relaxed and at peace. He saw and heard the world around him like never before.

"The Japanese samurai wrote a lot about death. Once you accept it, embrace it, and even welcome death, it is very enlightening. The world around you appears brand new as if you have just been reborn. All the senses become more acute. It happened to me all those years ago on the mountaintop with Aziz and my cousins."

"I saw a movie once where an Indian said 'today is a good day to die.' Always liked that line. Never thought I'd be using it myself though," Atal said.

"The Sioux were great warriors."

"Japanese samurai, Sioux Indians. For a Pashtun from the mountains of Khost you're an educated man Amir."

"Self-educated. I have always known that someday I would die for our cause. And as you said, with so many hunting me, that time is now. As a soldier of God I used my life to learn about the world and our enemies so my death will have the maximum impact."

Atal again picked up the photograph, carefully studying it this time.

"What's her name?"

"Maria Williams."

"My uniform's in the car. I'm going to change and I have to move fast. If the cousin dies before I get there they may all leave quickly, and the hospital is our only real shot at this."

"Hurry, Atal, hurry. Bring her to me."

"I will, Amir. On my life, I swear I will," he said over his shoulder as he ran to the garage.

CHAPTER 25
VOWS OF LOYALTY, VOWS OF VENGEANCE

Beth Israel Hospital

THE DOCTORS AND nurses desperately worked on Chris in front of his loved ones and the nation's Commander in Chief. There wasn't a dry eye in the room when they bowed their heads in defeat.

After regaining his composure the president stood over Chris and said a silent prayer. He gave his heartfelt condolences to the family and was walking down the hospital corridor with his Secret Service detail when a nurse came around the corner. The security team kept the nurse against the wall, but the president waved them off.

"Thank you for your service. Health care reform is a top priority for me and you nurses are this nation's unsung heroes," he said extending his hand.

"Thank you, Mr. President. This is a very special moment for me. I never imagined my work would lead to shaking hands with you, sir."

The president continued on, heading towards the stairs

to walk up the two flights to Marine One on the roof. The nurse looked after him.

"A very special moment for both of us. You're lucky your name's not on my list. Otherwise you would be dead right now, Mr. President," whispered Omar thoughtfully.

Further down the long hallway an NYPD Lieutenant passed through security after being carefully inspected by the Secret Service.

"Are you part of the detail assigned to protect Bishop and his family?"

"Yes Mr. President, Bishop and his family are my only mission now," said Adam Harbey, secretly known as Atal Wazir.

"Keep them safe," the president said as they shook hands.

"Yes sir."

Harbey passed the nurse who was carefully inspecting a patient's chart before he stopped to observe the crowd outside of Chris' room.

Omar moved silently, pausing a few feet behind the police officer that had just been greeted by the Commander in Chief. They both watched the large group of mourners. People were slowly coming out of the private room wiping their eyes and holding onto each other for support.

Lieutenant Harbey stiffened slightly when he saw Maria. She was huddled with several other women entwined in a big group hug. Despite the puffy eyes, the runny nose, and the grief etched on her face, he was instantly struck by her beauty. While pretty in the picture that Amir had given him and that was now tucked in his jacket pocket, Maria was truly breathtaking in person.

As Harbey was admiring his target from a distance several hard men with dead eyes and set jaws stepped into the hall. They were all a breed apart. Even if they hadn't been wearing their Special Forces uniforms, Omar would have instantly recognized them as fellow man hunters and killers.

Back inside the room the Valdez men stood silently in a semi-circle around Chris' bed. Macho Valdez was the first to speak.

"Goodbye, my son."

"We'll find them all Macho—every one of them," Gonzalo said.

"He was my life, hermano. Vengeance is all I have now."

"And you shall have it."

Already honored to be in the room during this very private moment Bunny walked around the bed and got down on one knee in front of Gonzalo and Macho.

"Don Valdez, I pledge my allegiance to your family. I'll do it on my own if you won't have me, but I'm going after the same people you are, either way."

"Young man, as you can see, everyone outside of our inner circle was asked to leave. You were not. We are a very private family that is closed to outsiders. If we didn't consider you one of us you wouldn't be here now." Gonzalo placed his hands on Bunny's shoulders. "Valentino Brown, we thank you for what you did for Chris, and accept your pledge of loyalty and vow of vengeance. Welcome to La Familia Valdez."

"Thank you Don Valdez. It is an honor," Bunny said as he rose up from the floor and stood towering over Gonzalo.

"Antonio, I need to talk to those men," John said.

"Benji is very skilled at extracting information."

"I know he is. He just may not know all the right questions to ask and I speak their native language. Believe me, you want me in the room."

"You're right. My men will take you there."

"I'll be going with him," Bunny said.

"Me too," said Felix.

"Good. Make sure they are not followed by law enforcement. The rest of us will meet with the consultants to see what they have learned," Gonzalo said.

John pulled down the sheet that was covering Chris' face. He leaned in, speaking softly so that no one else could hear his final promise to his dead cousin. He hugged him, then kissed him on the cheek. Each man stoically took his turn, whispering into Chris' ear a very private and solemn oath before kissing him goodbye. Everyone except for Macho headed towards the door. He sat on the bed, running his fingers through his son's hair, speaking quietly to him in Spanish.

The mission today was purely reconnaissance. Omar's breathing remained calm and steady when Sergeant Bishop walked slowly out of the room and joined the group. It was not time to act, but Omar had just identified many of the faces from Bishop's inner circle and saw the target in person.

Bunny was behind John and looked up just as the nurse disappeared out of sight. Sensing something, he hurried past the several police officers standing guard. He had an uneasy feeling as he stared down the long empty hallway.

John walked over to Maria and pulled her close, breathing in her scent with his face pressed into her hair.

"I have to go. I may be gone for a few days," he said.

"I know," she said. Reaching up, she held his face in her hands. "You do what you have to do, baby. Kill them all, but you bring your ass back to me. You hear me? I can't lose you now."

"I'll see you when it's over. Don't go home, stay with your mom and dad."

"I love you, baby."

"I love you too, Maria."

He kissed her and walked over to Bunny, Felix and Antonio who were waiting patiently for him. He didn't look back as they headed out to meet the enemy.

Before Gonzalo and his brothers left to meet with the Pro KEDDS team, a group of Chris' friends approached them. "There's an army behind us that's ready to put in work. How can we help you Don Valdez?"

Fiero looked to Gonzalo, who nodded his approval.

"They travel in taxi's posing as drivers," Fiero said.

Silently swearing their allegiance, the young men nodded and bowed their heads as the Valdez brothers walked away.

Almost an hour later, when people began to drift out, a lone police officer came over to the women who were still talking together.

"Miss Williams?"

"Yes," Maria said to the Lieutenant.

"I work with Captain Ryan," he said handing his card to her and another to Grassiella.

"The Captain said he'd help us, but you missed John."

"I have something for him."

"Is it important?"

"Yes, very. But Captain Ryan said I was to hand deliver it only to you or Sergeant Bishop. No one else."

"Okay, give it to me."

"It's very sensitive material. I can't be seen passing it to you. Will you follow me downstairs to my car?"

"Yes, yes of course," Maria said, then told her mother that she would be back shortly.

"Thank you for helping us," she said. They exited the hospital, walking right past the tight ring of Valdez security.

"I know you're good people that just got caught up in an ugly situation. And I'm very sorry for your loss. I'm parked right around the corner."

He held the passenger door open for her and she got in. Walking around to the driver's side he sat down and carefully closed the door. He exhaled deeply and turned to look at her.

"What is it?" she asked, suddenly uneasy.

"I'm very sorry, Maria."

"Sorry? Sorry for what?"

"For this," he said as he pressed a stun gun into her left side and zapped her. The electric jolt slammed her into the back of the seat before she slumped forward from the waist like a rag doll. Unconscious, her body continued to shake and twitch as Atal looked down at her.

"I'm sorry for us both. Now we're both fucked, pretty lady. But, I swore an oath to Aziz Khan many years ago, and I swore another one to Amir Khan just this morning," he said as he drove off.

Pedroza's Funeral Home
Lower East Side, Manhattan

Benji "Medicina" Medina was always deliberate and methodical in his interrogations. His technique was unconventional, but extremely effective. To start with, he didn't ask any questions. He simply removed things. He began with clothes so his subjects were completely naked. Next, he removed freedom, shackling them spread eagled to a cold steel mesh table that he designed himself. It allowed the table top to rotate, facing either the floor or the ceiling. Then, he took away the ability to speak by strapping a rubber ball tightly into the mouth. He then began removing things that his subjects never believed they would part with. He took the tips of their toes. Using razor sharp custom made shears, he slowly and methodically snipped off digits, going back and forth from one foot to the other.

He developed his process through trial and error. Years ago he had started with the fingers, but when one of his subjects managed to temporarily escape on foot he switched to taking the toes first. There was no running after that. The taking of the toes served a dual purpose. One, it emphatically stated to his subjects that all hope was lost. Two, it exposed the nerves that he would explore once the interrogation actually began.

Benji studied anatomy to learn the human pain points and had then tested the validity of what he'd read on the men he questioned. Once the toes were gone he would remove the ball from their mouths and let them speak. It was always the same. They began with lies. "I'm innocent." "It wasn't me." "This is all a mistake." Then the partial confessions. "I had no choice." "They made me do it." Next came the bribes that reached truly absurd numbers. "You can have anything you want. Five million, ten, twenty. A hundred million!" Then the begging and pleading. They begged him to stop. They begged God for mercy. Finally they just begged for death. Throughout the process he would remain silent, waiting for the truth to be revealed. It always was. No one could withstand the pain.

He used pain to strip everything away. He attacked each raw and open nerve with a mini blow torch. He took his subjects to places that they dared not dream existed. To levels of suffering and depths of horror beyond imagination. He touched them everywhere with the white hot tongue of flame. He merely started with toes and fingers, then moved on to the knees, the elbows, the teeth. Even the scrotum, the anus, and the eyes were slowly licked and probed by the torch's searing heat.

He didn't like this part of his job, but he was bound by his word. He had sworn an oath of allegiance to the Valdez family many years ago. Gonzalo had even tested his vow of loyalty by ordering Benji to question his own brother-in-law and lifelong friend. His friend had betrayed the family after being arrested by a dedicated narcotics detective. Benji himself had delivered the box of chocolates to the cop's house that contained his best friend's chopped off hands in the bottom. Hands that he had personally removed. He didn't like doing it, but he had to find out everything his former friend had said to the police.

Extracting information from the enemy was critical to the Valdez family's security and its very survival. Once assigned this important task, Benji took the job seriously. He made sure that he found out everything. Everything.

When Christmas, Boogie, Minty, and Danny brought the two terrorists downstairs to the embalming room of Pedroza's Funeral Home he examined each one carefully. One had a severely broken elbow and was whimpering in pain. The other had a knot on his temple from where Boogie hit him, but was otherwise unhurt. He was clearly the stronger of the two and stared back defiantly. Benji chose him to be the first one to share what he knew.

"I will tell you nothing. Nothing! Infidel swine!"

With a sad smile on face, Benji merely nodded in response.

Even with the ball deep in the subject's mouth they could still hear the distorted screams. Benji hummed a ballad of his fellow Panamanian, Rubén Blades, to tune them out as he continued snipping off toes. Even for seasoned soldiers like Christmas and his crew it was hard to watch. Boogie had seen this technique used once before, but along with the others in the room he flinched as one small appendage after another hit the floor. When there were none left Benji loosened the head strap and removed the ball.

"What do you want to know?!!!" screamed the naked, toeless, and once defiant terrorist.

"Whatever you want to tell me. All truths will be revealed," Benji said as he lit the blow torch. He narrowed the flame, turning it from a cool light blue to clear white hot.

"What are you going to do?" the terrorist asked. His whole body was shaking uncontrollably from the shock of the amputations and the terrifying realization that the worst was yet to come.

"I'm going to listen to you my friend. I am only here to listen," he said while zipping up the hazmat suit and lowering the dark goggles over his eyes. His head tilted slightly to one side, Benji looked like some form of curious insect when he slowly leaned forward with the torch and began the interrogation.

Danny held his ears to muffle the awful screams that filled the sound proofed room.

"Take away the stink from the burning hair, it really does smell like chicken," Boogie said.

"Thanks asshole. That's one thing I'll never eat again," said Minty.

Upon leaving the hospital, John, Felix, and Bunny were driven through a series of evasive maneuvers and eventually dropped off three blocks from the funeral home. They were then taken underground through dozens of connecting buildings before they entered a secret door in the basement of Pedroza's.

"What the fuck?!" said Felix when they walked into Benji's torture dungeon and saw what was happening.

"Why are you here?" Benji asked, lifting up his goggles.

"To make sure we get all the answers," John said.

"He will tell us everything he knows. Everything."

"Yeah, well, you do what you think you gotta do. I'll have a talk with the other one."

Benji shrugged. "As you wish."

John stepped out of the room and grabbed the other terrorist by his broken elbow. He cut short the high-pitched scream with a vicious back-handed slap and pulled him into the dungeon to witness the "interrogation."

"Allah, have mercy upon me."

"Allah may, but we won't. I always said that no one should ever be tortured, no matter what. You guys changed all that for me today. I need answers and I need them now. You tell me everything you know or you're next on the table."

"I swore unto God that I would never betray my brothers."

The screaming went to another level as Benji focused his attention on his subject's private parts. He touched the white hot flame to places where no man wants to feel searing heat and agonizing pain.

"Well, I just swore to Chris Valdez that I'd find all your friends. What's it gonna be? Me, or Benji's barbeque?"

"I will tell you what I know."

"Just so we're clear, you hold back, or if I think you're

bullshitting me for even a second, you go on the table and then we start over from the beginning."

"Yes, yes I will tell you everything. Please, I cannot watch this. He is my cousin. I cannot watch my cousin die."

"I just did," John said.

CHAPTER 26

GETTIN' BUSY

Baruch Housing Projects
LES, NY

NEW YORK CITY taxis work twenty-four hours a day with the drivers switching every twelve. They change shifts at 5AM and 5PM so that each driver gets to work either the morning or the evening rush hour and there's always a mad scramble to get last minute passengers in the late afternoon.

The driver cruised slowly through the projects after dropping off his final fare before going off duty. All day he had been listening to radio coverage of the terrorist bombings and the news of the president's surprise visit to the United Nations.

"Here comes one now."

"Drivin' slow, too."

"Let's do this."

"Remember, don't waste his ass."

"Unless…"

"The only unless is if the motherfucka's about to drop a hammer on yo ass. We ain't cappin' some innocent dude just cause he's drivin' a fuckin' cab. That just disses Chris' memory and puts more heat on his fam."

"You right. I'm just hyped and itchin' to get busy on these Jihad motherfuckers."

"We all are, but even if we do find one we keep his ass alive. We'll fuck him up good, but then we hand him over to Benji."

"I hear you. Yo, does that little dude really chop people up?"

"My nigga, you don't wanna know, and you most definitely don't wanna be asking."

"Yeah, my bad."

"Let's go."

The four young men had hoodies pulled over their heads and bandanas over their faces when they stepped in front of the yellow cab. Two held Mack 10 submachine guns, one held an Uzi, and the leader of the group had a Beretta 9 millimeter automatic in each hand.

"Step out the car Mohammed!"

"Please, I am working very hard for my family. Please not to rob me, please!" the driver pleaded as he held his hands up, and nervously got out of the cab.

"We don't want your money. We just need your ride. Check him, then look up front and in the trunk. If he's clean, and the car don't have none a that bomb shit, then he can step."

"You a terrorist, mothafucka?" one of the youngsters asked him. He held an Uzi to the driver's head while another emptied his pockets.

"No sir, no sir. No terrorist. I love America and working hard for my family."

The teenager inspecting the front seat area of the cab gave a sharp warning whistle. "He's one of 'em."

"You sure?"

"No doubt. There's a bottle a liquid nitro up here."

"Liquid nitro?"

"Yeah, check it out." He came up carefully holding a clear plastic bottle without a label. It was filled almost to the top with a dark yellow liquid.

"You ain't no bomb expert, and that ain't nitro."

"The fuck is it then, you so smart?"

"Piss," said the leader. Still holding his pistols, he scanned the surrounding rooftops for pigeons. Flocks of pigeons would be released to indicate a warning from the direction of any impending danger.

"What?"

"Piss mothafucka. Cabbies don't take bathroom breaks, they just piss in a bottle while they's stopped at a red light."

"That's nasty."

"It's way past nasty, but we ain't here to shake the man's hand. Give him back his cash and light it up."

They pulled out the plastic gas can from behind a tree and doused the car from bumper to bumper. The whoosh of flame ignited by a cigarette sent fire high into the sky.

"Liquid nitro? Where'd you come up with that shit?"

"I dunno. Musta seen it on TV."

"Dumb ass."

"Tell your friends, no more cabs," the leader said to the cabbie.

The four young men were confident on their home turf. They slowly tucked away their weapons and casually strolled into the maze of connecting buildings.

The driver stared at the burning car, unable to comprehend what had just happened to him. He quickly gave up trying to figure it out and took off running.

At area cab stands where off duty cars were lined up,

Molotov cocktails sailed through the air setting dozens of the closely parked taxis ablaze. All over the city, cabs were targeted. Kids on bicycles pedaled up to them, puncturing tires with knives and ice picks. Once disabled, the kids would jump onto the hoods and spray paint a simple three word message on the windows: "NO MORE CABS!"

New York FBI Headquarters
26 Federal Plaza, Downtown Manhattan

Captain Jimmy Ryan sipped his fifth cup of black coffee of the day. Since the initial attack on Union Square three days ago he'd only been able to snatch a few hours of sleep here and there. The coffee barely dented his fatigue, but there was just too much to do.

"What do you plan to do about Valdez's war on taxis?" SAC Terry Hall asked.

Like Ryan, Terry was exhausted. He hadn't slept at all. Though he'd showered and shaved, hot water couldn't erase the dark circles under his eyes, or the deepening lines in his face. Managing the search for Amir Khan while keeping Washington continuously updated was taking its toll.

"I'm not going to do anything about it."

"Come on Jimmy. They're attacking cabs all over the city. We can't sit back and do nothing," Terry said.

"My friend, as you already know, since I got the call we've arrested four terrorists. That's four so far. Four," he said again, holding up his fingers for emphasis.

Before the first cab attacks started, Jimmy received an anonymous call on his mobile phone. The caller suggested that once the cabs were disabled they would be part of a crime scene and could then be thoroughly searched. Jimmy had every available bomb squad member out in patrol cars inspecting the damaged taxis. Two had explosive residue in their trunks and the other two had pictures of both John and Felix in their glove compartments. All four drivers also had unlicensed firearms in their possession. They were immediately arrested and were now being questioned.

"We can't allow this shit to happen in our town. Look out the fucking window Jimmy! You can still see the smoke from the burning cabs."

"Yeah, I see it, and I'm good with it. Gonzalo's methods may be crude, but we needed some blunt force trauma to get things moving. Anyway, we've already arrested a bunch of his baby vigilantes. Not one over sixteen. The other thing is, they haven't injured a single person. They just disabled the vehicles. I asked them what they thought they were doing and they said they were, 'getting busy for Chris.' They said they were trying to help us and wanted to get back to what they were doing. I personally let two of 'em go and asked 'em to stop burning cabs so all the evidence doesn't go up in flames."

"You set them free?! You asked them to what?!"

"You heard me Terry. I let them go to pass on the message. Like it or not, this is one of those rare occasions where the good guys and the crooks have a common goal... and a common enemy."

"I should have you arrested for what you've done, Jimmy."

"You're tired, and I know you don't mean that. You've got the president and the whole world watching you on this, but the fires are gonna stop and now you've got four live terrorists in custody. That's a big win for you, buddy."

"Maybe. Maybe, you're right," Terry said wearily. He

leaned forward, his elbows on his desk, and rubbed his temples with the palms of his hands.

"Your guys making the other arrests?"

"Yeah, as we speak."

"That's another win and quick progress."

"The press and Washington don't see it that way."

"They don't know shit about investigating and you know it. You've done a great job so far, my friend, but you've gotta get some z's before you fall over or make a bad decision. You shut it down and I'll make sure everyone on our side keeps gettin' busy too," Jimmy said with a smile.

He guided his friend over to the couch and turned out the lights before leaving. Terry was already snoring when Jimmy carefully shut the door behind him and gave terse commands to the FBI agents and police officers that were waiting for him.

Fort Dix Army Base
Burlington County, New Jersey

"First a five mile run, and now this shit?"

"We've been standing out here for two hours."

"That sun is killing me."

"You two better shut up and get some focus. Something's going down."

"You think?"

"I know. This ain't no drill. All the officers are looking real tense man. They're waiting for something."

"What?"

"Dunno. But whatever it is, I guarantee you, it ain't gonna be good."

"Yeah, you're right. They're real tight. Something's going down, and it's gonna suck for us whatever it is."

The thirty-one-thousand-acre base was locked down on direct orders from its commanding general. The troops were wet with sweat, standing at attention with the hot late afternoon sun in their eyes. Most of them thought it was just another surprise drill in the never-ending routine of surprise drills. They were wrong.

The joint military, ATF, FBI and Homeland Security task force came through the main entrance with weapons drawn and ready. Two soldiers broke formation and took off running. Warning shots were fired, and one ended his futile attempt at escape by first throwing his hands up in the air and then lying face down on the parade ground as instructed. The other one wasn't going out without a fight. He did a crab walk while he frantically reached for the small caliber pistol stashed in his boot. He stopped, stood up, turned to face his pursuers, and pointed his gun towards them. Before he could fire a shot he was cut down by the ominous force of automatic weapons on full auto.

Another private, and a Captain were also rounded up and hand cuffed. They hung their heads, resigned in the knowledge that their fates were sealed. The captain had betrayed his country for his secretly held radical beliefs. The private had done it for money. Their motivations were different, but both knew their lives were over. They would never be free again and life without parole was the best they could hope for.

The origins of the C4 plastic explosives recovered from the Union Square Park attack had been traced back to the armory at Fort Dix. Once the source was identified it was clear that the conspiracy involved multiple military participants and that at least one officer had to be a key player. Three other soldiers were already in custody and the Special Ops interrogators were merciless in their quest for information.

The United Nations
1st Avenue and 44th Street
New York, NY

Diplomats and leaders from around the world listened intently to the harsh speech being given by the president of the United States. Word of his arrival in New York to visit victims of the attacks traveled fast, but no one at the UN anticipated this. The Secretary of State was scheduled to speak today. They had expected the focus to be on economic globalization, trade balances, and the need to reduce carbon emission around the world. Although everyone knew the terror attacks would be incorporated into the presentation, they did not expect it to dominate the speech. They were wrong.

The president had already been speaking for twenty minutes. His message was strong and clear, hard hitting and aggressive. He was a man known for his composure, and had often been criticized for his almost casual demeanor when confronted with controversy or crisis. Until today he was viewed as a man immune to pressure. Today he did not attempt to mask his controlled anger.

"I have always believed that engaging in war should only be undertaken when all other avenues of communication and diplomacy have failed. I believed that before I took office, and I believe it now.

"I also believe that once every other option has been

attempted, once every one of our overtures towards a peaceful resolution has been rejected, once the United States of America has been attacked by an individual, a terrorist organization, or a foreign country, we will spare no effort in bringing them to justice. So today I am speaking directly to those responsible for the cowardly attacks on the brave and innocent citizens of New York City. The world is not big enough for you to hide in. We are coming for you and those that support you. That is not a threat. It is a promise.

"Over the past forty-eight hours, through the diligent efforts of the Joint Terrorism Task Force, and through unprecedented multi-agency co-operation, we now have over thirty five individuals in custody that were clearly part of this conspiracy to kill American citizens. I will add that the arrests were not just made here. With the help of our allies, terrorists were captured in Saudi Arabia, The United Arab Emirates, London, and Canada. The United States of America thanks each one of those countries for their assistance and for their continued efforts in the war on terror.

"Now, for those countries that are harboring and assisting terrorist organizations, we have some bad news for you. You are now isolated and alone. The leaders of the free world have agreed in principal to sanction the twelve countries identified as terrorist allies. These sanctions range from trade embargos and forfeiture of assets amongst others. Taking the lead on imposing these sanctions, this morning the United States of America has confiscated over fifty-one billion dollars in assets. Believe me, this is only the beginning. The price of aiding and harboring terrorists has just gone up."

A dozen U.S. aides walked down the aisles handing the lists of sanctions and asset forfeiture packages to the twelve foreign delegations. Several got up quickly and raced out of the room, while others shouted out in protest. The president looked at them with fire in his eyes.

"So now you have something to say? Well so do I. The banks you have used to funnel money to murderers are now closed to you and the businesses you set up to finance terrorism are forfeit. The money is gone for good. It will be used against you, funding training and equipment for all the agencies involved the Joint Terrorism Task Force. If you don't want to lose more than you already have I suggest you hand us the terrorists."

He glared at the protesting delegations scattered around the room for another moment before resuming his speech and softening his delivery.

"I entered my presidency by addressing the world, and encouraging dialogue between friends and foes, between allies and adversaries. Very few of the self-proclaimed enemies of the United States of America accepted my invitation to sit down at the table. Instead, they have continued down a path of misinformation, lies, and ultimately violence.

"So now your assets have been seized and your countries are isolated and alone in the world. Turn over the terrorists you are harboring and we can discuss reintegration into the global economy. Nations from around the world are joining hands and working together as never before in this new war on terror. Over the past three days I have spoken with the leaders of France, the United Kingdom, Spain, Germany, Italy, Russia, China, Japan, Pakistan, India, Saudi Arabia, Jordan, Mexico, Brazil and Argentina. They have all committed to working together to eradicate terrorism by isolating and ostracizing those countries that harbor terrorists.

"There are no longer any gray areas. It is now time to

choose a side. You can get busy living by participating in the global economy based on fair trade, environmental responsibility, and a commitment to peace and prosperity, or you can bear the burden of leading your countries down a path of destruction. That is the price for promoting the murder of innocent civilians around the world."

There was a thunderous applause. Many world leaders were on their feet cheering, clapping and banging on tables.

New York State District Attorney Joshua Fishman's Office
Downtown Manhattan

"You know why you're here, Cindy?" Josh Fishman asked.

"Haven't got a clue, sir," answered Cynthia Weatherspoon, the NYPD Chief of Detectives.

"Sir? You've been calling me Fish since as far back as I can remember."

"That was when you were fresh out of law school, looking like a deer in the headlights, wearing that shiny polyester suit. You're the DA now, and you're lookin' razor sharp in that Hugo Boss," she said with a smile.

"I wore that poly blue pin for three years. Made it shiny from all the ironing. Seems like so long ago," Fishman said.

"That's 'cause it was a long time ago. We're both all grown up now."

"Yes we are, aren't we," he said, carefully avoiding eye contact.

"Look Fish, I know you've got something shitty for me. You didn't call me over here to stroll down memory lane. Just spit it."

"Yeah, you're right, Cindy. I was stalling. So here it is… John Bishop."

"The war hero?"

"The one and only."

"Is this 'cause of his Uncle?"

"I guess, in part, but it's more than that. Looks like he may have killed a Yale student seventeen years ago."

"Yale student? I just read about that case in the news. Didn't his cousin go down for that?"

"Looks like his cousin Felix took the fall for him," Fishman said, handing over the file. "Look at the four wit statements on top," he added.

After carefully reading through each statement given by the four student witnesses she slowly removed her glasses and sighed.

"This is thin Fish. Real thin. You'll need a lot more than this to convict Bishop."

"I know, I know. Look Cindy, this guy's not just a war hero. He saved a lot of lives at Union Square, and his younger cousin died this afternoon from wounds he received in the second attack."

"I heard the president went to see him," she said.

"The president pinned the Bronze Star on the kid's chest before he died and then said a prayer over him."

"And after that you want me to slap the cuffs on Bishop?"

"No, I want you to get a few of your best detectives to investigate. Subtly."

"Come on, Fish, what the fuck is goin' on here?"

"Look, you've read the smear campaign and heard all the stuff in the news. Some of the rags are printing more dirt about the Valdez mob and Bishop than they are about terrorist attacks in our own city. Bottom line here is that he pissed off some very powerful people. I've been presented with a potentially wrongful conviction in a murder case and I'm ordering you to investigate."

"This was never a murder case and you know it. At most it was negligent homicide, but it reads more like self-defense to me."

"My office is prepared to indict him on second degree murder. There also may have been a racial component, so we may up it to murder one with depraved indifference."

"What!? You're trying to send Bishop up for life without parole? I can't believe this," she said, shaking her head from side to side. "I feel sorry for ya, Fish. I miss that kid in the polyester suit that was gonna change the world. He'd never be part of this."

"I miss him, too." He looked melancholy as he stared down at his desk. When he raised his head his eyes were hard, his jaw was set. His decision was already made.

"I feel sorry for you too, Cindy," he said.

"Because you've got me doing you're dirty work?"

"Honestly, I hope it doesn't pan out, but if the evidence points to Bishop I want *you* to put the cuffs on him with the cameras rolling. You'll personally take him on the perp walk. You understand?"

"Asshole."

"Yeah, well, they say Fish always stinks from the head. Now get busy doing your fucking job. And don't ever think you can talk to me like that again if you want to keep it."

CHAPTER 27
SCHEDULE A MEETING

Campos Plaza, LES

THE CAMPOS PLAZA housing project is made up of four long connecting buildings designed in a fortress-like square with a large open courtyard at its center. With only two main entrances, the original architects had unknowingly created a layout that was custom made for urban warfare. It was easy to defend and ideal for ambushing intruders.

Neither law enforcement nor enemies of the family could enter the housing development without being spotted. It made it the perfect place for the brothers to conduct their business and Gonzalo had made Campos his flagship stronghold over thirty years ago. The family had dozens of individual and connecting apartments throughout the complex. It allowed them to move throughout the buildings and from floor to floor without using the hallways or the elevators. The many thousands of tenants were happy to be living under the Valdez flag. Drugs weren't sold there and the safety of everyone at Campos was guaranteed. It was truly a crime-free zone. At least at the street level.

Gonzalo Valdez sat at the head of a long mahogany table. His nephew Antonio sat at his right, his brother, and Antonio's father, Sesa, at his left. Fiero was too angry to sit, and instead paced menacingly around the large conference room. Carlos and Macho had been making Chris' funeral arrangements when they were summoned to Campos. Macho could barely control his emotions. He sat in silence, his eyes red and wet. He looked like he'd aged ten years over-night. The other brothers, Victor and Calixto, had been administering to the family businesses, but also returned for the mandatory meeting.

John, Felix and Bunny arrived and silently took their seats. John was fuming, his cheeks contracting and releasing, contracting and releasing, from unconsciously flexing his jaw muscles. The terrorist with the broken arm had given him several names and addresses. He'd passed the intel over to Christmas and his team and they immediately went into action. John wished them luck before they left, but really wanted to be by their sides on the front lines. He wanted to be on the hunt.

He stared down at the table, and noticed the dark red wood was embedded with a swirling pattern of rings from the original tree. The rings looked like a current flowing under the hard surface. A river of blood.

"Why am I here, Tio? I should be out there with the soldiers," he said angrily.

"John, your face is on every channel and on the cover of every paper. You could compromise the missions. If you think our troops can't handle the job then say so and we will find more competent men," Gonzalo said sternly.

"No Tio. They're excellent. The best. And I'm sorry. I wasn't thinking."

"Well, you better start. I taught you chess, not checkers. You selfishly want to go fight a battle when we need your help to win a war? A war on three fronts?"

"I was being selfish and stupid. It won't happen again, Tio."

"Good. Every one of us here wants blood for blood by our own hand. We don't have that luxury … Yet." Gonzalo's voice remained calm; his hands steady as he spread them wide to include everyone in the room.

"We have to protect the family and win all three wars in order to survive. To win, we must all think and plan strategically. And in the end each of us will taste the blood of our enemies. That I promise you."

John nodded at Gonzalo. His respect and admiration for the man was greater than ever. He served under many fine officers in the Army. None had the command, clarity, and vision of his own uncle and surrogate father. Gonzalo was a rock. As the head of the family, John knew he was as angry as any of them about Chris' death, but he didn't let his anger cloud his judgment.

They all sat up straighter and John, along with everyone else was now keenly focused. Even Fiero stopped his prowling. He took a seat at the table and waited for the presentation to begin.

Kevin Mitchell and Ed Taylor were the only members of the Pro KEDDS team attending the meeting. Their partner Danny Jones was backing up the troops, out with Christmas and Chepe's soldiers who were attacking the enemy. Kevin and Ed worked quickly and quietly. They set up the laptop, connected it to the seventy inch flat screen on the wall and passed out information packets to everyone.

"Don Valdez, Macho, before we get started please

accept our condolences. We are all very sorry for your family's loss," Kevin said.

"Thank you," Gonzalo said. His voice was flat, without emotion, but his yellow eyes glowed bright and hot. "Now please begin."

"Yes, of course. This presentation is in three parts. The first being Michael Meecham. The second is Amir Khan. And part three is his uncle, Aziz Khan."

"Why are we starting with Meecham?" John asked.

"Good question. The reason is you."

"Me?"

"Yes, you John. Don Valdez, I'm sure your sources would have informed you of this very shortly, but we just found out they're re-opening the investigation into the death of the Yale student. Mike Meecham must have some serious dirt on Fishman. The DA's planning to indict you on murder one once they find or fabricate enough evidence."

Felix slapped the table with a powerful blow. "Murder one?! What the fuck is that about!? They attacked us!"

"Felix, calm down," Gonzalo said. "The witnesses? Where are they?"

"We received this information only a short time ago and Danny is out with the troops. So, at this moment we only have addresses for three of the four witnesses. They are listed on page two of your packets. One is in Boston, another lives in Connecticut, and the third is right here in New York on the Upper West Side. Danny will find the fourth witness and we will provide a more detailed bio on each one later this evening with photos, bank records, family and medical histories."

"Your recommendation?" Gonzalo asked.

"Honestly, this one's a tough call. Meecham is also pressuring Fishman to get RICO indictments on every one of you, and that includes Felix, Carlos, Sesa, Antonio, Macho and Calixto. John is the exception, that's why they're going for the separate murder case. They're also going to use his military record against him. Say that he's always been a killer and the army just let him run free with it. They'll say it was a racially motivated killing and he used depraved indifference. Meecham's ultimate goal is for all of you to be in prison for the rest of your lives. That said, if four civilians suddenly disappear off the face of the earth it's going to make Meecham's and Fishman's job that much easier. So, first we need more intel on the witnesses. Bribe them or scare the shit of 'em and see how they react. We recommend holding off on anything past that at least for the next few days," Kevin said.

Ed followed up by saying, "We really just need to delay them from potentially giving any harmful testimony against John in a deposition until Meecham's gone. Once he's dead Fishman's motivation should rapidly diminish."

"Let me do it. I've already done time for murder and I've never killed anyone. I want Meecham to be my first," Felix said.

"You shot a terrorist last night," John said.

"He was already dead. You and Bunny hit him first. Anyway, Meecham is a piece of shit. He has to die. Please Tio, let me do it."

"Enough," Gonzalo said. "You will not be the one to end Meecham. I have something very special in mind for him. As for the witnesses, I agree with your recommendation. We will talk to them first. Antonio, get our people to them tonight. Find out if they've given any statements. Let us know if they have, and persuade them not to if they haven't. I want a diplomat to do all the talking, and two killers to stand there silently. Make sure our message is clearly received. Alive or dead, they will never testify against John. Next."

"Amir Khan. We've hurt him. We killed five of his men and captured two more in Redhook and we believe we have all his remaining explosives. Christmas and Chepe's crews have just killed three more that were a direct result of the information we received from Benji and John's interrogations. We have six more locations that we're targeting tonight."

"The facts are that he's wounded, thanks to John. We have his C4. He's lost a lot of men and safe houses. That's thanks to our own efforts, that of the FBI, and John's buddies in Special Ops. The actions against the taxis also resulted in four of Amir's men being arrested by the NYPD. He's being hunted by us, by every branch of law enforcement, and more than likely has been sentenced to death by his own uncle's hit squad. All these facts make Amir Khan more dangerous than ever," Ed said.

"Yes, I agree," Gonzalo said. "He will not run and hide. He proved that last night."

"We'll hit the six safe houses and we may find him there if we're lucky. If not, we keep tearing down his organization man by man, house by house. John's guy with broken arm gave us the name of their money man. He's an Imam that never leaves his Mosque in Brooklyn. We are looking at the structure to see if we can take him alive. If we get him, he'll know a lot more than the foot soldiers we've taken out so far."

"Anything else on Amir?" Antonio asked.

"Yes. Two things. One, beef up your security. While our guys our out hunting him, we have no doubt he's actively hunting you. Amir, despite his losses, is aggressive, resourceful, and takes quick, decisive action. We don't know how he tracked you to the bar, but somehow he did and he immediately went on the offensive," Ed said.

"Yes, after last night we have an army protecting us. No one's gonna be jumpin' out of a cab again. What's two?" Antonio said.

"Two is, you bring him here and finish him on your home turf. Give him a public event, like a memorial for Chris. It'll be hosted by John, in the middle of Campos Plaza. Even if he knows it's a set up, we think he'll bite. His life expectancy is a matter of days, so he's not gonna pass up on a final shot at revenge."

"Yeah, that'll work," John said. "No way he doesn't come for me. I want his ass and I'll gladly be the bait."

"Yes, he will come. Set it up," Gonzalo said.

"Now, if you turn to page six of your packets you will see what we've put together on Aziz Khan. There is no way we can get to him directly, or even find him in his mountain stronghold. So since we can't hunt him he has to want to see us. We make him schedule a meeting, inviting us for a face-to-face," Kevin said.

"How?" Fiero asked.

"Business," Ed replied.

"Business? What business?"

"Drugs," Gonzalo said.

"Yes, Don Valdez. Exactly. He's a warrior, but he's also a businessman. Therein lies his weakness. He sells dope to buy weapons. And we know where his next arms delivery is and what ship it's traveling on," Kevin said.

"Where?" John asked.

"Yemen. And it's a big one. Fifty-million dollars worth."

"We take the ship," Fiero said.

"Yes Fiero, we take the ship. Once it hits international

waters. Then, through your contacts overseas you make an offer. A truce. His weapons in exchange for a guarantee that there will be no more attacks on the family. Perhaps a distribution agreement as a sign of good faith and that all is forgiven."

"He will suspect a trap. I would. Whoever is sent will not return. Not unless he is very lucky," Gonzalo said.

"Yes, Don Valdez. It is a suicide mission. But we can't see any other way to get to Aziz. And you can't send an assassin to do this. As you said, he'll already be suspicious. An inner family member, one of you here in this room needs to go do it. And it can't be John since the whole world knows he's a trained killer. Also, this opportunity with the weapons may not present itself again for some time. We have to take the ship in three days or else we have to pass on Aziz for the foreseeable future," Ed said.

"Yes, we must act now. The ship is the key. Such a cargo will be well protected. How do we take it?" Carlos asked.

"It will be very well protected. So it must be taken at night, by air."

"Won't they just shoot down the planes?" asked Felix.

"We come in stealthy. Parachute onto the deck and commandeer the ship before they know what hit 'em," John said.

"Exactly," Ed said.

"Parachute at night onto a moving ship? You've done this before?"

"Me personally, no. But, it's been done. With the new laser guidance systems we can illuminate the ship and follow the green glowing line right in."

"I know I'm no soldier, but don't they have radar to see the planes?"

"Not from that height."

"What height?" Carlos asked.

"Thirty-five thousand feet," Bunny said.

"Hold up. Le'me get this straight. You're sayin' you're gonna jump out of a plane at night, seven miles above the ocean, land on a heavily defended moving ship, and kill all the bad guys," Felix said in disbelief.

"Sounds pretty thin when you say it like that, but yeah, that's basically what we're gonna do," John said.

"As long as it's not too windy, and there's no heavy rain we'll be fine," Bunny said.

"We checked. The weather forecast looks clear. Scattered clouds and winds at five to ten miles per hour. Only downside is the moon is going to be shining big and bright," Ed said.

"John, you think your pals on Team Razor will roll with you on this?" Kevin asked.

"Yeah, they will," Bunny said. "And so will I."

"How many years since you jumped out of a plane, Bun?" John asked.

"Like riding a bike, Johnny. If I don't land on the ship just make sure you turn it around and come get me before the sharks do."

"Then it is settled. Our friends at CIA will provide travel and equipment," Gonzalo said.

"We have several options for killing Aziz, once you've decided on who's going," Kevin said.

"It is already decided," Macho said. "I claim the right to kill him."

"Yes, it is your right, hermano. No one will oppose you. First we bury Chris. Then you will kill the man that's responsible."

Antonio left to assemble the teams that would meet with the witnesses. He was gone for less than five minutes when he ran back in with Grasiella following behind. Her hair was crazy, matted down in the front from the sweat on her forehead and sticking out in all directions on the back and sides. Her eyes were wide and she could barely catch her breath. Everyone stood up. They all knew that something was very wrong.

"What has happened?" Gonzalo asked her.

"Ma, ma, ma…" was all she could manage to choke out.

Felix poured her a glass of water and she drank it greedily. She looked first to her husband Gonzalo and then turned her eyes to her beloved adopted son, John.

"Maria! They took Maria!" she screamed.

"How? How could they get to her?" John asked, his voice almost a whisper.

"A policeman came to the hospital. He said he worked for your friend the Captain. He said he had some papers for you. She went with him."

"Pretending to be a cop!" Felix shouted.

"No, no. He was a cop. A lieutenant. All the other policeman there knew him. That's why we thought she was safe. We didn't think… we were all so sad about Chris and we just didn't think. I'm so sorry, John. I should have gone with her," Grasiella said, tears streaming down her cheeks.

"I'm glad you weren't with her, Auntie. Otherwise you'd be dead now," Felix said.

"He's right. They wanted Maria. That means Amir wants to trade her for his explosives. It means she's still alive," John said, talking through the logic.

"Yeah, you nailed it. He wants the explosives back. And one other thing," said Antonio.

"Let me take a wild guess. Me?"

"Yeah, you, primo. He called Marci's phone to let us

know he's got her and what he wants. He's calling back in ten minutes to speak to you directly."

"Where's the truck?" Gonzalo asked.

"It's close. Couple blocks away in a private garage," Antonio said.

"I'll need some time to wire it all to blow on a timer. As soon as Amir gives us the time and place you gotta get me to that Con Ed truck on the double," John said.

"No problem."

"Auntie?"

"Yes."

"Did you get the name of the cop that she left with?"

"Yes, yes. He gave me his card," Grasiella said, as she handed it over.

"Lieutenant Adam Harbey, NYPD," John read aloud. "I need a clean phone." They had all handed their cell phones over to Antonio before going to the funeral home to avoid being tracked.

Antonio left the room momentarily and then quickly returned with a new cell. John punched in Captain Ryan's number. Ryan picked up on the third ring.

"Hey Johnny, good to hear from you."

"I think you're gonna revise that statement. Adam Harbey, lieutenant. You know him?"

"Sure. Why?"

"He abducted my fiancé from the hospital and handed her over to Amir Khan."

"There's no way. Gotta be a mistake."

"You think I'd be calling if we weren't sure? All your men knew him and he gave my aunt his card. He wrote on the back, 'Bishop, Amir wants to meet you.' Sound like a mistake to you?"

"The guy's a twenty-year vet. He's about to make captain."

"That ain't gonna happen."

"No shit. But if Harbey's a terrorist mole then anyone can be."

"Yeah, well, let's focus on him for now. You said you wanted to help. What are you prepared to do?"

"John, I swear, this conversation stays between us. I'll get you everything we've got on Harbey. You want to meet?"

"I don't have time. Where are you?"

"Downtown, at One Police Plaza. The file will be waiting at the main information desk."

"Thanks, Cap. I'm sending a guy to pick it up. Give me everything. Especially anything that'll help me find him."

"Gladly," Ryan said. "And Johnny…"

"Yeah?"

"When you see him, put one right up his ass and tell him it's from me."

"Gladly," John said before hanging up. He turned to speak directly to his cousin. "Antonio, can you send one of your guys down to One PP to get the Harbey file?"

Antonio snapped his fingers and a Valdez soldier moved from his post against the wall and hurried out the door. The room became suddenly still. There was now only silence as everyone in the room stared at the phone on the table. They all tried to control their breathing, as every breath seemed amplified, disturbing the quiet. Anxiously, they waited for Maria's kidnapper and Chris' killer to call.

Grasiella jumped when it finally rang. John flipped it open and put it on speaker.

"Yeah?"

"Is this Bishop?"

"Yeah. That you Amir?"

"It is. So, you know I have your woman."

"Do I? Put her on."

Amir must have placed his hand over the phone because there was only muffled noise before Maria's voice came through the speaker.

"Johnny?"

"I'm here, baby. You okay?"

"That traitor cop tased me. My body's still shaking."

"Just hang tight, sugar, I'll be there soon."

"Please hurry up and kill these guys. I really have to pee."

Amir came back on. "Very brave and very beautiful. My compliments. Now, I don't want to hurt her, but you know I will."

"Let me guess. You want a trade. Me and the explosives for her?"

"Yes. You have my word that once I have all my C4 back, she is set free."

"Then let's schedule a meeting. When and where?"

"Midnight."

"Where?"

"First, get in the truck and park between the orange cones on Ninth Street and Fourth Avenue. You will stay in the driver's seat at all times. You have fifteen minutes from when we hang up the phone to get there. Once you are there I will call you back on this number and tell you where to go."

"Fifteen minutes isn't enough time."

"That's all you have. The timer starts when this line goes dead. At fifteen plus one I start slicing this pretty face. "

"Okay, okay. You're in charge."

"Yes, I know."

"See you at midnight, Amir."

"Bishop…"

"Yeah?"

"Your cousin Felix must come as well."

"Felix?"

"Yes. He comes too, or no deal."

"You got it. Make sure my girl isn't harmed or you'll never see your explosives. Understood?"

"Yes, yes of course. Until then."

"Until then," John said.

"Did you get a trace?" Antonio asked.

"Not enough time," Kevin said.

"We didn't think he'd be that careless, but we have to be ready for when he makes a mistake," Antonio said.

"So the man wants to kill us both," Felix said.

"Looks like it," John said.

"Do you think he'll let Maria go?" asked Grasiella.

"Auntie, I seriously doubt it. The only way to get her out of there is to take out Amir and his whole crew."

"Why midnight?" Felix asked.

"Not sure. Maybe he needs some time to get his troops in place," John said.

"The truck is on the way. It'll be downstairs in three minutes and it's only a five minute drive to Ninth Street and Fourth. I've already sent guys there to scout it out, but he picked a good spot. It's an open avenue and his guys can see you from a long way off. They can watch you from a high rise apartment anywhere within twenty or thirty blocks," Antonio said.

"At least we know where he'll be," Gonzalo said.

"Where?" Carlos asked.

Gonzalo walked over to the window and pulled back the heavy curtains. They all stared towards the East River and the massive structure of the Con Edison power plant.

The huge maze of pipes and chimney towers bellowed thick white plumes of steam into the night sky.

"You're right! The explosives are in a Con Ed truck, but there's five power plants in Manhattan alone. We can't be sure it's that one," Kevin said.

"That's the biggest. That's his target," Gonzalo said firmly.

"Do you think he knows we're only three blocks away?" Carlos asked.

"No, Con Ed was his target all along. We should have known from the truck," Antonio said.

"There is more to this. He knows we will to try to stop him," Gonzalo said, still staring out of the window.

"I was thinking the same thing," Kevin said. "The East 14th site produces power and steam for the Lower East Side and most of downtown. As I said, even if Amir blows it away, it's only one of five Con Ed plants in Manhattan. A lot of the city will be in the dark for a long time, but the rest of it, especially the big commercial centers in midtown won't be affected at all. There's gotta be more to his plan unless he's just trying to make it a symbolic act."

"For us, the only thing that matters is that we get Maria back safely. We get her and kill Amir. If we can stop a city-wide blackout that is good, but it is not our primary mission."

"Glad to hear you say that, Tio," John said. "Let's go, Felix."

"Johnny, how you wanna do this?" Antonio asked.

"Alright, here's what we're gonna do..."

CHAPTER 28
WELCOME HOME

East Harlem

KHALID MULAN KNEW he was going to die. Even if everything went according to plan, which rarely happened anymore, he still expected to be dead before sunrise. He also knew he shouldn't be going home. He'd done everything he could to protect his family and not even Amir knew where he kept them. Still, with so many safe houses already destroyed, he felt uneasy as he watched for signs of danger from across the street. Neighbors moved about as they always did. The old Puerto Rican woman who held court on her stoop was sitting at her usual post gossiping with another woman from farther down the block and local kids were playing a game of touch football that was constantly interrupted by the cars going west on 117th Street. Everything appeared normal. Everything except for his stomach which kept rolling over and the hairs on the back of his neck which were standing straight up.

A voice from deep inside his head whispered a single word over and over again. *Run. Run. Run.* He couldn't.

Forces beyond his control drew him to his wife and daughters. He had to say goodbye. He had to kiss them all one last time before he died.

Khalid paused before going up the final flight of stairs leading to their top floor apartment in the six story walk up. He strained to hear his wife's voice over the sounds of the building. The sounds of people talking and laughing. Of music playing. Sounds that came through the thin apartment walls, filling the hallway. He stared at the front door wondering if danger lay behind it. Everything seemed right. Only the rapid fire beating of his heart and the relentless voice in his head told him that something was actually very wrong.

His hand shook as he placed his key in the lock and carefully turned it, as if he could sneak up on whatever was waiting for him on the other side. The keys in one hand, his pistol in the other, he pushed the door open and took a quick step inside. He smiled and his whole body relaxed when he saw his wife and children sitting together at the table. His ears didn't register a warning from the whistle of the blade. His body didn't even react when it effortlessly sliced through skin, muscle, and bone without pausing. From what seemed like a great distance Khalid stared down at his own hand. Still holding the Berretta, it now lay at his feet on the floor. The fingers twitched slightly and the blood flowed steadily from the bloody stump.

His wife and daughters tried to scream. He hadn't noticed the clear tape that covered their mouths when he walked in. They made muffled sounds, distorted and unintelligible.

The initial shock wore off and the pain from his missing hand brought him to his knees. Khalid clumsily tried to reach for his pistol with his left hand as he turned to see his attacker. The blade whistled again, this time striking his left shoulder. His left arm hung limply at his side, now numb and useless from the precise cut that severed the tendons.

His featureless attacker was covered from head to toe, dressed in a black burka worn by many Muslim women. Only the dark emotionless eyes were revealed. Even the hands were covered in cloth gloves, though one held the thin, slightly curved eighteen inch blade that dripped blood from its tip.

"Welcome home Khalid."

"Who are you?" he asked.

"I am Omar."

"Hah! You are not Omar. The Sword of Allah is a giant of a man."

"I am no giant, and not even a man, but be assured Khalid, I am Omar."

"To die by a woman's hand," he said with disgust.

"You find irony in that?"

He sighed. "I do, but what does it matter in the end? Death is death."

"You could not be more wrong. It can be a swift and painless moment, or a long hard journey."

"Aziz sent you?"

"You swore allegiance to him alone. When you ignored his order to kill Amir your fate was sealed."

"I knew it was, but Amir is my brother. I couldn't kill him, even if it means my own death."

"What about the lives of your wife and children?"

"You are not here for them Omar. Kill me and be on your way."

"Yes, I will. That is what will happen once you tell me where the meeting is."

"What meeting?"

In a blur of motion Omar pulled a long thin dagger from somewhere inside the Burka and threw the knife across the room. Khalid screamed as it flew through the air and struck the chair just to the right of his youngest daughter's neck. The lightning fast throw was so precise that it pinned her hair and made a shallow cut across her throat.

"Please Omar. Mercy. She is only five," Khalid pleaded.

"I was her age when I began my training."

Omar granted herself the rare moment of self-indulgence, drifting back in time to the small Punjab village in India where she was born to a family of struggling farmers who barely grew enough to survive. On her fifth birthday an old man appeared at her father's door. Even by their meager standards he appeared poorly dressed, wearing little more than dirty rags. His brown skin was baked nearly black from the sun and he was layered in dust and dirt from his journey. Long tendrils of matted white hair cascaded down to his waist. Only the intricately hand-carved wooden staff that he carried indicated he might be something more than a wandering beggar.

Despite his appearance she had been drawn to him. When he spoke to her father he stared only at her and she boldly back at him. The old man said that he had traveled for months in his quest for her. He said that she was special. A rough jewel that he would shape into the finest warrior the world had ever known. The concept of their daughter becoming a fighter, or even that she was somehow special, was far beyond the reach of her parent's limited view of the world. They saw only a willful and belligerent girl who could not be disciplined no matter how often or how hard they beat her. They offered him one of their sons instead, but the old man merely laughed at their ignorance. He tossed a bag of gold and jewels to her father, ending the discussion and her father's life behind a plow.

She happily left with him the next morning. He walked ahead, moving fluidly, effortlessly. She remembered how he seemed to float silently across the ground, keeping a steady pace, never once looking back for her. Her little legs quickly tired, but he never slowed and when she fell too far behind she would sprint forward to catch up. Many hours and many miles later they stopped for lunch.

"How much farther?" she asked.

"A long way," he answered.

"Where are we going?"

"Does it matter?"

"My feet hurt," she said.

"I know they do, little one. Today is the first day of your training. There will always be pain at first. But remember, pain will pass. Not today, not tomorrow, nor the next. But soon your feet will no longer hurt and your legs will be strong."

"Where are we going?" she asked again.

He raised his hand, pointing a long boney finger to the north. "To Pakistan little one, to Pakistan. To your new home in the northern mountains. More than a thousand miles from where we sit."

"Should I be scared?"

"Are you scared of me?" he asked.

"No," she said truthfully.

"Good. Fear nothing in this world. Your training will be hard. Very hard. But fear nothing. I will be with you through it all."

On their second day of traveling the old man stopped

and had her sit on a fallen tree. He stepped into the middle of the road. As if immune to the terrible heat from the glaring summer sun he stood there silently, effortlessly. He never moved, letting the swarming, biting insects do their worst. They feasted on his flesh, crawling into his nose and ears. Sensing he was waiting for someone she too sat in silence, though she constantly smacked at the attacking flies.

After many hours they appeared in the distance. The old man remained a statue, his back to them as they marched forward. When they arrived, ten men from her village, led by her father, surrounded him. They had not come for her. Greed drove them. Not content with the fortune that the old man had so casually given him, her father believed there must be more for the taking.

As they made their demands the old man appeared to be in a trance, oblivious to any danger. He kept still, with his eyes half closed and the wooden staff held casually at his side when the first two men came at him. Like a fleeting shadow seen through the corner of an eye, his assailants barely saw the movement and suffered dearly for it. One received a vicious kick, the other an upward strike from his palm. Just one blow each and they both lay dead in the road.

The old man yawned loudly before resuming his sleepy stance. The remaining eight became enraged by his indifference. Brandishing long knives and hatchets, they charged him from all sides. He twisted the staff and pulled out a gleaming sword. With the blade in one hand and its wooden sheath in the other it took him only seconds to end them all. He swept through them as if they were blind men, dancing around and under their clumsy thrusts, then slicing open stomachs and throats with deadly precision. Not one attacker laid a hand on him before he cut them down. The dusty road was quickly covered by a thick, dark red river of blood that flowed from the men of the village.

"Why weren't they afraid of you?" she asked.

"Their eyes and instincts were blinded by their greed. They chose to see only a weak old man before them."

"They were foolish," she said.

"Yes, they were. Remember this lesson. People see what they choose to see. We will help them. We will hide behind their own stupidity and become invisible."

"Will you teach me to fight like you?"

"Yes, but first you must learn to walk. Are you ready little one?"

"Yes," she said.

Before following the old man she looked down upon her father's broken body and stared into his lifeless eyes. She felt nothing. Her father was a stranger. A part of her past.

Trotting eagerly up the road towards her new life, she never glanced back. Even at that very young age she knew she had to focus on what lay ahead.

The many months of traveling transformed her. Her body grew taught and lean, her legs strong and powerful. Her bare feet became coated with thick impenetrable callouses that were hard as stone. Every step along their long journey had been both a lesson and an adventure. He showed her the unseen world around her. How to read the land to find water, food, and shelter. How to see, hear, and smell all the living things that remain hidden to the untrained eye. How to walk in the dark, feeling and sensing her way through the woods. He taught her how to use the natural world as an ally rather than an enemy.

After six months of walking they finally arrived at his home deep in the mountains. The small, one story cabin was built into the cliff face, sitting high upon a flat stone shelf. It would be her home for the next sixteen years.

He stopped calling her "little one." She was instructed to call him Teacher, and he only addressed her as Student. He said she would be given a new name in time, but that time was a long way off. Again, he told her not to fear what was coming, only to survive it.

She learned to ignore and control pain. Pain from heat. Searing heat from long thin needles, glowing red from the fire, being pressed into her flesh by the Teacher. Pain from cold. Numbing cold from climbing snow covered mountains bare naked in the winter. Pain from thirst and hunger. Pain from the repeated blows she received in the daily combat drills as he taught her multiple fighting styles. Gut wrenching pain from the poison that he fed her in order to make her immune to it. Pain that took her near death over and over again.

In time she learned to use her body as an instrument of death. She could kill with her head, feet, elbows, or hands. Even a finger could deliver a lethal blow with an explosive force cunningly disguised within her diminutive frame.

She learned all manner of weapons. Pistols, rifles, explosives, the bow. An expert in all of these, she was truly a master of the blade. No one had ever survived a fight against her using a sword or knife.

Each evening, when the physical training was finished, the academics would begin. He taught her everything: from reading, writing and advanced mathematics, to economics, chemistry and linguistics. He taught her to cook, making her proficient in Eastern, French, Italian and Western creations. He even taught her how to drink without getting drunk. From a bare wooden table in the small cabin he showed her the world, spreading out maps and discussing every country and culture in great detail.

Every lesson drove her relentlessly towards one goal: molding her into a weapon and making her the world's greatest assassin. He told her of her legacy and the history of those that came before her. It was a legacy of unparalleled success. His family, the Tringas, had been training elite killers for twelve centuries, one pupil at a time. In twelve hundred years of service they had never failed to execute an assignment.

On her nineteenth birthday she was given her new name and the name of her first target. From there the mysterious and deadly legend of Omar was born. Like her predecessors, Omar had never failed to complete a mission. The old man was now a very old man. She stayed with him during those times when she wasn't working, though her visits were now infrequent. Her work kept her very busy.

After she was done with Khalid, Amir, and Bishop she would travel back to the cabin on the cliff, Omar thought wistfully. She wanted to see him one last time before he passed on.

Khalid groaned in pain, pulling Omar back to reality. She mentally scolded herself for losing focus. In her profession it was only her skill and discipline that kept her alive. Even a momentary lapse could prove fatal.

"One last time. Where is the meeting?" Omar asked, pointing the blade menacingly towards his family.

"You swear to me that they shall live?"

"You have my word." She seemed to glide across the room towards his wife and children.

"What are you doing!?"

"Do you want them to watch you die Khalid?"

"Thank you, thank you," he said.

He spoke softly to each of his daughters before Omar covered their heads with dark pillow cases from his bedroom. His wife struggled until he told her to stay calm and to remember him as he was in life and the love he would carry for her beyond death. He pursed his lips, sending her a kiss before her head disappeared under the dark cover.

"It is time," Omar said.

"Amir has Bishop's woman."

"I know. I saw her taken by Atal at the hospital."

"They meet at midnight at the big Con Ed plant on East 14th Street," he said quickly.

"Good," she said.

"You gave your word."

"And I shall keep it," Omar said. Before he could flinch the sword whistled above his shoulders, cleanly slicing through his neck and spine. His head stayed balanced for several seconds before toppling to the floor.

She wiped the blade on his shirt, then stepped into the hallway. Omar ignored the sound of Khalid's sobbing family as she closed the door. She was now completely focused on her next two targets.

The Upper West Side of Manhattan
Eighty Eighth Street and Central Park West

Bob and Karen Goldstein walked hand in hand down the street. After ten years of marriage and two children they were still very much in love. They were returning from a stroll through Central Park, which was a nightly summer ritual whenever their kids were away. A few feet from the entrance to their luxury building they were approached by a very distinguished looking man in his sixties. He had a thick mane of carefully coifed white hair, a thin white mustache dramatically curled at the corners, and wore a light blue seersucker suit accompanied by the mandatory bow tie. His broad smile completed the Colonel Sanders impersonation.

"Welcome home, Mr. and Mrs. Goldstein."

"I'm sorry, do we know you?" Bob asked.

"It is me who must apologize, sir, but I have something extremely urgent and very delicate to discuss with you."

"Is this about the case? Mr. Meecham said he'd be here at nine. You're early," Karen said.

"It is indeed, although I do not represent Mr. Meecham. Allow me to introduce myself, my name is Harvey Bascomb, Esquire," he said, handing them each a business card.

"In that case, Mr. Bascomb, we can't speak to you. Now, if you'll please get out of our way," Bob said sternly.

"As I said, this is a very delicate matter that deserves your complete attention," Harvey said. "I was asked to deliver this to you."

He handed Karen a plain unsealed white envelope. After pulling out a photograph, she tilted her head down and to the left as though the movement would help her to better comprehend what she was looking at.

"Oh my God!" she screamed. "Please! Please, don't do anything."

"Mrs. Goldstein, I assure you I am only a messenger. Would you be kind enough to invite me into your home so we can speak privately?"

"I'm calling the police," Bob said.

"Of course that is an option, though I find it quite disagreeable."

"Do as he says Bob. We don't have a choice," she said and handed her husband the photo.

"My associates will be joining us," Harvey added, just as two huge and dangerous looking men exited a black Ford Explorer that was parked at the curb.

The Goldstein's nervously greeted their doorman while Harvey Bascomb gave him a warm smile. The two killers offered only flat stares. After a silent elevator ride they all entered the plush three bedroom condo.

"Please don't hurt our children," Karen said. Tears streamed down her cheeks as she reclaimed the photo from Bob and firmly held it to her breast with both hands. Their sons, ages seven and nine, were at summer camp. The picture, taken from the woods, showed them toasting marshmallows with a counselor by their side. The time stamp in the lower corner showed the date and time of the photo. It had been taken less than an hour ago.

"I pose no threat to you or your family Mrs. Goldstein. As I said, I am merely here to discuss the case."

"What do you want?" Bob asked.

"Let's all have a seat," Bascomb said jovially.

Bob and Karen sat next to each other on the couch and Harvey took a chair facing them. His gruff companions remained standing. They each unbuttoned their dark suit jackets revealing the pistols that were tucked in their waist bands.

"First of all, I have to ask you, have you made any written or recorded statements that can be used in a court of law?"

"No sir. As my wife said, Mr. Meecham is coming here shortly with a court officer to take my statement."

"You are a lawyer yourself are you not?"

"Yes, I am."

"You are far too modest, sir. An extremely accomplished and highly regarded attorney, as I understand it."

"Let's cut the shit Harvey. You represent Gonzalo Valdez right?"

"I have heard the name, but have never had the pleasure of meeting the man you speak of."

"Look, we're right here. Just get to it."

"What are you going to say to Meecham?"

"That I can't be a witness."

"Could you elaborate as to why, sir?"

"Because I don't have any clear recollection of what happened. I was drunk and stoned. We had been drinking all day and night and even smoked a little pot."

"Is that all Mr. Goldstein? You seemed quite lucid in your original written statement," Harvey said. He removed a copy from his jacket pocket and placed it on the coffee table in front of Bob. "Would you care to read it?"

"I don't need to. It's worthless. The police grilled us for hours and told us what to say. They even typed up the statements and had us each sign them."

"I see. Anything else? There are many concerned parties that are very interested in the outcome of these proceedings. Any reassurances you can give them will be both welcomed and appreciated," Harvey said with flair.

"Yes. You can tell the interested parties that Hugh Packard was a bully. We all thought he was cool because he was from London, but really he was just an asshole with a mean streak made worse by the booze. He was always starting fights when he drank. The one thing I do recall clearly from that night is that Hugh assaulted a young man who was walking down the street. It was unprovoked. He broke a bottle over the boy's head. I moved away, wanting no part of it. The next thing I knew Hugh was dead and we were all being interrogated by the police."

"Yet your signed statement paints Hugh Packard as the victim and Felix Valdez as the aggressor."

"As I said, the police intimidated us, even threatened us with jail time if we didn't play ball. My father cut fabric in the garment center for thirty years. My going to Yale was the highlight of his life. They told me I would lose my scholarship at a minimum if I didn't sign."

"I see. Did you see anyone else that night?"

"Absolutely not."

"Even after all these years and in your admitted state of intoxication at the time, you can be so sure?"

"Yes. That I will swear to. Mr. Valdez was alone when he was attacked by Hugh Packard and I am very sorry that he went to prison. Mr. Valdez was defending himself. If I had been braver I would have testified on his behalf. He was railroaded by racist, small minded people, and it is my personal belief that it was also because of his last name. I heard the cops and the DA saying that they were finally going nail a Valdez, though I had never even heard of the uncle at the time. All I can say now is that it was a tragedy for everyone involved. Hugh lost his life and a young man was wrongfully incarcerated. It's haunted me ever since."

"Mr. Goldstein, it has been both an honor and a privilege to meet you, sir. I find your sincere remorse for your own inaction and your degree of empathy for the two victims here extremely refreshing. It reaffirms my belief in the good nature of mankind."

"You will assure those concerned and interested parties you spoke of that I pose no threat to them. In fact, they should consider me a staunch ally."

"I will assure them of exactly that. These are difficult times. Those small minded people you spoke of are still hard at work. They bend the truth without calling it a lie and create fear in others to mask their own evil intentions. At times like these, good God fearing people like ourselves need each other more than ever. I'm glad you are on our side Mr. Goldstein."

"Me too."

"You are clearly astute and I mean you no disrespect by asking, but do I need to caution you about making any written statements at this juncture?"

"You do not Mr. Bascomb. And if ever I do, it will be in your presence. I will rely on your guidance to ensure that none of us, as allies, could ever be injured as a result of such a statement."

"Excellent. Excellent. Thank you for your hospitality."

Bob handed Bascomb his business card. "Take this in case you don't already have it. My mobile number is on it. And please, call me night or day. I am always available to assist a friend."

Karen ran into her husband's arms the moment Bascomb and the killers left. She was shaking like a leaf and Bob held her close.

"I did all I could do, baby. They have to know that I'm no threat to them," he said.

"You were amazing. Bascomb was convinced. He knows you'll never testify."

"I just hope Gonzalo Valdez sees it the same way."

"What are we going to do?"

"We go get the boys, then come back here and wait for the phone to ring."

"And Meecham?"

"Fuck Meecham."

Michael Meecham's son, Caleb Meecham, walked into the Goldstein's building with a police detective and a court stenographer in tow. The doorman picked up the house phone and called to announce them.

"Mr. Goldstein says he can't see you."

"We have an appointment. This man is a police officer," Caleb replied. "I'll get to the bottom of this." He snatched the phone from the doorman's hand. Bob informed him that on advice from his attorney he would not be making any statements at this time.

"I can have you arrested," Caleb threatened.

"Really? Are you an officer of the court or in any branch of law enforcement?" Bob asked.

"I represent…"

"You represent your daddy, you little shit. Tell him to buy a warrant for my arrest if he can, otherwise leave me the fuck alone."

The line went dead in Caleb's ear. He put the phone down on the counter just as the ever smiling Harvey Bascomb and his stoned-face entourage exited the elevator and strolled passed the front desk.

"Who are you?"

Ignoring him, they continued on their way.

"Hey you! I asked you a question."

Stopping in his tracks, a slight nod of the head instructed his escorts to keep going. Once they were out of the building Bascomb spun on one heel with a flourish.

"Young man, are you ill?" His mocking tone conveyed contempt rather than concern.

"What? No, of course not."

"Are you quite sure? The lack of skin color, the degree of physical emaciation, coupled with your extremely rude behavior would indicate otherwise. Perhaps a brain tumor is responsible for your sickly appearance and this psychotic episode?"

"I'm asking you for the last time. Who are you and what are you doing here?"

"For the last time? Hmmm. That statement implies a threat. Young man, may I offer some advice?"

"What?"

"Tanning salon. You really do need to pink up a bit," Harvey said. He raised his hand, waved a pinky and said, "ta ta," then again turned elegantly on his heel and confidently strolled away.

"Why didn't you do something?" Caleb asked the detective.

"There was nothing for me to do, kid, except watch you make an ass of yourself."

Caleb watched Bascomb leave the building before turning to stare at the detective. He wanted to make sure he remembered him.

He got on his cell phone and said, "They got here first, Dad."

Trappe, Maryland

"We anticipated that some of the witnesses would not cooperate," Mike Meecham said to his son. "We only need one to swear he saw Bishop there and it's over. Don't worry, Caleb, we'll get him. I'm pulling up to the house. Call you later tonight," he said.

The silver Rolls Royce Phantom glided to a stop in

front of the ornately carved wooden doors that were the main entrance to the Meecham mansion. He had fallen in love with the doors when he toured Europe as a teenager. One of his first actions after his father died was to hire a team to steal the doors from the French castle they had been attached to for the last six hundred years. He simply had to have them.

His house servant, an elderly black man dressed in the mandatory butler's uniform, opened the rear door of the Phantom. "Welcome home, Mista Meecham, sah," he said. Meecham stepped out without replying.

An assistant immediately fell in beside him and began updating him on the events of the last two hours that he'd been away from the command center.

"Unless there's something new or urgent, you can save the update for later. I'm expecting someone."

"You're guest is here Mr. Meecham."

"Where's his car?"

"It's uncertain how he arrived, or how he entered the house. He tapped me on my shoulder in the hallway and said he would wait for you in your office, sir."

"And you let him?"

"I couldn't stop that man from doing whatever he wanted without an army behind me. Maybe not even then."

"I see," Meecham said. He walked down the long corridor decorated with priceless paintings and sculptures, then cautiously entered his own private office.

"Your security is for shit, Meecham. I hear you're going after some pretty nasty people and I just waltzed right in."

"Thank you for your concern."

"I could care less, pal. I just don't want you getting zeroed out before I get paid in full."

Mike Meecham carefully examined the man that was sitting in his chair blowing smoke rings from one of the fine Cuban cigars that were always locked in the humidor behind his desk.

As if reading Meecham's mind he asked, "I just broke into your house undetected and you're wondering how I got into the fuckin' humidor? You better get some focus or you're not long for this world."

"I plan on being around a long time and to outlive all my enemies. That's why you're here."

Constantine Bellusci stood up and stretched. He was half Greek and half Albanian, a massive man at six-six and two hundred-eighty pounds, none of it fat. He had a bald head, a crooked nose, the ancient facial and knuckle scars of a onetime brawler, combined with the stealthy movements of a trained soldier, which he once was. Now he was a full-time mercenary, an elite killer for hire, and anyone who came in contact with the man simply known as Connie instinctively gave him a wide berth. There was no disguising that he was one extremely dangerous and deadly human being.

He towered over Meecham, his crystal blue eyes penetrating and devoid of any emotion. Mike made a feeble attempt at staring up at him, but his neck began to hurt and his nerves quickly gave out.

"Why don't you take a seat so we can get down to business?"

Moving behind his desk and into his comfort zone, Meecham regained his composure. "I understand you go by Connie?"

"Yeah, that's right, Mike. Now, before you say anything else, I've got to ask if you're sure about this."

"You're the second person today to question my level of commitment."

"Just so you know, there's no turning back. You've been a business man and a government man up till now. After tonight all that changes."

"Do you always try to dissuade your clients from doing business with you?"

"I've found that people are extremely passionate and emotional. For a short time they can be angry enough at someone to hire me and then have regrets or a change of heart. By then it's too late and they somehow blame me for the outcome."

"What happens then?"

"I don't even waste a bullet, just bury them alive."

"I assure you I am firmly committed and upon successful completion of this action I would like to discuss a long term employment package for you."

"Okay, first things first. Who do you want clipped?"

"John Bishop and Felix Valdez for starters."

"The sons of the Don, huh? Okay, but what about the man himself? You sure don't want to make an enemy of Gonzalo Valdez and leave him hanging on your six."

"Very well, him too."

"You said for starters. I don't walk into anything without having a full picture of the playing field."

"I am considering adding Tony Kolter and General Marcus Palmer to the list."

"That's NSA Director Kolter, right?"

"Yes."

"Well, you sure aim high my friend. The first three are no problem. People get killed all the time and they've already made some serious enemies. The last two will require some finesse. If their deaths appear to be anything other than accidental they'll be called assassinations and neither one of us wants that kind of investigation. No one will buy it if they get taken out by street muggers."

"Can you do it?"

"Sure. As Michael Corleone once said, 'if history has taught us anything, it's that anyone can be killed.'"

"How much?"

"For Bishop, Felix and Gonzalo I'll give you a family package. Seven hundred-fifty k. Kolter and Palmer are bigger fish with a lot more risk. They'll cost you a million each." Bellusci handed over a slip of paper with his Swiss account number written on it. "Half now for all of them and the remainder for each one due upon completion."

"Done," Michael Meecham said, barely able to conceal his excitement now that he had ordered the deaths of his sworn enemies. "How long will it take Connie?"

"The Valdez mob is all in one spot up in New York. Could be as soon as a few days for them. A week or two max. Kolter and Palmer will take some time. Couple a months. Hard to say."

"For the last two the time factors are not as critical so take your time and do it right."

"That's the plan."

"Half down for all five of them is a million three hundred and seventy-five thousand. The money will be in your account tonight."

"Pleasure doing business with you, Mike." He placed his half smoked cigar burning in the ashtray and headed towards the door.

"You too... and Connie..."

"Yeah?"

"With Mr. Bishop and the young Mr. Valdez, it's very personal. Please make it as messy and painful as possible."

"Will do."

Meecham thought about Connie after he left. There was no doubt that the man was a lethal weapon, and that hiring him was a huge risk. But a risk worth taking. For years he had used information as a means of blackmail and intimidation and he knew that he inspired fear or at least a healthy degree of respect from everyone he dealt with. News of his being verbally abused by Bishop and his cousin and then getting fired by Kolter had spread throughout the community like a brush fire. His reputation had taken a huge hit from the events of the last week and it had emboldened many of his enemies. People who would normally run to do his bidding were no longer returning his calls. In order to maintain his power he knew he had to clarify in people's minds that he was not a man to be taken lightly before he became another water cooler joke.

He needed a strong statement and Connie was the man to deliver the message loud and clear. Once they all realized that crossing him was quite literally a fatal mistake, he couldn't wait to see the long line of grovelers who would spew apologies and invent wild stories about why they initially refused to obey his orders. After this first phase was completed he had a much longer secondary list of names and many of those who denied him were already on it. He had always known he was destined for greatness and the big bald headed killer was going to help him get there.

Connie reminds me of my lion, he thought, looking up at the massive head with its flowing mane and bared fangs that was mounted high on the wall. He would have to decide whether to have Connie killed before or after he became president. *I think I'll do him myself. Another gut shot? We'll see, we'll see.*

Meecham opened a side drawer in his desk and carefully removed five photographs, each in an eight by ten frame. His usually dull gray eyes sparkled when he looked down at the five men he had just given orders to kill. He wished he could be there to see it happen, but he smiled nonetheless. He rubbed his hands together with anticipation, staring at the empty placeholders on the wall that would soon display the heads of his latest trophies.

CHAPTER 29
CON ED

DESPITE HIS LACK of patience and bad temper, Amir Khan had always been a planner. He was only eleven when he devised the scheme to kill the Russian Colonel who had ordered the rape and murder of his mother and sister along with the gruesome death of his father. The Russian knew he was a hated and hunted man and was extremely careful. Just not careful enough.

The Colonel lay on top of his Afghan mistress, spent, sweating, and breathing heavily. He was still inside her when Amir steadied the heavy revolver with two hands, placed it next to his balls and fired. Even with his manhood gone the Russian had begged for his life. Amir had taken his time, using three more carefully aimed shots to maximize the man's pain and suffering. He saved the last bullets for the woman who had defiled herself by sharing her body with such a man. Only a boy, he stood over them, the strong taste of gunpowder in his mouth and the sad realization that revenge was bitter sweet. The joy he felt in having killed such a monster was tempered by the finality of the Colonel's death and his disappointment that it was something he could only do once. It was an act Amir would have gladly repeated over and over again.

Even then he had known it was only the beginning. His family, his entire clan, cried out for vengeance and their thirst for blood along with his own would never be satisfied. When he walked out of the room he had merely nodded at his uncle Aziz, who stood waiting for him with the bodies of three Russian soldiers at his feet.

Amir stalked New York as he had stalked the Colonel. Carefully and methodically. He started planning his attacks on the city more than five years ago when he was still in Syria. He knew that no matter how many security measures had been put in place after 9/11 there was no way to stop a committed group of fighters willing to lay down their lives to achieve their goals.

He despised Americans for their sense of entitlement and their expectations of luxuries he had never dreamed of as a child. New Yorkers were more arrogant than most and every one he met personified the "me now" mentality. He quickly saw that eight million self-absorbed people all living in a relatively small area created a lot of dependencies for the basic necessities of food, power, and water that they simply took for granted.

Initially, without a true plan in mind, he focused on recruiting men and creating a network of safe houses. He built his small army of dedicated soldiers and then sought a way to unleash them on the vulnerable citizens. Traveling throughout the five boroughs, learning all he could about the city, he was struck by how easy it was to blend into the crowds and maneuver undetected. Taxis were the perfect cover and many of his men were drivers. One afternoon while on a reconnaissance mission with Khalid they pulled up next to a Con Ed truck. The workers had put out a few orange cones and were pulling up a manhole cover in front of two police officers who neither questioned them nor paid them any mind. That night he started his online research and began to formulate his plan.

He discovered that New York was powered by multiple power plants, with five delivering electricity to Manhattan alone. He knew he didn't have the manpower to take over and cripple all five, but he could go after the two that were most critical to midtown and everything south of it. That would put more than a million people, all the major banks, the business centers, and the stock exchange in the dark and without air-conditioning or hot water for a very long time.

He narrowed his search, seeking fellow Muslims that worked for the big utility company that powered New York. Once he found them he began the slow and deliberate process of converting moderate middle class working men into radical soldiers of Islam that were ready to die for the Jihad. Or more precisely, men that would die for him.

Each stage of the assault had been planned down to the last detail. He believed it was foolproof. Even the first bombings at Union Square were designed to show his contempt towards the U.S. government and law enforcement. He wanted the city to be on full alert while all the leaders attending the global summit at the U.N. watched helplessly as an Afghan soldier of God ripped the heart out of the financial capital of the world.

The two things he couldn't see coming were his own arrest and John Bishop. The arrest was a stupid mistake that would not have affected the overall mission if he hadn't been blinded by his fury when he first saw the uniform, the medals, and that scarred face. They had all transported Amir back to his childhood. Like Bishop, the Russian Colonel had been a decorated hero and a member of the Spetsnaz elite Special Forces. For Amir it was as if he was confronting his father's killer all over again and he lost control. Years of planning were swept aside the moment he was placed in the cell with Bishop and things had rapidly deteriorated from there.

He had anticipated a body count surpassing the thousands that died on 9/11, yet between the attacks on Union Square and at the bar he had only managed to kill four people. He had a death sentence over him from his own Uncle. He was being hunted by the local police, the FBI, and Gonzalo Valdez. He had lost men, houses, equipment, and *most* of his explosives. Yet despite all these setbacks Amir remained optimistic. He knew he could still win. Tonight he would shut down New York and kill Bishop. After that he could die happy.

It was 11:57 PM. Amir sat in the control room scanning the multiple monitors that displayed the images from the security cameras covering everything inside and outside of the facility. Atal Wazir, still in his police lieutenant's uniform, sat in a chair nearby and five unconscious Con Ed workers lay bound and blindfolded in a corner. Amir's men had first taken over the control center, then worked their way through the power plant rounding up every one of the sixty-seven night shift employees without firing a shot. Nine true believers with automatic weapons was all it took.

He had two soldiers at the front gate and the others strategically placed in anticipation of the upcoming fight. Amir was no fool. He knew that Bishop would try something. He just wasn't sure what it would be.

He switched his view from the main entrance to the

plant's massive sub-basement. The monitor showed Maria standing with her arms wrapped around a vertical water pipe two feet in diameter that ran from the floor up to a much wider horizontal pipe twenty feet overhead. Wearing Atal's handcuffs, she was rotating her wrists and flexing her fingers to avoid losing circulation. Amir could tell her back was beginning to ache from the awkward position and watched her shifting her weight from side to side and from one foot to the other.

Amir tenderly touched his throbbing nose, reflecting on the promise he had made to Bishop. If he surrendered peacefully and handed over the explosives he would keep his word and let Maria go. On the other hand, if anything went wrong he was prepared to shoot her down without hesitation or remorse.

"Where's Khalid? He should have been here an hour ago," Amir said.

"He's either dead or in jail."

"You're right. He was a loyal friend and brother. Let us pray he died an honorable death."

"There they are, right on schedule," said Atal, pointing to the monitor that showed the truck coming towards them, driving east on 14th Street.

"I told you Bishop would come to me," Amir said. His men had been watching the truck from a distance for the past few hours in its designated spot on Fourth Avenue. They confirmed that both Bishop and Felix were in the front seats. Ten minutes ago Amir had called Bishop and instructed him to drive to the plant's main entrance.

"Unless one of us stays here to watch the screens we're going to be blind when they make their move."

"I know. I'm going over to the main building now. You stay here until I give you the signal."

"Okay. Be careful Amir."

"You as well my brother. Allahu Akbar."

"Allahu Akbar."

Amir walked out of the control room on the second floor of the command center. The circular three story building was glass enclosed to give the staff a three hundred and sixty degree view of the area. Recently built, its modern design contrasted dramatically with the windowless, dull red power plant next door that spewed smoke clouds from its four giant chimneys.

Security had been nearly nonexistent before 9/11. There used to be a lone unarmed guard sitting in a booth behind a single strand of chain at the main gate to the facility and there was even an entrance and exit to the FDR Drive that ran right alongside the Con Ed plant on East 15th Street. That exit had been closed off in 2001 and twenty foot high fences topped with barbed wire now surrounded the perimeter. The addition of reinforced concrete and steel barriers that retracted into the ground allowed only authorized vehicles to come and go and the old single sentry was replaced by two vigilant armed guards who manned the gate at all times.

Brushing aside the pain that came with each step, Amir quick marched through the tunnel that connected the command center to the power plant. He checked his pistol as he walked, then stuck it in his waist band. Then he gripped his still swollen arm. The bullet wound was sensitive to the slightest touch, but he pressed his fingers deep into the hole, reopening it. The jolt of pain heightened his senses and energized him. Blood flowed freely down his shirt sleeve. He howled once, then set his teeth, his eyes wild, his mouth stretched into a twisted smile.

"I am coming for you, John Bishop. I am coming."

Con Edison truck number 107
Avenue C and East 14th Street

"You know, we've lived down here our whole lives. This Con Ed plant's always been here like a smoking volcano in the background, but I never really noticed it until now. It's huge," Felix said.

"Look Cat, I know we've already gone over this a few times, but keep your eyes up. Like you said, that's a big ugly building and there's going to be all kinds of shit for the bad guys to hide behind. Amir will have a few guys at ground level, but count on most of 'em aiming down from the high ground. We've got three things to do. One, get Maria. Two, kill Amir and his crew. Three, stay alive."

"Works for me, cuz, but we may have to change the order and kill 'em all first."

"Spoken like a true soldier. Combat is unpredictable and you've got to be able to change and adapt to survive it. That's all that matters here. We live and they die."

Just then a bright green light flashed twice from a high rise apartment building south of the power plant.

"Johnny, there's the signal."

"I see it. Hey, before we go in I just want you to know... you're my brother. Always loved you and always will."

"Man, you know I've always felt the same way. Even when you were gone for so long I didn't sweat it. I knew we'd get back on track. Give me some love, baby."

They each leaned in and wrapped their arms around each other, sharing the moment. When they disengaged they nodded at each other once then turned their heads towards the main gate. Their yellow eyes glowed in the darkness and their jaws were set as they prepared to go to war.

"Here we go," John said, putting the truck in gear. He drove slowly towards the two guards that each held an AK-47 pointing directly at John and Felix.

The concrete barriers were lowered remotely and a section of the heavy fence slid to the side, allowing the truck to enter the compound. Once the cousins were inside, the barriers were raised and the fence closed behind them. One guard stood in front of the truck while the other opened the rear doors to check for any uninvited guests and to make sure the explosives were there.

The former Con Ed worker turned terrorist saw the stacked crates of C4 and gave a thumbs up signal. His companion called from his cell phone to pass on the all clear. Once the message was relayed he turned his attention back to John and Felix.

"Out of the truck. Now!"

They were each thoroughly searched and then roughly pushed from behind.

"Okay, here's what's going to happen. You two walk ahead of me. Slowly. My partner trails us with the truck. We're going to follow the arrows, go right through the entrance and into the main building. Remember, you try anything, anything at all, I'll blow you away and then your woman dies. We clear?"

"Yeah, we got it." John looked back at the terrorist that was about to get into the truck. "I'll give you a tip before you start her up."

"What's that?"

"Surrender."

"What's that supposed to mean?"

"It means don't say another word, just put down your guns and lay on the ground."

He took a step towards John and raised the AK menacingly. "Who the fu…"

His final word was cut short by the fifty caliber round that disintegrated his head, exploding it like a watermelon. The second terrorist had a split second to react to being coated with his partner's brains and skull before he was picked up and thrown aside by the heavy slug that punched a massive hole through his chest.

"Glad Christmas is a man of his word," Felix said.

"That was fine shooting," John said.

Christmas was in a tenth floor apartment in Haven Plaza, another housing complex only three blocks away. From that height he had a clear view of everything on the south side of the Con Ed plant including the main entrance to the compound. He'd promised to take the head off of the first terrorist at the gate and tear the heart out of the second.

The plan of attack was simple. No finesse. Just pure aggression. Come in hard and put the enemy down before he knew he what hit him. John and Felix each grabbed an AK. They opened the fence and lowered the barriers before getting back into the truck. They each reached under the dash for more weapons, NVG's and comm gear.

Outside on the street Kevin gave the go signal for the Mack trucks that blocked traffic on Avenue C north and south of the plant and along 14th Street. This was a private fight. No one wanted the police or any civilians getting caught in the crossfire.

"We're going in," John said into the headset he'd just put on.

"Right behind you," was the immediate response that both cousins heard loud and clear.

"Lights out in five, four, three, two, one, go!" Danny said into his radio.

John hit the gas hard. They bolted forward down the short driveway, made a sharp left turn that led to the fifteen foot wide and equally high open doorway, and onto the plant's main floor. John braked to a stop next to a massive generator just as the football field sized room went dark.

"Get your night goggles on. Look for heat signatures."

"Done," Felix said.

They each jumped out on opposite sides of the truck. John spotted two terrorists squatting down behind a forklift less than ten yards away. Their eyes still hadn't adjusted to the darkness. They were frozen, giving John clear stationary targets. He fired once, a direct hit to the forehead that flipped the first man backwards. The second target turned his head to the side. John squeezed once and put a round in his ear. The dead man made a long "eeeee" sound before he crumpled to the floor.

Felix saw three armed men on the second floor walkway along the south wall. They were spaced well apart, each about twenty feet away from the other. He fired twice and hit the first terrorist center mass right in the sternum. Felix didn't wait to see him fall, quickly turning towards the man in the middle and fired a three shot burst that took out terrorist two with one shot in the side, another in the back. The body tumbled over the rail and hit the main floor with a solid thud. The third terrorist ducked behind a network of pipes running along the wall and was out of sight.

"I've got one more guy hiding up there. I'm moving to get a shot."

"Be careful Felix. There's light coming from the doorway and his eyes adjusted to the dark by now. I'll circle around this way so we keep him pinned till one of us has a shot."

They each moved in opposite directions looking up and pointing their AK's towards the steel walkway. Felix saw a flash a split second before he heard the chatter of the machine gun on full auto. He dove behind a large tool box that got hit by a dozen rounds. He was breathing hard, trying to control his fear. His whole body tensed when he heard a short burst from nearby. He relaxed a little when he realized John was doing the shooting.

"He's down," John said. Felix was amazed by how calm and in control his cousin was, not even breathing hard.

"Let's find Maria."

"Think we got 'em all?" Felix asked.

"No. There's more hiding around here somewhere and we still haven't seen Amir. Shoot anything that moves. Unless it's my fiancé."

Felix chuckled. "You got it."

Time was short. They had to find Maria and find her fast. Their night vision sensors allowed them to move quickly through a green gloomy world of heavy equipment, pipes, cables, generators, and the giant transformer in the center of the plant that went down two stories below ground level. Halfway down the long main floor they came to the metal steps that led to the basement and sub-basement levels.

"She's down there. I lead, you follow. Stay sharp."

"I got you. Where's our backup?"

At that moment Boogie Washington and Minty Jackson ran through the main door. Boogie scanned left,

Minty right, both checking for overhead targets as they moved. Like John and Felix, they wore night sensors to see in the dark.

Back in the control room, Atal found the backup panel. Boogie and Minty were instantly blinded when Atal hit the switch and the bright lights came back on. Combat veterans, Boogie rolled to his left and Minty went right. Neither man panicked as they ripped off their goggles and blinked rapidly to regain their sight.

The shot rang out an instant before the bullet hit Boogie in the neck. He went down hard, blood gushing from both the entry and exit wounds. It spread quickly, the dark red in sharp contrast to the battleship gray colored floor. Minty knew his friend was already dead and focused on the shooter. The sniper was somewhere up high. Minty started his search at the top of the building and was looking at the fifth floor tier when the second shot echoed loudly. The impact of the bullet threw him backwards, slamming his head into the floor. He lay unmoving in the widening pool of Boogie's blood.

John and Felix had been blinded too. They struggled to get their vision back when they heard the voice behind them.

"Drop your weapons. Now!"

"That you Amir?" John asked, as he and Felix tossed their AK's down on the floor.

"It is. I was hoping you would wear your uniform one last time."

"Only for special occasions."

"Is death not such an occasion? Especially when you know it's about to happen. At least it won't be full of holes when they bury you in it. Did you bring my C4?"

"You think I would hand over the explosives before you let my girl go?"

"I thought it doubtful. But it no longer matters. I'm just glad you're here. And your faithful cousin as well. Now, down the stairs. Felix goes first. Move!"

Minty was only stunned by the fall and woke up to Christmas' voice in his earpiece. He knew the sniper was still up there looking for movement. He remained motionless, sprawled out on his back. His eyes barely open, he glanced down at the hole in his left shoulder. The initial numbness from being hit by a heavy caliber bullet was wearing off and the shoulder was starting to burn hot from the inside. It meant the slug was still in there.

He whispered into his earpiece. "Christmas, you there?"

"Here man. You guys okay?"

"Boog's gone and I'm hit. I'm out in the open playing dead."

"Shit. Where's the shooter?"

"He's high. Grid three. He's behind some pipes near the roof."

"Can you shoot?"

"Maybe. We'll know when he moves."

"Just tell me which way he runs and I'll nail him."

"Roger that."

Another shot echoed a millisecond before the bullet exploded into Minty's right thigh.

"Fuck! He hit me again. Fire, fire, fire!"

Christmas was lying down on a floor mat in the classic sniper's position with his legs splayed, his chest elevated, his left arm bent with his elbow resting on a pad, his left hand under the barrel that was also supported by a small tripod, the stock nestled into his right shoulder and his right index finger on the trigger. He'd removed the wall unit air conditioner from its sleeve. Using the dark hole in the unlit apartment as his hide rendered him completely invisible to the outside world.

He stared through his scope at the windowless brick wall of the five story high Con Ed plant three hundred yards away. He and Ed had prepped for battle by sectioning off the building into twenty pre-calculated grids. There were four grids for each floor. Starting at the top west corner, grid one, Christmas swung the Fifty Cal on its tripod over to the right, zeroing in on grid three. He was already on target when Ed aimed a green laser light that confirmed the spot. The high powered rifle had a range of over a mile. At this short distance he couldn't miss.

The rifle bucked as the heavy round flew out into the night at twenty-eight hundred feet per second. It punched right through the brick wall, creating a hole eight inches in diameter and kept on going. He edged the weapon a quarter inch to the right, firing again and opening up another eight inch hole three feet east of the first one.

The sniper bolted out of his concealed position, running east. The third shot came through the wall hitting him in the side just below the rib cage. His body tore in half, the torso silently sailed over the handrail while the legs and feet took two more noisy steps along the steel walkway before collapsing.

"You got him. Great shot Santa," Minty said into the mike.

"Hang tight Mint, help's on the way. Anymore targets?"

"Negative. And I don't see John or Felix."

They marched down three flights of stairs with their hands in the air and Amir covering them from behind with an AK. As soon as they reached the sub-basement they saw Maria at the end of a long hallway. She was about twenty yards away, still handcuffed to the wide cold water pipe. One of Amir's faithful stood behind her with a pistol pressed to the back of her head.

"Johnny!"

"I'm here, baby. Don't move," he said with a smile as Amir prodded him from behind.

"Funny man."

They walked towards her along a wide corridor that suddenly ended, opening up into the enormous transformer room. A labyrinth of pipes and cabling all converged on the giant mechanism that produced a thousand megawatts of electricity.

"That's far enough Bishop."

"I'm disappointed, Amir. I was expecting a lot more from you."

"Really? I thought watching your cousin die would be significant. This is what happens to any man who dares lay a hand on me!"

He turned the gun on Felix. Amir's left arm was nearly useless from where John had shot him three days earlier so he held and aimed the heavy rifle with only his right hand. Bracing himself for the recoil, he instinctively set his right foot back firmly. John jumped in front of Felix, expecting the familiar pain of bullets entering his body. He heard a loud crack, followed by a scream from Amir that was almost as loud as Maria's.

The sudden pressure had been too much for Amir's Achilles. It snapped completely, crumpling him to the ground.

John didn't hesitate. Diving forward into a roll, in one fluid motion he grabbed the AK with his left hand, rolled up onto his haunches, threw the butt to his shoulder, aimed and fired. He hit the terrorist standing behind Maria right on the bridge of his nose. The dead man lay flat on his back, his arms and legs spread wide, his feet twitching.

"God damn!" Felix shouted. "Not that I'm complaining, but what the fuck just happened?"

"You remember the little pin that our boy Fletcher stuck in this cocksucker's Achilles last week?"

"Back in jail? Are you for real?"

"Damn straight. Fletch just saved us all."

"Jesus."

"I think I remember you saying how you wished you could be there to see it pop."

"I did, didn't I? What a crazy world," Felix said, shaking his head.

Amir lay on his back. He dramatically groaned again from the pain trying to conceal his movement. John saw him reaching for the pistol and gave him a vicious kick in the head.

"Give it up, Amir. It's all over. Felix, go see if the dead guy has the keys to those handcuffs."

"Freeze Bishop!"

"Son of a bitch! That you, Lieutenant?"

"It is. Now drop the weapon. You let it fall, then kick it to Amir or you're dead where you stand."

John tossed the rifle and slowly turned to face the man he was very eager to see. Unlike the dead terrorist with the hole in his face, Harbey kept himself well concealed behind Maria with his Glock extended past her head and pointing at the two cousins.

"You know, even if we live through this shit I'm still gonna die of a heart attack just thinking on it," Felix said.

Amir picked up the AK once again. He used it to help himself stand up, then hopped on his left foot until he reached a hand truck and held on to it for balance.

"Rest assured Felix, you won't live through this."

Amir was breathing hard from the effort and sweating heavily from the pain. He hung the rifle by its strap over the handle of the hand truck and pulled his Berretta out of his waistband.

John started laughing hard and said, "Damn, you look like shit, Amir."

"What is funny?"

"You dude. We kicked your ass from head to toe."

"Let's see you laugh when I kill your woman. Bring her here Atal."

"Just shoot them and be done with it Amir. Can't you see he's playing with you?"

"Do it!" Amir screamed.

Harbey shook his head in frustration while he unlocked the handcuffs. He walked Maria forward, staying crouched behind her the whole way.

They were five feet away when Amir shouted, "Laugh now, Bishop!"

John moved to tackle Amir before he could turn the pistol on Maria, but Felix grabbed his arm, holding him back. John and Felix both stared wide-eyed at the beautiful woman dressed in black who appeared out of nowhere.

Amir sensed something too, and turned awkwardly. He was only halfway around when the blade whistled, severing his right arm just below the elbow. He hopped around to face his attacker. His scream of, "Omar, wait!" was cut short with finality by the second slice that cleanly severed his head from his shoulders.

"Thanks!" Felix said.

"She ain't with us!" John shouted, just as Omar lunged forward. He threw himself backwards, barely avoiding the thrust that would have gutted him. Amazed by her speed and balance, he scrambled to his feet, frantically twisting away from the eighteen inch blade that cut through the air an inch short of his Adam's apple. Her attack was relentless. Stabbing and slashing at him from all angles, in only a few seconds he was bleeding from cuts on both shoulders and his forearms.

John ducked under a big yellow water pump to try and get away from her. It was a mistake. As if herding cattle in a slaughter pen, she had driven him right where she wanted him to go. Omar jumped over the pump and stood over John, raising the blade for the death blow.

A split second seemed like an eternity as he prepared to die. He could see her clearly. She was gorgeous, with high cheekbones, a perfect nose and cupid lips. A single strand of dark hair had come loose and lay gracefully across her forehead. She was slim and tiny at five-three or five-four at the most, yet she radiated an almost superhuman strength and power. He looked into her black lifeless eyes. There was nothing there. No mercy. No compassion. Just the empty orbs of a killing machine.

The blade was arching downwards towards his neck when Felix threw a nine inch length of pipe at her back. Omar twisted away from it and in one fluid motion made a quick back handed throw that sent a double edged knife at Felix's head. His years of Kendo and Karate training saved his life. He ducked below the blade and kept on coming, picking up a three foot long steel jack handle as he ran to save his cousin.

Felix's distraction delayed the death blow from Omar's sword hovering above his head and gave John the split second he needed to go on the offensive. He pulled his belt buckle which became a handle for the flexible two inch wide and five inch long piece of razor sharp metal that he'd kept sheathed inside his thick leather belt.

He sliced up at her frantically from his prone position, cutting into her calf and hamstring. His efforts were unrewarded. Omar didn't react at all to the deep wounds to her legs and the sword arched down once more towards his neck.

Omar sensed Felix close behind her, but this time she did not turn to avoid his attack. She had one target. One mission. She was duty and honor bound to kill John Bishop and she could not fail. Even if it meant sacrificing her own life, she simply would not fail.

Felix swung the heavy jack handle with all his might, cracking her in the head. The impact knocked Omar off of the pump, yet even after absorbing such a vicious blow, she still stabbed at John as she fell. He turned his head just in time to avoid the thrust that would have ripped his throat open. She hit the ground hard and didn't move. The sword came free from her open hand and skidded across the floor.

"That bitch is no joke," Felix said.

John pushed himself up and grabbed the sword. He hesitated for a second, then said, "Fuck it." He went to stab her, but she rolled away, then flipped up onto to her hands and feet like a cat.

"I busted her fuckin' head open with this pipe. She should be out cold."

Blood ran down Omar's face and neck from the open wound on her scalp, and flowed freely down her leg from where John had slashed her. She staggered backwards trying to shake off the effects of the blow so she could finish her work and go home. No Tringa had ever failed. She would not be the first. Bishop had to die by her hand.

"I've got this," Felix said. "You get Maria. I saw that traitor cop drag her away when Amir lost his head."

"Take this." John handed him the sword. He heard shouting in the distance and took off towards the sound of Maria's voice.

Omar was regaining her senses, but drunkenly staggered forward to get closer to Felix. He held the jack handle vertically in his left hand and had the sword raised over his head in his right. He'd always been confident in his combat skills. He'd battled and beaten the best in the gym, on the streets, and in prison. But this was a different kind of fight. He'd seen what she did to Amir and what she'd been about to do to John. Holding two weapons against an unarmed and wounded woman, Felix still felt uneasy. She was a stone-cold killer. He knew if he didn't put her down for good he was a dead man.

He didn't see her move until she threw the knife. Turning his head to the left saved his life, though he wasn't quick enough to dodge the blade all together. He felt the sting of the razor sharp edge slicing open his cheek as it flew by.

She's too quick, he thought.

She jumped to her left, forcing him to move, firing another knife at him when he did. Felix saw the flash of silver and then looked down at the blade sticking deep in his right thigh.

The moment of shock was short lived when she

immediately charged in for the kill. Felix swung wildly; Omar ducked under it and raised another knife, driving it towards his eye. The blast from the Heckler & Koch .45 echoed loudly and Omar was thrown back and away from Felix like a rag doll. She rolled once then disappeared behind the base of a crane used for lifting heavy equipment.

"You okay, Felix?" Bunny asked. Not stopping to check, he ran after Omar and fired two more times before he came trotting back.

"I saw that bitch at the hospital. Knew on sight that she was bad news. Hey partna, you've got a knife in your leg."

"No shit. Did you get her?"

"Hit her with a high chest shot. Lotta blood. Missed with the other two, but she's just gonna crawl into a corner and die."

"I'll believe *that* when I see a dead body, then I'll drive a stake through her fuckin' heart just to be sure."

"Yeah, well maybe later we'll have time to come back and check, but not now. Where's Johnny?"

"Ran that way after the cop who's got Maria."

"Ready?"

"For wha..?!!!!" Bunny yanked out the blade and cinched his belt tight around Felix's leg.

"Thanks for the warning."

"Like a Band-Aid baby. Right off!"

"Damn that hurts!"

"You'll be fine, and we gotta move."

"Not sure I can walk Bunny."

"You can wait here with that shiny sword if you want to. Doubt it'll do you much good if your vampire bitch comes back for a kiss."

Bunny spun and took off in the direction John had

gone. He didn't look back to see if Felix was coming, but heard him thumping along a few feet behind. They both stopped when they heard John's voice above them when they reached the stairs. Bunny took them three at a time.

"Look Harbey, or whatever your name is, it's all over. Amir's dead, your men are dead, your cover's blown. Hasn't there been enough killing?"

"I'm not spending the rest of my life in Gitmo. I'm walking out of here. I'll let her go after I get some distance."

"It's not gonna happen and you know it. Just put the gun down."

Atal Wazir had his forearm wrapped tightly around Maria's neck and his gun pressed firmly to her head. He twisted and pulled her back, moving farther away from John in an awkward dance as he desperately searched for a way out. They were on the basement level in the center of the plant with the transformer behind them. High Voltage warning signs were posted everywhere.

John had Amir's pistol and calmly angled for a shot. Harbey was moving a lot, bobbing and turning like a boxer to avoid exposing himself. John was about to put a round in his knee cap when Maria let out a piercing scream and then bit down with all her might on the forearm that held her. When Atal released his grip she snapped her head back into his nose and then twisted her body. Facing him now, she slammed up with her elbow. Her pain masked by adrenaline and anger, Maria didn't feel her elbow shatter when it hit him in the chin. Like a bully finally getting an ass whipping in the schoolyard, Harbey didn't try to shoot or fight back. He just covered himself up to fend off her blows and kept retreating until he ran out of road. Maria shoved him hard.

He flipped backwards over the rail and sailed off the edge of the platform. Tumbling down onto the transformer, sparks flew when he hit, his body shook, and his hair and uniform burst into flames.

"How do you like it!? You tased me, so I tased you back, fucker!" Maria screamed over the edge.

"You okay, honey?" John said, putting his arm around her.

"Ouch. I think my arm's broken," she said, gently touching her elbow.

"Where'd you learn to do that?"

"Felix taught me. Needed to get out my aggression while you were away," she said with a smile.

"Didn't realize I'd done such a good job," Felix said, limping over and staring down at Harbey's smoking and blackened corpse.

"That is a badass lady you've got there, Johnny boy," Bunny said.

"Speaking of badass women, how's the little ninja?"

"Put a forty-five slug in her chest, but she got away."

"Forty-five usually keeps someone down."

"Usually does."

"Alright, we can't worry about her now. Felix, you get Maria upstairs and both of you get outta here."

"Where you going?"

"Bunny and I are gonna go free the Con Ed people that are pounding on that door over there and then find the bomb."

"Bomb? What bomb?" Felix asked.

"Amir didn't care when I told him we didn't bring the C4. Means he had more explosives all along and they gotta be around here somewhere."

"Sneaky little fuck."

"That he was. Now get her out of here."

"Johnny please come with us!" Maria pleaded.

"I'm right behind you, baby. I can work faster if I know you're safe. Now go!"

John and Bunny took off running towards the door that was being hammered from the inside while Maria helped Felix up the stairs. The key was broken off in the lock. John put two shots in the cylinder and Bunny kicked open the door.

"Who's the chief engineer?" John asked as the men streamed out.

"Right here. Name's Ivan Petroff."

"I'm John, this is Bunny."

"I know who you are young man. Is the plant safe?"

"No. We think there's a bomb here somewhere, but need your help to find it. Where would an explosive charge do the most damage?"

"Most people would think it's the transformer or the turbines, but they can be replaced pretty quick. It's the oil tank."

"Big tank?"

"The building next door *is* the tank. Holds over a million gallons. If that blows the plant and most of this neighborhood will be gone for good."

"Okay, Ivan. Show me. The rest of you men get outta here."

They ran out of the main plant to the long flat one story building next door. Ivan led the way to the main control system and they quickly worked their way around the massive flow pipes. Ivan said, "Sweet Jesus," and made the sign of the cross when they saw the thick wads of C4. The digital timer on the detonator was placed up high, over seven feet off the ground. It showed forty nine seconds, blinking each time it counted down to blast off.

"We don't have time to find a ladder. Bunny, hoist me up."

Bunny grabbed John low around his shins and lifted him up easily to get a clear view of the mechanism. With the clock ticking right in front of him he took his time, carefully examining each wire and checking for booby traps.

"Shit. Whoever designed this was a real asshole. All the wires are the same color," John said.

"Time?"

"Nineteen seconds."

"How many wires?"

"Three."

"One in three and ain't all that bad. Pick one Johnny."

John knew that this one was out of his hands. It was too late to run. He picked the middle wire and bent it against his knife.

"Here we go." He cut the wire cleanly and held his breath in anticipation of what would happen next. The clock counted down from six, to five, to four and then froze on three.

Bunny was still holding him up by the legs, with John's ass resting on his forehead for support.

"Dude, did you just fart in my face?"

"Think one mighta slipped out."

"Was it a slip or a push?"

"Slip."

"Really? I felt your cheeks tighten on the release. That makes it a push."

"Like you care. I defused the bomb like an hour ago and you're still talkin' into my ass crack."

"Don't flatter yourself cowboy."

"I've got another one in the chamber ready to fire."

"You guys are nuts!" the Con Ed engineer said.

Bunny put John down and they laughed long and hard on the walk back to the main plant. They stopped laughing when they saw the wide, thick pools of blood. Blood that came from Boogie and Minty.

CHAPTER 30
GOODBYES

AFTER DISARMING THE bomb and leaving the plant, John and Bunny hopped into the van waiting for them at the curb. Benji was driving, Maria and Felix were inside, and they drove off just as the cops arrived on the scene. After giving his soon to be bride a kiss and a clap on the back for his cousin, his first call was to General Palmer to give him an after-action report and to see how things went for Team Razor.

Earlier that night during the meeting at Campos Plaza they had figured out that Amir was going after two of the five Manhattan power plants. There was overlap and built-in redundancies between the 14th Street plant and the one on 39th Street and First Avenue. In order to create a significant disruption of power to the city Amir had to take them both out.

John had called Palmer and given him the 39th Street location on the condition that there would be no interference at 14th Street. Palmer kept his word. The FBI and NYPD had quarantined the area for ten blocks and did not converge on the scene until after the fight was over.

The attack on the second utility plant had not been an inside job. It was a commando raid with a full frontal assault on the gate. The seven terrorists were expecting limited resistance from the two armed guards that were always on duty. Instead they faced the deadly skill and overwhelming firepower of four battled tested Special Forces operatives. They never made it past the gate. Only one of the terrorists had surrendered. Another was in critical condition. The other five were dead.

The van carrying John, Felix, Bunny and Maria away from the scene passed through the police blockade without incident. John told Benji to pull over when he saw Captain Ryan. He stepped out and gave him a quick and private update about Harbey. John figured that they'd probably tout the lieutenant as a hero rather than a terrorist mole to save face. In the end he didn't really care as long as the man that kidnapped his girl was dead and gone.

Terry Hall was there too. He was a by the book type of guy and had a hard time accepting the order to let a civilian army engage in a gunfight with terrorists while his people were relegated to crowd control. John could see the man was conflicted.

"I tied a ribbon on it for you, Terry. Ten bad guys down, including Amir Khan, a bomb defused, the power plant saved, and no civilian casualties. We were never here. You and your team get all the credit."

"I'm happy with the result, but next time you stay out of it, and leave it to the professionals."

"Next time? I don't ever expect my fiancé to be captured by terrorists again, so we're good." He didn't add that his team had more operational expertise than anything the FBI could have deployed. "Lighten up man, this is a big win for you. You're looking at a big bump up for killing Amir and his crew."

John turned away and got in the van without looking back. Ryan came over and squeezed Terry's shoulder. They both watched Bishop and his family drive off into the night.

"Quite a guy, huh?" Ryan said.

"Yeah, he sure is."

"He's right, you know. You're going to be a legend after this."

"But, you and I both know the truth about what really happened here."

"I'm good with it. How 'bout you?"

Terry smiled for the first time. "Yeah, I'm good, and you're helping me with the press conference pal."

There was a lot to do after the battle, starting with patching up all the wounded. They didn't go to the hospital this time in order to avoid the wait and all the questions, especially about the bullet wounds. Two of the connecting apartments in Campos Plaza were setup for surgery and the doctors were already working on Minty when the rest of them arrived to get patched up. The bullet in his shoulder broke his clavicle and the one in his leg had shattered his femur. He was going to be on the Injured Reserve for at least three to six months, depending on how the leg healed.

Felix was next with eight stitches in his cheek and the repairs to the deep stab wound in his leg. He kept both the short sword and the knife that Bunny had pulled out of him as souvenirs. The doctor told him that the blade had missed the artery by a hair. If it had been pierced there would have been no saving him. He would have bled out in minutes.

Maria's broken arm was X-rayed and re-set and she had

a big knot on the back of her head. The wrist to shoulder cast kept her left arm bent at a forty-five degree angle in front of her stomach. She was pissed. The arm encased in plaster was already starting to itch.

John had lots of bumps and bruises and received twenty more stitches from his fight with Omar to add to the thirty-six he got from the bomb blast and building collapse at Still Bar.

They all knew that their collective survival had come down to the skill of everyone involved and a lot of luck. They were all happy to be alive, but their joy was tempered by the knowledge that one of their own, Boogie Washington, had given his life to save theirs.

Gonzalo, Grassiella, Maria's mom and dad, Silvi, Marci, and all the other uncles were there to congratulate them and welcome Maria home. There were hugs, laughs, tears, cheers, and toasts all around.

John, Felix, and Bunny met with Gonzalo and Antonio to give them their version of the battle, but they had listened to most of the action over their secure radio transmission and had already been briefed by the Pro KEDDS team. There was also the live video. Kevin and Danny removed all the security tapes from the Con Ed command center before leaving so they could be reviewed later, and also to make sure that there were no records left for the police. Gonzalo was most interested in the assassin. There was no clear image of her on the tapes. He had a sketch artist come in and between the three of them they created a detailed picture from memory. Hers was not a face any of them would ever forget. After that the adrenaline started to fade they all crashed hard into a deep, dreamless sleep.

There was no time to relax on Wednesday morning.

John and Bunny were up early to meet with Team Razor and General Palmer to go over logistics for the next phase of the multi-tiered operation. They laid out the timelines, reviewed satellite images and close-up photos of the ship, and went over weapons and equipment requirements for each man. They would all meet later in the evening to begin their covert journey to the Middle East after Chris' funeral.

The funeral was held in the family cemetery on a high bluff overlooking Calixto's house on Long Island. It was a beautiful bright sunny day without a cloud in the sky and the flowers were in full bloom. No one noticed. Putting such a wonderful and vibrant young man in the ground was a sad and solemn affair.

Each family member took his turn to speak, recounting stories about Chris. His spirit, character, and independent nature all bespoke a life lived to its fullest. Bunny spoke in detail about Chris' heroics after the bombing and his eternal love for a young man he had just met. No one could hold back their tears and even the ever stoic Gonzalo sobbed openly.

Chris was buried next to his mother and everyone shivered when they stared at the next plot over. The newly placed head stone ominously read:

Macho Valdez
Loving Father and Husband

It's where his spirit or his body would be laid to rest in a few days. The odds for recovering his remains were about fifty-fifty.

After the service Gonzalo put on an old white straw hat and walked slowly up the hill with his brother Sesa. They stopped at each headstone along the way to say a prayer and pay their respects. When they reached the crest of the hill they stood before two graves that lay above the others. Maria and Juan Valdez were side by side in the places of honor. Gonzalo never forgot the promise he made to his mother all those years ago back in Panama. He kept the family together. Both the living and the dead.

"So much death, hermano," Gonzalo said softly.

"It is the Valdez way," Sesa said.

"I failed our family."

"You don't say that. You never say that. We chose a bloody business and some of us paid with their lives. We mourn them, and we never forget them, but we move forward. Always we move forward. We live and we fight until our time comes, and we are placed beside them. "

Gonzalo nodded to his older brother, but remained silent. He stared down at all the dead and then lifted his eyes to see all the living family members spread out on the lawn.

"Our four brothers died fighting for our cause. That I accept. But, Christina and Michael and now Chris. That's different. I can't forgive myself for not protecting them," Gonzalo said.

"War is war, Zalo. Look down there," Sesa said pointing to their family below. "Do you think you can protect them all? You can't, and you know it. More may die. More probably will, but the family lives on. After you and I are gone the Valdez family will still be strong. That is what you have given us. You're a great leader, my brother. I wouldn't say it, and I wouldn't have followed you all these years if that wasn't the truth."

"Gracias, hermano. You have always been here to give me strength and help me see."

"I got tired of getting beat up by my little brother when we were kids, so I decided way back then it was safer to become your advisor." Trying to lighten the mood, Sesa smiled, his teeth bright white in contrast to his dark and wrinkled face.

Gonzalo smiled back at his big brother, and then carefully placed the Panama hat back on his head.

"Is that grandfather's hat?"

"It is," Gonzalo said.

"I know Poppi is happy that you still have it after all these years."

Their grandfather had only taken the hat off to sleep until the day he died and then their father had worn it the same way. Gonzalo kept it in a glass case and only wore it on very special or very solemn family occasions.

Gonzalo turned around and tilted the hat at his father's grave.

"Ready?" he asked.

"Yes Don Valdez. I'm ready, and we have work to do," Sesa said.

John and Maria walked hand in hand up the hill and passed Gonzalo and Sesa who were on their way down. Like his uncles, John stopped and paid his respects as they moved through the cemetery. Off to the right there were two tall head stones that stood slightly apart from the others. They were surrounded by red and white rose bushes and statues of winged angels.

The names Maria Valdez Bishop and Michael Barrington Bishop were etched deeply into the stones. It had been more than four years since he had come to see them.

"This is such a beautiful place, Johnny. I know they must be happy here."

"I know mommy's happy that we're finally getting married."

"And finally giving her a grandchild."

"What!?"

"That first night we were together. It's too soon to be sure, but I know I'm pregnant."

"If you didn't have that broken arm I'd pick you up and spin you around," he said beaming.

"I'll settle for a kiss."

They stood there together, kissing and caressing each other, taking in the moment, pushing away the grim realities of the outside world.

"If it's a boy we're naming him Chris," she said.

"And if it's a girl?"

"Even better. Christina, for him and your mother."

John bent down, laid his hand gently on his father's grave and then kissed the grass over his mother. He whispered a prayer and made the sign of the cross.

Maria stood behind him looking down upon the man she had loved her whole life. She saw him not as the trained killer that protected her and the world like a comic book hero, but as a simple man of honor whose heart overflowed with love and respect for family and friends. Standing there in the Valdez cemetery reminded her of the violence and tragedy that had surrounded him since childhood. Only three of the eleven dead Valdez family members had died of natural causes.

"I don't want you to go," she said.

"Me either, but we both know I have to."

She placed his hand on her belly. "Come back to us."

"I will, baby. I will."

They made their way down to the main house where everyone was gathering for an early dinner. John pulled Felix aside so they could talk alone.

"How you holding up partner?"

"Funny, the leg's starting to swell, but it don't hurt as bad as I thought it would. It's my cheek that's killin' me."

"Believe me, that stab wound is gonna be screaming by morning and you'll need something a lot stronger than Tylenol to take the edge off."

"What, Superman feels pain like us mortals?"

"What're you talking about, Cat?"

"Man, first we were dead, then we were saved, dead again, then saved again, over and over. Too many times for me to count and you breezed through it like we we're shoppin' for tee shirts at Old Navy."

"Look, I know last night was insane. And you're right, we probably shouldn't be here. But the fact is we're alive, and they're dead. I'm just real thankful it worked out this way and I don't pick at it."

"That whole sequence with Amir drawing down on me and then his Achilles poppin' was crazy."

"Yeah, it sure was."

"Don't think I forgot about how you jumped in front of me to take those bullets."

"You've done the same for me more than once. And speaking of Amir's leg, don't forget to get Fletch out of jail. We owe our lives to that little Puerto Rican."

"Made the call to our lawyers this morning. He'll be out tomorrow."

"Good job."

"You think she's still alive?"

"The head chopping psycho bitch? I sure hope not."

"She sure was fine."

"What do you mean?"

"I'm just sayin'… she was gorgeous," Felix said.

"Don't tell me."

"What?"

"You caught feelings for her?"

"I was just thinking that maybe under different circumstances... well, you know."

"Oh my God! She was about to cut my fuckin' head off and she nearly killed you and *now* you wanna take her out to dinner?"

"Come on J, you saw her. She was beyond beautiful."

"Don't let the looks fool you. I stared into those eyes and there was nothing there."

"You don't have to say it... I know... I'm sick."

"Dude, seek therapy. And if you ever see her again you best not hesitate. Put two rounds in her fucking head. You can feel bad about it later. Hold onto her sword while you jerk off to her memory, but make sure she's dead first. You hear me? Make sure. Otherwise she'll kill you, cuz."

"Yeah, you're right. Forget I ever said it. I'm bugging."

"Yeah, you are. Remember, don't hesitate. Two in the head. We clear?"

"Crystal."

"Good. Hey, another thing. I know Tio will take care of it, but find out where Boogie's people are. We'll go pay our respects in person when I get back."

"Can't believe you're going right back to the front lines. Wish I could be there to watch your back."

"Felix, listen. I've fought all over the world with the most highly trained professionals there are and I'd take you as my battle buddy any day. You were great. You've been great since I got back. Actually, you've been great my whole life. You saved me when I was a kid, went to prison for me, saved me from being shot by the cop in Union Square, and saved me again when that crazy bitch was about to cut my head off. What do I say? How do I thank you for all you've done for me?"

"Just come back safe. That's all I need, bro."

"You got it. Now let's get some food and talk to Uncle Macho."

"Seeing him standing next to his own grave was beyond heavy."

"You know, it ain't just revenge either. He's willingly giving up his life to protect us all."

"He's some kind a man."

"The best kind there is. Come on. Time to say good-bye to him."

Though everyone tried to put on a good face, the heaping platters of food were only picked at. The family was full of comedians and the few jokes that would normally have the whole table laughing were met with polite chuckles that quickly faded. Chris was dead, his father would soon follow, and John was heading into combat halfway around the world. It was a dark day for the Valdez family.

When the men gathered for a final meeting his uncle Macho was short and to the point.

"John, you do your part, and I'll do mine. You get that ship."

"We will, Tio… We will."

"Tomorrow I fly to London to meet with our CIA friends. They'll help set up the meeting with Aziz."

"Listen, Uncle Macho, I know the chances are slim, but if you see a way out, or a place to hide, you go for it, okay? I'll find you."

"I've thought of that. I'll be on his home turf surrounded by his men. I don't see them letting me walk out of there, but like you said, if I can get out I will… Wait, what do you mean you'll find me?"

"After the ship I'm headed back to Afghanistan with the team."

"We both are," Bunny said.

"I'm bringing you home, either way. Once we have your location there'll be Marines and Special Ops on the ground in minutes. Find a hole and wait for the troops, Tio.

"Yes sir."

"Good hunting, Uncle Macho."

"Same to you. Love always."

"Te amo, Tio."

They could hear the helicopter in the night before they saw the lights.

"That's our ride," Bunny said.

"Bring him back safe to us, Valentino," Gonzalo said to Bunny, gripping his arm and staring hard into his eyes.

"I will, Don Valdez. I swear I will."

"Last thing before we go. We took out Amir and most of his men, but don't any of you let your guard down." John spread his arms wide to include everyone when he spoke. "He may have more assets, and me and Felix barely survived our meeting with one of Aziz's assassins last night. We don't know if she's dead and there may be more where she came from."

They said their goodbyes once more. John kissed Maria and then Grassiella before he raced after Bunny. They both ducked low below the rotors and jumped in. A second later they lifted off and were gone in the night. The family stood together staring into the darkness, straining for a final glimpse of the helicopter.

A single cloud rolled in obscuring the moon on the

far horizon. A bolt of lightning lit up the sky like a camera flash revealing the helicopter in the distance for less than a second. A strong wind came out of the darkness, blowing hot across the lawn. The gust knocked the hat off of Gonzalo's head, setting it down gently near Sesa's feet. Sesa quickly retrieved it and placed it on his own head for a moment.

Suddenly, the lone cloud disappeared and the moon shone bright once more, sitting low in the clear night sky. The entire family was touched by what they had just seen and heard. For a moment no one said a word and no one moved until they each reached out and grasped the hands on either side of them creating a continuous connection. Everyone stayed huddled together staring into the night except for Felix who went to find to a chair. Just as Johnny had predicted, the pain in his leg was getting worse. It hurt too much to stand.

Out of respect for their privacy, Kevin, Ed, Danny, and Christmas were all standing quietly in the back, well behind all the Valdez family members. Everyone turned towards them when Ed shouted out a warning and Christmas pulled his pistol and fired a shot in the air.

CHAPTER 31
CONNIE

IT WAS A combination of home-grown skills and years of training that allowed a man of Constantine Bellusci's size to move so easily and silently through the woods. His father and grandfather were hunters. He spent his childhood in the forest with them and they taught him what he believed were the three keys to success. Be prepared, be patient, and be quiet.

Preparation meant training your mind and body and planning for the unexpected. Know the terrain. Study maps or see it firsthand. Always have extra food and water in case of emergencies. Always look for an edge by finding the weakness in your prey and using it to your advantage. Never carry less than three weapons.

Patience meant knowing how to wait. Though contrary to the nature of modern man, the ability to wait for the right moment for hours, even days, is one of the most critical requirements for the successful hunter. Always focus on the target with calm and clear intentions, but never lose an opportunity by rushing or acting too soon.

Quiet. Quiet was the hardest. He would spend days upon days out in the wild with his grandfather without a single word being spoken. Every time he would try to speak a calloused and crooked finger would press against his lips, then gently touch his ears, then his nose and finally his eyes. He understood his grandfather's message. Speaking, noise of any kind, masked the other senses.

The tough and weathered old man taught him how to move without disruption, like a ship slicing through water without a wake. He taught him how to hear the story being told by the land. How the rustling leaves indicated wind speed and direction. How birds were the guardians of the forest, their constant singing giving the all clear, while their silence was an alarm bell that put every creature on high alert. How to smell the rain long before it came. The quieter you were the more you were tuned in to the natural world.

He called his childhood lessons PPQ and he made them the foundation of his life. Mastering them gave him the edge he needed in a profession where failure was not an option. Success offered great rewards, failure meant death. Before he began a new "project" he checked his PPQ status to make sure he was ready.

He grew up in Albania, raised by his father after his mother abruptly moved back to her native Greece when he was four. Constantine was mercilessly bullied and tortured for his name and the local kids shortened it to Connie to add to his humiliation. Then he began to grow and by age ten he was nearly six feet tall. He paid back the bullies in full, but kept the name as a badge of honor.

His father died of a heart attack when Connie was fifteen and he buried his grandfather a year later. He was a big angry teenager alone in the world and he quickly joined a local gang to find a home. He loved the violence, but soon realized that gang life wasn't about brotherhood, it was simply about money. Money that enforcers like him didn't get to enjoy since all the cash got kicked upstairs to the gang leaders. Within a year he moved on. Hopped on his motorcycle, hit the road and didn't stop until he reached Germany. At eighteen he was a drunken bar brawler living life from day to day on a fast train to prison or the morgue. That all changed when he joined the army.

The army gave him purpose and clarity. Connie excelled at everything they threw at him and two years later he was a member of the Kommando Spezialkraefte, the elite German Special Forces. He fought in Croatia, Iraq and Afghanistan until he walked away after eight years of service. He was tired of taking orders and tired of killing civilians. Then the Bundesnachrichtendienst, the German foreign intelligence service, came calling, offering him big money to eliminate threats contrary to national interests. He excelled at this too and quickly left government service to become an independent operator.

At age thirty-two he was at the top his game. A professional hitman that chose his jobs carefully and guaranteed success. All thanks to preparation, patience, and quiet. PPQ.

He worked on a client referral basis only, meaning that if any former client passed on his name without his consent they immediately became his next target. He cautiously researched potential employers before ever agreeing to meet with them to avoid dealing with fanatics or the mentally unstable.

He almost passed on talking to Mike Meecham. He was ambitious, ruthless and a loose cannon. After meeting him, Connie still wasn't sure if the man was crazy or not, but Meecham hadn't even blinked or haggled over the fee, which was triple the normal rate.

Connie was a pragmatist. He would take out Bishop, his cousin, and Don Valdez, but he would stall on General Palmer and Director Kolter. Hitting those two would make him famous, but quickly end his career and his life. He wasn't into suicide. He took the million for a job that he couldn't do and wouldn't do even if he could.

He was already following the events on the news and his network of informants helped him fill in the blanks. He knew it was Bishop and his crew that blew away the terrorists at Con Ed and he figured they'd all head to the Long Island estate to recover and regroup.

He studied maps of the area and found two potential locations to set up shop. The first was a hilltop four hundred away from the house and Connie immediately ruled that one out. It was too close and too exposed. Valdez security would be all over it. Not that he couldn't by-pass any alarms and take out the sentries, but it wasn't worth the risk when he could work from the second position farther out. Fourteen hundred yards farther out, making it eighteen hundred yards, or just over a mile to the main house.

At six-six and over two hundred-eighty pounds, Connie drove big SUV's whenever he could. He needed a spacious interior and extra leg room. He parked the dark blue Navigator at a public beach lot more than three miles from his destination. Camouflaged as a surfer wearing a cut off wetsuit with a short board tucked under his arm, he took the long hurried strides of a wave rider trying to catch the final set before nightfall.

The first part of the walk was easy, following the bike paths over mostly flat terrain. It was the end of the day and the few cyclists that were still out were all headed in the opposite direction towards their cars. When the last of the bikes passed him he stepped off the path and into the woods. Leaving the board hidden behind a tree, he moved slowly, carefully, and silently, while the world around him changed from green to gray in the dusk before the full dark of night.

He arrived at the tree exactly as he planned it, right after the sun set and before the moon rose too high to provide maximum cover. He took night vision goggles out of his back pack and put them on to scan the area and look for the best way to climb the giant spruce that rose over a hundred feet straight up. Moving carefully and quietly, it took him twenty minutes to make the ascent and find a perch that met his requirements. He needed to stand on a heavy branch at least fifty-five feet up that could take his weight without too much bend or sway. Then he needed a second branch at chest or shoulder height above the bottom one so he could use it to steady the sniper rifle.

He checked his surroundings once more before hanging the back pack on a broken limb and removing the scope and range finder. Looking through the scope he was pleasantly surprised to see all three of his targets standing with a large group of people on the big lawn at the back of the mansion.

Assuming you have the right gun for the job, which he did, long range shooting combines marksmanship, training, and mathematics to calculate distance, trajectory, wind speed, humidity and elevation. Factoring in the moonlight and his standing position high in a tree made it a near impossible shot that only a few other people in the world could make. He regularly practiced night shooting in environments just like this to keep his edge. Preparation! Connie knew he'd make the shot.

Connie forced himself not to rush. He took his time setting up the Accuracy International L115A3 long range rifle. He had just finished attaching the telescopic sight and sound suppressor when a helicopter came in fast and landed at the house. He punched home the magazine, set the rifle in his shoulder and peered through the scope just in time to see Bishop run towards the bird. It was up and moving the second he got in.

Your lucky day Mr. Bishop.

He scanned the crowd for the other two names on his list: Gonzalo and Felix Valdez. He could see Gonzalo wearing his Panama hat near the front of the group, but he was partially blocked by a taller head in front of him so Connie zeroed in on Felix. He aimed, exhaled and fired just as a bolt of lightning momentarily blinded him.

The fuck was that?

He'd checked the weather and knew there was no chance of rain. He was baffled by the rogue lightning strike, but had experienced nature's unpredictability time and time again. He looked up at the clear night sky and shrugged before pressing his eye back into the circle of the scope. He knew he'd missed because everyone was still standing huddled together. Large gatherings of people don't remain calm when there's a body at their feet. He looked for Felix again and let out a soft sigh of frustration as he watched him limp from the front to the back of the group. Felix sat down heavily in a chair and there was now a woman standing right in front of him blocking the shot.

Connie moved on, breathing easy and maintaining the second P in his PPQ philosophy. Patience. He eyed the Valdez family from high in the tree and over a mile away until he finally found his man. This time there was no blinding flash of light to spoil his aim. He steadied himself, slowed his breathing and fired on the exhale. He watched the man in the white straw hat crumple to the ground from the head shot.

The old Don, rest in peace, must be slipping.

He smiled at the private joke as he methodically disassembled and packed up the rifle. He hurried down the tree and made his way back to the car. Driving off into the night he was already planning how and where to take out John and Felix.

CHAPTER 32
WE GO ON

"WELL?"

"They found tracks in the woods leading to and from the big pine tree more than a mile out. The shooter had to climb high up to get a clear view," Kevin said. He was stating the facts, his voice flat. He stood there along with the rest of the Pro KEDDS team and the other members of Valdez security feeling empty and defeated. They had failed. Many of the men in the room were already expecting the worst, silently saying their prayers and a final goodbye to their loved ones.

Gonzalo had his back to them. He stared out into the night waiting for it. It happened faster than he expected. The giant tree had been doused in gasoline. The flames hungrily raced up its trunk and quickly reached the crown. It burned tall and bright, a giant candle that could be seen from miles and miles away.

"Spruce," Gonzalo said.

"Spruce?"

"Yes Kevin, a spruce. You called it a pine."

"My mistake, sir."

"Mine for not cutting it down years ago." Gonzalo stared at the burning tree for a long time after that without saying another word. The silence was heavy and it began to unnerve some of the hardened men in the room. They stared at the back of Don Gonzalo Valdez wondering if they would leave the room alive or if he had something more gruesome in store for them.

Finally, he turned to look at them. He wore no shirt. He had wrapped it around Sesa's head to try and stop the bleeding. His muscled forearms and chest were painted dark red and his pants were stiff where the blood was beginning to dry. His scarred face was an unreadable death mask, but his fearsome yellow eyes glowed hot, seeming to radiate their own heat. No man in the room could hold his stare or dared to try.

Kevin was looking down at the floor, lost in thought and replaying the sequence of events in his mind.

Saved by a gust of wind blowing off his hat?

Then his brother puts the hat on and takes the bullet?

How many times have they tried and failed to kill this man?

They don't call him El Gato Negro for nothin'.

The legend lives on and as the saying goes, "You come at the king, you best not miss."

Kevin looked up when Benji marched in with Christmas at his side. Both men walked directly up to the Don and bowed formally.

"I know who's responsible Don Valdez," Christmas said.

"Wait," Gonzalo said. He waved his hand dismissively and the room cleared out. Only the Valdez brothers, the Pro KEDSS team, and a few trusted associates remained.

"First, your warning shot. How did you know?

"The assassin missed with his first shot. It ricocheted off the patio right in front of me and Ed."

"But you weren't behind me and my brother were you?"

"No Don Valdez. We were behind Felix. He was the first target."

Gonzalo turned his back on Christmas and faced the burning tree once more. "You said you know who is responsible. Is that the shooter or the man who hired him?"

"Both. The shooter is an Albanian named Constantine Bellusci. He goes by Connie."

"How do you know this?"

"There are very few men that could make that shot or even try. He's one of them and he's the only one with size sixteen feet. I've tracked him before. It's him. He's a very expensive and very, very good gun for hire. Maybe even the best," Christmas said.

"And now he works for Aziz Khan," Gonzalo added.

"I don't think so, sir."

"Why?"

"He has his own code and picks his clients carefully. He's been approached by the Saudis, the Iranians and a few other Middle Eastern extremist groups. They all offered him a ton of oil money to carry out hits and he turned them down every time."

"Very well. I defer to your expert opinion on this Connie Bellusci." Gonzalo turned back around and stared hard at the soldier in front of him. Christmas held his gaze, waiting for his boss' brilliant mind to process the information.

"That can only mean that I have seriously underestimated the threat from Michael Meecham."

"Yes, it's got to be Meecham. But with all due respect sir, there is no way anyone could anticipate that a Deputy

Director of Homeland Security would hire an assassin to settle a personal score. He's one of those wild cards that blindsides the best of us on the battlefield. You can't anticipate a guy like Meecham, but once he's in your gun sights you empty the clip in his ass," Christmas said. "It will be my honor to gut him for you Don Valdez."

"Thank you Christmas. We will speak again later. In private."

"I'm at your service."

At that moment Felix came limping into the room.

"He's alive Tio."

"How? The wound was terrible."

"The Doctor said Uncle Sesa's head was turning away at the moment he was hit. We all moved when Christmas fired the warning shot. That and the metal band on your hat saved him. The bullet didn't penetrate, it only gouged deep into the skin and creased his skull. That's the good news. The bad news is that he's still critical. They said they expect his brain to swell from the impact and there's no way to know how much damage there is until he regains consciousness."

Gonzalo carefully examined the bloody straw hat and the hole in the heavy metal band that his father Juan had installed years ago for a day just like today. He thought it might give him an edge and save him from the certain death of a head shot. Juan had been killed by multiple shots to his chest and stomach so the metal band couldn't save him, but at least for now, it had saved the life of his son Sesa.

"My brother has always been strong. If any man can survive such a wound it is him. But whether he lives or dies, we go on as planned."

"One more thing Tio."

"What?"

"They don't know it's Sesa. Everyone at the hospital assumed it was you. Antonio took his wallet and then gave them your name," Felix said.

Good thinking Antonio. The fact that his nephew could think clearly and make strategic decisions after seeing his own father shot truly impressed Gonzalo.

"Excellent," Gonzalo said. "We follow Antonio's lead. Put the word out that I am not expected to live much longer. No one goes to work. Stop collecting money from the street. Make our enemies think we're weak. Let the sharks circle close."

"And then kill them all." Fiero hissed.

"Sí hermano. Todos."

"What about John?" Macho asked. "Do we tell him?"

"After they take the ship. He's a professional. He'll understand. We can't have him distracted before he goes on a mission," Gonzalo said.

"Bueno," Macho said in agreement.

"Okay, get to work. I'm going to shower and change. Don't disturb me for twenty minutes unless it's with news about Sesa. I want an update from each of you when I get back."

"Yes Don Valdez," they all said to his back as he exited the room.

Felix looked to his father Carlos who was also covered in Sesa's blood.

"Go with him Felix. He needs you now," Carlos said.

Felix nodded his head and limped quickly away to catch up to Gonzalo. Macho broke the silence after he left. "Like Zalo said, we go on. Whatever happens, we go on," Macho said.

"Yes we do… we always do," said Fiero.

Gonzalo walked mechanically up the stairs, then down

the hallway, through his office, and into his bedroom with Felix in tow. Felix of all people knew how close Gonzalo was to his brother Sesa. He was there for silent support and there to help if needed. Felix sat down in a chair against the wall and watched his uncle carefully strip naked and then enter his private bathroom. Gonzalo closed the door behind him. He turned the hot water in the shower on full blast and then stood at the sink staring at himself in the mirror. He held on tight to the edge of the counter while his body shook uncontrollably from rage and anguish. He continued to cry for his brother long after the steam had fogged away his reflection.

CHAPTER 33
LIGHTNING GODS

The Arabian Ocean
200 nautical miles off the coast of Yemen

THE HELICOPTER DROPPED John and Bunny off at LaGuardia Airport in Queens, where they met up with General Palmer and Team Razor. They all boarded a private jet owned and operated by a CIA front company that flew them directly to Germany. Landing on an isolated runway at the massive U.S. Air Force base in Hamburg, the jet taxied next to a big C-130 Hercules cargo plane. All four of the C-130's massive propellers were spinning and its wheels were turning before the door closed. The team spent a total of three minutes on the ground.

There had been little time to rest on the trip across the Atlantic. Every moment was spent on mission prep and review. Now that they were on the last leg of the journey they did equipment and weapons checks before shutting it down for a team nap. Only General Marcus Palmer and his aide, Colonel Steve Masters, stayed up. They weren't jumping with the team.

"What's your honest opinion Steve?"

Masters took another look at the satellite photos taken earlier in the day. Though they were covered with tarps, the silhouettes of mounted machine guns could be seen fore and aft and eight armed men were grouped together on the open deck of the cargo ship.

"Surprise is the key to this Op General, and I believe we'll have it. Their security detail is spread out randomly in some of these pics and then they're often all huddled together amidships for meals and gambling. The heavy guns aren't manned at all. They're not expecting trouble, least of all a night attack by an airborne Special Ops team."

"I still wish we had more back up in place," Palmer said. "One bad guy staring up at the moon is all it will to take to eliminate the surprise factor. Then the team'll be at an extreme disadvantage. They'll be exposed and out in the open."

"I wish we could bring more forces to bear too sir, but we can't risk an international incident and Aziz has to believe that Gonzalo Valdez hijacked his weapons. Otherwise we'd just sink the damn ship and be done with it," Masters said.

"I know… you're right Steve. There's no other way."

"General, we've been together a long time and put together Black Ops missions that faced longer odds. What's really bothering you here, sir?"

"Honestly, I just don't want to lose any of these guys. I've been sending soldiers into battle for more than twenty-five years. I've seen a lot of good men die along the way. Far too many. Through it all I've always kept my perspective. Mission first. I've never been reckless with a man's life, but mission success was mandatory. Now, maybe for the first time in my military career, I can't be objective. I love these men and I don't want to lose them. That's God's honest truth."

"I know how you feel, sir. There's always been something real special about Team Razor. And after losing Tommy and the other sergeants last week I don't want these guys in harm's way either."

"But that's their job, isn't it?"

"Yes sir, it sure is."

"Well then let's make damn sure we've done everything we can do to help them from here. Let's go over it all one more time Steve."

"Yes sir!"

John lay on his back with his eyes closed on a steel framed cot that folded down from the wall of the plane. He could feel the engines and every bounce of the C-130 through the thin plastic covered foam pad under him, which was a perfect conductor for vibrations and turbulence. He'd slept in mud holes with bugs and rats climbing over him so it wasn't the shabby mattress that woke him up. It was his dreams that made him uneasy.

He'd had vivid dreams all his life. Dreams that always seemed so real. Too real. After his parents were killed the dreams became nightmares. Eventually the horrors faded, but the dreams were a constant and in them his mother often appeared with a message. On nights before he went into battle he would see her directing him to go a certain way or whispering a warning. Today she said one thing over and over again in Spanish. "Don't open the door. Don't open the door. Don't open the door."

He didn't understand it and it scared the shit out of him, but he didn't dismiss it either. John knew from experience that his dreams could save his life as they had many times in the past. Was it really his mother protecting him by showing him which way to go or which path to avoid on his next Op, or was it simply his own intuition combined with hours of mission prep guiding him along? He didn't know and he didn't care. All he knew was that so far his dreams had given him an edge and helped him survive. And if it really was his mother speaking to him in his sleep so much the better. He hoped it was.

John never told anyone about the dreams, not even Maria. He wasn't sure if anyone would understand, let alone believe him.

"Sergeant Bishop, did you hear my order to move your team?"
"Yes sir."
"So you willfully disobeyed a direct order?"
"I did, sir."
"And why would you do that sergeant?"
"My mother, sir."
"Your mother?"
"Yes sir, my mother told me not to sir."
"She's here?"

"Not exactly, sir. She's been dead for more than twenty years, but she comes to me in my dreams and gives me advice about combat tactics. That's why I disobeyed your direct orders and thereby saved my team from walking into an ambush, sir. My mommy warned me not to go that way."

It sounds so ridiculous even when I think it, there's no way I'm ever sayin' it out loud to anyone. They'd put me in a psych ward for sure. Sorry Ma, this stays between us.

John was smiling when he sat up after his internal chat session. He went to the head, relieved himself and washed his hands and face before walking over to General Palmer and Colonel Masters. Bunny woke up next and then all of Team Razor seemed to put their boots on the floor at the same time, every man instantly alert and focused. They all joined the group at the planning table and started examining photos.

"Steve, let's do a final mission review before they suit up," General Palmer said.

"Yes sir," Colonel Masters said, moving in front of a large white board that was bolted down to the floor. "Gentlemen, this is the Al Badir. She's a Chinese made and Yemeni owned and operated cargo ship. She's currently carrying ten thousand tons of weapons and explosives heading for Afghan front line terrorists. She has a light crew of seven including the Captain and you will treat them as enemy combatants. Is that clear?"

"Yes sir," they all said.

"Good. There's an additional eight man armed security team protecting the cargo for this haul which means there's a total of fifteen hostiles on board. Your mission is to eliminate the opposition, detain any survivors before they can call for help, and then secure the weapons cache for pick up."

"Let's start with the ship herself. The Al Badir's a Handy-size which means she's a midsize model in the world of cargo vessels. Approximately two hundred-twenty meters long and thirty-four wide. Her max speed is fourteen knots and they've been running full out in daylight, but slowing her down to a steady nine knots at night. Even at nine knots you're aiming for a small moving target on a big black ocean so you're all going to need to bring your A game to hit the mark."

"Is she running with her lights on?" asked Bunny.

"She is and that's going to help hide your silhouettes when you get close. Using your night vision and lighting up the ship with the laser guidance system will lead you in, but the biggest challenge is the gear on the deck. Take a look here," Masters said pointing to a three foot by five foot enlarged color photo of the Al Badir.

"She's a smuggler and therefore designed to carry any-thing and offload it quickly. They even added some cranes so they can anchor offshore and transfer any illegal cargo to small fishing boats before going into port."

"Doesn't give us much of a landing zone," John said.

"No it doesn't Johnny. As you can see, there are four containers stacked near the bow and two more at the stern leaving a good portion of the main deck open. The only way for you all to get down on the deck is to come in from the rear making sure you don't hit the cranes. Once you clear the booms you'll have to drop down quickly onto the main deck. Be careful on your approach. The ship's going to appear to be almost stationary until you get right up on her. If you come in too fast you're going to bust an ankle or a leg when you touch down."

"I thought this over Colonel. I did a HALO onto a ship in daylight and barely made it," said Maceo. "All six of us trying to hit the same spot on a small moving LZ just isn't going to work. Even if we all make it onboard we're going to be stacked up on top of each other. How are we going to take these guys out if we're all tangled up in chute lines?"

Masters looked over at General Palmer who was digest-ing Maceo's assessment of the situation.

"I've been looking at these photos and thinking about this mission for the past three days. Bottom line, I don't like it. The only way to avoid landing in a big pile is for each of you to deploy your chutes at different altitudes and if you go in using that staggered approach it means splitting our forces and reducing firepower. Gentleman, unless we come up with something better I'm pulling the plug on this Op. Any suggestions?" Palmer asked.

"I agree sir. We need to modify our plan," John said. "The only way to do this right is to double up."

"Tandem," Mace added, nodding his head in agreement.

"A tandem jump?" Palmer asked.

"Yes sir. Three chutes instead of six reduces our profile on the way in and we'll have three shooters who won't have to worry about steering," John explained.

"Bear?"

"We've all done tandem HALO jumps in training. I like it, sir. I believe we can take out the tower and the armed guards before our feet hit the deck."

"Colonel, finish the presentation and then let's run some calculations with the Jump Master for the increased rate of descent based on the extra weight on each chute."

"Yes sir," said Colonel Masters. "As I mentioned, she's Chinese made, which helps us on this Op. Most cargo vessels are designed with the tower bridge aft... that means in the back by the propellers for you non-seamen. The Chinese built this one with the bridge tower fore, or closer to the bow of the ship. This means that whoever is on night watch manning the controls will be facing forward and therefore won't see you landing on the deck behind him. With or without the element of surprise, the bridge tower needs to be taken out before any radio transmissions can be sent. Find your targets on the way in, if possible, and if not make sure you hose it down to prevent anyone from making a distress call."

"Colonel, me and Mace will hit the tower hard on the way in. Once we land the two of us will assault the bridge on foot to neutralize any survivors and the comm gear. At that point we'll hold the high ground to assist the rest of the team if needed," Bear said. "How many guys should we expect up there on night watch?"

"With only a seven man crew, I'll bet there's only two. This is a ship flying a don't-fuck-with-me flag, meaning Yemeni. But they are sailing through pirate infested waters. The good news again for us is that Somali pirates don't attack ships from Yemen, since they receive so much financing directly from the government or from terror groups based there. In addition, the pirates usually attack in daylight so the guards and the crew should be more relaxed at night," Colonel Masters said.

"Okay, since I'll be riding in on Bear's lap I'll take out the tower crew before we land," Mace said without bravado, just stating the facts.

"You sure Bear's fang on the back of your neck won't mess up your aim?" Able asked.

"At least I'll be gettin' poked in the back. I hear you're jumpin' with your face on Bobby's package," Mace replied with a smile.

"Well played," Bunny said.

"Alright, let's talk about the guards. All eight are carrying AK's. Only one has an additional side arm. Looks like they're eating and sleeping on deck and pissing over the hand rails. They go below to the head one at a time to take a dump. The majority of the time they stay grouped together at the center deck, but we do have a few photos of two or three of them joking around at the stern on the smaller rear deck. The two heavy machine guns aren't manned and have been kept covered. "

Colonel Masters nodded to Bear who stepped forward and took over.

"Okay team, we've got eight armed targets on the deck, two or three more enemy combatants in the tower, and the rest more than likely sleeping in their bunks below the bridge. Bunny, you remember how to operate a chute?"

"Yes Chief, I'll hit the mark."

"Good. You fly Johnny in. He's the shooter. You vector in from ship's ass and come in from the right side. Bobby, you're the flyer and Able's on guns. You come in from the rear and glide in along the left side. Johnny, Able, watch your cross fire. You'll be comin' in fast, taking targets from opposite sides of the deck. Don't shoot each other."

"Yes Chief," they both said, nodding to each other.

"Okay. I'm flying Mace in right over the deck and the bridge tower. We'll take out our targets and then back you up to search the ship and secure the weapons. Now remember, below decks there's lots of places to hide. The hallways are narrow and there's a lot of doors we have to go through one by one. We take our time and do it right. Stay together. Don't go chasing any runners on your own. They could be leading you into an ambush. Remember, they're on a ship, and there's nowhere to go. Be patient, stay sharp, and we'll get 'em all."

"How much time do we have before the fishing boat with our backup arrives on scene?" Bobby asked.

"Ten to fifteen minutes," Masters said. "She's trailing a few miles behind the Al Badir, far enough out so the enemy's not nervous and on full alert. As soon as you land she'll be racing towards you. There's a SEAL team on board just in case you need them and they'll assist with off-loading the weapons."

"You guys ready?" Bear asked.

"Ready Chief!" They all echoed.

"Suit up and put on the oxygen. We go in forty-five minutes."

All six of them walked over to the equipment area and

clamped on oxygen masks. Before executing a High Altitude Low Opening or HALO jump they all had to breathe in pure oxygen for at least half an hour to purge nitrogen from their bloodstreams and avoid the Bends from the air pressure and the rapid rate of descent. They all sat together breathing deeply and mentally reviewing every detail of the mission. After five minutes the Jump Master walked over and ran his hand across his neck. They peeled off their masks and stood up, waiting for an explanation.

"New plan, gentleman. Follow me."

Masters, Palmer, and the Jump Master had been busy running calculations. Weight was the key concern. Each two man team had to weigh the same to ensure that they descended at the same speed. Adding too much extra dead weight to the lightest team, which was Bobby and Able, could cause serious injuries.

"HALO is out, due to your weight variance. There's some good scattered cloud cover at eleven thousand feet so you'll jump from there. This'll reduce your equipment requirements since you won't need the oxygen tanks or the cold weather suits. You'll be traveling light with just your altimeters, flak jackets, guns and ammo. And I want all of you wearing knee and elbow pads along with the night vision crash helmets."

"I like it," John said. "We'll be able to move better without those heavy suits and the extra gear."

"That's the idea," Palmer added. "Everything else goes according to plan. We'll illuminate the ship and the laser guidance system will lead you right to her. Get ready, we're starting our rapid descent in fourteen minutes. You jump five minutes after that."

The team marched off again to change into the new lighter jump suits.

"Hey Bun, can I have a word?" the general asked. He was now alone, standing with his hands behind his back and his feet spread apart.

Bunny trotted over, his brow knotted and his body tense. He was pretty sure he knew what the general was going to say: after five years of civilian life his fighting ability was about to be questioned. He'd expected it, but he sure wasn't happy about it.

Standing at parade rest, the general was all business. Palmer's fierce piercing blue eyes revealed nothing.

"Sir?"

"I want you to stand there at attention. I'm about to tell you something. When I do you keep your head up and your eyes stay fixed on me. Understood?"

"Understood, sir."

"Look Bunny, we just got the word. Gonzalo Valdez took a head shot from a sniper right after you two dusted off."

Bunny's head swam, instantly overwhelmed by the news, but the general's eyes bore into his, bringing him back and forcing him to focus.

"Is he dead?"

"He's hanging on by a thread. That's all we know. I can't tell Johnny right before a mission. I'm leaving it up to you to break it to him when you think the time is right."

"Yes sir, I'll tell him after."

"I know I don't have to say this, but you stay close to him when you do. He left the Army after Sammy died in his arms. Last week Major Burke and four Team Razor sergeants were blown away. He just buried his cousin Chris and now he's about to lose his uncle and surrogate father. These were all his closet friends and family. Every man has a breaking point and I don't want him losing it and getting himself killed when we get back to the Stan to take our final run at Aziz."

"I will, General. I won't leave his side. I'll help him through it."

"Good work, sergeant. You be careful down there on that ship tonight."

"Thank you, sir."

General Palmer came to attention and saluted. Bunny returned it with crisp formality. He turned on his heel and trotted back to the team. They all worked silently, putting on flak jackets and loading up on ammo.

"What was that about?" John asked as he helped Bunny with his chute.

"He told me that things just weren't the same without my guiding hand, and how happy he is to see me back."

"I could see that. I feel the same way," John said with a smile.

The plane went into a steep dive, quickly dropping from thirty-five thousand to fifteen thousand feet where it leveled off and began a more gradual descent. Before heading to the jump station all six combat veterans strapped on altimeters, combat knives, pistols and short barreled P90's. The submachine guns with sound suppressors were designed for close quarter combat.

Lights flashed and a muted alarm sounded throughout the massive cargo bay as the C-130's ramp lowered. Each team member pulled his visor down and moved forward towards the gaping black hole in the belly of the plane. General Palmer and Colonel Masters stood along the wall but were still engulfed by the howling wind that buffeted their clothes and wildly blew their hair back. They saluted each team member and placed a hand on their shoulders as they passed. At the end of the ramp all six soldiers stared into the night, waiting for the countdown. They did a final sound check into their mikes and activated the night vision sensors in their helmets before giving each other the thumbs up. The three shooters, John, Able, and Mace stepped in front of the three flyers, Bunny, Bobby, and Bear to get hooked in. They all listened to the countdown from ten. On one they stepped out and off of the ramp, free falling at one hundred and twenty-eight miles per hour into a world of wind and stars eleven thousand feet above their target.

You wouldn't know it was June in the Middle East. At more than two miles above the ocean the cold cut them to the bone. They plummeted down together in a tight group, holding hands to form a circle. There was a layer of clouds below, but from that height the night was crisp and clear. A billion stars were shining bright and the moon was a giant glowing ball in the sky.

Straining against the air pressure and the numbing cold, the team held on tight to each other as they fell through the clouds. They all felt the powerful jolt from the lightning strike that suddenly filled the air with a force that gave them all a full body muscle spasm and punched each of them hard in the stomach. Every team member stared wide-eyed in amazement at the electric blue light that surrounded them in a protective bubble.

"Look at us!" Able shouted in awe.

"Gods of War," Bear said.

"What!?" John asked.

"The lightning God is the God of war. Tonight we're his brothers," Bear said.

CHAPTER 34
THE AL BADIR

THE TEAM SHOOK off the shock of the rogue lightning strike as they passed through the cloud ceiling and into the clear night sky. They stared down at the huge expanse of dark ocean dotted with tiny lights that glowed green through their night sensors. Each scattered green spot represented a ship and they waited for their target to get lit up.

General Palmer watched the live action unfold on the big screen in the Command and Control Center on the C-130 circling above. All the calculations for wind, the target ship's speed and position and the team's rate of descent were fed into the computer in front of Colonel Masters. At this stage of the operation Masters and Palmer maintained control. Once the shooting started the team became an independent unit.

The Special Ops vessel disguised as a fishing trawler hit the Al Badir with its advanced radar system, making it flash red on the screen in front of General Palmer.

"Light 'em up Colonel."

Masters turned on the infrared laser guidance system

that sent a laser beam of invisible light directly down from the plane to the Al Badir.

"Team Razor, you are on target. Do you have visual?"

"Roger. We see the target," Bear said into his mike.

Glowing like a spear reaching down from the heavens, the guiding specter of infrared light pointed directly down at the Al Badir just over a mile ahead of the team. Following Colonel Masters' instructions they tucked their arms to their sides and flew head first to a position a thousand feet behind and fifteen hundred feet above the ship. Once there, Bear, Bobby, and Bunny pulled their rip cords.

Coming to a complete stop after falling from such an extreme height at such an extreme speed was a painful exercise. Bunny stifled a groan as he and John were violently yanked skyward the instant he deployed the chute.

John could clearly see the Al Badir below. The ship appeared much larger up close than it had in the photos. Bunny guided them in, gliding silently above the high angled booms of the cranes at the stern and then steering along the starboard side to make the landing. John listened for warning shouts or shots, but saw only the prone bodies of sleeping men. While the world raced by in a blur, his training decelerated everything into a controlled flow of motion that allowed his mind to process and react to every detail. He almost smiled when he realized they were about to nail a near impossible approach and landing.

His moment of self-congratulation was cut short when he locked eyes with a fat bearded sentry who suddenly appeared at the rail in front of him. John could clearly see the man's crooked, smoke stained teeth when the guard's mouth fell open in disbelief. They couldn't leave an enemy at their backs, but they were moving too fast and went right past him. John twisted as far to his left as he possibly could and shot the P90 one handed. He knew when he fired that it was a split second too late. The two shots from the silenced three round burst that hit the sentry in the side weren't enough to stifle his warning shout before he died. The rest of security team woke up when they heard the scream over the roar of the ship's engines.

Bunny used all his might to fight against a powerful gust of wind that came across the deck and almost pushed them back out to sea. He worked the chute controls, turning directly towards the group of seven men that were now on their feet. John ignored the few guards who stood there frozen, too stunned to move. He aimed and fired at the three seasoned soldiers who reacted quickly enough to raise their AK's. He saw two go down before he was thrown forward when Bunny hit the release on the tandem rig the moment before impact. Bunny timed it perfectly, giving John the freedom to fight while he made a solo landing and then struggled out of the parachute harness on his own.

"Go get 'em, Johnny," Bunny said aloud. He hadn't seen Johnny Bishop in action in a long time and it was a sight to see.

John felt Bunny reach for the release button before they hit it so he knew what to expect. He flew down and forward, leading with his legs and surfing on his back four feet above the deck. He snapped both his boots up in a vicious double kick that nailed the man in front of him right on the chin. The guard slammed backwards into the three men behind him, pulling the four of them down in a tangled pile. The impact helped slow John's momentum allowing him to tuck and roll into a tight summersault. Coming up in a low crouch he spotted a skinny dark skinned guard taking aim at Bunny.

John fired twice hitting the man in his bony left check with both shots. John didn't waste time watching the dead fighter go down. He turned to face the last man standing, quickly firing a three shot burst. The guard was tall and powerful. He dropped his weapon, but stayed on his feet staring down at the three blooming red flowers that spread across his chest just above the Nike emblem on his white tee shirt. Slowly lifting his head, he stared at John with a look of surprise, resignation, and sorrow. With the last of his strength he raised his right hand and seemed to be waving goodbye when his legs gave out. He collapsed to his knees, then fell over sideways, his face smacking the deck with a heavy thud.

The guard that John had kicked lay with his head twisted at an unnatural angle, dead from a broken neck. He had killed six men in less than fifteen seconds and the last two survivors slowly got up with their hands raised in surrender. John kept them covered and didn't bother turning when he heard the familiar sound of size fourteen feet running towards him from behind.

Bunny was moving fast. He fired twice without slowing down, hitting each of the prisoners in the center of the forehead.

"Come on!" he shouted.

John didn't look back at the bodies of the men his friend had just executed. He sprinted after Bunny and said, "Holy shit," when he saw where they were headed. In the back of his mind he knew that Bobby and Able should have been on the far side of the deck at the same time he was, but he'd focused all his attention on the enemy. Now he saw them. Six feet above the deck they swung in a wide arc, their chute stuck and tangled in the boom of one of the cranes at the stern of the Al Badir. Bobby hung limply with his head slumped down and arms dangling at his sides, while Able struggled to get free, madly cutting away at the harness. John watched Able sheath his knife and brace for impact when the wind and motion of the ship slammed him and Bobby into the solid metal wall of a large red cargo container.

Bunny got to them first. Reaching up, he grabbed Able's legs and tried to hold his friends in place. He couldn't get any leverage and was dragged along with them across the ship's small rear deck. They were headed for the railing and the open ocean when John jumped onto Bunny's back and scrambled up to cut the chute strings above Bobby's head. John knew he had to cut them free before they went over the rail or they'd all be in the water watching the Al Badir continue on its way without them. The four of them moved steadily towards the edge while John sliced through string after string. When he cut the last pair everyone tumbled down onto the deck. Everyone except for him. The forward momentum took him out and over the ship's railing.

Flailing wildly as he fell face down towards the black water below John desperately threw his hand back and managed to catch the edge of the deck with just the tips of three fingers. Despite the pain and pressure on his fingertips he dangled above the water willing himself to hold on. The ship hit a swell and thousands of tons of steel were pushed upwards by the unrelenting force of the ocean. When the ship was at its apex he lost his grip, falling down and away once more until he was suddenly yanked back up by a vice like grip around his left wrist. Hanging above the waves, John looked up at Bunny's smiling face.

"You can bathe after work Johnny. Right now we need you on board."

"Your dumb jokes made me abandon ship."

Bunny hauled John up and helped him back over the rail.

"How's Bobby?" John asked.

"Out cold. The helmet saved him, but he really smacked his head the first time we hit that container," Able said.

"How many times you hit?"

"Three. I knew you had your hands full with the guards and didn't want to distract you with a distress call."

"Shit. Well, let's move him to a safe spot while we clear the rest of the ship," John said.

Bear came running over. For him and Mace the landing had been uneventful. There had only been one crew member at the helm and Mace had taken him out with a perfect shot through the window of the tower bridge on the way down. From there they swooped in silently onto the front deck and secured the rest of the crew without another shot being fired. The prisoners were bound, blind folded, gagged and tucked away in a storage room before Mace made his way up to the bridge to reduce the ship's speed and guide her to the rendezvous point with the Special Ops vessel. He was staying up there to provide covering fire while Bear came down to assist the team.

"We took out the First Mate on the way in and we secured the rest of the crew, and the Captain in a storage room below the bridge. That should be everyone, but let's take a look around before we assume the ship's secure," Bear said.

John looked down at the heavy metal plates on the deck that covered the cargo bay. He saw that they had been carefully welded in place.

"We're going to need a torch to cut through these welds," he said.

"I saw one behind the main door in the tower," Bear said.

"We can get in from below to take a look at the weapons before we start cutting," Able said.

"Roger that," said Bear.

They carried Bobby over to a corner of the main deck away from all the bodies where Mace could watch over him from the bridge. They made a bed from a pile of life jackets and tucked him in before they all walked cautiously towards the steel door that led below decks.

"Kill the lights," Bear ordered before he pulled opened the door and stepped inside. The four of them did a thorough search of every compartment and the engine room before they turned their attention to the hold under the main deck where the weapons were stored. Able spun the wheel to release the water tight seal then pulled down on the handle. He leaned in and then quickly jumped back to draw fire. He looked back at the team with a big grin on his face just as John recalled his mother's warning.

When Able stepped into the doorway John's scream of, "No!" was drowned out by the report of the large caliber rifle. The shot threw Able back against the far wall of the corridor. The bullet hit him high in the stomach and went right through his flak jacket. His hands pressed the wound while he fought to catch his breath.

Bunny dove at Able, knocking him down just as the second shot exploded into the wall where his head had been only a split second before. He pulled Able farther down the hall and checked the wound. It was bad and they both knew it. Able looked up at him with resignation.

"Don't give me that look, Mex. I was hit way worse and we just went sky diving," Bunny said, his hands already slick with Able's blood.

"I guess we'll be bartending together," Able said. He tried to smile, but his mouth was clenched in a tight line.

"Bartender? That's skilled labor. You'll be washin' dishes for a few years before you ever see the front of the house, amigo."

"Asshole." Able grabbed Bunny's arm, fighting the pain and trying to remain conscious. "Bun, I saw the muzzle flash. It came from pretty far back and high up. Unless this was a lucky shot he's got a night scope."

Everyone was still mic'd so they all heard Able's report.

"You ready Mace?" Bear said.

"Ready."

"Lights on in three, two, one, go!"

The second Maceo turned the lights on from the bridge John dove low through the door with Bear right behind him. Just as planned, the sniper in the cargo bay had been blinded by the lights. The two shots that came a second after John and Bear were already inside were off target, hitting high on the wall above them.

John and Bear crawled forward and found cover behind some unmarked crates. They gave each other a here-we-go-again look when the familiar sound of AK's fired on full auto sprayed the open doorway.

"Looks like we've got a sniper in the back and at least two more shooters, one on either side of the room," John whispered. "Mace, lights out again on three."

"Roger."

The cargo hold once again became a dark steel cave. John went left and Bear right to go after the two fighters that were blindly firing away, revealing their positions in the process. Moving along the wall and below the sniper's line of sight John spotted his target five feet away. His man was out in the open standing straight up and shooting from his hip one handed like Stallone in a Rambo movie. John aimed through a small space between crates and put him down with a single head shot.

"Mine's down," he said, keeping Bear and the team updated.

Two more loud shots came at him from the open side of a large crate stacked high near the ceiling along the back wall. Both slugs penetrated the wooden box in front of him and then clanked loudly off of something metal stored inside.

I better not be hiding behind a box of grenades.

The second AK fell silent and Bear announced his target was off the board.

"The sniper's in the big crate with the open face high up in the back," John said softly.

"Let's go," Bear said.

John moved fast and low. He reached the corner of the far wall and started climbing. The crate was right above him when he reached up and fired a full clip into the opening. Bullets ricocheted wildly back out of the sniper's hide that had been designed with a heavy steel plate set back from its one open side. Bear climbed up next to him and they both heard curses from inside the box.

"Fuck this," Bear said, pulling the pin on a smoke grenade. Red smoke filled the air before he pushed it through the hole where the shooter's rifle barrel was sticking out. Frantic screaming came from inside and then the font plate fell forward. The rifle was thrown out, followed by two terrorists who fell ten feet down to the steel floor below. They rubbed at their eyes and clawed at their throats, hacking, coughing, and trying to catch their breath.

John and Bear hopped off their perch, landing on either side of the two men who were now on their hands and knees.

"These guys are hard core Afghan fighters for sure. Can't tell which one was the shooter," John said, carefully looking them over.

Bear shrugged and stomped hard, first on the right hand and then on the left of the Afghan closest to him. The heavy soled jump boot easily shattered and splintered the bones beneath it, but he ground down even further to make sure the hands could never again be used for accurately aiming and firing a rifle.

The second terrorist knew what was coming and tried to protect his hands by hugging them against his body. Bear kicked him hard in the side, then knelt on his back to pin him down. He held the man's arms out, forcing his hands palm down on the floor. John picked up the sniper rifle and repeatedly smashed each hand with the butt of the heavy weapon. Ignoring the screams, he kept pounding away until they weren't hands anymore. Just two bloody misshapen lumps of torn flesh and crushed bone.

During the fire fight inside the cargo bay Colonel Masters had patched in the medic en route on the Special Ops ship. John and Bear had been busy taking out the four terrorists, but they still heard Bunny describing Able's wound in detail. They all knew he was critical and needed immediate surgery.

They quickly hogtied the two Afghans, putting plastic zip cuffs around their ankles, then cuffed their ruined hands behind their backs before tying their hands and feet together. They put black sacks over each of the soldier's heads and then ran out to help with Able.

"Get those lights back on!" Bunny shouted. When they came on it was a shock to see how pale and frail his friend was.

"Take me topside," Able said softly. His voice was so weak Bunny had to read his lips to understand what he said. Despite Bunny's efforts to stop the blood flow he was squatting in a wide red puddle as Able bled out.

"Medic's on the way brotha. You hold on. Hold on Able. You hear me?! Hold on!"

Running through the doorway, John reached them first. "Bear, grab his legs! Come on Bun, pick him up! Let's go, let's go!"

They made their way to the stairs and carefully brought Able up on deck.

"I can taste the salt in the air," Able whispered, slowly licking his lips. "Lay me down next to Bobby."

"There's the ship!" Mace said over the radio. "Medic on board in two minutes."

John kept pressure on the wound while they laid Able down on the make-shift bed next to his best friend Bobby, who was on his back with his arms spread wide. Bobby stirred, moving his head gently from side to side. He opened his eyes and blinked slowly, trying to clear away the cobwebs. Staring up at the night sky he said, "Man, my brains are scrambled. Where are we?"

"On a cruise," Able said.

"Did we get hurt?"

"Yeah, but you're gonna be fine."

"You too?"

"Me? Nah, I'm gone, man."

"But you're my brother."

"Always will be, partner. Gimme a squeeze."

Bobby bent his left elbow and wrapped his arm around Able.

"I'm going back to sleep," Bobby said.

"Adios, hermano," Able said.

Bobby closed his eyes and fell back into unconsciousness. Able closed his eyes and died. Still on their knees in a semi-circle around the two brothers, John, Bear, and Bunny sat there in silence. Finally, John spoke softly into his mic.

"Able's dead. Bobby needs evac for head trauma."

They all heard Mace scream out into the night. John looked towards the tower, shook his head, and exhaled deeply. He stood up and placed his hand on Bunny's shoulder. "Come on Bun, we still have to get the weapons and the prisoners offloaded. Let's get the torch and start cutting these deck plates open."

Bunny dried his eyes, gently touched his bloody hand to Able's cheek, and then hopped up and followed after John. Bear stayed on his knees speaking quietly to Able. After a few moments he got up and walked to the rail. He stood there alone staring into the night. He never looked at the twelve Navy SEALs when they boarded and they knew instinctively to keep their distance.

In the C-130 five miles overhead General Palmer smashed his fist down over and over again onto the desk in front of him.

"How many more good men have to die before we get Aziz Khan?"

"I don't know General... I just don't know," Colonel Masters said.

CHAPTER 35

WITNESS FOR THE PROSECUTION

Manhattan Court District
District Attorney Joshua Fishman's Office

DON'T LET THIS fool get you shook. He don't know you. Be cool BD. You just be cool and we're home free, Brendan Donahue said to himself.

He'd been ready to answer questions, but the DA just sat there looking at him, not saying a word. Brendan gave up trying to hold his stare and kept glancing nervously over at Mike Meecham for support. Brendan and Meecham sat next to each other in matching high-backed leather chairs in front of Fishman's huge mahogany desk. Meecham nodded, smiled easily and placed a hand on Brendan's knee to get him to stop furiously pumping his leg up and down.

"You need a towel?" Fishman asked, still gazing upon the scrawny, scabby, cadaverous human being who was sweating so heavily that drops fell from his stringy black hair and dripped from his thin fingers down onto the grey carpet. Fishman made a mental note to have the carpet steam cleaned. Meecham handed Donahue a handkerchief and Fishman watched his star witness pat his face, neck and wrist with quick, jerky motions. Fishman finally looked away in disgust while he weighed his options.

Brendan Donahue's life had been marked by a series of wrong turns, poor decisions and according to him, "Just a shit load of bad luck," since his glory days at Yale almost two decades ago. He came from a wealthy New England family who tolerated his drunken playboy lifestyle until the day he'd graduated with a solid 2.0. He thought he was headed for a cushy job in the family business, but his father quickly closed that door. He told his son that if he made something of himself in the world he would find a place for him. Until then he was on his own.

Thus began the freefall. He'd been fired from every job he ever held until he was finally deemed unhireable. It was just his bad luck that every boss he'd ever worked for had been a complete asshole and every person he'd ever worked with had been a jealous backstabber.

Throughout his steady downward spiral he'd briefly taken three different Mrs. Donahue's along for the ride. Once again, it was just his bad luck that he happened to marry "The three most cold-hearted bitches that ever lived."

He partied hard through it all, drinking socially from noon to 4AM. He dabbled with the coke at first, gradually increasing his consumption until he became a daily, but still functional user. He stopped functioning after his father died and completely cut him out of the will. In the last five years since his old man gave him a final "fuck you" from the grave he'd become a full blown junkie, mixing crack, heroin, and anything else he could get his hands on. He'd been shacked up with an equally addicted and emaciated hooker in Atlantic City when Meecham's men dragged him out and cleaned him up two days ago.

He had completely forgotten about the fight that left his college bud from London dead on the street in Manhattan all those years ago. Meecham himself had gone over everything. Brendan recognized his own handwriting in his signed statement, but he'd been cooking his brain for so long that large segments of his life were completely erased.

Hugh's death had actually been far less traumatic than his father humiliating him in front of his friends and the cops by calling him a total loser unworthy of the Donahue name. As if that night was somehow all his fault.

Meecham kept reminding him about the kid he'd described in his statement and showed him some pictures. He pointed to the one guy that had a scar on his face. He remembered the kid who hit Hugh had a scar, but not much else. He worked for hours and hours with Meecham going over it time and time again until he could recite the story like it happened yesterday.

Now you're sitting here with this asshole eyeballing you. Thinking he's better than you? Better than you? You're the man! You're the king!

God damn right I am. I'm the king that's about to get paid. Cha ching bitch. Meecham money motherfucka. That's real chedda you broke ass DA. When I get my paper I'm gonna come back here and take a shit on your fuckin' desk. Have you wipe my ass while your secretary's sucking my fat dick. I'm Brendan Donahue. You're gonna remember that name for the rest of your life you grey haired punk!

He's scared a you.

He fuckin' should be.

Fishman didn't know what was going on inside

Donahue's head, but he knew from the crazy look in his eyes that it wasn't good. He didn't want a psychotic skeleton having a fit in his office so he reluctantly broke the silence to give Meecham the bad news.

"Mike, this just won't work."

"Make it work, Fish," Meecham said venomously.

"How? John Bishop has more medals than Audie Murphy. Last week he became a national hero after what he did to those terrorists and now it seems he's a personal friend of the president of the United States. You think we can put this skel on the stand to testify against him in open court? Come on."

"Who you callin' a skel?"

"I'm talking about you, junkie, and if you say another word without being asked a direct question I'll have the two officers outside that door haul you down to the Tombs."

Donahue was about to stand up in protest, but Fishman kept him in his seat by raising his palm like a stop sign. "Asshole, I've seen your sheet. Fifteen arrests and two outstanding warrants. It'll be ninety days before you even see a judge. You sure you want to kick dope in city jail?"

Donahue slumped back down with a sigh. He pantomimed pulling a zipper across his mouth and then dramatically throwing away a key, which would have been funny if it hadn't revealed more about the depths of his dementia.

He can't talk to us like that! Don't just sit there! Do something!

I'm just waiting for my moment. He's about to get his.

That's why you're the king. Cause you're smarter than everyone else. You're right BD. Be patient. Then bam! He won't know what hit him.

He's gonna be on his ass lookin' up at my dick.

Spit on him when he's down. No, no! Piss on him, yeah piss on him!

That's the plan.

"Come on Mike, what do you expect me to do here?"

"I expect you do what you're told. First, we get his statement on the record. Do the deposition now and then I'll get him straight for the Grand Jury."

"Mike, let me state this clearly so there's no misunderstanding here. There is no way we can depose Mr. Donahue in his current condition, so today is out of the question. First we'll get him detoxed and then we'll determine how stable he is in a few weeks."

"A few weeks? Don't be ridiculous. We're on a schedule here and Bishop's indictment is just one component of a much broader plan. I need this to happen now."

"What is your grand plan for Bishop and his family?"

"That's above your pay grade Fish."

"I'm hearing some disturbing things."

"I have always embraced the nasty rumors that surround me and used them to my advantage. In any event, what you may have heard is irrelevant and what you think about what you heard is meaningless to me," Meecham said, waving his hand dismissively.

"Meaningless. Hmmm. Why's that?"

"Look at me as the CEO of a multi-billion dollar corporation and yourself as a low level employee in the mailroom or mopping floors."

"Well thanks for clarifying things for me. Never realized that you had such little respect for me or this office."

"The DA's office I respect. You I don't. It's only my benevolence that lets you sit behind that desk and keeps you out of jail. And let me assure you, the moment you stop being useful to me you'll be headline news. Neither of us wants that, so I suggest you keep me happy Little Fish."

Josh Fishman's eyes watered and he turned away. Meecham's triumphant stare and condescending tone sliced him to the bone. The fact that Meecham had spoken to him like this in front of a low bottom junkie made the wound that much deeper.

"No pouting now. And it's time you expressed some gratitude. Who would you rather have own you? Me, or the sexual predators in state prison?... Well?"

Meecham sat there waiting for the DA to compose himself while Donahue pretended to smoke a cigarette, blowing imaginary smoke rings towards the ceiling.

"You," Fishman said.

"Say it," Meecham said.

"What?"

"As I said, an expression of gratitude."

"Uh, thank you?"

"Was that a question?"

"No. I mean yes. Thank you, Mr. Meecham."

"Good. I'm glad we're friends again. And since we're friends you can call me Mike."

"Thanks Mike," Fishman said while he contemplated the best way to kill himself.

"Look, we've got work to do and you understandably missed the big picture here. Mr. Donahue is another victim of Bishop's homicidal behavior. Poor Brendan was so traumatized by witnessing his best friend's murder that he fell deeper and deeper into depression and a pattern of self-destructive behavior that ultimately manifested itself in his drug addiction... I'm just free forming here, but that had a nice flow to it. You should be writing this stuff down."

Fishman picked up a pen and started writing the word ASSHOLE over and over again on his desk pad.

"What about the other three witnesses? I understand they haven't been as co-operative as Mr. Donahue here."

"That's not your concern. Don't worry about them, they won't be a problem. Just focus on Brendan's statement and getting the indictment."

"Okay. But, you agree that we can't take his official statement today. Let me work with him overnight and hope-fully his condition will improve by the morning."

"Very well. I leave him in your hands, but you stay with him at all times. He doesn't leave your sight. Understood?"

"Don't worry. There are two beds in the main bedroom of the safe house. I'll bunk with him and we'll have a SWAT team in the living room."

"Good. You keep him protected and guard him as if your life depends on it. Because in reality… it really does."

Meecham gave Brendan a reassuring pat on the shoul-der and told him he'd see him in the morning. He nodded at Fishman on his way out and the three men from his private security detail were on their feet and ready to move when he came through the door.

After Meecham's departure Brendan sat there beaming with a big grin on his face.

"You have something to say?" Fishman asked.

"Yeah I do. Watching you get bitch slapped like that made me hungry. Order me up a ribeye, medium rare, with mashed potatas and a couple a Heinekens."

"That it?"

"I like your attitude man. I was gonna kick your ass a few minutes ago, but now I see we're on the same team here. Tell you the truth, this whole deal's got me stressin'. Get me a chick with some big titties. A redhead if you've got one handy, but I'll settle for dark hair. I need to plug a wet hole so I can get my mind right for tomorrow."

"You want a date?"

"Yeah man. Companionship asshole. Set it up!" Brendan said snapping his fingers.

"My pleasure." Fishman leaned back in his chair and said, "Come on in." Looking back at Brendan he said, "Here comes your companionship dipshit."

Clayton Unser, the CIA Deputy Director and Valdez family friend, came in through a side door. He was followed by two linebacker sized CIA leg breakers in dark suits with flat dead eyes.

"He's all yours," Fishman said.

"Let's go turd," one of the CIA muscle men said as he effortlessly dragged Brendan out of his seat, threw him up against the wall, and cuffed him.

"You fuck! You can't do this to me! You heard what Meecham saaiiidd!" Brendan's shouting was cut short by the liquid contents of a tiny needle injected into his neck that instantly slumped him down to his knees. The two goons picked up his limp body and carried him out.

Clayton waited for his men to leave and the door to close before he began speaking: "Great performance Mr. Fishman. Really well done."

"Yeah, well, if I hadn't fought him on this he would have known something was wrong."

"You sold it."

"Do you really think Meecham's going to kill the other witnesses?"

"I think he's going to try," Clayton said.

"And then blame it on the Valdez mob…"

"Exactly. Contrary to what that sociopath thinks you do see the big picture quite clearly."

"I guess. Just hard to think of the Valdez family as allies, even with the war on terror and all that."

"The ironies and complexities of life are a wonder to behold," Clayton said, then pulled out his cell phone and dialed a number.

"We're all set here. The package is secure…" Looking at Fishman as he spoke, he continued the conversation. "Yes, I'm here with him now. I will share your concerns, but I believe Mr. Fishman understands the gravity of the situation and the National Security issues involved here… Yes sir." Carefully placing the phone back in the inside pocket of his suit jacket he asked, "Do you?"

"Do I what?" Fishman replied.

"Understand the gravity of the situation."

"I understand I'm between a rock and a hard place and when I get thrown under the bus, which I definitely will, it won't be a soft landing. But I gave you Donahue didn't I? And you've got Meecham on tape. I'm probably going to end up in prison, but I've done everything you asked me to, haven't I?"

"You have and if it comes to that I see a presidential pardon in your future or worst case a short visit to a minimum security facility. More like a fat farm. Lift weights and jog for six months and sell your book for a million bucks when you get out."

"It's still prison pal."

"There are worse things."

"What could possibly be worse than a disgraced DA walking the yard?"

"Death my friend. Painful and violent death," Clayton said with a pleasant smile.

The Hudson River

Meecham didn't consider himself a short man, but because of his lack of height he liked it better standing up. It gave him more leverage. He made her stay on her knees while she frantically stroked him with her hands, desperate to end it. She even tried to take him in her mouth to get him to come faster, but he didn't want contact with any of her bodily fluids so he gave her a crisp slap that made her back off. Although his right arm was tiring from the effort, he hit her again and again and again with the hand crafted leather belt. Each satisfying crack of the belt drove him into a frenzy that engorged him further. His eyes wild, he finally he spasmed and groaned with pleasure, releasing onto her face and breasts.

Meecham put on a black silk robe monogrammed with his initials and ran his fingers through his thinning gray hair. The cocky, statuesque blonde bomb shell that had so confidently walked into his stateroom an hour before now lay curled up in the fetal position, shaking uncontrollably on the king sized bed. Indifferent to her sobbing, he stood there admiring his work. The Madame who sent the girl over had insisted on no scars this time so he'd only used a belt instead of his preferred whip. Part of him was disappointed that the bright red welts across her back, buttocks, and thighs would heal in a few weeks and she wouldn't have a permanent mark to remember him by. Meecham made a mental note to have her again. Next time he would brand her for life and gladly pay the agency the extra fee for damages.

She was already gone and back on dry land when he came out of the bathroom after a long hot shower. His assistant came in and informed him that his dinner guest had arrived early, as Meecham knew he would. Dressing quickly, he put on a pair of jeans with a white dress shirt and loafers.

The sun was setting, sending golden rays across the Hudson when Meecham came topside. He stepped onto the lower deck of his luxury yacht and saw the massive figure of Connie Bellusci standing near the rail smoking one of his Cubans.

"Stealing my cigars again, Connie," Meecham said, looking down at the three foot high glass humidor. It had a four digit combination lock on the door that was now wide open.

"I'm glad you buy the best. Nothing worse than stealing a cheap cigar."

"How did you crack the code so quickly?"

"It's one of my many talents."

"You'll have to teach me that one."

"Maybe someday." Connie didn't mention that the humidor in Meecham's home office had been left unlocked just like this one on the yacht. Nothing wrong with letting a rich client believe he had magical powers to crack a four digit combo in five seconds.

Yeah dumbass, opening an unlocked door is one of my many talents.

"Alright, let's get down to business," Meecham said, pouring himself a glass of wine and sitting down in a pillowed deck chair. "I paid you to kill Gonzalo Valdez, not wound him."

"Well, he's more than just wounded. I hit him in the

head. Don't know why that bandito is still alive, but he's in a coma on life support."

"I want him dead, but he wasn't even number two on my list. I only added Gonzalo at your suggestion and paid you quite well for it, as I recall. Bishop and Felix are my priorities."

"Understood. The Don is off the board for now which is a good thing. It leaves the family weak and vulnerable. If he doesn't go on his own in the next few days I'll personally finish the job."

"And the cousins?"

"Bishop is off hunting terrorists with his Special Ops pals, but they must be keeping him in the dark about his uncle, or he'd be at the hospital right now. They can't keep it a secret much longer. Maybe you can nudge things along. This has been big news here in the northeast, but there's not a lot of national or global coverage. Can you spread the word so our boy comes running home?"

"That I can." Meecham got on the phone and gave quick instructions to his son Caleb. After he hung up he asked, "And Felix?"

"No sign of him yet."

"Frankly Connie, I'm disappointed. Based on your stellar reputation I expected faster results here."

"Mike, when it comes to taking lives for a living the most important of the many lessons I've learned is that it pays to be patient. Targets don't usually stand still and say shoot me when you want them to. I understand we're just getting started here so let me reassure you. I've completed every single assignment I've ever accepted, and believe me, these three clowns aren't going to be around much longer. As you said, I have a stellar reputation to uphold."

"Okay, just understand that I have my own reputation

to maintain and everyday those two cousins are still breathing puts a big shit stain on me."

"Understood."

"Where are you with the witnesses?"

"The teams are about to go in. The contractors will all speak Spanish during the assault just as you instructed. I have to hand it to you on this one, Mike. Brilliant plan. Everyone's going to blame this on the Valdez mob."

"As long as there are no more slip ups. I want these witnesses gone and Gonzalo cuffed to his bed in the ICU."

"These guys are pros. All ex-military and heavy hitters. You want to listen in?"

"Really?"

Connie nodded. Pulling a small radio out of his pants pocket, he switched on the speaker button so they could both listen. Meecham's eyes were wild and wide. Connie killed for a living, but seeing Meecham lick his lips and eagerly rub his hands together in anticipation of a family being slaughtered made his stomach turn. He knew he would have to be very wary of this man in the future.

The Upper West Side
The Goldstein residence

Three hard looking men with light backpacks all wearing dark jeans and black shirts stepped out of a Land Rover double parked a few feet past the building's entrance. The driver kept the engine running and ready to move. He stayed behind the wheel, peering through the windows, and scanning the mirrors for any sign of trouble.

"All clear," a voice said in Spanish over the radio.

"We're going in," was the quick response. Meecham sat on the edge of his chair listening to the action unfold.

An elderly woman screamed, then collapsed on the sidewalk. She cried out for help and the uniformed doorman ran out to assist her. The three men moved fast. They entered the building without being seen, crossed the empty lobby, and headed up in the elevator. They exited on the Goldstein's floor, and checked the hallway in both directions before removing their packs. Opening the folding stocks on three matching machine guns, each man slapped in a thirty round magazine, cocked his weapon, and put it on full auto. In front of the Goldstein's door one of them stepped forward and blasted the locks with a short burst before he kicked it in.

They ran in firing at the four figures sitting on a couch in the living room. The shooters were stunned when the mannequins they had just killed exploded into white dust. The last thing they heard were the three shots that ended their lives.

Christmas walked over to the dead assassins while his team looked down the hallway for more targets. It wasn't necessary to check any of them for a pulse. All three had big ugly gaping holes in their heads. He quickly went through each man's pockets, placing everything he found in a large plastic bag. When he was done he reached down and removed the only earpiece that wasn't covered in blood. He put it in his own ear and spoke into the mic.

"These guys were chumps Connie. Hope they weren't you're A Team."

"Who is this?" Connie asked.

"We met a few years back."

"Refresh my memory."

"A dark alley in Barcelona."

"Christmas?"

"That's me."

"I put a bullet in you the last time you interfered with my business. You should've learned your lesson pal. Now I'm gonna make a very nasty example of you."

"Hey Connie, you and Meecham enjoy the cruise. I'll be you seeing you both real soon," Christmas said, then ended the transmission.

Connie looked at Meecham and shook his head.

"What the fuck just happened here?"

"It was a set up."

"So the Goldstein's are still alive?"

"Yep, either in protective custody or more likely in a Valdez safe house. I'm sure the two other teams that went after the witnesses in Connecticut and Boston are dead too."

"That's unacceptable. Goldstein along with the other witnesses all have to die so they can't contradict Brendan's testimony. How are you going to fix this Connie?"

"Don't you see what's happened here? Christmas is Gonzalo's top soldier and he's one of the best there is. The game just changed in a big way. They knew we were coming. My troops are dead and there's a team of Valdez hitters coming for me... and you."

"Me?"

"You heard what the man said. When a man like Christmas says he'll be seeing you it ain't for a social visit. I'd advise you to get off this boat and hire an army to protect you. Your rent-a-cops won't cut it in this fight." Connie got up and headed to the rail.

"Where are you going?" asked Meecham, his brow wet with fear.

"It's a war now. I've got to kill them all before they kill me. Good luck Mike. If you live I'll come back for the rest of money when this is over."

Connie climbed over and launched himself off and away from the fast moving yacht. He went feet first into the dark waters of the wide Hudson River. Meecham ran to the spot where he'd jumped. His eyes straining to see, he got a brief glimpse of Connie swimming hard towards the Jersey side of the river more than five hundred yards away before the night swallowed him up.

Meecham shivered. He told the Captain to stop and within minutes he was motoring towards the 79th Street Boat Basin in a dingy with a four man security team. They tied up to the main dock and bolted up the stairs, two guards in front and two following, with Meecham in the middle. Guns drawn and ready, they ran over to a stretch limo that was decorated with pink and white flowers waiting to pick up passengers from a wedding party. The short Latin driver with a pock marked face put up only token resistance against the force of armed men. He even tipped his chauffer's hat and held the door for them after Meecham pressed a thick wad of cash into his hands. He was whistling beautifully when he got behind the wheel.

"Driver. What song is that?" Meecham asked.

"It's called 'Pedro Navaja,' a ballad by Rubén Blades. From his early days."

"It's lovely. Now stop the fucking whistling and raise the divider so I can speak to my men in private."

"As you wish sir," the driver said pleasantly. He pressed the button on the dash board to raise the partition.

Sitting back comfortably in the plush rear seat, Meecham let out a sigh of relief when the car pulled out and sped away. The men on his security detail relaxed as well. None of them noticed the solid click from the door locks being set or the thin wisps of smoke that rose up from the hidden vents until it was too late. They all hammered away at the tinted, shatter proof windows until one by one they passed out in a heap on the floor.

Benji Medina resumed his whistling while he drove the limo through Central Park. He continued east until he reached the southbound entrance of the FDR Drive, then headed downtown to LES with his five passengers sleeping peacefully in the back.

CHAPTER 36
DINNER

GONZALO VALDEZ'S NORMAL routine was a series of daily rituals designed to keep his mind sharp and his body strong. Each morning he was up at 5AM for a two hour workout followed by a steam, shower, and shave before breakfast. But the war had kept him busy. He hadn't exercised or steamed in days, and this morning, for the first time in more than twenty years, he forgot to shave.

It was time to get back to basics, though tonight he was changing the order of the routine. At nearly 10PM he was shaving first before he entered the gym. Gonzalo shaved the way he tried to live his life. Slowly and precisely. He carefully drew the straight razor across his skin, scraping off the stubble and avoiding the numerous scars that marked his face. When he was done he removed a hand towel from a bowl full of ice water, closing his pores with the cool cloth. Continuing the daily the ritual, he dipped the towel in again and applied it to his face once more.

Still taking his time, he put on black shorts and laced up his black boxing shoes. Flexing his feet to test the shoes as he walked, he made his way over to a massage table where he sat down and held out his hands.

Felix's leg was swollen tight and throbbing from Omar's knife wound. He'd been sitting in a metal chair with his leg up on a stool in front of him watching Gonzalo prepare. He got up, used his cane to hobble over, and began taping his uncle's hands. His uncle grew up fighting without protection in bare knuckled matches. The knuckles were still covered in callouses and the strong dark hands were like stones, but Felix taped them anyway. When he was done he helped Gonzalo put on the thin gloves that were designed to inflict the maximum amount of damage.

"Hurt him, Tio. Make him suffer," Felix said.

Gonzalo didn't say anything. His smoldering eyes held those of his nephew and adopted son. Finally he nodded his head in response and hopped down from the table. Bare chested, he walked out of the locker room with Felix limping behind.

The Lower East Side gym simply called "Gladiators" was usually crowded and noisy with hard-core training going on twenty-four hours a day. Tonight the gym was deathly quiet and empty of everyone except the Valdez mob. And the man who sat in a chair in far corner of the ring.

The Valdez brothers, Antonio, Benji, the Pro KEDDS team and Christmas eagerly watched Gonzalo make his way over. He passed through them and climbed into the ring without a word being spoken. His opponent, also dressed for battle in white shorts and black shoes, jumped up from his chair.

"You? This is impossible! You were shot in the head."

"The man you hired shot my brother, Sesa. He fights for his life, just as you are about to fight for yours."

"I know you're low life street scum, Valdez, but you can't be serious. Let me go now and I promise I won't say anything to the authorities. Otherwise, I can assure you that you and everyone in this room will be arrested for kidnapping. Do you hear me?" he said, spreading his arms to address everyone outside of the ring. "You will all be incarcerated for the rest of your lives. I walk out of here now I will protect you. You have my word."

"Your word?"

"Yes. I am an educated man with a family history that goes back hundreds of years. My word counts."

"Our family history goes back much farther than yours and education comes in many forms. All that matters here is that I am a man of honor and, as you say, my word counts. There is only one way out of this for you."

"I fight you."

"No. You kill me."

"Kill you?"

Gonzalo nodded. "That's the only way you walk out of here."

"I doubt it, old man. After I beat you to death your men will rip me apart."

"Every man in this room begged me to let them torture and kill you. I refused them all. I'm the head of this family and what I say goes. My commands will be honored... even after death. Kill me here in this ring and you live."

"Fair enough," Michael Meecham said.

"There is only one condition."

"Which is?"

"Confess."

"Confess to what?"

"There's no point in lying, Meecham. We already know

most of what you have done, but I need to hear it all here and now. Tell me everything, truthfully. Then we will see if you are man enough to end my life."

"And if I don't?"

Gonzalo pointed across the room. "You go there," he said. "We all sit and watch you die. And I have one more promise for you… it will last a very long time."

Meecham stared at the long table that looked like it came straight out of a torture dungeon from the Dark Ages. He recognized his limo driver when Benji Medina lit the mini blow torch and tightened the flame. He held it up in a menacing display and with his free hand he silently beckoned Meecham over.

Michael Meecham, like many of the Meecham men before him, was born without the key ingredients that allow human beings to socialize effectively. He didn't feel empathy or compassion. He was incapable of compromise and he rejoiced in the suffering of others. These defects of character or missing strands of DNA had been swapped out for an innate ability to sense weakness in his fellow man. He preyed on those weaknesses to advance his own position and to hurt as many people that he could. On the flip side, he was a calculating man. For those that were too strong or too powerful he lay coiled like a viper, waiting for the opportunity to strike them down.

He stared down into the hard, hate-filled eyes of the men surrounding the ring. He knew each and every one of them wanted him dead, but these were street thugs and small time gangsters far below his station. Dying by their hands was not an option. It would dishonor his family. And he still had so much to do. He was going to change this country, perhaps the entire world.

Meecham knew his superior breeding and intellect would keep him alive. He weighed his options and quickly went on the offensive.

"Before I say anything I think you all owe me some gratitude."

"What!" Felix shouted.

"Please explain," Gonzalo said.

"My team did extensive research on you and your family. In the course of the investigation we uncovered something very interesting."

"I'm listening."

"It seems extremely likely that our families have crossed paths before. My great, great, great grandfather was a ship's captain. He sailed regularly to Panama and kept meticulous records, which I still have. One of his clients was a wealthy land owner named Porfirio Valdez. I believe some of your ancestors were in his employ."

Gonzalo stared at Meecham in disbelief.

Could it be?

Can this be true?

"So, he was a slave trader."

"Importer, exporter," Meecham said with a smile.

"And he sold his human cargo to the murderer Porfirio Valdez."

"Porfirio is credited with taming vast portions of the Panamanian frontier. He was and is a hero in the history of your country."

"Not to us." Gonzalo said. Outwardly he remained calm and in control. Only the heat in his yellow eyes intensified as he recalled the stories about Porfirio. Horrific accounts of suffering and death passed down through the generations by the lucky few who managed to escape into the mountains. The plantation had been a death camp where the then Don Valdez raped, tortured, and murdered his own slaves.

"You need to stay objective," Meecham said, edging closer and gaining confidence. Gonzalo was almost thirty years older than he was and the man was clearly rattled by their dialogue.

"At the very least you owe the man a debt for your name. More importantly, you owe me and my family your thanks. Without my forefather's help you would not be where you are today enjoying the luxuries of life in this great country. You would still be living in your natural habitat."

"Our natural habitat?"

"Do I really have to spell it out for you? Africa of course. Eating termites, and climbing trees like the monkeys that you are."

Though Gonzalo had anticipated the attack, he was surprised by Meecham's speed and accuracy. He dodged two of the blows, but the third, an overhand right, caught him on the side of the head.

"And so we begin," Gonzalo said, baring his teeth.

"You underestimated me Valdez. I've been training in the ring for years."

"On the contrary." Gonzalo stepped in and peppered Meecham with four light punches to the face and body before moving away. "Now let's see if you've trained hard enough."

Meecham was amazed by Gonzalo's speed and balance, but was unimpressed by his punching power. Visualizing a quick victory he charged forward. He didn't see the punch that stopped him in his tracks. The body shot sent him backwards and dropped him to his knees.

"Stand up so I can keep thanking you."

Meecham realized that it was he who had underestimated his opponent.

"If you can't rise on your own my men will hold you up for the remainder of the session."

"I am a better man than you in every way," he said, steadying himself and bouncing on his feet like a pro boxer.

"Prove it."

Gonzalo moved in again, ducking and blocking Meecham's increasingly desperate blows with his shoulders, wrists and elbows. Growing bored with the charade he fired back one devastating shot after another.

"I thank you." Two vicious punches sent Meecham's front teeth flying from his mouth.

"The Valdez family thanks you." Thwack, thwack. Meecham felt his ribs break.

"My brother Sesa thanks you." Bam, bam, bam, bam. Meecham managed to block those four, but the bones in both his forearms fractured from the impact.

"My nephews thank you." Crack. His nose was broken.

He ran, but there was nowhere to go. Gonzalo followed his every twist and turn, hitting him again and again. Finally Meecham stopped and leaned heavily against the ropes. Blood poured from his nose and mouth. His broken arms dangled uselessly at his sides.

"No more," Meecham said, shaking his head.

"Final offer. Confess and you live. Otherwise we continue."

"You swear to let me go?"

"I promise you will live."

Meecham stared hard into the eyes that glowed like fires in Gonzalo's dark face. He knew he was out of options. His only hope was that the old Don was a man of his word.

"Okay, okay. It's not like I'm telling you anything you don't already know."

"Say it."

"Yes, I hired Connie Bellusci to kill you."

"Me alone?"

"You, John and Felix."

"Why?"

"They insulted me and got me fired."

"So this was all about your pride and ego?"

"I don't know. Maybe. It is who I am."

"You had already hired the hit man. Then why bring up the case against my nephew with the DA?"

"Just being efficient. Making sure I had a backup plan in case Connie didn't come through."

"That's it?"

"That's it," Meecham said.

Gonzalo cracked him again, breaking another rib. Meecham screamed in pain and began crying hysterically.

"No, no, no! You swore."

"There is more. What else?"

"The witnesses."

"We know about them. Tell me what I don't know."

"Palmer… and… Kolter," Meecham blubbered out in between sobs.

"General Palmer and Director Kolter are on your hit list?"

"Yes, yes, yes! That's everything, I swear! Now let me go so I can see a doctor."

"Yes, you will get your doctor. Later. First you will join some friends for dinner."

"Dinner?"

"Yes Michael Meecham. After all you're the guest of honor."

Christmas and Antonio climbed into the ring and roughly dragged him out. His legs were gone so they carried him to the locker room and stripped him before throwing him in the shower. Naked, terrified and suffering terribly from the pain he managed to speak in a shaky child-like voice.

"What're you going to do?"

"Just getting you cleaned up man. You know it's important to wash before every meal," Christmas said.

His body was vigorously scrubbed with a long handled brush until his skin was red, then soaped and rinsed in scalding hot water. They weren't really concerned with Meecham's hygiene. They were removing any of Gonzalo's hair, skin, or DNA that may have been transferred in the one sided fight.

Despite the heat from the shower Meecham was shaking uncontrollably. "I need a doctor. I think I'm dying."

"Not yet. This will help with the pain," Benji said. He injected Meecham with a short needle that sent him floating into oblivion.

The Bronx, New York

"How long do you think they will wait?" Felix asked.

"Not long," Gonzalo said.

The Valdez men and their soldiers stood together watching through the high fence. No one else spoke. They watched and waited in the darkness. All of them stared at the lone figure that lay unmoving in a field of green grass on the other side of the fence and across a wide moat.

Mike Meecham opened his eyes and was immediately shocked by the intense pain in his nose. That pain was quickly overshadowed by the agony of each breath as his lungs expanded into his broken ribs. He tried to move, but his body refused to respond. He could blink. He could open and close his mouth. He could even move his head from side to side. Other than that he was completely paralyzed.

He felt the wind on his skin and knew he was naked. All he could see from his prone position at ground level was thick grass and tall trees around him and a cloudless night sky above.

"Where the fuck am I?" he said aloud.

He thought he heard movement in the bushes to his left.

"Help. Help me! I'm over here!"

Other than the loud screeching of birds in the distance his calls went unanswered. Then from behind his head and out of his line of vision he felt the impact of footsteps running towards him.

"Thank God! I'm here. I'm badly hurt. Hurry."

Meecham strained to see who was coming to his rescue, but the steps came to an abrupt halt beyond his line of sight.

"Please, please. I can pay you. Anything you want. Just help me!"

The heavy feet moved closer.

"Believe me, today is your lucky day my friend," Meecham said.

Sensing he was about to be saved, his fear vanished, and a sudden calm came over him. The moment was short lived when he looked up at the massive head above him. Hot, heavy breath beat down into Meecham's face. The thick yellow and black mane shook when the four hundred pound lion roared in triumph.

"Oh God. Please no."

The lion walked around Meecham, baring his fangs and sniffing him as he moved. The steady flow of blood from Meecham's nose and mouth was driving the big cat into a frenzy. His powerful muscles rippled with tension and excitement.

"Get away! Get away!!! You get away, God damn it!!!"

The lion was unimpressed by the orders. He put a heavy paw on Meecham's chest and then lay down next to the man who expected to become president of the United States of America. The lion's rough tongue was designed to scrape meat from bones. With each lick large patches of skin were ripped away from Meecham's face.

"Nooooo!!!!"

The lion didn't seem to mind or notice the frantic screaming that increased when he sank in his teeth and tore off Meecham's right cheek.

"Oh God, oh God. Please no!!!"

Meecham didn't hear the other two lions when they came charging in. One female bit into his left arm and the other sank her fangs deep into his right leg.

"Ahhhheeeeeeyyyyeee!!!"

The male didn't want to share his dinner and a violent snarling tug of war ensued. Each female ran off with an appendage while the king of beasts gorged himself on the remainder of Michael Bascomb Meecham.

"I think he's still alive," Christmas said.

"Good," Felix said.

"The man claimed he was a lion," Gonzalo added.

"Those cats didn't recognize him," Carlos said.

"Maybe they did," Fiero said. "Maybe they did."

The lion opened his mouth wide and clamped his teeth down on Meecham's head. He picked him up and dragged what was left of him into the bushes to finish his meal in private. The Valdez men and their soldiers lingered for another minute, staring through the fence and into the night. Then they all turned and headed back to their cars in the big empty parking lot. Driving away, they all passed the big green sign at the exit.

WE HOPE YOU HAD FUN AT THE BRONZ ZOO COME BACK SOON!

CHAPTER 37
FRIENDSHIP

Khost, Afghanistan
FOB Lone Wolf

AFTER THE TAKING of the Al Badir the weapons and prisoners were off loaded and the ship sunk. The cache was impressive and the inventory of sophisticated land mines, detonators, IED's, RPG's, mortars, sniper rifles, machine guns, ammo and advanced communications gear had been kept out of enemy hands. Everything was carefully photographed and placed on disc. The disc, along with a scripted video recorded message from John describing how he and a handful of Valdez soldiers had captured the weapons and killed the crew, was placed in the right hands to make its way to Aziz. The response from Aziz Khan came back sooner than expected and the meeting was set.

"Keep pushing! Keep pushing!" Bunny shouted.

John's whole body was shaking. He struggled up time and time again, willing himself to finish.

"Forty eight, forty nine, fifty! Great job, Johnny."

John rolled over on his back, sucking wind and trying

to recover from the insane workout that began at sunrise with a five mile run and concluded with five hundred sit ups and ten sets of fifty pushups.

"Dude, you're killing me. We're gonna be too tired to fight."

"Keeping you razor sharp, man."

"More like wearing me down to a dull blade. I'm hitting the showers."

"Hey, we're not done."

"I am. I sent Maria an e-mail yesterday to let her know we were okay and I could tell from her response that something's wrong."

"What she say?"

"It wasn't what she said, it was how she said it. It might be nothing, but I'm going to call her after I clean up just to make sure," John said. He dried himself off with an extra tee shirt and headed back to the barracks. Unsure of what to do, Bunny hung back for a moment, then jogged after him to catch up.

"Hey Johnny. Hold up."

"What's up Bun?"

"I… uh… man, I just don't know how to say this."

"You know you can tell me anything man."

"I'm sure she's fine."

"Dude, you're talking, but what's coming out of your mouth don't make sense."

Bunny was struggling. He didn't know how to tell John that Gonzalo was in a coma. Before he could say anything else they saw two of their wounded Team Razor pals making their way towards them. Sergeants Brian Ilchuck and Jimmy Waters called out on the way over. They had both been shot the week before when the team got ambushed in

Khost. Ilchuck's arm was in a sling and Waters was walking with crutches.

"Hey guys," Brian said.

"Heard you were back in town," said Jimmy.

"How you guys healing up?" John asked as they all shook hands.

"Ah, you know. Feels better each day," Brian said, gently moving his arm.

"Can't wait to get back into the shit," Jimmy said. "Wish we could roll with you Johnny."

"Me too, brotha," John said.

"You hurt 'em before you put 'em down. You hear me man? You hurt 'em. The major died in pieces and DC got burned alive. That's no way for good men to die," Jimmy said.

"We're on it," Bunny said.

"Alright, we'll leave you to it. Headed over to the CP to see if there's anything we can do. Man the comm gear or something. Anything."

They said their goodbyes and were turning away when Jimmy stopped and gently hit Brian with one of his crutches. They came back looking very uncomfortable.

"Look Johnny, we just want to say how sorry we are about your family."

"Thanks guys, I really appreciate it."

"Any word on how he's doing?"

"Chris? No, uh, he died from his wounds. We buried him on Wednesday."

"Yeah we heard. Our condolences. But, what about your uncle? Is he going to make it?"

"My what? Jimmy, what are you talking about?"

"Ah fuck! Man, I'm sorry. I thought you knew."

"Say it."

"Your uncle Gonzalo man. He was shot a few days ago. We read it in today's paper. It's right here."

"Tio? He was…" John didn't finish the sentence. His hands wouldn't stop shaking while he gripped the newspaper. He blinked away the tears so he could read the article describing the assassination attempt and the details of the head wound. When he was done he looked up at his friends, nodded his head and then stumbled away. Jimmy and Brian called after him, but he never stopped or turned back.

"Damn, Bunny. We just assumed he knew."

"He didn't, but I did. Just couldn't bring myself to tell him after all the shit that's gone down and everything we still gotta do."

"What now?"

"He needs to refocus."

"How's he gonna do that?"

"I'm gonna give him something to get mad at so he can keep going."

"What's that?

"Me," Bunny said.

Bunny trudged along following his friend's trail until he caught up to him. He gently put his hand on John's shoulder to hold him in place. John kept his head down. The paper was still gripped tightly in his right hand.

"They shot my Tio in the head Bunny."

"I know."

"They say he's in a coma."

"I know."

"Doesn't say when or how."

"It happened at Calixto's house the night we left. Sniper was in that big tree a mile out."

"How do you know? It doesn't say anything about that here," John said, finally looking up at Bunny.

"I already knew."

"You knew? You *knew*?"

"Yeah. I've known for a few days now."

John launched himself at Bunny, punching him over and over again in the face. Bunny kept his hands at his sides while John battered him to the ground. John knelt over him. Bunny lay there unmoving and made no attempt to avoid the blows that kept on coming until John finally ran out of gas. His rage purged, he suddenly stopped hitting the big man and collapsed down onto his friend's chest. Bunny wrapped his arms around John and let him cry it out. There was no shame or embarrassment. They were friends and brothers.

"Why? Why didn't you tell me?"

"You know why, Johnny. We were heading into the shit. We still are. You gonna be okay?"

"Yeah man. I'm okay."

"Then you better let me up. This ain't a "don't ask don't tell" Army anymore, but we're lying here hugging it out in broad daylight."

"Asshole. Let's see how bad it is."

John got up and helped Bunny to his feet. He had a split lip, blood was dripping from his nose, and there was a big cut above his left eye.

"Damn, I'm sorry man. That's gonna need a few stitches."

"Glad you still hit like a girl."

John smiled. He knew what Bunny had just done for him. How do you thank someone for being that type of friend?

"You going to be alright?"

"Yeah, yeah, no worries. Go call Maria."

John nodded and took off running. Bunny dabbed his face with a handkerchief to keep the blood out of his eyes.

Ouch. That little man just kicked your ass dude.

Yeah, but we love that little man don't we?

Yeah we sure do.

Gladly take a beating to help him get his head right and keep him in the game.

We promised to get him back home safe.

We did and we will.

Way to take one for the team, Bunny Rabbit.

Yeah, yeah, I'm a legend in my own mind.

Let's find a medic.

You know I'm scared of needles.

Then tighten up your panties boy.

CHAPTER 38
MACHO

Khost Province, Eastern Afghanistan

MACHO HADN'T SLEPT in the two days since his armed escorts had picked him up on the Pakistani side of the border. As expected, his clothes were taken and he'd endured an invasive search where they'd roughly examined every crack and orifice of his body. There were numerous starts and stops, car switches, and directional changes. Eventually he was locked in the back of a minivan without rear seats or windows and driven on what must have been the bumpiest roads in the world. They traveled for hours and sweltering mid-morning sun turned his confined space into an oven. The metal floor and roof were hot plates. For most of the ride he tried to keep himself balanced in a painful squat with his hands at his sides to avoid touching anything.

He felt sick to his stomach and he knew what it meant. The CIA doctor had told him to expect it. It meant he was running out of time. It meant he was dying. He just had to stay alive and on his feet until he reached Aziz.

After nearly cooking to death in the van they began

the long uphill march. His guts were on fire, his legs were cramping, and his tongue was thick from dehydration. He dismissed the nausea, pain, and thirst by thinking of his son Chris. Willing himself up higher and higher into the mountains, he thought only of Chris. Forcing each foot forward one step at a time he thought only of Chris. He traced back every memory, every image of his baby boy from birth to death. In the end, after mentally burying his son once more, he thought only of Aziz Khan.

Macho knew they were getting close. The mountain region they were traversing was harsh and barren, but they weren't alone. There were sentries on the slopes above them and the attitude of his security detail had suddenly shifted from relaxed and bored to tense and alert.

The shadows were growing long when Macho spotted a plateau farther up along the steep trail and he assumed that was the meeting place. He was looking up at it when he was suddenly yanked off the path and pulled through a hidden crevice between two massive boulders. Immersed in total darkness, he stumbled forward blindly until an unseen hand grabbed him by his wrist and another roughly shoved him from behind. Barely wide enough for a man, the passage twisted and turned taking them deep inside the mountain. Macho bumped and scraped his way along the narrow rock walls until they gradually widened and then opened up into a huge high ceilinged chamber.

Bright lights strung along the walls illuminated the massive cave that looked like an ant farm with many smaller side chambers and numerous tunnels branching off in different directions. Standing at its mouth Macho could see that it served as a barracks for the insurgents. He estimated there were at least sixty armed men moving about and sensed that there were many more beyond his line of sight.

His escorts marched him to a rough wooden table in the center of the room. Although everything he was originally wearing had been confiscated and replaced with the dirty clothes and old sandals he now wore, he was thoroughly searched again and scanned for electronics. Satisfied that he posed no threat, the men stepped back, but AK-47's remained pointed at him from three sides.

Macho noted how well trained and disciplined his guards were. They never took their eyes off him. Not even when a curtain was thrust aside and Aziz Khan stepped out of a side room. Macho had carefully studied the CIA case file and the few pictures of the man he came half way around the world to see. From where he stood twenty feet away there was no mistaking the fearsome face. Aziz's forehead was creased and scarred, his dark eyes were deeply set under a heavy brow, and his long hooked nose reached down towards his thick full beard.

As always, Aziz wore simple clothes and dressed all in black. His frayed turban, torn shirt, loose dusty pants and old boots exemplified his meager lifestyle and his fanatical commitment to his cause.

I get it. You want everyone to know you're the bad guy and you dress the part.

Aziz walked towards him with several men in tow. He stopped on the opposite side of the table and stared quizzically at Macho. Macho held his gaze, giving nothing away.

"You are a boxer," Aziz said.

"Was. A lifetime ago."

"Once a fighter always a fighter. The fire may grow weaker with time, but it never truly dies. Is this not true?"

"It is. You speak good English."

"And Russian. A true soldier must always know his enemy."

"Good policy."

"It seems I now have to learn Spanish," Aziz said with a slight grin.

"Not after tonight," Macho replied with an easy going smile.

Aziz snapped his fingers and two of his soldiers raced over with chairs. He gestured for Macho to sit and he did the same. The rest of his men remained standing.

"Coffee?"

"Why not."

Macho had been told to expect this ritualized greeting before any meaningful discussions took place. He was happy that Aziz adhered to Afghan custom. It gave him time. While he waited and watched the brief pouring ceremony he repeatedly ground his right front incisor against his bottom tooth until the new lead-lined cap came off. The liquid that had been stored in it gently slid down his throat and he immediately felt the heat as his body temperature begin to rise. He had to focus to keep his hand steady when he reached for the cup of thick, sweet, scalding hot coffee.

"Good?"

"Very."

"Excellent. Now tell me Mr. Valdez, how do you plan to kill me?"

The question caught Macho off guard, but he kept his cool. "Kill you? I'm only here to negotiate."

"I don't believe you."

"I'm alone and unarmed. How could I kill you Aziz?"

"Yes, how? That is what I have asked myself."

"Then why am I here?"

"Curiosity. And my weapons of course."

"We have them. It was the only way to get your attention."

"You have it. What do you propose?"

"Do your men understand me?"

"No. None that are here."

"Then what I propose… what my family proposes is a trade."

"I checked. Your family is no longer involved in drugs."

"We're getting back in. We see inefficiencies and weakness in the global heroin markets. My family, and me personally, have suffered a great deal from the events of the past week. We've suffered, but we're strong. Our eyes are dry, our minds are clear and we see a great opportunity. An opportunity for us both."

"You lost a son?"

"I did."

"Your only son."

"Yes."

"Yet you claim you are only here to discuss business?"

"That's the truth," Macho said shrugging his shoulders.

Aziz had an uncanny ability to see the hidden truths that people tried to hide, but he found the small dark skinned man in front of him hard to read. Confounded, he continued to stare, casually stroking his beard while looking for any signs of deception.

Could it be? Could it be?

He didn't think so. Aziz knew that very few men in the long history of men could be ruthless enough to sacrifice their own blood for the greater good. Men who could take control of their own destiny by placing personal gain above the violent death of those they held most near and dear. He knew because he was one of those rare few.

He reflected upon how he had betrayed his own family

so many, many years before. His older brother Aman had been the leader of their clan, but he was born a hundred years too late, looking back in time for all his answers and blind to the changing world around him. Despite being the second son Aziz always knew in his heart that he was the chosen one and it was he alone who must lead. He had the vision to take his people out of the Dark Ages and the cunning to defeat their enemies. He would rule his tribe and one day, with Allah's blessing, the entire country.

Aman was reckless, and with so many hunting him his reign should have been brief. He was a fearsome fighter who led from the front lines, but a man who just wouldn't die. Aziz had tried to be patient. For years he watched and waited for his turn. Many times he had come close to shooting Aman himself. Staring at his brother's back he reached for the pistol time and time again only to withdraw his trembling hand and sneak away in shame.

Ultimately Aziz had known that he could never pull the trigger. When he secretly met with the Russians the Colonel had assured him that they only wanted Aman. No one else was to be harmed. In the end the Russians had betrayed him just as he had betrayed his brother.

Aziz remembered standing high above the Korum Valley with his two young sons and his nephew Amir looking down on the clan. He remained strangely detached when he watched his mother, his wife and his daughters executed along with every person he had ever known and loved. Did he take his sons and Amir to scout in the mountains because some deep dark part of him had suspected the Colonel's intentions? He didn't know and it didn't matter. In the end it was Allah's will. His sons didn't survive the war with the

Russians and now Amir was dead. Killed for his own stupidity and failure.

When Aziz looked inward into his heart of hearts he knew that the massacre at Korum had set him free. A cruel blessing from God. With all the hard work ahead there had been no time to mourn. He had accomplished so much since then and there was still so much more to do. He would beat the Americans. Then all of Afghanistan would lay down before him. But first he would kill this little man and his entire family for stealing his weapons.

"Tell me what you propose," Aziz said. He felt like a cat toying with a mouse.

"We will give you back your weapons as a sign of good faith. You will sell us uncut heroin at twenty percent below your market rate for the next two years so we can solidify our position. After that we will pay you ten percent below market."

"What else?"

"As we are giving you a sign of good faith we will need one from you in return." Macho looked cautiously up at the lieutenants that were standing nearby.

"Speak freely. They cannot understand your words."

"First, call off the assassins who hunt my nephew."

"Consider it done."

"And then we will need you to turn some of your people over to us."

"To be killed?"

"Of course. We have taken losses that demand a very public display of vengeance. Give us one or two key people and a few soldiers so our enemies will see our power. Then we can start our business without any bad blood between us."

"Before we get to that let us go back to the twenty percent. That is too much. More coffee?"

"Please."

Macho Valdez and Aziz Khan continued negotiating and making promises that neither man intended to keep.

Khost, Afghanistan
FOB Lone Wolf

John felt awful for losing his cool with Bunny. He'd let his emotions take control and he'd used the big man as his personal punching bag. It was unacceptable behavior, especially in a war zone where clear thinking was the key to survival. More importantly, it was contrary to everything that his uncle Gonzalo had ever taught him. He promised himself that no matter what else life had in store for him never again would he lose focus by having such an infantile public meltdown. He also swore to somehow make it up to Bunny after all this was over.

When John finally called Maria they both knew they had to keep it short. He'd prepared himself for the worst, but during their brief conversation he was faced with a whole new set of conflicting emotions. At first he was relieved and beyond happy when Maria told him that Gonzalo was in fact unharmed. That relief was quickly erased and a dull pounding began at his temples and then spread across the front of his head when he learned that his uncle Sesa was the one barely clinging to life from the assassin's bullet.

After the call he hit the showers, geared up and headed over to the mobile Special Operations Command center. General Marcus Palmer, Colonel Steve Masters and three A-Teams were already there for the briefing. Bunny came in a few minutes later, stitched up, swollen and bandaged.

"Okay, listen up. Our man is in these mountains here," said General Palmer pointing out an area on the wall map that they were all familiar with.

"How are we tracking him, sir?" asked one of the Special Forces sergeants.

"He's radioactive."

"Sir?"

"The man that is leading us to Aziz Khan ingested a small dose of a radioactive isotope. It gives off just enough of a signature so that we can track him by air from long range."

"Don't we expect the meeting with Aziz to take place in a mountain cave? How do we track him then?" another sergeant asked.

"When our man is absolutely certain that he's next to Aziz Khan he will break off a recently placed false lead-lined cap on his tooth. Inside of that cap is a much higher dose of the liquid isotope that will combine with what is already in his system. We will then know exactly where he is, wherever he is. Even if he's deep inside a mountain we'll see him."

Everyone in the room mulled this over for a second. Another Special Forces sergeant said aloud what everyone else was thinking.

"Just to be clear, General. This man is intentionally ingesting a lethal dose of radiation so we can pinpoint the meeting place with Aziz… and then he's waiting for our bombers to dump their payload on his head?"

"That's correct," Palmer said stiffly.

"Who is this guy?"

"The brave man giving his life for this mission?"

"Yes sir. I'd like to know his name."

"His name is Macho."

"Macho? That's for sure. Is he a local asset?"

"No he's not. Macho Valdez is a civilian volunteer. He's also the uncle of the man standing right behind you. Sergeant John Bishop."

Every man in the room had turned to face John. They all nodded in unison, conveying their respect and admiration. A silent gesture far more powerful than words.

After the briefing the teams went to their barracks to wait for the go signal. It was a steamy summer afternoon in the Stan. Even with the AC on full blast the barracks felt hot and stuffy, but they all kept their gear on. Sitting on their bunks checking their weapons each of them thought about one thing: a man named Macho Valdez.

When General Palmer stepped through the door several hours later they were already on their feet locked and loaded. He spun his finger in the air and they all followed him out to the heliport.

Ten minutes later John and Bunny were sitting in the back of the fast moving Blackhawk flying low through the ravines. There were four other Special Ops helos racing behind them in a staggered formation. Wearing headphones, John stared straight ahead while they listened to the radio traffic between Bagram and the bombers cruising high above.

"We have target acquisition," said the lead pilot of the B-2 Stealth Bomber squadron.

John gripped his M4A1 assault rifle a little tighter. His uncle was about to die and he was listening to it happen in real time.

"You are free to engage Easy Rider. Repeat, Easy Rider, you are weapons free, over," said the voice from Special Operations Command at Bagram.

"Roger. Going into attack."

Bunny looked closely at his friend's face and felt a

familiar chill run through him. He'd seen the look before. The usually soft yellow eyes had turned a cold dark amber. The deep scar that carved through John's brow and ended in his cheek appeared to pulse like a thick red vein engorged with blood. The square noble jaw was usually set firmly, yet now seemed deceptively relaxed and at ease. Bunny had seen this look before. It meant that Aziz and his men were better off dying from the airstrike. Death from the sky was far easier than facing the wrath of John Michael Bishop.

"Coming down," the Stealth pilot said.

CHAPTER 38
PROMISES KEPT

"ARE YOU SICK?" Aziz asked.

"Never better," Macho said.

"You do not look well, my friend."

Macho was fighting the last fight of his life against the poison that was quickly killing him. Despite the coolness of the cave his clothes were soaked through and sweat dripped from his face.

"I am not the man I once was Aziz. City living has made me soft... and the journey here was... difficult," Macho said waving his hand dismissively.

He knew he was almost out of time. His vision was blurring and the slightest movement sent shock waves of pain through his body. He took a few deep breaths, trying to steady himself, when a vicious stabbing in his guts doubled him over in his chair. Macho was determined to die on his feet and used the edge of the table to pull himself up. He stood there swaying on shaky legs, staring at the man he was willingly giving his life to kill.

"What is this? What is wrong with you?"

"I came a long way to see you Aziz."

"Yes you did."

"To tell you something… before…"

"Before what?"

"Before I die."

"Before I kill you little man," Aziz said, removing his pistol from its holster.

"I am Macho Valdez."

"I know."

"You don't. If you did, you wouldn't have let me come. My family is proud and strong. We were once kings and once slaves. We survived hundreds of years of death and suffering. Our promises kept us alive. The promises to each other that we would stand together… face anything together… and the promises to our enemies that we would kill anyone who ever hurt our family."

Aziz smiled at the threat, then casually shot Macho once in each leg. Macho looked down at the blood pumping from his thighs, but stayed on his feet. Looking up at Aziz he continued speaking as if nothing had happened.

"I am the son of Juan and Maria Valdez. Father to Christopher Valdez. You killed my son Aziz. I came here to keep my promise to him. I came here to kill you."

Aziz quickly shot him once in each shoulder, but Macho still held his ground.

"I came here to watch you die."

"Then you should have stayed home my friend," Aziz said, pointing the pistol at Macho's chest. Before he could fire the world exploded all around them. The bunker-busting bombs dropped from the planes above penetrated deep into the mountain's face before detonating. When they did, the high ceiling and walls of the cave immediately collapsed sending razor sharp rock fragments and huge boulders down onto the men below. There was no time to duck or move. Some were ripped apart or flattened by the blast while the lucky few stood dazed, but untouched by the massive explosions.

Macho opened his eyes. Flat on his back he stared up through the huge gaping hole in the mountain and marveled at the myriad of colors in the sky. The setting sun had created a pallet of yellow, pink, orange, and purple hues across the clouds. A beautiful parting gift.

He heard a groan nearby and turned his head towards the sound. Through the dust and smoke he saw Aziz lying on his side only a few feet away. Long splinters from the wooden table were stuck in his face and eyes, his left arm was gone and his legs were pinned under a heavy stone slab.

Macho was beyond pain. He couldn't feel anything as he inched his way along using his hands and feet to move slowly towards Aziz. Whether it took minutes or hours to get there was beyond him. He was in a void without any sense of time or space: only purpose.

"Aziz. Aziz, can you hear me?"

Macho thought he was too late until he felt the warm rancid breath being exhaled into his face and saw the pistol being raised towards him. He smiled and easily pulled the gun away from Aziz, then raised himself up to a sitting position with his shot up legs extended straight out in front of him.

"Like I told you pendejo, I'm Macho Valdez of la familia Valdez, and we keep our promises."

It took everything he had to cock the pistol. Once he did he placed it firmly up against Aziz' head. Aziz was blinded by the splinters that had pierced his eyes, but still turned his face up towards Macho.

"Your nephew is still marked for death."

"We already killed your assassin, the woman named Omar."

"No matter. More will come. The Tringas have never failed. Not in a thousand years."

"As you said, no matter. All you need to know is that you are dead and I am the man that killed you."

"Let me live and I will stop them. The life of your nephew is in your lands. Let me live and save him from certain death."

"Let you live, huh?"

"Yes."

"Who are these Tringas? Where do they come from?"

"An ancient family of assassins."

Macho pushed the pistol harder into Aziz' temple.

"Where?"

"Pakistan. They come from Pakistan, but you will never find them."

"Unless I let you live."

"You know you must. There is no other choice." Aziz raised his open hand. "Give me the gun and all is forgiven my friend."

Macho pulled the trigger. He didn't flinch at the sound or blink from the recoil. He watched Aziz convulse and smoke drift out of the black hole in his head. The pistol felt suddenly too heavy to hold. It fell from his hand, landing in his lap. With a final effort he dipped his finger in his own blood and began writing a message on his shirt. He had to warn John before he died.

Special Ops Airborne Assault Team

In fading light just before sunset the five Special Ops birds flew over the target area.

"Holy shit! It's hollow. The whole top of the mountain is hollow," Bunny said.

John didn't respond, but was no less amazed by what the bombing raid uncovered. The Bunker Busters had ripped the face off of a large section of the mountain, revealing the huge honeycombed network of caves, chambers and tunnels. They also revealed the dozens of armed men who survived the blast.

"There's a fuckin' army down there!" shouted the helicopter co-pilot.

"All I see are live targets," the pilot said calmly. Pushing the stick forward, he took them into a steep dive.

The soldiers below raised their weapons skyward. John's helo along with the others immediately began taking hits from AK-47 rounds pinging off their fusillades. The pilots went into attack. Firing rockets and mini-guns, they flew right into the mouth of the crater, mowing down anything that moved.

They made six runs at the enemy before landing on the plateau a hundred yards above Aziz's formerly hidden headquarters. John was the first man out, with Bunny right behind him. He ran down the rough narrow path moving fast with his M4A1 at the ready. John fired twice at a flash of movement to his left and saw an enemy soldier flop backwards. He kept going, jumping from rock to rock and sprinting forward whenever the trail evened out.

Bunny watched his back. He matched John stride for stride, but stayed ten feet behind to guard against an enemy sneak attack. Bunny froze in place when he saw John stop short and his raise his fist in the air, signaling him to stay put. A second later three armed fighters popped up, standing on top of a large boulder overlooking the path. Bam,

bam, bam, John hit all three center mass and took off again. Bunny knew all three shots were fatal, but kept his weapon trained on the bodies until he was absolutely sure none of them were getting back up. He did a final scan of the area before running after his point man.

The path narrowed and took a sharp turn. When they came around the bend they saw the huge smoking hole in the side of the mountain. They both knew they were going in and they knew there were still dozens of live enemy soldiers hiding down below.

"We waiting for the troops?" Bunny asked.

"Negative. I'm on point. You're on guns."

"Got it."

"And Bunny," John said without looking back at his pal.

"Yeah?"

"Maria's pregnant."

"What? You're going to be a father?"

"Yeah, and I'd really like to be there when my kid is born. So do me a favor. When these guys start shooting at me… don't miss."

"You got it, pops."

The three A-Teams were close behind, but John couldn't wait. Standing on what was once the roof of the main cave he used the smoke billowing up from below as cover and eased his way over the side. Holding onto to the lip, he lowered himself down and hung for a second before releasing his hands. Dropping into the semi-darkness, he landed like a cat fifteen feet down.

"Uncle Bunny. Got a nice ring to it," he said out loud before he followed John into the abyss.

John was adjusting his eyes to the darkness with his

M4A1pointed out into the gloom when Bunny crashed down hard onto the ground right next to him.

"You okay?" John asked.

Bunny groaned, but jumped up and unslung his rifle. "Never better. Let's move."

"Central blast point is at my twelve o'clock. That where we'll find Macho."

"Lead on Sarge."

The birds were back on station, hovering fifty feet above them. Even with the roar of the helo engines they both heard the shouts of trapped and wounded men all around them. Bright pockets from the spotlights helped them see, but they were moving down into a dark murky world filled with sharp edges and armed insurgents.

There was no running here. John moved cautiously with Bunny right on his ass. He mentally calculated they were about fifty feet down. That's when the roar of AK's came straight at them. Bullets ricocheted off rocks and thudded into the dirt at their feet. John dove left and Bunny went right, ducking away from enemy fire that didn't let up.

"Cover me Bun."

Bunny got behind a stony ridge and put down suppressing fire. Aiming just above the AK-47 muzzle flashes ten yards away, he heard several men scream and their guns go silent. Bunny ducked down when, as planned, all the remaining fighters turned their weapons on him.

John crawled fast and low coming around on their left flank. There had been nine of them all together. The three bodies on the ground were a testament to Bunny's marksmanship while the remaining six gunmen blasted away at him from behind a waist high wall. From fifteen feet away John shot two of them in the head and hit three more in the heart when they turned to face him. He swung his weapon towards the last target a second too late. He was too close to duck or run and that made him a dead man. The Afghan was looking right at him, already firing his AK. John exhaled deeply when the shots went wide. He watched the short bearded man sink to the ground from the three rounds that Bunny put in his back.

Bunny ran over with his rifle at his shoulder moving in a semi-circle to make sure there were no more hidden threats. They both looked up at the familiar sound of M4A1 fire coming from above.

"The troops are here," Bunny said, his weapon still at the ready.

"Let's keep moving," said John.

He led them to the center of the blast zone. They had both seen the effects of artillery strikes and bombing raids before, but never like this. There were body parts everywhere. Feet, heads, hands, arms, legs and sections of human beings that were beyond recognition were piled together in some areas and scattered about randomly in others. John felt something wet hit his shoulders. He knew he shouldn't even look, but did anyway. Bunny followed his eyes up to the torso impaled on a spear shaped stalactite twenty feet above them. The intestines hung down to just above their heads, dripping blood one thick glob at a time.

"If this ain't hell on earth I don't know what is. Never seen anything like this, Johnny."

"Me neither."

At that moment spotlights illuminated an open area farther down in the crater. At first John wasn't sure what he was seeing. He squinted and rubbed the dust out of his eyes. Then he sprinted over to the man that was sitting up with his finger on his chest.

"Tio?"

John looked down at his uncle. The powerful figure he had last seen three days ago in New York was gone, replaced by the broken body at his feet. Under a layer of dust and dirt, Macho had cuts all over him from the explosions. Blood flowed steadily from the four bullet wounds and more oozed slowly out of his eyes, nose, and mouth from the radiation poisoning.

"John?"

"It's me, Uncle Macho."

"I can't see you," he said, trying to blink the blood from his eyes.

"It's okay, Tio. I'm right here."

John bent down and reached out to touch him, but Bunny grabbed his arm and pulled it back. He shook his head no. Any contact without protective gear could be fatal.

"Don't come close. The poison. It... it can..."

"I know Tio. It's okay."

"You see Aziz? You see the body?"

"I see it."

"I killed him. He killed my Chris and I came here and killed him."

"You did."

"He didn't believe I could do it."

"We all knew you would. We all knew it."

"I'm glad you're here."

"I promised to bring you home Tio. I'm a Valdez. We keep our promises."

"You remember."

"Always. You taught me well."

"Have to tell you... the message..."

"Tell me what?"

"Listen. Very important. The Tringas… Tringas are coming."

"Tringas?"

"Pakistan… coming… coming for … you…"

"Tio? Tio!"

Bunny placed a hand on his friend's shoulder. "He's gone Johnny," he said. "What a man. My God, what a man."

They both stood there staring down at Macho, then crouched and turned at the sound of men running towards them. They lowered their weapons when General Palmer came trotting over with a large group of Green Berets behind him.

"Is that your uncle?"

"Yes sir."

"He did it. He actually did it."

"His whole life, he never let anyone down. If he said he was going to do something, it got done. No matter what, it got done," John said.

"That's a life well lived." Palmer looked down at Macho again. "I want four men to form a perimeter. Eyes out, ears open. Everyone else gather round and take a knee."

All the men formed a semi-circle and knelt in prayer.

"Look at this man before us. He gave his life for a true and just cause. We honor this fallen soldier as one of our own. Rest in peace Macho Valdez, rest in peace."

The general crossed himself, stood up and said, "Don't worry, John, we'll take good care of him. There'll be private plane ready for you and Bunny in the morning so you can bring your uncle home."

"Thank you, sir."

"Son, it's me and every man here that owes you and your family a debt I doubt we'll ever be able to repay. This was your mission from start to finish. With the backing of two presidents and every military resource at my disposal

I've been trying to kill Aziz Khan for the past eight years. I failed. But there's that piece a shit lying there dead and gone. You and your family got it done in four days."

"We couldn't have done any of this without you General."

"John, we've just been your backup. I'm just glad you let us be a part of it. The public will never hear about it and it'll never be mentioned in the history books, but we all know what you and your uncle did here and we're all real proud to have fought in your private war. Now it's over. Me and the men are going to finish what you started and clean this place out, but your war's over. You hear me? Bishop's War is over."

"Yes sir," John said. He quickly glanced over at Bunny and he could tell the big man shared his thoughts. Macho didn't fight that hard to stay alive just to say goodbye. He knew his uncle. It was the message and the message was important. He wasn't sure who the Tringas were, but he was definitely going to find out before he declared an end to hostilities.

Everyone turned towards the sound of heavy fire coming from the far side of the crater. They were all combat veterans and instantly recognized the signature echo of AR-15's.

"That's the Marines. I had them climb up the back side of the mountain to hit any squirters with some blunt force trauma," Palmer said. "We've got these rats trapped in their own nest. Aziz and his army are finished. This is a big win for Special Ops and the U.S. of A."

Twenty feet above their heads Tariq Hassan lay nestled in a natural crevice that had been undisturbed by the aerial attack. He scratched at the thick burn mark on his face that he carried since childhood while he watched and listened intently to the conversation below. He listened and swore a silent oath of vengeance.

Tariq was a senior officer, but to him Aziz Khan had been much more than just his commander-in-chief. Aziz had been a mentor and a father figure. Tariq revered him and was a true disciple of the man that lay dead at the feet of these Americans. Every true soldier of God expected to die on the battlefield someday. But to lose someone like Aziz to this ex-soldier and his family was unforgivable.

You are wrong general.

We are not finished.

I will rebuild the army.

I will give you a war like you have never seen.

The name of Aziz Khan will live forever.

And someday, someday soon, I will watch John Bishop die at my feet. I promise you, as Allah is my witness, he will die at my feet.

Islamabad, Pakistan

Amongst the many thousands of refugees and homeless living on the busy streets of Pakistan's capital city no one noticed or paid attention to two more beggars sleeping in a dark alley. The few locals who did notice them didn't seem to mind. Though the two men were filthy and dressed in rags they were quiet and kept to themselves. Both were crippled. One walked with a severe limp and the other was bent in half from a broken back or defect of birth.

Since moving in two days ago they kept themselves busy. Constantly moving about, they cleaned up the alley removing trash, stacking, organizing and even sweeping up where they could. They worked until it was too dark to see. Tonight, with only a crescent of light along the horizon they were still at it, struggling to move an old stove across the street. The stove was either too heavy or stuck in a hole. They rocked it back and forth trying to get it moving again, but it wouldn't budge.

The headlights of a long black Mercedes sedan illuminated their efforts. The car pulled up just a few feet behind them. With no room to go around the driver flashed his high beams and honked his horn loudly in frustration. The two cripples pushed and pulled with everything they had, but the stove remained in the center of the road.

"Go help them. Both of you," said General Mohammed.

"Yes General."

The driver and the front seat passenger left the cool interior of the Mercedes and stepped out into the hot evening air. Although they were both majors in the Pakistani Inter-Service Intelligence Agency (ISI) they wore civilian clothes whenever they were part of the general's security detail.

"You bums step aside," the driver said. He reached down and grabbed one side of the stove.

"You are too kind," replied the beggar with the crooked back.

"And too dumb," said the beggar with the limp. Both ISI majors froze when they saw the silenced automatic. Neither had time to speak before Mace shot each of them in the head.

Bear stood up straight and Mace's limp disappeared as they walked purposefully towards the car. Going along opposite sides, they each opened a rear door and watched the general fumble with his holster, trying to draw his pistol. Bear shot him in the hand and Mace shot him in both ankles. Neither man paid any attention to the high pitched screaming.

"Do you know who I am!?"

"You're General Gulam Mohammed aren't you?" Bear asked.

"Yes, yes. You are Americans. This is all a terrible mistake. I am your friend and ally."

Bear shot him in the side of the right knee. The general shouted out again in pain, but Bear gave the man credit for his quick recovery.

"Why are you doing this!?"

"The Special Forces mission in Khost last week."

"What mission?"

"The one you warned Aziz Khan about. You got our friends killed."

"No, no, no. Khan is my enemy and yours. Why would I warn him?"

Mace shot him in the left leg.

"We don't know. That's why we're here. Why General?" Mace asked.

"These are lies! Lies!"

Mace looked over the roof of the car at Bear and shrugged. Bear nodded back.

"Okay, I guess we're done then," Bear said. He pulled a quart sized bottle from under his robes and began pouring its contents all over the back seat and the wounded man sitting on it.

"What are you doing?"

"In case you don't recognize the smell, that's jet fuel."

Mace leaned in, looked at him and said, "A whole bunch of good men went up in flames because a you. We promised them you'd do the same." He pulled out an identical bottle and poured more fuel onto the general.

"We're Team Razor and we keep our promises," Bear said, striking a match.

"No, no please!"

He might of said more, but they only heard the whoosh of flames and screaming after Bear tossed in the match. The two Green Berets turned away and walked off into the night. Neither of them looked back.

CHAPTER 39
NEW BEGINNINGS

Long Island, NY

THE PLAN WAS to have a small private ceremony. Plans changed once the word got out and everyone demanded to be there. A week after they buried Macho in a lead lined coffin next to his wife and son, John and Maria were married in front of three hundred family and friends.

The groomsmen were a tuxedoed parade of walking wounded. The three surviving members of Team Razor, Bear, Mace and Bobby bore the marks of recent battles. Felix, the best man, still limped from his stab wound. Bunny's face was cut and swollen and John was covered in band-aids to hide the stitches. Even Maria was in a full arm cast, yet somehow managed to make plaster and lace look breathtaking.

Security was intense around the church. Captain Ryan supplied off-duty cops from his trusted inner circle, Terry Hall was there with an FBI team, heavy hitters from Special Ops and the CIA tried their best to look inconspicuous, while the entire area was blanketed by Valdez soldiers.

After saying their vows they were quickly shoved into one of the long line of waiting limos. John held his new bride's hand while the caravan traveled back to Calixto's Long Island estate for the reception. He didn't need to be married long to know his wife wasn't happy.

"This is a circus. Are we celebrities or criminals?" Maria asked, staring through the tinted back window at the police cars racing along beside them.

"I know baby, and I'm sorry. I wanted this day to be special for you."

"For me? Not us?"

"You know what I mean. Yes, for us."

She turned to look at him and gently ran her fingers across his face. He tingled from the sense memory. It was the same tender touch she had been giving him since high school.

"I'm sorry honey. I don't mean to be a brat on our wedding day. I just never imagined us getting married surrounded by armed guards."

"I think the priest had a MAC-10 under his robe," he said with a smile.

"You're a funny man, Mr. Bishop."

"From now on it's your job to laugh at my jokes, Mrs. Bishop."

"That'll be tough, but I promise to try," she said batting her eyes at him.

"Listen hon…"

She cut him off. "I know the reception will be great. I just can't wait until the honeymoon so we can finally have some time alone."

He immediately started sweating before he gave her the bad news. "Yeah, umm, about that."

"What baby?"

"We may have to delay our trip for a few days," he said, his voice barely above a whisper.

"*What* did you just say?"

"Just a few days honey. We may still be in danger. I'll know more after the meeting today."

"When will it end? Oh God, when will it end?" she buried her face in his chest and cried the rest of the way to the house. She pulled herself together when they passed through the main gates.

"Okay, I feel better now," she said wiping her eyes with his handkerchief. "Don't know why I'm all emotional."

"Honey, we've all been through two weeks of hell. You don't have to justify anything to me." He hugged her and gave her a long lingering kiss.

"You just do what you have to do to keep us safe. You hear me? Don't worry about the honeymoon. You just keep us safe."

"I love you, wife."

"I love you, husband," she said, just as the limo stopped in front of the main house.

The party kicked off after Maria's bridesmaids touched up her hair and redid her makeup. It was an amazing reception with great music, gourmet food and plenty to drink. They laughed and danced together for hours, sharing the moment they had both been dreaming of for so many years. Felix made an incredible speech that had everyone in tears and there were dozens of toasts after that. When things began to slow down a little John saw his uncle Fiero nod his head towards the house. He excused himself and followed Fiero to the meeting room where everyone was waiting.

Kevin, Ed and Danny, the Pro KEDSS team, stood at

the front of the long table. Gonzalo beckoned him over and John took a seat at his side.

"John, congratulations again. And we're very sorry to have to have this meeting on your wedding day," Danny said.

"Thanks Danny, but I'm real eager to hear what you've got to say."

"Yeah, well I wish we had some good news. Ed?"

Ed stepped forward. "It took us the better part of a week to find out about the Tringas. Bottom line is they're a highly secretive family of assassins. They hand pick one child at a time and train them to be the best at what they do. And when I say the best I mean it. These kids are trained to ignore pain, they are masters of disguise, experts in all weapons and can kill with their bare hands."

"So the woman named Omar was one of these Tringas?" Felix asked.

"Yes, she was."

"I have to agree with you about their skills," John said. "I've never seen anyone that could fight like her. If it wasn't for Felix and Bunny she would've killed me for sure."

"You're right, she would have," Kevin said. "And since we don't know if she's dead let's assume she's not."

"I shot that bitch with a .45. Clean shot right in the chest," Bunny said.

"But she took the hit and kept on going didn't she Bun?"

"Yeah she did. She ate the slug and took off running. Never seen anything like it."

"Look, we're not saying these Tringas can't be killed. But until we see a body, let's assume she'll come at you again once her tit grows back. Either way this ain't over."

"And why is that?" John asked.

"Our research uncovered one very important thing

about the Tringas. They've been in the game doing murder for hire for a long time. More than a thousand years."

"Fuck," Felix said, shaking his head.

"Fuck is right. In all that time they've never failed. That's a heavy rep. Even if Omar is dead another one will come to take her place," Danny said.

Gonzalo stood up and spoke for the first time. "We will not sit and wait for assassins. You must find them. You find them and we will destroy them. Macho said they come from Pakistan."

"They do. We just don't know where," Kevin said.

"Find out. Quickly."

"Yes Don Valdez."

"Is there more?"

"Yes sir, quite a bit more. First, Meecham's hired killer is still out there. He knows you're hunting him, but he's not going to run. Just as you're going after the Tringas, Connie will go on the offensive."

"Yes, Christmas told us the same thing. We have taken every precaution, but in the end we will just have to see what he does. Unless we find him first. What else?"

"The Russians from Brighton Beach. They view your move away from narcotics as a sign of weakness. Expect them to try to push you out of everything else. And soon."

"Yes, we expected this. Not this fast, but we knew they would come," Gonzalo said, nodding to his nephew and heir apparent, Antonio.

"Don Valdez, we know and respect you. We've seen a lot of men wear the crown, but none like you. You're the best. Hands down. That said, you're opening yourself up to attack from all sides. The Tringas, Connie Bellusci, the Russians and maybe even the Chinese. Like I said, we know you. We know you've got a plan. We just can't help unless we know what it is," Kevin said.

"Antonio and I will speak to you in private after this meeting. I want everyone, especially the groom, to enjoy his wedding night."

"Understood. Well then the last thing we have to discuss is your brother."

"You speak of Nestor?"

"Yes sir. Nestor is getting out of prison next week. He's been inside for thirty years and he built his own army."

"And?"

"You may be out of the drug game, but he's deep in it and getting deeper every day."

Gonzalo sighed. "I will speak to my brother. No matter how many years he's been away he is family and he will understand."

John got up and stood next to uncle. "Tio, I'm going back to the party. Maria and I will stay here until... until we come up with something better." He nodded to everyone then turned and walked heavily out the room. Bunny and Felix followed him out.

"You okay, primo?" Felix asked.

"How do I tell my pregnant wife that I'm marked for death by an ancient order of Pakistani killers with a perfect track record?"

"You don't," Bunny said. "Let her have tonight. Tell her tomorrow or the next day. In the meantime you can sleep easy. Me and Felix will be right outside your door."

"Right outside the door?"

"Yep."

"Outside the door on my wedding night," John said, finally cracking a smile.

Maria was dancing with her father when they went back outside to the reception. He passed his daughter over to John and she held him tight.

"Is everything okay, baby?"

"Everything's, great honey. Everything's great."

She reached for a glass of seltzer and handed him a flute of champagne.

"Then here's to new beginnings."

"To new beginnings," he said, clinking glasses before they each took a sip.

"I've got an idea. Let's walk up the hill so you can introduce your new bride to your mom and dad. After that you can take me to bed and rip this gown off me."

"That's my girl."

Maria kicked off her heels and John put away his fears about the future as they walked hand in hand up the hill to the family cemetery. Felix and Bunny trailed them silently from behind, keeping enough distance to give the newlyweds their privacy, but close enough to act in case an assassin was waiting in the night.

CHAPTER 40
CALEB AND CONNIE

Trapp, Maryland

CALEB MEECHAM SAT at his father's desk and looked around the study. It was the first time he ever sat in the big captain's chair that had once been in the stateroom of his great, great, great grandfather's three masted frigate. His father had told him that he was never to sit in it as long as he was alive. Caleb never had.

After the police had given him the unpleasant details of his father's demise the lawyers had given him the very pleasant details of his inheritance. He was unemotional when he saw the pictures and was told how his father had been severely beaten before he was eaten alive. He was equally unemotional when he saw the will and was told that he was now worth over two billion dollars. The only thing that lit his fire was when the New York detective said that there were no suspects at this time.

No suspects my ass! I know who did this and they're going to pay! If it costs me the entire fortune they're going to pay! You hear me, Dad? I'll get them all for what they did to you. There won't be a Valdez left when I'm done. I swear it.

Caleb's thoughts of his personal vendetta were cut short when Connie Bellusci opened the door and walked in unannounced.

"I take it you're Caleb."

"That's right."

"I worked for your dad. My name's Connie."

"I know who you are."

"You know who your father hired me to kill?"

"I do, and I know that if you'd done your fucking job my father would still be alive."

"I'll give you that. I missed, and your father's dead. I can't change any of that. All I can do is keep moving forward."

"Moving forward. What exactly does that mean?"

"It means I have a plan."

"Let's hear it."

"I'll get to it. First, I have a present for you, Mr. Meecham. Let's take a walk."

Mr. Meecham... hmmm.

It was the first time anyone had ever called him that, and Caleb liked the sound of it. He followed Connie through the house to the garage. The big man led Caleb to the back of his Chevy Tahoe and opened the rear hatch. Three Latin men lay there bound, gagged and struggling to get free.

"These guys are Valdez soldiers. I need two of them for the plan I'm going to tell you about later. In the meantime I brought the extra one for you in the event you might want to..."

"What?"

"Entertain a guest?"

"That one," Caleb said pointing to the biggest of the three. "Bring him inside and follow me."

Connie lifted the two hundred-twenty pound man up and casually threw him over his shoulder. He followed Caleb back through the house and then down the stairs into the basement. The mansion was huge and the basement was like a maze, but Caleb knew exactly where to go. He stopped in front of a large wooden door with two heavy locks to keep it closed up tight.

"I don't have the keys."

Connie shrugged his shoulder to drop his human cargo onto the floor then pulled out a .45 caliber pistol. The booms were deafening, echoing down the hallway. Three shots and a swift kick got them in.

"Damn. Well you sure picked the right door."

Caleb had never been in the room, but heard whispers about what his father did to any unsuspecting woman who had the misfortune of venturing inside. A big cozy bed with thick pillows was placed invitingly the near the door. The bed faced out towards the far brick wall. Painted bright white, the bricks had hand and leg irons bolted into them and near the restraints, whips, chains, belts, pliers and power tools hung down ominously from wooden pegs.

"You know where to put him," Caleb said.

Connie dragged him in. He reached behind his back, pulled out a Special Forces combat knife, and used it to cut the man free before roughly locking him up against the wall. Caleb grabbed the bullwhip and took a few practice swings.

"Pull the tape off his mouth so we can hear him."

The stream of curses was short lived, replaced by agonizing screams as each crack of the whip sliced through clothes and flesh. An hour later the new Mr. Meecham lay on the bed panting and exhausted. Wet with his own sweat and Valdez blood, he felt dizzy and giddy. He had just flayed a man alive. When there was nothing left but raw meat he had taken Connie's knife and cut the man's throat. Something warm and tingly released inside him when he felt the thick flow of blood pour over him. He killed a man with his own hands and there would be no consequences. He knew it was something he would have to do again. And again.

"Feel better?" Connie asked.

"It's a start, but my father was eaten alive by fucking lions. Killing a few street soldiers doesn't come close to evening the score. I want them all. You hear me? Every last Valdez. I want them all."

"Well, then let me tell you what I have in mind..."

Brighton Beach, Brooklyn

Nicholai Skobelev sat at his regular table in the VIP section of Club Raz. It was one of the many clubs he secretly owned throughout the city. The place was packed, the music had everyone in a frenzy and there was a long line of hard men on the stairs below. The men weren't lined up to get into the VIP section. They were lined up and waiting to see him. Waiting their turn to kiss the ring and pay homage to the new king of New York.

"Nicky" was the only son of Yakov Skobelev, the wealthiest and most powerful gangster in all of modern day Russia. For years Nicky had lived the self-indulgent lifestyle of a spoiled golden prince in Moscow. Under his father's protection and above the law he had flaunted his power until one night he went too far. Drunk and high, he beat his father's mistress half to death after she refused his advances. As punishment Yakov banished his son to New York.

Cast out and disgraced he had arrived in Brighton Beach five years ago with a lot a to prove and a big chip on his shoulder. Through cunning, brutality, and a surprising knack for leadership, he rose to the top of Russian organized crime on the East Coast without any help from daddy. This morning his last remaining rival was found dead, drowned in a bathtub filled to the rim with Petrossian Caviar.

The news had traveled fast. Friends and foes had come to personally congratulate him, but to Nicky the call he received in the afternoon from his father was all that mattered. Yakov told him how proud he was of him. He told him that all was forgiven. He told his son how much he loved him and to hurry home to take his rightful place by his side.

Nicky was reveling in it all. Tonight, the party for his wife's birthday at Club Raz. Tomorrow, with his honor restored they were flying back to Moscow. He left in shame five long years ago. Now the prodigal son would return home to a hero's welcome.

It was just after midnight when Nicky, his wife, and three body guards walked out of the club. There was still a long line of people waiting to get in and everyone cheered and tried to touch him when he passed by. This was his neighborhood. His enemies were all dead and he had nothing to fear as they walked down the street to get a late night coffee.

His wife didn't react to the sound, but Nicky and his men spun around when they heard the safety click off. Connie mentally complimented them for their reflexes. They almost got their guns out. Almost. Connie flattened them all with the spay from the silenced Uzi. They were all dead before they hit the ground, but Connie walked up to Nicky and his wife and emptied the magazine into their faces.

No open caskets for you two. Yakov's going to be one very angry Rusky. Very angry indeed.

Connie reached into Nicky's jacket and removed his pistol. He walked over to the back of his SUV and shot each of the Valdez soldiers in the heart before he dumped them in the street. He walked back and put Nicky's gun in his hand, then dropped the Uzi next to the Valdez boys before he drove off into the night.

CHAPTER 41
THE DEATH OF NESTOR VALDEZ

Elmira, NY

CORRECTIONS OFFICER FRANK Moore was already sweating through his uniform and breathing hard. Universally known as "Big Frank" for his three hundred and eighty pound frame he lumbered up the stairs, grunting from the effort. He paused when he reached the top tier.

I hate this fuckin' job.

After he caught his breath and wiped his face, the gate guard buzzed him through the steel doors. Big Frank was usually calm and cool, but today was a big day. He felt nervous. He saw that all the hardcore cons felt the same way. They stood silently outside of their cells, tense and waiting.

This was Elmira State Prison. D Block. Tier 4. Every inmate on this level had violently taken the life of at least one other human being. Many of them had killed more than once. Each man nodded at him when Big Frank made his way through the heavily muscled and tattooed lifers.

He was cool with most of them. Seasoned cons that did their time and didn't break his balls. He treated these guys with respect and didn't fuck with them. He even over-looked their extracurricular activities and most of their minor infractions.

There were a few trouble makers who sometimes got in his face and tried to give him shit. Not today. Even the ass-holes were standing at attention with their backs to the rail. Frank walked his slow walk along the tier until he came to the last cell in the line of thirty. No one stood outside of that one. He paused for a moment before announcing himself to Nestor Valdez.

Being alone in a cell with Nestor was like being locked in a closet with a cobra. The cobra knows it can kill you any-time it wants to, and you know you can't dodge the strike. Every time you walk out of the closet you thank God you're still alive and try not to think about the next time you have to visit the snake again. The thing you always had to keep in mind when you dealt with Nestor was that his fangs were long. You didn't have to be anywhere near the closet to get bit.

Since Frank's first day on the job fifteen years ago, Nestor Valdez had always been polite, friendly, and respect-ful, but Big Frank never felt comfortable around the man. Especially after he heard about what happened to his prede-cessor. The officer had been a hardass who made the critical mistake of giving Nestor a rough time one day. That night in the middle of a family meal he was abducted from his home. A box containing the officer's head was delivered to the war-den a few days later.

"'Scuse me Mr. Valdez. Okay if I step in your house?"

"Sure Frank. Come on in."

"Anything I can help you with Mr. Valdez?"

"No, but I appreciate you asking. I'm just taking the photos and a few paintings. Everything else is for my friends."

Everything else was a lot. Nestor's house was not like any other cell in the prison. There was a Persian rug on the floor, a flat screen TV on the wall, a toaster oven on the shelf, and even a small office space with a desk, swivel chair, and laptop computer.

"Frank, how old is your boy now? Sixteen?"

Shit, I don't wanna be talkin' about my son with this dude.

"Turning eighteen next month."

"Senior year, huh?"

"Yeah, and thank the lord he's way smarter than me. We're looking at colleges in the fall."

"Tuition's expensive."

"We've been saving. Student loans, maybe a scholarship. He's going to college one way or the other."

Nestor handed him a slip of paper.

"What's this, sir?

"It's a full scholarship in your son's name from Ford Motors. Use that savings to fix that hole in your bedroom wall or buy yourself a new car. That old Honda you drive needs to be put down."

Man's sayin' his people have been in my fuckin' house and they know my ride.

"I can't take this."

"Of course you can, Frank. Your son just got a free ride from the oldest car company in America. That's a big deal. You should be proud. Either way, I insist." The eyes of the cobra didn't blink.

"Thank you, sir, Thank you very much."

"Alright, let's get out of here."

"You mind if I ask a question?"

"Sure Frank."

"How do you feel?"

"About leaving?"

"Yeah."

"I've been in this cell for thirty years. Thirty years, seventeen days. Made some great friends while I did my time. How do I feel?... I'm overcome with emotion." The cobra's eyes were clear and dry. "You see," he said, pointing to the tiny black tattoos shaped like tears that ran down his face. "I cry for all the friends and family I have lost, and for the many men I have killed."

Nestor stopped to speak briefly with every man lined up along the tier. Others called out to him from below. They cheered and clapped for him. They stomped on floors and banged anything that would make noise against the bars. In an almost religious frenzy they chanted his name over and over again. "Nestor! Nestor! Nestor!" echoed loudly off the walls as he made his way through the prison.

Following the warden's orders, the guards had pre-processed his paper work to speed things along and get him out of Elmira. He could still hear the chanting when he walked past the last gate and out into the world. More than five hundred men standing outside the prison joined the chorus with their brothers on the inside.

He stood there staring at his soldiers while they softly chanted his name. Their volume steadily increased until they reached a crescendo, screaming, "Nestor! Nestor! Nestor!" over and over again.

His expression never changed as he moved forward, a prophet amongst his disciples. Like the parting of the Red Sea, they opened a wide space for him to pass. When he reached the center he stopped and raised his hands up to silence them.

"I am glad you're all here to share this moment. None

of our lives will ever be the same after this. You who are here with me now will go out and tell your brothers what you have seen." He slowly began taking off his clothes.

"People said that they were sorry. Sorry that I lost my freedom for all this time. What those people don't understand is that no one can take away your freedom. I was in a cage for thirty years, but I was always a free man!" The crowd roared. "And if I go right back to that cage tomorrow I will still be free!"

The men went into a frenzy, raising their fists and shouting. After a few moments Nestor raised his hands again to silence them.

"You who are here with me, never forget this moment. You are here to witness my death… and my resurrection."

He kept taking off clothes until finally he stood there in his boxers. He turned slowly so all of them could see the ferocious tattoo that completely covered him from the neck down.

"Nestor is no more… witness the rise of Geronimo!"

As he continued to turn in a slow circle with his face turned up to the sky, his eyes seemed to project a bright light, his tattoo began to glow and thunder boomed from the clouds. Five hundred men dropped down onto their knees and began a new chant of, "Geronimo! Geronimo! Geronimo!" From inside the prison his new name pulsed through the air like the steady beat of a base drum.

He stopped his turn and walked forward to one of his trusted soldiers who handed him a knife. Geronimo sliced two deep diagonal gashes across his own chest.

"I am Geronimo and you are my Apaches! Come! Come share my blood!"

All the men surged forward to touch his chest. They streaked their faces Indian style with his blood. Many cut themselves to mix their own blood with his. Throughout the ceremony his expression never changed until at last he saw his brothers in the back behind his frenzied followers. Then he smiled.

Still bleeding he walked up to them and raised his hand. The instant he did the chanting stopped, creating an eerie silence. Nestor opened his arms wide and hugged Gonzalo.

"I am glad you were here to see that," he said finally.

"Welcome home, hermano," Gonzalo said.

"It's good to see you. All of you," Geronimo said looking at the rest of his former family.

"Come. Everyone is waiting. There is big party for you."

"No Zalo, I can't go."

"What do you mean?"

"Weren't you watching? I have my own family now... and my own business."

"You would turn your back on your own blood? On me and La Familia Valdez?"

"I know you won't understand, but I built something while I was inside. I have thousands of soldiers out here. Like me, they've been waiting a very long time for this day."

"So you are no longer with us?"

"No."

"You choose them?"

"Like I said big brother, you won't understand. But, since I know you need to hear it... yes, I choose them over you."

"And the business you spoke of?"

"Is none of your business."

"What if our interests should conflict with yours?"

"They won't. Just stay out of narcotics. I will let you keep some of the gambling, but not all of it."

"You will let us?"

"Yes brother, I will let you. I already run every prison and all the drugs east of Chicago. Soon I'll have the whole country. When I come to pay my respects to Macho and Chris I will explain everything to you in detail."

Gonzalo frowned.

"And don't make that face. I am Geronimo and you and the family are under my protection. Be grateful."

He touched his chest, then reached up and made two red diagonal slash marks on both of Gonzalo's cheeks. "There, now you're one of my Apaches. I'll see you soon."

With that he turned and walked away. When the messiah was back amongst his people the chanting started up all over again.

Gonzalo stood there for five long minutes composing himself and thinking through all the moves on the chess board. His brothers and Antonio waited quietly until he was ready to go. When he was, Benji Medina started the car and they all got in. Gonzalo carefully wiped the blood off of his face with a handkerchief, then took off his blood stained blazer and shirt, and then tossed everything out the window. No one said a word during the two and a half hour drive back to the City.

CHAPTER 42
NOT TODAY

Moscow

YAKOV SKOBELEV DIDN'T try to hide his emotions and wept openly for his only son. His brother sat beside him and passed him a large glass of vodka. Yakov drank it greedily.

"So tell me brother. Who did this?" Yakov asked.

"It was the Valdez family in New York."

"I have heard the name. Why did they massacre my Nicky and his wife?"

"A dispute over territory, Yakov. Nicky was pushing them out."

"Territory?"

"Yes brother."

"How many are they?"

"Perhaps eight hundred, with ten in their inner circle and one man at the top."

"What is his name?"

"Gonzalo Valdez."

"Does he have children?"

"Two adopted sons."

"Kill the sons first and their wives if they have them. Then all of the soldiers."

"Yes Yakov."

"I want Gonzalo Valdez to be the last one to die. I will kill him myself, but first he must know he is responsible for the destruction of everyone and everything he has ever loved."

"It will be done."

"Nicky demands blood for his blood and so do I. Blood! I want great rivers of blood!"

The Northern Mountains of Pakistan

"You sent for me grandfather?" the young man asked.

"Yes, I need you."

"I am yours to command grandfather."

"My student Omar has failed."

"No Tringa has ever failed."

"She did and she must be dead or she would have sent word to me by now."

"Who was her target?"

"This man," said the old man. He held out a press clipping in his bony wrinkled fingers.

"John Bishop."

"Yes."

"A famous man. Easy to find him."

"Easy to find, yes. Maybe not so easy to kill."

"I will not fail."

"You cannot. Our family honor is in your hands David."

"Rest easy grandfather. I am a Tringa and you taught me well. I will find John Bishop and when I do he will be dead."

Trapp, Maryland

"So now we just sit back and wait?" Caleb asked.

"Believe me, I know Yakov Skobelev. We won't have to wait long."

"This all started with Bishop. I want him dead! As much as I want his uncle for what he did to my Dad, if it wasn't for Bishop none of this would have happened."

"Yakov is an old school Rusky. His way is to kill your family first. I still have an open contract on John and Felix that I plan to close myself, but now with Yakov's army hunting them there's no place on earth where they can hide. That Russian would drop a nuke on New York just to take them out."

"I can't wait," Caleb said, rubbing his hands together just like his father used to do. "Hey Connie?"

"Yeah Caleb."

"Do you think you can get me another Valdez soldier to put on the wall?"

"Sure kid. I'll get you another one."

Blakesly, PA

The heavy slug had done a lot of damage, costing her a breast and a lung. She knew she had to be patient. She had to wait, rest, and let her body heal. But she couldn't wait very long. Her teacher would send another to replace her. Tringa honor demanded it. Her own honor demanded that she complete the mission herself.

Omar knew she couldn't travel yet so she lay on the bed, willing herself to recover. She lay there staring at a picture of the man with the jagged scar on his face.

It will be Omar that kills you.

It can only be Omar.

I will see you soon John Bishop.

Khost mountains, Afghanistan

After the bombing raid and the Special Forces assault on Aziz's headquarters, Tariq Hassan watched and listened from his hide until all the U.S. forces had cleared out. Already enraged by the assassination of his commander and father figure, he screamed in anguish when he discovered that the Americans taken Aziz's body with them.

For what? He asked himself. *To be displayed like some trophy at their base, or at the Whitehouse?*

He climbed through the mangled remains of his fellow soldiers and emerged from the demolished mountain stronghold with more focus and determination than he'd ever had. Other survivors of the attack sensed Tariq's power and fell in line behind their new leader. He spoke silently to Aziz as he marched his fledgling force higher and higher into the mountains.

I will rebuild the army and my men will chant the name Aziz Khan as they charge into battle. We will avenge you here Aziz, and we will avenge you in America when we kill the infidel dog John Bishop!

Unnamed Island
190 miles off the coast of Venezuela

They lay side by side on the white sandy beach while light waves lapped at their feet and a cool breeze took the edge off of the hot mid-morning sun. The crystal clear water looked too inviting to pass up. He reached for his homemade spear gun and sat up.

"I think I'll go catch us some lunch."

"Sounds good honey."

He looked down at his wife. The sun had turned her complexion from creamy mocha to dark cocoa, making her somehow more beautiful. If that was even possible. He couldn't tell whether her eyes were open or closed behind the dark shades.

"You going to be okay?"

"I've got you… and them," she said, pointing her thumb behind her.

John turned to look back at Felix and Bunny. They were sitting upright in deck chairs on the bungalow porch. They both gave him a mock salute, which he returned crisply.

Amazing. When do they sleep?

They were always on duty. Guarding them from a discreet distance against the terrible danger that might one day appear out of nowhere.

One day, but not today. Definitely not today.

He bent over and kissed her, then stood up and put his goggles on top of his head. He strapped the spear gun across his back and carried the fins with him into the water.

"I'll do a lap around and then bag us some fryers."

"Hurry back honey. I miss you already."

"Will do."

He put on the flippers and stroked his way out past the surf to where the water was deeper. He began the short swim around the tiny island that was only three hundred feet across at its widest point. Their trip to Atlantis had been cancelled, but thanks to Gonzalo, John and Maria got a honeymoon after all. Two weeks alone on this very private and secluded island. Well, almost alone.

John swam hard across the surface. He pushed aside the sad memories of the past two weeks and his strong sense of foreboding about the future. He focused only on the present and what he had right now. A beautiful wife. A baby on the way. Felix, his cousin and brother by his side, and Bunny, his best friend in the world here to share it all. These people, these things, and this time were precious gifts. He wanted to keep them all for as long as he could.

He stopped and dove down into a pristine blue world of multi-colored fish, plants, and coral. He had never felt so at peace. No death, no killing, no sorrow. Just beauty all around him and the love he felt for his family and friends.

John wanted this moment to last forever, but he knew deep down in his heart of hearts that it never would. Once again there were dark forces on the horizon. Dark forces that were coming for him and those he loved most. That was his curse. They were coming and he would kill them all or die trying.

But not today.
Definitely not today.

About the Author

Rafael Amadeus Hines is a native New Yorker with Panamanian, Jamaican, and Irish roots, who was born and raised on Manhattan's Lower East Side. Dipping into his early Alphabet City memories, he loosely based many of the characters in his first novel, *Bishop's War*, on the people he grew up with, and adapted many of his own experiences into the book as well.

A former Jazz club owner and restaurateur, Rafael has worked in the financial and energy markets for over twenty years. On 9/11 he watched his office along with all the others in the Twin Towers come crashing down and, like many New Yorkers on that day, he anticipated follow up attacks to take place throughout the city. Years later he envisioned a lone citizen soldier preventing these attacks and the hero Sgt. John Bishop appeared on paper.

Rafael is the father of three and still lives in the New York neighborhood where he grew up. A voracious reader of suspense thrillers, his writing career was inspired by legendary artist-authors Elmore Leonard, John Sandford, Stephen Hunter, James Lee Burke, and Tom Clancy. He is currently working on the second novel in the Bishop series, *Bishop's Law*.

Visit his website: www.rafaelhines.com
Follow him on Twitter: @RafaelWrites
Like him on Facebook: www.facebook.com/Rafaelhines.Author